Amidst the vast wastelands, devastated orgs, and isolated arcologies of a ravaged Earth in 2436, Terran ha-
tred of their RAM persecutors seethes openly. But these
scattered pockets of resistance remain almost totally
powerless until a daring band of freedom-loving Terrans under the fledgling banner of NEO forms. In the
midst of this tension-packed scenario, two young NEO
undercover agents race RAM for control of a new breed
of super-gennies called Barneys, whose leader emerges
as the most powerful and notorious of them all: Black
Barney.

More than twenty years later, as a much-
strengthened NEO united under Lt. Col. Anthony
"Buck" Rogers waits to hear from their leader in deep
space, the struggle for control of the Barneys takes on
even more far-reaching urgency. . . .

ARRIVAL

THE MARTIAN
WARS TRILOGY

THE INNER
PLANETS TRILOGY

INVADERS OF CHARON

Invaders of Charon, Book One

THE GENESIS WEB

C. M. Brennan

TSR Inc.

THE GENESIS WEB

Random House and its affiliate companies have worldwide distribution rights in the book trade for English language products of TSR, Inc.

Distributed to the book and hobby trade in the United Kingdom by TSR Ltd.

Cover art by Continuity Studios

Interior artwork by Mike Hernandez and Albert Deschesne

BUCK ROGERS and XXVc are trademarks owned by The Dille Family Trust. The TSR logo is a trademark owned by TSR, Inc.

First Printing: May 1992
Printed in the United States of America
Library of Congress Catalog Card Number: 91-66502

9 8 7 6 5 4 3 2 1

ISBN: 1-56076-093-1

TSR, Inc.
P.O. Box 756
Lake Geneva, WI
53147
U.S.A.

TSR Ltd.
120 Church End
Cherry Hinton
Cambridge CB1 3LB
United Kingdom

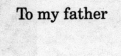

To my father

SOLAR SYSTEM

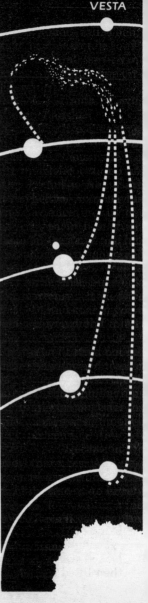

The Asteroid Belt

A scattered anarchy of tumbling planetoids and rough rock miners, where every sentient has the right to vote, and the majority rules among five hundred miniature worlds.

Mars

A terraformed paradise, Mars was reborn through the most sophisticated technology. Yet, the ruthless Martian corporate state of RAM spreads its evil tentacles throughout human space from this paradise.

Luna

An iron-willed confederation of isolationist states, the highly advanced Lunars are the bankers of the Solar System, "peaceful" merchants willing to knock invading ships from the skies with mighty massdriver weapons.

Earth

A twisted wreckage despoiled by interplanetary looters, Earth is a declining civilization. Its people are divided and trapped in urban sprawls and mutant-infested reservations.

Venus

A partially terraformed hellworld, where only the highest peaks can support human life. As the Uplanders build their great ceramic towers, the nomads of the vast, balloonlike Aerostates cruise the acidic skies. Far below, in the steaming swamps of the lowlands, reptilian humanoids struggle to make the world to their liking.

Mercury

Home to an underground civilization of miners, its surface is paved with huge solar collectors, massive mobile cities, and gaping strip mines. Far overhead, the mighty orbital palaces of the energy-rich Sun Kings spin in silent majesty.

CHAPTER ONE

Identify yourself!" the red-uniformed guard snapped, legs braced. His right hand rested on the rocket pistol holstered on his belt. Vincent Pirelli refrained from wetting his lips, which had gone sandpapery. It wouldn't do Rachel Wydlin any good if he were found out now.

"Lieutenant Ivan Vronsky, RAM prison, Deimos." His tone carried a healthy dose of the arrogance that the Martian military were taught to use with their inferiors. Vince detected an infinitesimal adjustment in the guard's posture and extended a red microdisk. The guard accepted it without comment, stepped to the wall-mounted computer terminal, and inserted Vince's offering into the disk slot. Vince waited tensely, staring at the computer screen. It remained mostly blank, except for the line identifying the guard post—"Number 3 Erebus Station"—and the date—"20 Mai, 2435."

"Release prisoner C2509 for transfer," said the computer in a clear, inflectionless voice. The cell block door behind the guard whooshed open.

The guard paused, his eyes narrowing to slits as he looked at Vince. Vince returned the look for a moment, then lifted an eyebrow. The guard shifted his feet uneasily. Apparently something didn't seem right to him, but as an ordinary trooper, he had come from the laborer caste. It went against the conditioning of a lifetime to challenge an officer. Vince had counted on that. Still, the trooper was probably puzzled. Though Vince wore the uniform of a lieutenant in the Russo-American Mercantile's Security Division, he didn't have the thin, delicate bone structure of a true Martian, and at six foot two, he wasn't as tall as most Martian males. Finally the guard said, "Only one of you?"

"Sir!" Vince prompted, his voice even and menacing.

"Only one of you, sir?" repeated the guard.

Vince's right fist shot out toward the guard's face. When the guard brought up his own fists to block the blow, Vince snatched the pistol from the guard's belt and aimed it at him. The guard held his hands up, palms forward, in a gesture of surrender. Vince considered killing the guard, then decided the empty guard post would bring pursuit too quickly. He handed the pistol back to the guard, sneering as if disgusted by the guard's incompetence. "Release the prisoner," Vince said.

The guard walked halfway down the corridor to a cell and punched a code into a keypad next to it. The door slid open and the guard entered. Vince heard the guard's growled commands, a low murmur from a woman, and then a slap.

A tall, thin blonde shuffled from the cell, followed closely by the guard. Vince barely recognized Rachel Wydlin from the holograms he'd studied while preparing for this mission. She was considerably thinner, and her dull blue eyes showed none of the spirit he'd seen in the holos. She stood blinking, her jaw slack, until a vicious prod from the guard sent her stumbling toward Vince. Vince caught and steadied her, then gestured to the trooper. "Now finish it."

The trooper approached a small microphone set under the computer screen. "Transfer complete," he said into it. The computer whirred briefly, then spat out the microdisk. The trooper gave it to Vince.

Vince repressed the urge to grab Rachel Wydlin's hand and run. As the trooper watched, Vince put the restraint cuff on her wrist and guided her from the cell area.

When the guard post door closed behind them, Vince stopped and looked into Rachel's blue eyes. "Hello, Rachel," he said softly. "I'm Vince Pirelli, from NEO." She made no response other than to stare at him vacantly, so he explained more fully, in case she hadn't understood the acronym. "New Earth Organization. I've come to take you home."

Rachel cringed away from him, avoiding his eyes. Vince frowned. Maybe he shouldn't have admitted his allegiance to NEO, but they'd told him she would know all about them. Hell, hadn't Beowulf said she wanted to join?

Maybe her RAM captors had convinced her that NEO was a terrorist group. It was RAM corporate policy to call NEO operatives terrorists, though they knew better. NEO was a revolutionary army that would one day break the Russo-American Mercantile Corporation's stranglehold on the solar system. He tried again. "Rachel? What's wrong? I'm not going to hurt you."

Rachel still wouldn't look at him. Vince had figured her imprisonment would be tough on her, but not this tough. She didn't seem to understand a word he was saying. "Rachel, we've got to go. Do you understand? I'm taking you to your brother, Noah." She still said nothing, but Vince couldn't wait any longer. He led her toward the prison asteroid's spaceport, where his ship waited.

O O O O O

Remus Wydlin turned on the holo projector and sat in his favorite chair, an aging curved recliner covered with synth-tweed. He didn't have to put a cube in the projector. The holocube of Rachel was already in the machine, just as it had been since she'd been imprisoned six months ago.

Her image sat Indian-style on the holo surface. She was looking at him as if they were really in the same room together.

"Dad, I hope you understand why I'm doing this," she said. "I won't tell you where I'm going or what I'm going to do, because that would mean trouble for you. But I can't stay where I am, or I'll still be part of the problem. Someone has to say no to the corporation. Someone has to start people on a better way. It might as well be me."

She leaned forward, a small crease forming between her brows. "I don't blame you for what RAM has done with your creations. I give you credit, Dad. You've had as much integrity as possible on Mars, and you've taught me a lot about concern for others and dignity."

Remus tried to swallow past the lump in his throat. He'd watched this holo countless times since Rachel had left it for him nine months earlier, but hearing her praise always saddened him.

"If I blame anyone, it's Noah. He never learned anything from you. He's as greedy and uncaring as—" Rachel had nearly risen from her seat, but she seemed to realize what she was doing and settled back down with a self-deprecating grin. "Hey, who am I to judge? He has a family and his own concerns. He's no worse than most people with his advantages and connections to RAM. But I just can't let things go on like they are, Dad.

"There are others who think like me. They'll think I'm a real Russo-American princess at first, I'll bet. But I'll make them accept me. Someday we'll make a difference, Dad, and I hope you'll be proud of me. And, Dad"— at this point the image of Rachel blinked back tears—"I love you."

As Remus watched Rachel's image fade, he became aware of a beeping from the terminal on the wall. "What is it?" he snapped.

"Visitor, sir."

"On screen," Remus said.

The terminal's view screen immediately filled with the image of a tall man with the same strong cheek-

bones and prominent nose that Remus had. The man—
Remus's son, Noah—pushed back a strand of thick
brown hair. Remus's late wife had insisted that their
children have every advantage, including genetic engineering to insure that Noah would not be susceptible to
baldness like Remus was. Noah spoke. "Come on, Father. I know you're there. Let me in."

Remus sighed and stood. He had hoped that taking
this tiny retirement flat on the unfashionable rim of Coprates Chasm would help keep his visitors to a mini-
mum. Noah, however, still managed to drop in and
harass him every few weeks. Remus wouldn't mind if
Noah wanted to talk about Rachel, but Noah seemed to
have completely forgotten he'd ever had a sister. His only concern was to persuade his father to come back and
head the laboratory division of Wydlin Corporation.

Remus pressed the key sequence that allowed Noah
access to the apartment, closed the door to his study,
and went into the front room. As he expected, Noah was
already there, with a pained expression on his face as if
he smelled something bad.

"Hello, Noah," Remus said. "How are Katya and the
children?"

"They're fine. They wanted to come along, but I didn't
want to expose them to this neighborhood."

Remus doubted that Noah's elegant wife Katya had
shown even the slightest interest in accompanying him,
but there was no point in challenging Noah's statement. "To what do I owe this . . . pleasure?"

"I think you *will* find it a pleasure, Father," Noah
said. "I have some good news."

"Oh?" Remus was already finding this meeting a
pleasure, comparatively speaking. At least Noah
wasn't begging, bribing, or bullying him to come back
to work.

"I've found someone to rescue Rachel. We should have
her back within a week."

"How? I mean, who?" Remus stammered.

"I don't know many details about the fellow," Noah
said. "It didn't seem polite to be overly inquisitive. He's

from the Asteroid Belt, probably a pirate. But he convinced me he could get Rachel out of prison, and it seemed worthwhile to hire him."

"Noah." Remus sank into a chair. "I didn't expect— Do you think he can succeed?"

"Obviously I do, or I wouldn't have come here to tell you about it." Noah sat on the chair next to Remus's.

"Son, if this works, I'll be so grateful. You have no idea."

"Oh, I think I do." Noah leaned back in his chair, propping his feet on a small ottoman. "I also hope you'll be less depressed—perhaps willing to come back to work."

Remus's spine went rigid. "I see. You had a motive, as always. Even with your own family."

"Spare me!" Noah said sharply. "Do you treat me like family? You've favored Rachel for as long as I can remember."

Remus felt guilty at that, as he supposed Noah had meant him to. It was true. He had never been as close to Noah as he had to Rachel. His work had always come first while Noah was growing up. Rachel was born twelve years after Noah, and Remus's wife had been killed soon afterward in a cruiser accident. Following the accident, Remus had become an involved parent, largely because there had been no alternative. He'd discovered that he enjoyed it more than he'd expected, and he tried to make up for lost time with Noah. But it had been too late. He stared at his hands, not knowing what to say. Finally Noah spoke.

"Well, if you want to see Rachel, she'll be at our research station in the Jovian Trojans. Maybe you'll find that you want to work again. If so, you'll have every opportunity to see Rachel."

"Rachel will come to see me," Remus said.

"Oh, that's a great idea!" Noah said. "As soon as she arrives on Mars, she'll be arrested again. This time I probably will be, too, for having her rescued. Then you can have both your offspring in prison."

Remus wanted to smack Noah's sneering face, but it wouldn't help. And Noah was right—the Jovian Trojans, two groups of small asteroids that shared Jupiter's orbit, should be remote enough to keep Rachel hidden for a while. The asteroid fields there were said to give nightmares to even the most jaded pilots.

Rachel would be safer at Wydlin Corporation's secret research station, which Noah had named Genesis. And it wouldn't hurt Remus to visit her there, though he wasn't sure he'd resume his work. True, he missed it. And without being immodest, he knew he was the foremost cybergeneticist in the solar system. But after what had happened to Rachel, he'd had to think twice about what he was doing.

Genetically engineered beings, or "gennies," as they were called, did most of the labor in the solar system. Unlike the engineered human races—Martian, Mercurian, and Venusian—which were mildly altered to help them adapt to their different terraformed worlds, gennies were more radically modified, often combining characteristics from different species.

Remus had worked on the cutting edge of species design. His specialty was cybergenetics—the combination of biological species with enhancing hardware and computer elements. He'd been working on a gennie that would have been stronger than any other known species and as intelligent as many "pure" humans. For lack of a better name, and to show Noah that he cared about him, Remus had called the series "Barneys" after a Coprates Duelpit gladiator whom Noah admired. Then Rachel had been arrested, and suddenly gennies—even incredibly advanced ones—no longer seemed important to Remus.

Rachel had always said gennies were slaves, another symptom of RAM's domination of the solar system. Remus had never thought about it until she was convicted of treason. Then he realized Rachel must have been right about a lot of things—otherwise, why would RAM act so swiftly and harshly against a young woman whose only crime had been some expensive property damage?

"Noah," Remus said slowly, "I think you're right

about keeping Rachel at Genesis Station for now. I'll come and see her there if your rescue succeeds. I'm glad you thought of it, Son. I can't promise I'll come back to work, though."

"Wonderful!" Noah said sarcastically. "I go out on a limb to bring your precious daughter back to you, and all you can say is 'thank you.' Remind me to do you another favor real soon."

Noah stormed out the front door. Remus put out his hand, wanting to say something to soften Noah's mood, but it was no use. The door slid closed, leaving Remus inexorably alone.

He stared at the door, wishing he knew what to do. He couldn't thoughtlessly go back to creating gennies. If he got Rachel back, he wanted to do something to earn the respect and love she'd always given him. Yet he missed his work.

Remus knew that Wydlin Corporation, which he had formed as something to leave to his son, had been foundering badly ever since he left. That didn't surprise Remus, and he didn't think it was Noah's fault. Improved gennies came along so quickly that a cybergenetics company that had been on top for years could find itself defunct almost without warning.

Wydlin Corporation had been more stable than most because Remus was so well respected. Once he was gone, however, it didn't take long for the carrion-eaters to gather. Maybe if he just finished the Barney project, the most ambitious thing he had ever attempted, he would leave Noah in a stronger position. Noah was doing a lot for him. Remus sighed. He would have to consider returning to work.

CHAPTER TWO

Vince nodded curtly to the guards at the spaceport checkpoint. They had accepted his disk
without question and waved him through. He
guided Rachel past the lowered field fence. His ship, a
RAM scout cruiser called the *Hermes*, was in the third
launch bay.

He opened the air lock entry, then helped Rachel
through it. She still seemed disoriented, but at least she
wasn't difficult to guide. The hatch of his stolen RAM
scout cruiser opened at his approach.

"How you doin', Ivan?" Gina Cahill—like Vince, dressed
in a RAM uniform—peered out, grinning at him.

Now that it was almost over, Vince could return Gina
s smile. "I'm fine. But I don't think Rachel is doing so
well. Help her up, okay?"

"Sure." Gina turned serious. "Come on, Honey. Take
the restraint off her, will you, Vince?"

Vince felt his face turn hot. He still felt like the new
kid on the block. "Sorry." He unlocked the cuffs that en-
circled Rachel's wrists and removed them. Gina held
her hand out for the young woman to grasp. Rachel
looked puzzled, then seemed to understand and allowed
Gina to help her up the ladder.

Vince closed the hatch and joined Gina and Rachel on the cargo deck. Gina was clucking over Rachel. "Geez, Honey, you musta had it rough. Never mind, it's all over now. Vince, did you tell her what's up?"

"I don't know if she's ready," Vince said. "She needs some food, I think, and rest. I—"

Vince was interrupted by the clanging of boots on the metallic ladder. He saw a bulky male in a red uniform descending and caught his breath, then expelled it with a foolish grin. It was the ship's engineer, Jacques Garonne, wearing a RAM uniform. Vince had known Garonne would be dressed as a RAM trooper, of course, just as he and Gina were. He must be more nervous than he thought. Rather short and stocky, Garonne didn't look at all Martian.

"Victory, my friend?" Garonne asked, in his French-Canadian accent.

Vince grinned, feeling better now that he was back with his NEO comrades. "*Mais oui*, Jacques." He indicated Rachel with a sweep of his hand. Gina had stepped away from Rachel and was looking at her, frowning.

"What's the matter, Gina?" Vince asked.

"Rachel," Gina said, taking Rachel by the chin and looking into her eyes, "are you in there? Come on, Honey."

Rachel pulled away and refused to look at Gina. Gina dropped her hand and swore.

"What is it?" Vince asked. "She is Rachel Wydlin, isn't she?"

"Oh, yeah, Vince," Gina said bitterly. "She's Rachel Wydlin, all right. Or what's left of her. They did a mind scan on her."

"Are you sure?" Vince asked.

"Yeah," Gina said. "My brother had one, so I should know what someone looks like afterward."

Vince had wondered what had brought Gina to NEO. Almost every recruit had a story of some horror RAM had perpetrated that led to his decision to work against the giant corporation that controlled Mars and Earth and had tentacles reaching everywhere else in the solar system. Vince's own parents, descended from farmers in the American Midwest, had been reduced to slaving in RAM's agricultural domes. The only way they could get anything for themselves and their son was to scratch away at a patch of ruined earth that had not been protected by RAM. Eventually the exposure to the toxic environment killed them.

Vince shook his head, not wanting to remember. He didn't want to stir Gina's unpleasant memories, either, but he had to ask. "Gina, will she get over it?"

Gina's mouth was a thin line. "My brother never has. He's finally learned to eat with a spoon again."

Vince couldn't speak. He felt a firm pressure on his shoulder and saw that Garonne had put one arm around him, the other around Gina. "Come on," Garonne said. "We're not safe yet."

Gina patted Garonne's hand. "You bet. Let's blow." She looked at Vince. "You ready, Rocketjock?"

"Rock steady." Vince took a deep breath and mounted the ship's ladder for the control deck. Beneath him, he could hear the others. Garonne would be going to the reactor level to monitor the engine for takeoff. Gina, he figured, would get Rachel settled in a crew cabin before coming up to monitor the sensors.

Gina came huffing up the ladder a few minutes later. "I couldn't even put Rachel in a regular cabin," she reported. "She freaked when she saw how big it was. She didn't quit screaming until I put her in one of the emergency chambers in sick bay."

Vince shook his head. The tiny chambers were designed to continue life support during an emergency for helpless or unconscious patients. They were almost womblike.

He programmed coordinates for Deimos, one of the moons of Mars. It had been transformed into a prison for RAM's more recalcitrant criminals. Heading toward Deimos would be consistent with the story Vince had given the officials at the prison asteroid. They could alter their flight plan when they had put a few thousand more miles behind them.

Garonne joined Vince and Gina on the control deck. "Well done, Vince," he said.

"Oh, come on," Vince said. "Easy takeoff. Nothing to it."

"Yeah, I wasn't particularly impressed," Gina cracked.

"No, I meant the rescue," Garonne said. "You pulled it off like a veteran."

"You make it sound as if you've belonged to NEO a lot longer than I have," Vince said, smiling at his friend.

The New Earth Organization had only been formed two years earlier when a few formerly separate resistance groups had decided to band together to defend their beleaguered planet from RAM's depredations. Garonne had belonged to the group from the beginning. Vince had joined about a year ago and had quickly become an excellent pilot.

"Ah, but I had experience before that, my friend. If only I looked more Martian, I would have gone inside and spared you all that." Garonne smiled. "But I think you didn't mind the danger, eh?"

"He loved it," Gina interjected.

"I tried not to think about it," said Vince. "I just did what had to be done."

"That's the best way," Garonne said. "Beowulf thought you'd pull it off. He asked us to evaluate your work in order to see if you could handle the next part of the assignment. We had to see how you would do at deception."

"Deception? You mean passing as a Martian?"

"Yes. And also convincing Noah Wydlin you were a pirate and that he needed you on his payroll," Garonne said. "We hope you can stay on at Wydlin Corporation for a while, Vince."

"If you want me to," Vince said. "What then?"

"Wydlin Corporation is working on a highly secret new project. We'd like you to find out what it is," Garonne said.

"We hoped Rachel could help you," Gina said. "But obviously that's not going to happen."

"I've never done any information piracy," Vince said. "I can see how Rachel might have gotten the information, but how will I go about it?"

"It may be difficult," Garonne admitted. "But you won't be alone. A contact has been arranged for you at Wydlin Corporation—an insider. Don't seek this person out unless you have to, though. His cover is extremely sensitive. Let him approach you."

"Who is it?" Vince asked.

"I don't know the person's real name," said Garonne. "But the code name is 'Dekalb.'"

"You're kidding!" Vince said. He had an ancient metal sign, the only thing he'd saved from when he lived with his parents. It was a yellow ear of corn, with green wings on it. The word "Dekalb" was emblazoned in red letters across the corn. The sign hung above his bed back in his quarters in Chicagorg.

Gina smiled. "Beowulf thought it would be appropriate. Especially since they told Dekalb to call you 'Farm Boy.'"

"Aw, geez." Vince smiled at Gina teasingly as he echoed her characteristic expression. "So I report to this—Dekalb?"

"I don't think so." Garonne said. "I think you get information from Dekalb, but you report to someone else. Dekalb can tell you who. But at least you won't be alo—"

"Whoa, baby!" Gina's exclamation interrupted Garonne. "We've got company."

Vince looked at the tactical monitor. Two bright green dots stood out against the dark screen, coming toward them from the prison station. "Damn!"

A shrill whistle came from the commo board. "Lieutenant Vronsky, or whoever you are, we are RAM Security. You have removed a prisoner without proper authorization. Prepare to be boarded."

"The hell we will," Vince growled under his breath. "We're out of here!"

Gina was already out of her seat, heading down to the weapons turret. Garonne took over her position at the sensors.

Vince throttled the cruiser into a higher speed and began to pull away from his pursuers.

Garonne scanned the tactical sensor. "We have two light cruisers following us, Vince."

"How close are they?"

"Not in weapons range," Garonne said. "Not likely to catch us, either. So far, so good."

Vince nodded. All he had to do was stay ahead of them.

"You might as well return." A voice from one of the RAM scouts came through their comunications system. "You can't escape."

"Oh, yeah?" Vince said, flicking on his transmitting switch. "Who's going to catch me?"

"We've contacted every RAM ship between here and Mars. You can't possibly get past them all."

"We'll see about that!" Vince said and pulled the *Hermes* up into a steep, curving climb.

Their pursuers seemed to be having problems getting their act together. The first ship went into a climb, apparently hoping to block his path. The other eventually swung around, but it was far behind.

Vince sighted through his targeting computer, watching for the cruiser to come into range. At the steady blip indicating that he was on target, Vince fired. His computer registered a hit, and he let out a whoop. He heard Gina yell from the weapons deck. "Not bad, Rocketjock! Did you see mine?"

Before Vince could reply, an explosion shook their cruiser and brilliant light flashed in his peripheral vision.

Garonne leaped to his feet and headed for the ship's ladder. "We're hit—engine level! I'll check it out."

Vince glanced over at the tactical sensor. It must have been the ship that had tried to block their path. The other one was still too far back to use its weapons. He accelerated, shooting forward. Gina yelled triumphantly as she scored another hit.

Vince looked at the tactical screen and saw the blip

representing their nearest pursuer dissolve. The other cruiser had no hope of catching the *Hermes*, provided they could maintain speed. And now they were heading away from Mars.

Genesis Station was cored into one of many asteroids in the Jovian Trojans, a collection of asteroids that shared Jupiter's orbit. Why Wydlin had chosen such a remote area for a research station was unclear to Vince, but it afforded some built-in protection for him. The orbiting rocks would be difficult to navigate through, even for a small cruiser like Vince's. The remaining cruiser was unlikely to leave its Asteroid Belt post for such a long chase, and RAM didn't keep many small craft this far out in space. He might have some problems with the bigger ships while they were still in the Asteroid Belt between Mars and Jupiter, but he could probably outrun them.

"Vince?" Garonne's voice came over the commo board.

"Problem, Jacques?"

"Some of our engine shielding was damaged in the hit we took. It's not dangerous for now. Unfortunately, it'll be difficult to repair before we land."

"Will it hold?"

"Sure . . . as long as we don't get hit there again."

"Understood. I'll do my best," Vince said. He called down to the weapons station. "Nice work, Cahill."

"Yeah, well," she said. He could almost see her shrugging as she said it. "How we doin'?"

"All right for now. You want to come up and watch the sensors? We're way ahead of the other cruiser, but you never know what might come up."

"Sure." A moment later, she came up the ladder. She leaned over to whisper in Vince's ear. "I'm sure you're just trying to get me alone."

He put a hand up to cup her cheek. "You know all my secrets."

"Not yet, Rocketjock," Gina said, grinning. "But I'll work on that when the mission's over."

○ ○ ○ ○ ○

"Vince! Vince, are you awake?"

Vince's eyes flew open and he shook his head to clear it. Garonne, seated at the tactical sensors, looked at him with concern.

"Sure, Jacques. Well, almost."

"Maybe Cahill can watch the controls for a while," Garonne said. "You need rest."

"That's not a bad idea," Vince said, yawning. "She in the crew quarters?"

"Yes. I'll get her." Garonne went down the ladder. Vince blinked, trying to keep his eyes open. The trip to Genesis Station would be a long one, but the coordinates had been fed into the ship's computer. There was no reason why Gina couldn't watch things for a while. At least she'd had a little sleep. He looked at his wristchrono. She should be relatively fresh. He'd sent her, protesting, to the crew quarters about six hours ago. It would be another two days before they reached their destination and the next part of his assignment.

He yawned and stretched, scrunching up his eyes. A tiny light registered just before he closed them. He sat up, startled, and looked around. There was nothing out of the ordinary on the control deck as far as he could see. Frowning, he looked at the sensor screens. What he'd seen was the green blip of an approaching spacecraft on the tactical scanner. He switched on intraship communications. "Jacques, Gina . . . we have company."

"We're on our way," Jacques said.

Vince turned back to the tactical monitor and requested information about the other ship. As Vince heard his comrades coming up the ladder, gold letters began scrolling across the top of the screen: "RMS *Regius*, medium Argyre-class cruiser. Weapons: 5 beam lasers, 3 gyrocannons, 1 heavy acceleration gun, 1 K-cannon."

Gina had just come on deck and was standing behind him. "We've gotta get out of here, Rocketjock."

The ship was obviously moving to intercept them. A RAM medium cruiser this far out was probably on routine patrol, but it would have been informed of the prison break. Vince stared at the blip. He might be able to outrun the ship if he made a break for it, as Gina suggested. The fact that the larger ship hadn't hailed them led Vince to believe their intentions were not friendly. Vince reached for his helmet. "You're right, Gina. It could be tight, though. Where's Jacques?"

"Right here," said Garonne. Vince turned and saw Garonne standing behind Gina, one hand on her shoulder.

"Looks like battle stations," Vince said, looking at their sober faces. "Though I hope to hell it doesn't get to that point."

"Right," said Garonne, releasing Gina's shoulder to grab his helmet. "You want me on tactical or weapons?"

"Weapons," Vince decided. "I can keep track of that crate." The medium cruiser couldn't match their ship for speed or maneuverability, but it could destroy them in three minutes if given the opportunity. They needed Garonne to shoot down incoming missiles.

Garonne nodded and followed Gina down to the weapons level. Vince turned the nose of the *Hermes* up so that it would leapfrog the path of the larger vessel. The enemy cruiser would undoubtedly try to come within weapons range, but with luck, they wouldn't be able to get many clear shots at the *Hermes*. Gina and Garonne signaled they were ready; Vince accelerated to maximum speed. A deep, chuckling voice came from the commo board. "Lieutenant Vronsky, I presume?"

"Who is this?" Vince asked.

"Captain Vladimir Holst, of the RAM cruiser *Regius*. If you don't surrender immediately, we will destroy you."

Vince checked the scanner. The *Regius* had increased speed, but it couldn't catch them. In another minute, they would come within the RAM cruiser's weapons range, but only briefly. Vince decided he would rather take his chances against the cruiser's superior weaponry than hope that RAM would be merciful once he was captured.

"Sorry, Vladimir. I've seen how RAM treats prisoners. No thanks."

"As you wish. My men could use the target practice, anyway."

Vince turned off his ship-to-ship transmitter, then called down to Garonne and Gina on the commlink. "You ready?"

"Rock steady," Gina said. Garonne grunted affirmatively.

"All right," Vince said, more for himself than for them. Gina would launch a missile, he knew, while Garonne swept across incoming projectiles with the beam laser. Vince would wait until Gina's missiles were launched before he released a chaff shell to confuse any incoming "smart" missiles from the *Regius*.

"Missile launched," Gina announced over the link. Vince glanced at the tactical display and saw Gina's missile speed toward the *Regius*. The *Regius*'s lasers shot out to intercept it. However, the missile streaked through the web of beams and exploded against the enemy ship's hull.

"Outstanding, Cahill," Vince said, and released the chaff. It bloomed, shimmering, behind them. He watched his scanner anxiously. Four missiles were streaking toward them. Within moments, three of the four missiles entered the chaff field, lurched drunkenly, and fell away. "Come on, Jacques!" Vince sucked in his breath as he watched the sweep of the beam laser intercept the last incoming missile, exploding it in a brilliant flash.

"How was that, Vince?" Garonne asked.

"Great!" Vince said. "But stay alert—we won't be out of range for another minute or so."

"I copy," Garonne said, and Vince heard Gina mutter affirmatively.

Vince looked at his scanner. Another minute at this speed and they would be out of danger. The *Regius* might chase them, but it couldn't hit them. And it was unlikely that RAM would continue the chase as far as the Jovian Trojans. It wasn't worth it to brave the rocks and pirates there. Wydlin must have been either crazy, obscenely wealthy, or both, to choose such a remote area for his research station. But the fact that he had was certainly working in their favor now.

"Missile launched." Gina's voice came over Vince's headset.

"I copy," said Vince, releasing chaff. He watched his scanner for incoming missiles. The *Regius* fired off another trio of gyrocannon shells, followed by a giant missile from their K-cannon. Vince could see numerous smaller projectiles as well, shot from an acceleration gun.

The *Regius* managed to knock out Gina's missile. Vince frowned and concentrated on his screen. His chaff took out two of the three gyrocannon shells this time, and Garonne finally got the last one. The chaff exploded most of the acceleration pellets, but a few got through. Garonne, forced to concentrate on the more deadly K-cannon missile, couldn't do much about them. Vince held his breath as they battered the *Hermes*.

A thunderous boom shook the ship. Vince's body slammed against his safety harness. It took him a moment to get his breath back. When he could speak again, he said, "What the hell was that?"

"They got our missile launcher," Garonne said over the link.

"Gina? Are you all right?"

"I'm okay," Gina's voice crackled through the comm-link. Apparently her space suit link had also taken damage from the hit.

"She's wounded. Can't tell how bad," Garonne said.

"Hang on," Vince said. "We're home free in another minute. Just keep shooting down those missiles, Jacques." Vince had access to only one weapon, an acceleration gun. He fingered the controls, debating with himself. If the *Regius* was close enough to use her acceleration gun, so could the *Hermes*.

"Well, Vronsky?" the cruiser captain's voice came over the speaker. "Are you ready to give up?"

"Not likely, Holst," Vince growled. He targeted the *Regius*, aiming for the control center. Then he fired.

"Vince!" Garonne said.

"Leave him alone," Gina gasped. "Good going, Vince."

"Right." Vince knew he'd lost it for a moment. He belatedly released the chaff, then watched his scanner. Another load of projectiles were heading for the *Hermes*, but Vince paid more attention to the progress of his shot. By the time the *Regius* could launch any chaff, the pellet was almost home. He watched as it effortlessly sailed into contact with the *Regius* and tore a hole in the control section.

Garonne, muttering French curses, was shooting down incoming missiles. Vince checked the scanner to see how many missiles were still coming in. Several gyro shells had made it past the chaff, but what horrified Vince more was the speck of a K-cannon missile, clearly visible on his screen and very close.

A flash so brilliant that Vince tried unsuccessfully to shut it out with both arms illuminated the sky around the *Hermes*. Vince heard only the beginning of the explosion before everything went black.

O   O   O   O   O

Vince wasn't sure what was more troubling—his throbbing head or the waves of nausea. He didn't know how long he could remain conscious.

"Gina? Jacques?" he whispered into the commlink, unable to make his voice any louder. There was no reply. He tried to focus on the systems monitor to see what part of the ship was damaged. Red, glowing dots swam before his eyes, but he couldn't see well enough to make any sense of it.

The flight computer, as far as he could tell, looked all right. And the ship was still moving, undoubtedly on its previous heading. He blinked, trying to keep the controls in focus. He couldn't move his right arm, so he used his left hand to punch in the coordinates for Genesis Station. Then darkness descended again, blocking everything else out.

CHAPTER THREE

I t really was the dullest party, Noah. I couldn't even
trash Ardala Valmar. If I'd tried to talk to anyone
else about how tacky she looked, I'd be in Deimos
prison and the children would be RAM wards."

Noah smiled at his wife's image on the screen. He
wasn't really looking at Katya, of course. It would take
about an hour for his words to reach her; he was really
talking to a toy of hers, a digital personality she'd had
programmed to keep in touch with him. After he finished talking to this digital double of his wife, it would
return to Mars to report the conversation to Katya. He
performed this ritual once or twice a week whenever he
was on Genesis Station. "I dislike being apart as much
as you do, my dear."

In reality, Noah didn't think their separation was particularly hard on either of them. Katya had a few dis-
creet diversions on Mars, and Noah's personal
assistant, a particularly lovely pleasure gennie named
Marcie, kept him from getting too lonely. Even at this
godforsaken research station.

"When are you coming home?" Katya's double asked,
flipping a brunette wave over her shoulder and thrust-
ing her lip out provocatively.

"Katya," Noah sighed, "we've been all through this. I'll be home when I get this new project straightened out."

"I wish you'd tell me what it is." The image widened its green eyes, as Katya always did when she wanted to look innocent.

"It's too soon," Noah said for the hundredth time. He wanted at least a few flawless Barneys decanted before he let the news of their existence leak out. It was incredibly annoying; he'd had to order another one destroyed just that morning. It had been a grotesque, unintelligent mutant, impossible to control or train. Without his father, the project seemed doomed to failure.

"Have you gotten Remus to help you with it yet?"

"Not yet. Soon, though." As soon as Pirelli delivered Rachel. Rescuing Rachel would be the wedge Noah needed to deal with his father. Remus had always seemed susceptible to guilt-inducing tactics. As well he should be. It wasn't fair that Remus had always cared more about Rachel.

But if Remus finished his work on the Barneys, it would be years before any other cybergenetics firms could hope to catch up. Wydlin Corporation would have the kind of power and independence that very few RAM subsidiaries could boast. In addition to being able to name their own price for the Barneys, they could always use them for defense in the event that RAM tried any of its nastier takeover tricks.

Noah looked forward to the time when he'd have a personal army of inhumanly strong gennies. RAM would find him a force to be reckoned with then. Noah had no present plans for an out-and-out takeover of RAM itself, but he wouldn't rule it out, either. With the Barneys under his control, there was literally nothing to which he couldn't aspire.

A red light flashed at the upper left-hand corner of the screen, alerting Noah that he had a message on his private channel. "Darling," he said, "I'm terribly sorry, but something's come up. I'll call you back, all right?"

"Oh, all right," Katya's image said, pouting. "I have to go to Ardala's theater party tonight, so you'd better wait till tomorrow."

"Good-bye, Katya." Noah terminated the connection and switched to receive the incoming communication. "Wydlin here," he said.

"Gretsky," said a man's voice tersely.

Noah employed Gretsky to keep him informed of seemingly unimportant events that might not otherwise come to his attention. So far, Gretsky had never wasted Noah's time.

"What is it?" Noah asked.

"There's a small cruiser entering our sector. It appears to be damaged, but we don't know if there are survivors on board. The consensus here seems to be to let it break up when it hits the rocks, or to let the pirates have it. Thought you'd like to know."

"Check it out," Noah said. The ship could be Pirelli's. The situation definitely required the most delicate attention. Gretsky could be trusted not to say any more than he ought to.

"Yes, sir," Gretsky said.

"I'll call the commander. You volunteer for the assignment."

"Understood, sir."

Noah hung up and then called the spaceport.

"Commander Andreyev here."

"Commander, this is Noah Wydlin. It has come to my attention that there is an unidentified ship in the asteroid field, possibly in distress."

"Yes, sir. We think it's a ghost ship. It's leaking radiation, and there's no communication from it."

"Are there any survivors? Have you scanned for life forms?"

"Survivors are highly unlikely, though I can't say for sure. It's not in range of our infrared sensors, Mr. Wydlin, and it probably won't make it that far. It appears to be operating on ship computer. Without a real pilot, it'll never navigate the rocks."

"Send someone out to look at it," Noah said. "And have the pilot report to me."

"Yes, Mr. Wydlin."

O   O   O   O   O

Noah tried to work but found it impossible to concentrate. If Rachel died, he'd never get his father to come back to Wydlin Corporation. Perhaps he should have kept his job in the Biosciences Department at RAM, instead of encouraging his father to start Wydlin Corporation. But it irked him to see his father getting so little material reward from his work. A man with such unique abilities deserved better, and Noah was clever enough to see that they all profited.

With Remus gone, Wydlin Corporation had had to scramble for every contract. Noah had tried to see the Barney project through to completion, but without Remus, it was hopeless. None of the other scientists he employed had the ability to fulfill Remus's vision. They tried, but all they achieved were grotesque mutations of what Remus had first described to Noah.

Damn Rachel! When she had lived at home, she had taken all their father's attention. And when she left, Remus had been useless for months, hoping for some word of her. Then when she was finally convicted of terrorism, he had given up his work completely.

Noah wondered if it was a good idea to rescue her, to bring her back to wreak havoc on their lives again. Well, it was pointless to wonder. Remus was no good to anybody the way he was. Noah had to relieve the situation somehow.

He leafed through the reports on his desk, not really seeing them. Finally a soft chime sounded on the comnet. Noah flicked it on. "Yes?"

"Call from Gretsky, sir," Marcie said.

"Put it through," Noah replied.

After a moment, he heard Gretsky's voice cutting through static. "I'm calling from the derelict."

"What have you found?"

"The ship has extensive hull and engine damage. Life support, except for auxiliary in sick bay, is nonfunctional. Four aboard, but two of them are dead. The other two are still alive. I've alerted the med unit to stand by."

"Any identification on the vessel or crew?"

"RMS *Hermes*, sir. The badges on the two dead officers are unreadable."

Noah nodded. The identificatioin badges RAM's security division used only functioned while their wearers were alive. "What about the others?"

"There's a young woman—blonde, maybe early to mid twenties. She's unconscious . . . seems to have some burns."

"Is she a RAM officer?" Noah asked.

"She's wearing a plain brown jump suit, sir. No identification. She's in an emergency support chamber in sick bay. Only place in the ship with life support." Noah felt a leap of excitement. It was Rachel; he was sure now. "You said there was someone else?"

"The pilot. He has a broken clavicle and some contusions. Possibly a concussion. His space suit is functioning, or he'd be dead, too. He's been that way for a day or two, it looks like."

"Do you know who he is?"

"His ID reads 'Lieutenant Ivan Vronsky.' "

Noah chewed his lip, thinking. It was probably Pirelli, or one of his crew. He didn't want the med unit personnel to think they were treating a RAM security officer; it would have to be reported to RAM Central and would complicate matters unnecessarily.

"Is there anything you can put him in besides his uniform?"

"There are some civilian smart suits here."

"Very good." Noah felt almost euphoric. Gretsky could easily insure that Rachel's breakout wouldn't be linked to him. If only Rachel hadn't been injured, he would have been completely satisfied. However, Genesis Station's med unit was as sophisticated as those of many major hospitals on Mars. He spoke to Gretsky. "Get them off the cruiser. Then do one more thing for me."

"Yes, sir."

"Destroy the ship."

"Yes, sir," Gretsky said.

Noah terminated the connection and had Marcie put a

call through to his father's retirement flat on Mars.

"Rachel's here, Father," Noah said over the comnet. He considered how best to state his message, to make it most likely that his father would come to Genesis. "She's very seriously injured, however. I don't know if she'll survive." Might as well add a little drama to the situation; his father would feel all the more urgency to arrive quickly. "I thought you'd want to know so you could arrange to be with her."

Then Noah clicked off, supremely satisfied with his handling of the situation. If he knew his father, Remus would come as quickly as possible. When he arrived, Rachel would be on the way to recovery, and Noah would be the hero of the hour. Remus would do anything for him then. The success of the Barney project was assured.

He ought to go down to the med unit, he supposed. When Rachel woke up, he could explain the situation to her. Knowing her, she'd probably want to go out and start blowing up weapons manufacturing stations again. He'd have to convince her to wait at least until Remus arrived and saw her. Once Remus had expressed his gratitude by promising to finish the Barney Project, Rachel could do whatever she wanted. Noah would have Gretsky personally ferry her to the next trouble she wanted to create.

O O O O O

Noah let himself into the viewing room next to the emergency section of the med unit. He switched the viewer on and scanned treatment rooms until he found one in which a large group of personnel were particularly active. He set the camera to zoom in on that area. As he expected, the patient was Rachel. He was shocked to see how thin and drawn she looked. He frowned, turning his attention to the monitors above her treatment table. They were a bar graph of disaster. He watched as the vital sign indicators dropped slowly and inexorably. Irritated, he punched his access code into the keyboard below the screen.

"Yes, sir?" the computer's soothing voice responded.

"Put me on the speaker to treatment room A."

After a moment, the computer voice said, "You're on the speaker now, sir."

Noah spoke into the unit's microphone. "Renner?" He couldn't really tell who any of the medics were under their garb, but Dr. Renner was the chief medic on the unit and therefore was likely to be directing Rachel's treatment.

One of the white-swathed figures at the treatment table stepped toward the wall-mounted communit. A terse voice came over Noah's speakers.

"What is it?" a voice asked irritably.

"Noah Wydlin here. I want a report."

"What the hell are you talking about? Report on what?" Renner was even more brusque than usual. "In case you didn't realize it, we're rather busy down here right now."

"Yes, I'm watching." Noah pressed his hands together in an effort to calm himself. "What is the patient's condition?"

"Hopeless," Renner answered bluntly. "In addition to the trauma of the crash, she's been subjected to massive radiation. If we do everything possible, she might last the night. No longer."

Noah stared helplessly at the monitors above Rachel. He hadn't gone to all of this trouble to let her die. He remembered a time, over twenty years ago now, when Remus had told Noah to watch Rachel while he took an important call in his study. Noah had kept only half an eye on his year-old sister as he watched tri-dee. Ignoring Noah's repeated warnings to stay away from a flight of stairs, Rachel had taken a nasty tumble down them. Remus had seemed angry at first, but then quickly blamed himself for relying on a twelve-year-old boy. Noah was surprised at how clearly the memory of that day came back to him—the day when he knew his father would never trust him again. He heard the doctor sigh impatiently. "Do you mind if I get back to work? Unless, of course, you want us to just give up on her."

"No!" Noah barked. "No, do everything possible, Renner. I'll be in touch."

He switched the communit off abruptly, then pounded his fist on the wall. He couldn't lose Rachel. He had to think of how to save her. He knew what he'd want done for himself in the same situation. He'd ask to be downloaded into the computer. He knew of several people—obviously, those who could afford it—who had chosen to have a digital personality created as a repository for their consciousness once their bodies were no longer viable. The most obvious example was the head of RAM, Simund Holzerhein. Holzerhein had been chairman of the board of RAM for many years when he decided to have himself downloaded fifty years ago. He'd continued as the chairman of RAM since that time, and he showed every indication of continuing indefinitely. He'd even continued to run the board meetings, since he could appear almost anywhere there was a holographic projector.

There was no way of knowing whether Rachel would appreciate becoming a computer personality. She had such strange ideas. And Noah couldn't be sure what Remus's reaction would be. However, there was nothing else to do. Noah addressed the console. "Get me Programming."

Moments later, he heard a tenor voice. "This is Grushkov in Programming, sir."

"I need someone downloaded into the computer as soon as possible."

"I'll see to it, sir."

"Fine. Get any equipment and assistants you need and come down to the medical unit."

"Sir?" Grushkov's voice was doubtful. Noah assumed Grushkov didn't usually involve himself with such details. Well, he would this time.

"Is there some problem?" Noah asked coldly.

"No, sir. We'll be down immediately."

CHAPTER FOUR

Grushkov stared at his communit in dismay. He'd never downloaded a personality. He could have lived forever without Noah Wydlin finding that out. His strength was in management—always had been. Now Mr. Wydlin wanted someone downloaded, and it seemed urgent.

Grushkov gripped the edge of his console. He simply couldn't do it. He would have to find someone else, but then he'd have to convince Mr. Wydlin that the substitute was the most qualified person for the task. Mr. Wydlin wouldn't be amused if Grushkov pleaded his own inability, but if he were able to tout the excellent qualifications of the person he assigned . . .

Grushkov called up his personnel list on the computer and scanned it. Dieterich was capable, but there was nothing special about him. Nothing Grushkov could impress Mr. Wydlin with. He thought about Karenin, briefly, but realized Karenin did every critical task that came along. If Karenin—however improbably—failed at this, Mr. Wydlin might fire him, and then Grushkov would be left without his lead programmer. He should look for some other possibility.

He went through the other names quickly, trying to

see one that stood out. He noticed Trask's name. She was new to Genesis Station. He had a vague recollection of a young woman with straight, mousy hair and colorless eyes—eminently forgettable. But something niggled at the back of his brain, telling him she might be the answer.

He called up her employment record. Jovanna Trask. She had come here to replace Semprini, who had some sort of neurophysical problem related to extended time inside a space station. Trask had been out of school about a year and had been performing routine programming tasks at Wydlin Corporation ever since. No complaints about her work, but no commendations, either.

Grushkov frowned. Nothing impressive there, unless it was her university record. He called up her transcript and letters of recommendation. She had graduated from the Artificial Intelligence program with highest honors. What was she doing on a remote space station, performing simple software maintenance and updating?

He flipped through the letters. One professor praised her effusively, saying that her abilities were particularly amazing because of her "humble beginnings."

Grushkov read further and discovered that Jovanna Trask's parents had apparently belonged to the manager caste of Martian society—a caste that ranked below the powerful, wealthy executive caste and above the laborer caste. Trask had won the Ingrid Zetzen Scholarship to Coprates University, a scholarship bequeathed by an eccentric Martian heiress to reward talented but impoverished aspirants to higher education. Grushkov doubted that Ingrid Zetzen had really meant for anyone outside the executive caste to receive her scholarship, but Trask had won it. And she had justified her selection by earning every honor available.

He examined her other references until he found one that nearly made his heart stop. There was a brief memo to Wydlin Corporation's personnel chief that said simply, "Please hire Jovanna Trask and give her something suitable to do." It was signed, "Remus Wydlin."

Grushkov squirmed uncomfortably. He'd had this ge-

nius in his department for the past four months and had
made scant use of her talents. Well, that would change
immediately. He put a call through to Trask.

$$\bigcirc \quad \bigcirc \quad \bigcirc \quad \bigcirc \quad \bigcirc$$

Jovanna looked up, startled, at the chime from her
console. It sounded as if someone was calling her, and in
the middle of the day. She couldn't remember the last
time that had happened. The lead programmer, Andre
Karenin, usually left a list of tasks for her via the computer network. He called only to scream at her when he
thought she'd fouled up. Since she was always able to
prove that she hadn't, he had stopped calling her. Instead, if he had a question about something she had
done, he'd leave it on the computer net, with instructions for her to answer on the net. It was a less terrify-
ing way to communicate, but a lot lonelier.

Jovanna would have liked it if Karenin, or Dieterich,
or anyone else on the station had stopped by her cubicle
to speak to her in person. But she knew now that it
wasn't going to happen. She was of a low caste, with no
connections. Well, that wasn't exactly true. She had
met Remus Wydlin through her friend Rachel, but she
was too proud to ask the others to accept her on that
basis. Executive-caste Martians flashed their connections around like jewels, but she just couldn't do it.
Maybe that was the real difference between the classes.

The console chimed again insistently. Her fingers fal-
tered as she reached for the switch. She took a deep
breath and flipped on the comm. "Jovanna Trask."

"Hello, Jovanna." The pale, pudgy man on the screen
looked like Stephan Grushkov, the head of Programming, but that was ridiculous. If Karenin wouldn't
speak to her, why would the boss?

"Hello," she said cautiously.

"This is Stephan Grushkov. I'm sorry we haven't
talked before this. Could you stop by my office, please?"

"Yes, sir. When?" It was all Jovanna could do to get
the words out.

"Right away, please."
"Yes, sir."

O O O O O

Stephan Grushkov had a large office in the executive
pyramid, which jutted up right through the surface of
the exterior. One wall was of glass, admitting paler sun-
light than Jovanna had been used to on Mars. Genesis
Station was in the core of a hollowed rock. The areas in
which Jovanna worked and lived were small and
tunnel-like, but the executive offices were larger and
made to look almost like those back on Mars. Of course,
from the station's orbital path, shared with Jupiter, the
sun wasn't as strong as it was at home. Still, Jovanna
was mesmerized by the pale natural light, so different
from the greenish artificial light below the surface.

"I'm glad you could come," Grushkov said. "I have
what I think you'll find a challenging assignment."

"Yes, sir," said Jovanna, glad that she had done nothing wrong.

"I wish we had more time to talk, but it appears to be
rather urgent. Noah Wydlin called me from the med
unit a few minutes ago. He needs someone downloaded
into the computer matrix. Do you have any experience
with that procedure?"

"I did it for practicum my fourth year at Coprates,"
Jovanna said, feeling dizzy. In a matter of moments, she
had gone from being completely unknown and unappreciated to being asked to perform a special task for the
CEO. "It's been about a year, but I think I could still do
it. The med-tech does most of—"

"Great!" Grushkov rose and walked from behind his
desk. "Well, it's urgent, so we'd better go down."

Jovanna bumped into the doorframe in her hurry to
keep up with her supervisor. He turned around and
peered at her anxiously. "Are you all right?"

"Yes . . . I'm sorry," she said, startled by his apparent
concern. She was even more startled when he took her
arm and helped her through the door.

O O O O O

The patient hadn't arrived yet. Jovanna occupied herself by accessing and examining the digital encoding program. It appeared to be in order, at least as up-to-date as the one she'd used at Coprates. The electroencephalograph link was being tested by a med technician; he nodded to Jovanna when he was finished. "All set," he said briefly.

Grushkov was pacing the long, pale gray room. Jovanna wondered why everyone seemed so tense. The treatment room seemed unnaturally quiet. She was used to being ignored, but usually when her coworkers ignored her, they continued to talk to each other.

The door swung open and admitted two white-garbed men pushing a wheeled cart, which presumably held the patient. When the cart came to a stop in front of the EEG link, Jovanna drew in her breath sharply. The patient looked just like Rachel Wydlin.

Jovanna looked closer but saw nothing to change her mind. The woman was thinner than Rachel had been when Jovanna had known her, and certainly far less healthy, but Rachel had been in prison for six months.

What was Rachel doing here? She'd been sentenced to life imprisonment. It hadn't been easy for Jovanna to learn that, since RAM was determined to keep the case quiet. RAM couldn't admit there was any discontent with them, especially among the upper class.

Jovanna's monitoring of the case, by infiltrating a supposedly secure database, amounted to information piracy. For long afterward, she had lived in terror that RAM Security would find her out and she'd join Rachel in prison. But she'd covered her tracks well, and now it was unlikely that the deed would catch up with her.

Jovanna looked pityingly at Rachel as the medical technician applied the electrodes that would download her brain waves into the computer matrix, forming the basis for a digital personality. How did this happen? she asked her friend silently.

She imagined she heard Rachel's ironic laughter inside her head. "Why not, Jo? You know how I feel about RAM. I gambled and lost."

Rachel had been Jovanna's best friend at Coprates University. A few people in her department treated Jovanna with some respect, but almost everyone at Coprates had ignored her, just as they did here. When Jovanna worked as the environment design technician for a university theater production, Rachel took her under her wing.

"You're really quite talented," Rachel had said.

"Oh, no!" Jovanna had stammered. Rachel had one of the lead parts in the play and was admired by everyone in the cast. "You—you're the talented one. I'm just—"

"Just too modest," Rachel had finished. "You're the only one who's ever been able to make the environmental software do anything even remotely predictable."

It had taken Jovanna a long time to trust Rachel. At first she had assumed that Rachel just didn't know that she was lower caste. After it became clear that Rachel knew all about it, Jovanna thought that perhaps she was making some kind of a political statement. Jovanna's friendship might be a way to demonstrate her broad-mindedness. Once, during an argument, Jovanna had accused Rachel of using her to boost her own ego.

"I am not!" Rachel had declared angrily. "You make me crazy sometimes, following me around like a puppy, hanging on my every word. I hate it when you do that!"

"What do you want, then?" Jovanna had asked.

"I want you to be honest and give me the benefit of the doubt! I truly like you, Jo. Except when you're being a pain in the ass."

"Like now?" Jovanna was beginning to calm down. She could see the humor in their argument. How many people screamed their admiration for each other?

Rachel had laughed. "Yeah . . . like now."

After graduation, Rachel had been angry when Jovanna couldn't find a job. It wasn't that she was offered work that was unworthy of her talents. She received no offers at all. No one wanted to deal with a university-trained expert in artificial intelligence who wouldn't fit in socially with her colleagues.

Finally Rachel had insisted that Jovanna apply to Wydlin Corporation. Jovanna resisted at first, just as she had resisted going on for further academic work. She'd gone to the university to prove she was worthy of the best Mars had to offer. Maybe someday she would return to an academic setting, but not until she'd made Martian society accept her on her own terms.

Thinking about it now, Jovanna almost laughed aloud. She had been infected by Rachel's idealism and naivete. RAM had defeated them both. RAM would always win.

As Jovanna sat at the console to begin the encoding process, a shiver went through her. Rachel could be vulnerable in the computer matrix, depending on how vengeful RAM really was. Well, not if Jovanna could help it. She would give Rachel as much protection from electronic sabotage as she could.

When the program asked for the name of the new personality, she turned to Grushkov. "What name do they want?"

Grushkov's brow furrowed, and he went over to the wall communit. "Mr. Wydlin, are you there?" Immediately Jovanna realized why everyone in the room seemed to be walking on eggshells. Noah Wydlin was watching the entire process.

"Yes, what is it, Grushkov?"

"What's the lady's name? We need to know for the encoding process."

There was a pause, then Noah Wydlin's smooth voice came over the speaker. "She was rescued from a ship, which later blew up. We found no identification."

Grushkov relayed Wydlin's statement to Jovanna, even though she had heard it clearly. She frowned at her computer screen. It didn't make sense. She knew it was Rachel; why did her own brother deny knowing her? Perhaps Noah didn't want it known that Rachel was out of prison and had somehow made it to Wydlin Corporation's research station. He would face criminal charges himself if RAM ever found out. Still, Jovanna was angry at his denial of his sister. She typed, "RW."

Grushkov, at her shoulder, looked puzzled. "Why 'RW'?"

Jovanna nearly told him the truth, but her native caution returned. "For 'Reborn at Wydlin.' "

Grushkov smiled nervously and patted her shoulder. "Very clever."

Jovanna monitored the encoding program until it ran the message that the process was complete. "All done," she told Grushkov. "It'll take her some time to get used to computerspace, but at least she's there."

"Are you sure?" Grushkov asked.

Jovanna smiled. Her superior was either not very experienced in the digital translation of personalities or extremely nervous or both. She said, "Yes, I'm sure. Whether she'll communicate with us is another matter, though. I'll try to contact her through the computer, but she'll reply when she's good and ready. Because we didn't use the name she had during her biological life but made up a name designation for her, she may not respond right away."

Jovanna leaned forward, speaking into the computer's microphone. "RW? RW? Please respond." There was no reaction. Jovanna felt a mild alarm, but reminded herself that it might take some time. She keyed in the new digital personality's identification code, "RW." This time the blinking insertion point moved to the line below Jovanna's typed request of its own accord. It was a rather small, unsatisfying response, but at least Jovanna knew she'd made contact. It might be easier if she could use Rachel's real name, but she didn't dare do that in front of the others. She turned to Grushkov.

"She's not talking much yet. I'll keep working with her until she does. We don't need the medical people anymore. I'll do just as well with her back in my office."

"Fine, Jovanna," he said, clasping his hands together tightly. "But first let me introduce you to Mr. Wydlin. Then you can go back."

Jovanna was mildly terrified at the thought of meeting Noah Wydlin, but she attempted a smile. "Yes, sir."

She followed Grushkov down a corridor and into a small room outfitted with a computer and video setup. A tall, handsome man with thick brown hair sat at the screen. Grushkov pushed her forward. "Mr. Wydlin, this is Jovanna Trask. She's our artificial intelligence expert, the one who performed the translation."

Jovanna blinked. She had been trained in artificial intelligence, but since coming to work at Wydlin Corporation, her job title had been "Software Maintenance Technician." She wondered when she'd gotten the promotion. Probably when she agreed to encode Rachel.

"Hello," Noah Wydlin said. "I've never seen a person digitally encoded before. It was a success?"

Jovanna had the impression that he was more keenly interested than his casual words indicated. She made her voice as light and unconcerned as his. "Practically routine, Mr. Wydlin. Her response has been minimal so far, but considering how far gone she seemed to be at the time of the encoding, that's not unusual."

"I'll be interested to see how it all turns out," Wydlin said.

"I'll keep you posted," Grushkov said. "I understand Ms. Trask is a friend of the family. Perhaps you'd rather she contacted you directly."

"A friend of the family?" Wydlin turned to look at her with a puzzled expression. Jovanna felt her face grow hot. It would be dangerous to mention Rachel, of that she felt certain.

"Not really," she said, trying to sound amused. "I was introduced to your father by a mutual friend. Very kindly, Dr. Wydlin arranged a job for me with Wydlin Corporation. But I don't suppose he's spoken more than two or three times to me in my life."

"Remus has always been very kind," Wydlin said in the same tone he might have used to imply that his father was a fool.

Jovanna sensed that the interview was over. Apparently Grushkov thought so, too, because he nodded and moved toward the door. It whooshed open and he indicated to Jovanna that she should precede him.

As the door closed behind them, Grushkov said, "That went rather well, I think. It seems that the operation wasn't as urgent as I thought. I'm glad you were available, though."

"Any time, Mr. Grushkov," Jovanna said. Her duties weren't so pressing that she couldn't leave them to encode an occasional digital personality.

"I'd like you to follow up on this until you get a positive response from RW. Please, keep me informed," Grushkov said as they walked out of the med unit.

"Of course," Jovanna said politely. She was struggling to keep her mind off her conflicting emotions—joy at finally being asked to work with a digital personality again, sorrow that that person was Rachel, and fear that she wouldn't be able to reach her friend.

○ ○ ○ ○ ○

When Jovanna was back in her work cubicle, she typed "RW" into the terminal once more. The blinking cursor moved down to the next line, seemingly of its own accord, and remained there, unrevealing. That was something, at least. Jovanna tried again, this time typing "RACHEL? IT'S JOVANNA. ARE YOU THERE?"

This time there was no response at all. Jovanna sat back, chewing her lip. She knew of no reason for Rachel not to respond, if she understood. Perhaps her time in prison or the trauma of the accident had done something to Rachel. Jovanna sighed. It would take time, but it might be profitable in the long run to make sure that Rachel's language use was at the standard level.

Jovanna keyed in the two command sequences that would run the English and Cultural Background tutorial programs for RW. There was little else she could do tonight for her. The real Rachel Wydlin was dying. Jovanna couldn't be with Rachel without arousing suspicion, but at least she could be alone, to think of her. She went to her room.

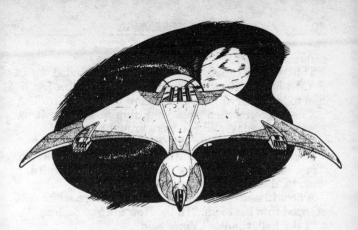

CHAPTER FIVE

Vince's head ached. Actually, his whole body felt as if someone had bounced him down the side of a mountain. A groan escaped from him as he considered whether to risk opening his eyes.

"Are you awake?" a perfectly modulated voice asked him. He decided to open his eyes. He was lying in a bed, a sheet covering him to the shoulders. Seated on the edge of the bed was a thin, short-haired digital personality of indeterminate gender. Glowing a pale orange, it smiled at him. "You are awake. You had us wondering."

"Who—who are you?" Vince croaked. His throat felt as if it had rusted. He wondered how long it had been since he last spoke.

"How original. Most people's first words are 'Where am I?' I am Monitor. I was supposed to keep an eye on you and let them know at the primary care station when you woke up." Monitor's eyes flickered. "I just signaled them. They'll be coming soon."

"Where am I?" Vince asked, too miserable to care if Monitor was disappointed in his lack of originality.

"You're at Genesis Station. I'm afraid I'm not allowed to tell you any more than that. The director will want to speak with you before you're cleared for more sensitive information."

That was a relief. At least he hadn't ended up in RAM's hands. He wondered why Noah Wydlin felt he had to be "cleared," however. "How did I get here?"

"You were rescued from your ship just before it exploded yesterday, and you were brought here."

"The others—how are they?"

Monitor took on a routinely sorrowful expression. "Two of them died before we found you. The third, a woman, died this morning. But they—"

A door hissed open and a woman wearing a white coat stepped into his room. "Hello. How are you feeling?"

"Like hell, thanks," Vince said.

The woman smiled sympathetically. "That's to be expected." She turned on a small, hand-held light and shined it into his eyes. "You had a very narrow escape, Mr.— I'm sorry. We had no way of learning your name."

"That's sensitive information." Vince smiled at her crookedly. "I can't clear you to hear it until I've talked with Wydlin—excuse me, your director."

"How did you—?" the woman began, then stopped herself. She finished examining him without speaking. Then, apparently satisfied, she said, "You'll live."

When she left the room, Vince closed his eyes to shut out Monitor's hovering orange form. He willed himself to relax. Dropping Wydlin's name should get him an interview with Noah sooner than he otherwise would. Maybe then he could get some real answers.

$$O \quad O \quad O \quad O \quad O$$

Noah Wydlin looked down at Pirelli as he slept. Now that Pirelli had begun talking, Noah realized they should meet as quickly as possible. Pirelli would just have to delay his nap. "Hello, Mystery Man."

Vince Pirelli started awake and blinked several times. He looked up at Noah. "I'm no mystery to you."

"No," Noah said, "but I have to be sure you'll help me before I admit to knowing you."

"Help you? How?"

Noah pulled a chair close to the bed so that he could speak softly. There should be no malevolent eavesdroppers here on his own space station, but he still felt better keeping this conversation intimate. "You're the only survivor of the RMS *Hermes*. Only you and I—and one other person, whom I believe to be trustworthy—know the name of your cruiser. Only you and I know why you're here. I want to make sure it stays that way."

"Works for me," Pirelli said.

Noah wasn't surprised at Pirelli's calm acceptance. He had angled for a permanent job at Wydlin Corporation before he undertook the rescue mission. It would be in his best interests to keep Noah happy.

"Good," said Noah. "Then here's your story. You're a free-lance pilot, working out of the Asteroid Belt. "You had an assignment to deliver a cargo to Jupiter. However, some pirates ambushed you. You barely escaped. The others on the cruiser were all members of your crew. You don't know much about them. In the Belt, you rarely ask for full employment histories."

Pirelli nodded. "True. And if I tell this story, it saves you the trouble of trying to explain how I got here."

"Yes," Noah said. He was glad Pirelli was proving to be moderately intelligent. Maybe there was a place for him at Wydlin Corporation. Once his father decided to resume work on the Barneys, Noah would need a pilot he could trust. He had Gretsky, and he knew he could trust Andreyev, the commander of the spaceport on Genesis, to a certain extent. But until some of the Barneys themselves learned piloting, it might be helpful to have another pilot in reserve.

Pirelli said, "I was told that one of the women survived until this morning."

"Yes. It was Rachel," Noah said, answering Pirelli's unspoken question.

"I'm sorry," Pirelli said.

Noah answered absently. "I had her digitally encoded before she died. I hope that will be good enough."

Noah had no idea how Remus would react to finding that Rachel was now a digital personality, but it would have been far better to have her whole and sound. The report from Jovanna Trask had been depressing. "RW," as Trask called Rachel, seemed to have no memory of her past life. Trask had spent hours just getting Rachel to understand human language and common points of reference. He stood and walked to the door.

Pirelli stopped him. "May I ask you a question?"

"You may ask," Wydlin said.

"Why not just have me killed?"

Wydlin looked at Pirelli, momentarily stunned. Then he realized why Pirelli had asked. He was Terran. Most non-Martians believed RAM executives or executives of RAM subsidiaries, like Wydlin Corporation thought of their own power above all else, including legal or moral obligations. In many cases, Noah had to admit, that perception was correct. Yet until he'd hired Pirelli, Noah had never done anything illegal. And his family's opinions notwithstanding, he'd tried to be reasonably moral as well. Maybe Remus had more influence over Noah than either of them realized. It was a depressing thought; softhearted RAM executives didn't last long.

"So far, I've never had to have anyone killed. I'm sure you don't want to be the first."

"No, sir," Pirelli admitted with a smile.

"Then we'll get along fine," Noah said, cutting off further conversation.

○ ○ ○ ○ ○

Vince lay quietly for several minutes after Noah Wydlin's visit. It seemed as if Wydlin was going to let him stay at Genesis Station for a while. It was difficult to tell how long he'd have, though. How long to—what? Jacques told him what his assignment was, but that seemed years ago. He was supposed to get Rachel Wydlin out of prison and recruit her to NEO during the flight to Genesis; that part was easy to remember. But RAM had wiped out all of Rachel's memories. She didn't remember anything about NEO. In fact, she had the approximate mental ability of a newborn baby.

Vince frowned, trying to remember. After Rachel, what had Jacques told him to do? There was a secret project, he remembered. Vince's eyes, casting about the room as he thought, settled on a compdex on a small console against a wall.

He pulled himself to the terminal and punched up the user directory. There were listings for the station bulletin board, Mediabloc and Infonet, as well as the standard listing of access codes for different departments. He stared at it stupidly for several seconds, then laughed weakly at himself. What had he been expecting? If he weren't so disoriented, he might be able to think of some way to attack the vast information stores before him. As it was, he couldn't imagine how to begin.

Noah Wydlin said Rachel had been translated into a digital personality. Vince wasn't sure what to expect of her in that form, since she'd been pretty helpless in human form when he'd last seen her. But maybe she could help Vince now.

The directory of digital personalities consisted of one direction, which should have been simple: "ENTER NAME OF DIGITAL PERSONALITY." But when Vince entered "RACHEL," nothing happened. He tried again, typing "RACHEL WYDLIN." The computer screen flashed the message, "RACHEL WYDLIN IS A RESTRICTED ACCESS INFORMATION CATEGORY. TO REQUEST INFORMATION, EXIT DIGITAL PERSONALITY MENU AND ENTER YOUR ACCESS CODE."

"Maybe later," Vince muttered. He entered "WYDLIN" and read the computer's reply: "WYDLIN IS AN INFORMATION CATEGORY. TO REQUEST INFORMATION, EXIT DIGITAL PERSONALITY MENU AND ENTER YOUR ACCESS CODE."

"Damn box," Vince said, resisting the urge to hit the compdex. He stared at the screen, trying to think around the headache that was worsening by the minute. "All right, how about this?" He typed "RW."

After a moment, a message appeared below his last line. "I'M BUSY NOW. I'll BE WITH YOU AS SOON AS I CAN."

"Bingo!" Vince said, then corrected himself. "I hope."

Several seconds later, another message appeared on his screen. "CURRENT USER, PLEASE IDENTIFY."

Vince frowned. Was Rachel being coy or what? Or was someone onto him? He wished he could think more clearly. With a groan of frustration, he switched off the compdex and staggered back to bed.

O O O O O

Rachel, now RW, sat perched on the edge of Jovanna's console, her holographic legs crossed at the knee.

"I wish I understood what was going on," Jovanna complained. "Why can't you remember anything?"

"I'm sorry," RW said. "I have no idea. But if I really have this past life as a human, as you say, why don't you just point me toward the data on me? I'll learn it, and you'll be happy."

"First of all," Jovanna said, "there's more to you than was stored in the computer matrix. But more importantly, it'd be dangerous to call up data about Rachel Wydlin. If RAM is looking for you, they're just waiting for a move like that."

"All right," RW said and shrugged, looking a lot like Rachel.

Jovanna tried to ignore the pang RW's characteristic shrug sent through her and apply her mind to the current problem. "I've run every diagnostic test on you I can think of. There was nothing wrong with the encoding process. You should be fine."

"Jo-*van*-na," RW said, rolling her eyes. "I *am* fine. If you'd just—" Her eyes went momentarily blank, and Jovanna sat up. Usually a digital personality looked blank when it was accessing information from the matrix or when someone at another terminal was trying to access the digital personality.

"What is it?" Jovanna asked.

"What do you know?" RW said. "Someone wants to talk to me. I'll be right back."

"No!" Jovanna cried quickly. "You don't know who it

is. Go into secure mode, and I'll take care of it." RW made a face at Jovanna and vanished.

Jovanna typed a request for user identification. She waited a moment for a reply, but none appeared. "Why doesn't that surprise me?" she muttered. She keyed in a sequence that would trace the terminal that had tried to access RW. In a moment, a message appeared on her screen: "NO CURRENT REQUESTS FOR RW."

"Oh, don't give me that!" she said. As she considered the problem of finding out who had recently requested RW, she heard the quiet slide of the Programming Department door opening. No one should be here at this hour; the others had been gone for over two hours.

"Who is it?" she called out.

"Jovanna Trask?" asked a somewhat familiar male voice. Jovanna frowned, trying to place it.

"Yes?" she said.

"It's Remus Wydlin."

Jovanna let out the breath she wasn't aware she'd been holding. "Oh, Dr. Wydlin. I'm in the fourth cubicle." She hastily swept stray papers from her console and rose to greet him.

Remus stood in the small space between the edge of the console and the temporary wall that divided Jovanna's workspace from her neighbor's. "It's nice to see you again, Jovanna." He looked around her tiny cubicle. "They don't give you much room around here, do they?"

"I'm told space is at a premium on Genesis Station," Jovanna said. She didn't mention that the one executive office she'd seen—Grushkov's—had plenty of room.

"Perhaps," Remus Wydlin said, with a skeptical look. He gestured toward her chair. "Could we sit down?"

"Sure," Jovanna said. "I'll get a chair from the next cubicle."

"Allow me," he said, stepping around the partition.

When they were both seated, he said, "I understand you got the job of encoding Rachel."

"Yes," Jovanna said, then stopped, wondering how much Noah had told his father.

"I'd like to speak to her," he said.

"Dr. Wydlin, she's not exactly . . ."

"Noah said she'd been through a lot."

He looked calm, but Jovanna noticed that his hands were tightly clenched together. She didn't know what to say to him. What came out, to her horror, was "She has no memory." He looked at her with his mouth slightly open, as if someone had punched him in the stomach. Quickly she tried to lessen the damage. "But she's better than she was at first, Dr. Wydlin. I had to run the language systems they use to design generated digital personalities on her before she could even communicate. Now she talks very fluently. She has a real personality. She's just not . . ." Jovanna stopped herself.

"Just not Rachel," Dr. Wydlin finished for her. "Noah said she wouldn't be. But he said you were working hard. Do you think she'll come back?"

Jovanna looked down at her hands. It was a measure of Dr. Wydlin's sorrow that he even asked the question, just as it was a measure of her own that she'd been working so hard to find out what had happened to Rachel's memories. If Dr. Wydlin were thinking more clearly, he'd realize that the trauma of Rachel's experiences had affected her physical body. The damage was there at the time of the encoding, and there were no memories to retrieve. It was next to impossible for the things Rachel had experienced in her past life to come back to her now that she was in digital form.

"Never mind," he said, seeming to understand her silence. "I know. I just— Could I see her?"

"Sure," Jovanna said, relieved to be able to answer something in the affirmative. She keyed in the code that would recall RW from her secure position.

"Hi, Jovanna," RW said, popping into existence in front of the console. "Did you find the bad guys?"

"No," Jovanna said.

"Hey, who's he?" RW pointed to her former father.

"Rachel!" said Jovanna, embarrassed.

"No kidding! Your name is Rachel?" RW looked at Dr. Wydlin, her head cocked inquisitively to one side. "Jovanna calls me Rachel sometimes. She says my name was Rachel when I was human."

"I'm Remus Wydlin," he said, smiling.

RW shook her head sympathetically. "She just calls everyone Rachel, I guess. Well, I suppose it's easier than remembering a lot of names."

"That's true," Remus said, smiling. Jovanna saw a sudden moisture in his eyes and his shoulders sagged. He blinked rapidly a few times, then turned to Jovanna. There was a catch in his voice as he said, "Could I stay while you work with her?"

Jovanna hesitated. It would be hard on him to see how like, yet unlike, Rachel RW was. Still, after he saw RW for a while, he'd know that Rachel wasn't coming back. "All right," she said. "Though I wasn't going to do much more tonight.

"You promised I could learn about computer security," RW reminded her.

Jovanna glanced guiltily at Dr. Wydlin. "I'm concerned that RAM might discover RW's whereabouts. I want her to be able to protect herself."

"What did you think, Jovanna Trask?" he said. "That I'd suspect you of ferreting out Wydlin Corporation secrets? You don't seem like an industrial spy type to me. Please, go ahead."

Jovanna smiled at him, then said to RW, "All right, I'll open the file for you." She punched a few keys. "Have at it."

RW disappeared once again. "She's studying the program," Jovanna explained. "When she finishes it, she should be pretty well able to take care of herself. Not a moment too soon, either."

"What do you mean?" he asked.

"Just tonight, someone tried to access her. It wasn't you, was it?"

"No."

"That would have been all right. Or if it was Mr. Wydlin—your son, that is. But whoever it was, he wouldn't identify himself. I don't like that."

"You think someone's trying to hurt her?"

"I can't tell," Jovanna said. "But I'm going to try to

find out."

"That could be dangerous for you," Dr. Wydlin said.

"I hope not. I'm a devout coward."

"Oh, no," he protested politely.

"I've known people with courage. I'm not anything like—"

Again Dr. Wydlin finished for her. "Like Rachel."

"I'm sorry, Dr. Wydlin." Her eyes stung, as much for his sake as for hers. When would she learn to keep her mouth shut?

"Don't be. It's nice to meet someone who feels that way about her," he said. "Everyone else thinks she was either evil or insane."

"Well, they're idiots then," Jovanna said emphatically, surprised at her own passion.

RW appeared again. "That was interesting. What else can we do?"

Jovanna looked at Dr. Wydlin. He looked worn out, and she'd put in a long day herself. "That's it for tonight. Try to stay out of trouble. I'll see you in the morning."

RW pouted, pushed her chin up into the air, and disappeared.

"Just like having a kid," Jovanna said, turning to smile at Dr. Wydlin. He was wearing a shocked expression and seemed much paler than he had been. "Dr. Wydlin, are you all right?"

"Yes, Jovanna," he said. "She just surprised me. When she pouted like that, it was as if she was four years old again."

"Maybe you should go to the med unit," she said. He still looked terribly pale and suddenly much older.

"No. I'm just tired."

"Well, I'll help you to your room, then," Jovanna said. "Or should I call your son?"

"No," he said, smiling weakly. "I don't feel up to seeing Noah tonight."

Jovanna wasn't surprised he felt that way. Noah Wydlin had seemed brusque and preoccupied in the few short conversations she'd had with him. If she weren't feeling well, Noah Wydlin would be the last person she'd want to see.

○   ○   ○   ○   ○

Remus Wydlin's suite was on the top floor of the station's exterior pyramid. The pyramid was an extravagance. They hadn't really needed to build any part of the station on the exterior of the asteroid, but Noah had wanted windows. Noah enjoyed surrounding himself, and those he favored, with luxury, even in deep space beyond Jupiter. Remus had protested about the expense, but Noah assured him it was necessary for business. If they were going to ask employees to spend a long time on Genesis Station, they'd have to make it as pleasant as possible.

Remus had noticed, however, that only the higher-ranking employees lived and worked in the external pyramid. Jovanna's room, for example, like her cubicle, was in the tunneled interior of the asteroid.

Putting a blanket over Remus as he lay on the couch, Joanna asked him for perhaps the tenth time if he didn't think he ought to go to the med unit.

"I'm fine," he said. "Do I really look that bad?"

"No . . . of course not," she said, looking miserable. Her eyes, neither blue, green, nor gray, were deeply shadowed beneath a fringe of mousy brown hair. It suddenly occurred to Remus that Jovanna was grieving for Rachel just as he was. Noah had been particularly insensitive to make her work on Rachel's digital personality.

"I can't believe Noah was heartless enough to make you work on RW," Remus said. "I'm going to speak to him about it."

"No, please don't!" Jovanna said. "He doesn't know that I was Rachel's friend. And I want to work with her."

"Jovanna," Remus said, "you can't bring her back. You've said so yourself."

"I know." Her face started to contort. Remus hoped she wouldn't cry.

"All we can do for Rachel is to make her death mean something." Remus tried to distract her.

"How?" Jovanna asked.

"Rachel hated RAM. After what happened to her, I'd say she had good reason."

"I'm beginning think so." Jovanna's forehead began to pucker again.

"So we'll just have to find a way to make RAM pay for what they did to her." Jovanna was staring at him, her mouth an **O** of surprise.

Suddenly Remus realized what he was saying. Then he thought, why not? He still had a few good years in him. And he had the beginnings of a weapon the Barneys. He'd thought the corporation would market them, but now he had a better idea. The Barneys could form the basis of an invincible corporate army. Noah had mused about the possibility of using them in such a way. Remus was beginning to agree with him, though admittedly for different reasons. Remus himself knew little of the necessary strategies, but the Barneys could learn all they'd need to know. And Noah, with his understanding of Martian politics, would know how to best take advantage of the Barneys' abilities.

"I don't know . . ." Jovanna began uncertainly, bringing Remus back to himself.

"Shh, shh," he said, patting her hand. What had he been thinking of, talking that way in front of the girl? He had no business involving her. Still, he wanted to comfort her. "Don't worry, Jovanna. Everything will be all right. Rachel didn't die for nothing."

"What are you going to do?"

"It's better if you don't know too much," he said. "Someday you'll realize, and you'll feel better. Now, you go on home. I need to think."

Looking puzzled, Jovanna let him guide her to the door. "Good night, Dr. Wydlin."

"Good night, Jovanna," he said, letting her out. Then he went straight to his study.

CHAPTER SIX

Jovanna listened as the Programming Department door shut behind Karenin, who was the last of her colleagues to leave. Her computer screen still showed columns of digits from the diagnostics he'd asked her to run. Her usual list of tasks had been on the net this morning. It was the only indication she received that her work with RW was no longer considered necessary.

But Jovanna wasn't finished with RW yet. And since no one had specifically told her not to work with the digital personality, she planned to continue. Dr. Wydlin's reaction to RW made Jovanna realize she couldn't simply leave RW as she was. It was time to teach the computer personality about her past life. Jovanna didn't expect RW to turn back into Rachel, but at least she might learn to be more sensitive to people who'd known her in the past.

She leaned forward to speak into the microphone, then sat back abruptly. Last night when she'd worked with RW, some unknown person had interrupted them, trying to access RW. Jovanna still hadn't learned who it was. It wouldn't hurt to be cautious. Instead of accessing RW directly, Jovanna could approach her through a "back door," entering a command sequence that would allow her to locate RW within the matrix and discover whether—and where—she might be interacting with any humans. Jovanna's fingers flew over the keys.

○ ○ ○ ○ ○

"This is interesting." RW looked out at Vince from the compdex screen, her head tilted to one side. "Jovanna never told me Rachel was a terrorist."

"Not a terrorist, a revolutionary," Vince said.

"RAM says anyone who'd destroy a weapons plant—"

"I know what RAM says," Vince interrupted her. "But it was RAM that killed Rachel. Are you going to believe everything they say?"

"I can only go on the data."

"Well, I'm trying to supply you with some new data," said Vince. "But I don't want to duplicate things you already know."

"I'm only four days old. I don't know all that much," RW said.

"Do you know anything about Rachel Wydlin?" That should be a relatively safe topic, Vince figured. He didn't want to say anything to her about NEO unless she seemed sympathetic to their cause. Her reaction to what he told her about Rachel should tell him what he needed to know.

"All I know is that I used to be a human, and my name was Rachel Wydlin. Jovanna did say RAM would be looking for me. She's always telling me I have to be careful. You're not from RAM, are you?" RW's blue eyes widened at the thought, but she looked more excited than worried.

"No, I'm not," Vince said.

"Oh. All right. So tell me about Rachel Wydlin."

"Well, Rachel would be about twenty-three years old. She—Wait a minute." Vince frowned. He'd activated a simple alarm program before he contacted RW. After his last attempt to talk to her, he wanted to know if anyone had detected him interacting with her. A small dot flashed on and off in the upper right corner of the screen. Someone was eavesdropping.

"Excuse me, RW," he said. "I need to do something with a program I'm running."

He typed "LOCATE," then tried to figure out what to do next.

"Hey!" said RW. "Aren't you going to finish telling me about Rachel?"

"Well, I'd like to," Vince said, "but I need the answer to a question to finish this other thing I'm working on. Do you think you could help me out?"

"And then you'll tell me about Rachel?"

"Then I'll tell you about Rachel."

"All right," RW said. "What is it?"

"I have to know how many stars there are in the universe."

RW frowned. "What database will that be in?"

Vince smiled. He hoped the task would keep her busy for a while and whoever was following her would stay at his terminal to monitor her movements. "I'm no computer expert. You'll just have to look around."

"All right," RW said. "See you later." Her image disappeared from the screen, leaving only the blinking light in the upper right corner. Several seconds later, a map appeared on the screen, and the blinking light appeared on a section of the floor plan. Vince studied the map and satisfied himself that he could find the area, which was labeled "Programming Department." The eavesdropper wasn't Noah Wydlin, then. If it wasn't a RAM agent, it was probably some loyal Martian who'd lead RAM to Vince. Unless Vince stopped him.

O O O O O

Jovanna watched as her screen spelled out the message, "RW ACTIVE AT TERMINAL IN MED UNIT PATIENT ROOM." She sat back, frowning. Who in the med unit would be interested in Rachel? It was probably an industrial spy. RAM was rumored to have spies in many of its subsidiary companies. What if a RAM spy had figured out who RW was?

The screen changed. Jovanna read the new message: "RW IN TRANSIT THROUGH COMPUTER MATRIX." Where could she be going? She was so trusting; the spy could send her straight to Simund Holzerhein.

"RW!" Jovanna nearly shouted into the speaker. "Come back here!"

Then she realized shouting wouldn't bring RW back. Jovanna typed, "RW, RETURN TO PROGRAMMING TERMINAL."

Nothing happened. RW was ignoring her; it was just like having a stubborn child. Jovanna could try reasoning with RW, but first she'd have to preempt whatever suggestion RW was following. Which meant she had to learn what it was. She watched her screen for the next message, hoping it would give her some clue how to get RW's attention.

$$\bigcirc \quad \bigcirc \quad \bigcirc \quad \bigcirc \quad \bigcirc$$

Vince could hear only the blood pounding in his ears. He'd never killed anyone with his own hands before, though he knew how. NEO was a strange group in many respects, but it didn't allow its operatives to go out unprepared. Well, his training would be tested now. He had found his smart suit and boots, but his pistol belt wasn't with them. He suspected the med unit personnel wouldn't return it on such short notice. He went through the door marked "Programming Department."

The room was long, with low, light-emitting ceiling panels. Just ahead was a long corridor, while to his left were semipermanent walls three-quarters of the way to the ceiling, with doorlike openings every few feet. He stepped up to the first opening. Behind the wall was a workstation, consisting mainly of a computer console. It was empty.

He stood still and listened. As he expected, from somewhere close by came the low hum of a working terminal. He walked slowly and quietly, glancing up at the ceiling. At the fourth partition, he saw a faint glow reflected in the ceiling panel. That must be the one he wanted. He inched toward the opening.

Then, taking a deep breath, he lunged around the corner. To his surprise, the workstation was empty. A screen flickered, but no one was there.

Could his adversary already have escaped? The chair was pulled close to the console, but it wasn't flush against it. Vince's lips straightened in a tight smile. He pulled the chair out suddenly, revealing a crouching form huddled beneath the console. "Throw your weapon out," Vince growled, gambling that his adversary wouldn't guess he was unarmed.

"I—I don't have one," the figure under the console said. The voice was that of a woman, with a trembling voice.

"Either you're stupid or you think I am," Vince said.

"I don't think anyone's stupid," the woman said. She sounded as if she was about to cry, but she could just be trying to con him.

"All right, come out. On your stomach, with your arms out in front of you," Vince directed. Two hands emerged from under the console, followed by arms encased in dusty brown sleeves. The woman's hair, a nondescript brown, was tousled and hung down just below her ears. She was sobbing softly. When she'd come halfway out of her hiding place, Vince put his foot on her back, stopping her movement. "That's far enough."

He considered what to do with her. She was at a terrible disadvantage; he felt strange about breaking her neck when she hadn't shown any sign of resisting. Yet. Still, she knew more than was good for him. Finally the woman spoke into the tense silence. "What do you want?"

"I'll ask the questions," Vince said. His head throbbed. "Why were you eavesdropping on my terminal?"

"I—I was just looking out for Rachel . . . I mean RW. I encoded her, and I . . . worry about her."

Vince's eyes narrowed. There was more to it than that, he'd lay odds. "Why did you call her Rachel?"

The woman was silent, confirming Vince's suspicions that she was covering something up. She'd stopped crying, but he could feel her body shaking under his foot. Well, he wasn't very comfortable in this situation himself. The safest thing would be to kill her, but something made him hesitate.

A three-dimensional image winked into being beside him, causing him to jump almost out of his skin. "Vince! What are you doing here?"

RW was looking at him with a puzzled expression. Then she looked down on the floor. "Jovanna? Is that you down there?"

The woman looked up, her face streaked, eyes red. "Y-Yes," she gulped.

"What's going on here?" RW asked.

The last thing Vince needed right now was a conversation. "This woman is a RAM agent," he told RW, then wondered why he was explaining things to a digital personality.

"Jovanna, a RAM agent? I don't think so. She doesn't even like RAM. She's always warning me about them. I told you that. Don't you remember?"

"This is Jovanna?" Vince remembered RW talking about a Jovanna . . . which didn't necessarily mean she could be trusted. RW seemed extremely gullible to Vince.

"Aren't *you* a RAM agent?" Jovanna said suddenly to Vince, then reddened, as if she realized how naive her question sounded.

Vince looked at her through narrowed eyes. If this woman was acting, then she was good at it very good indeed. Still, if she wasn't RAM, who was she?

If he were to judge on appearances alone, he'd have said she was no agent at all. She had no self-possession that he could see, and she was flabby. But why was she keeping such close tabs on the political prisoner he'd just rescued?

He remembered Jacques telling him there would be another NEO operative at Genesis Station. Could this flustered, overweight, but apparently determined woman be his contact? He frowned, trying to remember the code name Jacques had given him. The crash had played hell with his memory. Decoy? No. Dekalb!

"Do you know anything about Dekalb?" he asked her.

She looked at him blankly, then looked away, as if trying to think. After a moment, she looked back at him uncertainly and said, "It's an ancient brand of hybrid grain. If you know what Dekalb means, you must be a farmer."

Farmer! My contact name, he thought. "Right you are," he said, relieved. He helped her up. "I'm glad I found you. What's next?"

○ ○ ○ ○ ○

Pale green light from the ceiling panel formed a nimbus on Vince's curly brown hair, giving him the look of an angel in an old Terran painting. And he was Terran, Jovanna realized. He wasn't as thin and fine-boned as a Martian man. At his question, Jovanna felt her jaw drop open, then closed it firmly. She had gotten this far by convincing him that she knew what he was talking about. This wasn't the time to confess her ignorance. "I was hoping you could tell me," she said experimentally.

"You mean Beowulf didn't give you instructions?" Vince asked, frowning.

RW had taken up her usual perch on the edge of the console and was watching their interchange with a fascinated expression. Jovanna ignored her. "I thought you'd know," Jovanna said.

"Damn!" Vince said. "NEO's as bad as RAM. Why don't they trust us?"

Jovanna nodded sympathetically, but filed away the snatch of information he'd inadvertently given her. When she got a chance, she'd find out about this "NEO."

Vince was looking at her the way some Martians looked at gennies they were considering buying. His brown eyes might have seemed warm in other circumstances. To Jovanna, they just looked calculating.

"You're a programmer?"

"Well . . . yes," Jovanna said. Despite her short-lived promotion to artificial intelligence expert, she seemed doomed to be a low-level programmer forever.

"Good. I know just enough about computers not to embarrass myself," Vince said. "In other words, not enough."

Jovanna nearly said, "Enough for what?" until she remembered that she was trying to convince him she knew what was going on. She nodded knowingly.

"I don't know how we're supposed to get any reports back to headquarters, but we can at least start collecting intelligence. Maybe Beowulf will get a message to us."

"Mm-hm," Jovanna mumbled, as if the name Beowulf meant something to her.

"What do you know about Wydlin's new project?"

"Not much," said Jovanna. She saw what looked like suspicion in Vince's eyes and quickly amended her answer. "I've been looking into it, but I haven't been able to discover what it is yet."

"Well, keep working on it," Vince said. "I'll contact you in a couple of days. I should be settled by then."

"Where?" Jovanna asked.

"I'm one of Wydlin Corporation's new pilots. I'll bunk wherever they do." His smile was winning, conspiratorial. She smiled back, in spite of herself. "I'm glad we made contact, Dekalb," he said, patting her cheek. "I'll talk to you soon."

Jovanna nodded as he left the workstation. Then she heard the department door close. She reached around in a daze, feeling for her chair, and sank into it weakly.

CHAPTER SEVEN

W ell, what did you think of him?" RW appeared on the other side of Jovanna's kitchen nook counter. Jovanna had started to set her teacup down; at RW's appearance, she jumped. The cup clattered in its saucer.

"RW! You frightened me!"

As soon as she could get her legs to function, Jovanna had left her cubicle and headed for the relative safety of her room. She had no intention of touching her compdex tonight, not even to access Mediabloc. Maybe that way she'd be safe from spies for a while. She forgot that RW could turn on any terminal she wanted to and lacked the tact to know when a visit would be unwelcome.

"Sorry." RW shrugged. "So what do you think?"

"I think you should review the section on basic courtesy in the Cultural Background program. I don't appreciate your just appearing without warning." Jovanna rose and stalked into the far corner of her kitchen.

"Later," said RW, moving her holographic image onto Jovanna's couch. "Right now I want to know what you thought of Vince."

"I thought he was scary, all right? I'm not used to worrying that someone might kill me at any minute."

"Oh." RW sounded disappointed. "I rather liked him."

"He found me because you'd been talking to him. RW, didn't I warn you to be careful?"

"He didn't kill you," RW said, reasonably. "He didn't do anything to me, either. He said he'd tell me all about Rachel." The last sentence was accompanied by a pout.

Jovanna frowned as realization hit her. How, and what, did Vince know about Rachel? She addressed RW. "What do you want to know about her?"

"Everything there is to know," said RW.

"The only way to do that is to talk to everyone who ever knew her, and even then you'd come up short." Jovanna didn't feel up to telling RW about Rachel tonight. "I'll tell you what. I'll tell you how to access information about Rachel. But use the Genesis computer. Don't go anywhere near RAM Main. Promise?"

"I promise," RW said.

"Look up the Wydlin scrapbook file . . . any references to Rachel Wydlin. Your access number is 08-15-2412." The number was Rachel's birth date. Usually family albums could be accessed using any family member's birth date, and Jovanna doubted that Rachel's access number had been expunged yet. "If you have any trouble, let me know. Otherwise, I'll see you tomorrow."

"Thanks, Jovanna!" RW exited through Jovanna s compdex, leaving it on. Jovanna moved leadenly across the room to shut it off, but by the time she got there, she found that the unanswered questions from her encounter with Vince were preying on her. Her hand hovered over the keyboard as she considered whether she ought to involve herself further.

She didn't know why she hadn't called Security after Vince left. It couldn't just be his smile; she wasn't that susceptible. She'd embarked on her career as naive as any young person fresh out of college, but she'd learned a few things since she'd left school. The most important was that she wasn't the type of woman to whom exciting things happened. Her social caste handicapped her career progress, but her dead-end job was due to the fact that she was hardly beautiful. If she'd been attractive, it would have been easier for her to gain recognition for her abilities. As it was, she was mostly ignored. After a while, she'd gotten so used to it that it began to feel comfortable. Vince made her forget how unimportant she was, but only briefly.

So why didn't she turn him in? Was it because she was so tired of being unappreciated? Or maybe she was looking for a way to make a stand, to honor Rachel's memory. Jovanna stared at the blank screen. It couldn't hurt to learn a little about this Vince and the group he called NEO. She pulled a chair up to her terminal.

She started with Infonet, requesting any news items during the past year about Vince, though she realized that only having a first name might make her search pretty difficult. There were too many references to people named Vince to pursue. She decided to let it go for a while.

For Beowulf, Infonet had no listed references whatsover. It suggested she try Biblionet.

Jovanna found several references to a Beowulf in Biblionet, but they referred to an ancient Earth saga. She didn't think that was what she wanted. She exited Biblionet and returned to the Infonet interface.

Next she requested a search for NEO. She located two references, and she requested that both items be run.

The first, dated 08-08-2434, was the account of an attack on a Terrine headquarters on Earth, in Chicagorg. Bombs were placed in several strategic spots within the structure and detonated, effectively demolishing the building. Later a group called NEO—or "New Earth Organization"—claimed responsibility for the blast. NEO claimed that Earth belonged to its inhabitants, and listed grievances with RAM, including what they called the "deliberate pollution, rape, and destruction of Earth." NEO promised that attempts to rebuild the barracks would be met with more attacks.

After the NEO statement there was a quotation by Ludwig Holzerhein, who administered the Bio-Mechanized Assault Force and had ordered the building of the Terrine headquarters. He promised that the headquarters would be rebuilt and that if there was any further terrorism, reprisals would be swift.

The second reference was a recorded panel discussion held about three and a half months ago, on 01-22-2435, among several economists, historians, and experts on terrorism. NEO was mentioned several times by a Dr. Gruber, a historian who had spent some time on Earth. He seemed to believe the group had legitimate grievances. He opposed the use of the Terrines, who, he claimed, "were genetically engineered to enforce RAM's will on a resisting population." The moderator of the discussion stated that no grievance justified the use of terrorism and spent the remainder of the discussion ignoring every attempt Dr. Gruber made to speak.

Jovanna's heart pounded. It seemed as if she was committing treason just watching the discussion. Dr. Gruber seemed well informed and passionate about his subject. She wanted desperately to speak with him, to see what else he could tell her. She terminated the second item and initiated a search for Dr. Gruber. She began by requesting a link to the Coprates University directory. Dr. Gruber was listed as being on a leave of absence. She requested his forwarding address. It was listed as Serenity Residence, with an address in the Argyre region. Jovanna sent him a message there, leaving her access code and requesting that he contact her.

As she tried to get up, she realized that one leg was asleep. How long had she been at it? She looked at her wall chrono, which read 0144. She groaned; she'd probably be no good at all at work tomorrow.

Stretching to relieve the kinks in her back and neck, she took a few unsteady steps and flopped wearily onto her couch, which doubled as a bed.

○ ○ ○ ○ ○

"Jovanna! Are you taking the day off or something?"

Jovanna forced her eyes open. RW was seated on the arm of her couch. The glow of her holographic image was hard on Jovanna's eyes, and she closed them again and rolled over, pulling a cushion over her head.

"Jovanna, you're going to be late!" RW insisted.

"What time is it?" Jovanna mumbled.

"0630," RW replied.

"That's not late," Jovanna said loudly, so that RW could hear her through the cushion. "Go away."

"But you promised I could come back in the morning. It's morning now."

"I was up late. Give me another half hour, all right?"

"But, Jovanna, I want to tell you something. It's about that Dr. Gruber."

"How do you know I'm interested in Dr. Gruber?"

"Oh, I finished with the scrapbook in no time. But you said not to bother you last night, so I just watched what you were doing from inside the matrix. After you went to bed, I thought I'd keep working on your questions."

"RW, I left a message for Dr. Gruber to call me. He can answer my questions himself."

"I erased it," RW said.

"You *what?*" Jovanna sat bolt upright.

"I erased your message. Sorry," RW said. "But when I tell you what I found out, you'll be glad I did. I wondered what Serenity Residence was, so I looked it up."

"And?"

"It's an asylum."

"An asylum! I doubt that very much," Jovanna said. "Dr. Gruber seemed perfectly sane from what I saw."

"But it is. It's a very special asylum, for people who seem sane but who say insane things. Like Dr. Gruber saying that the Terrans have legitimate grievances against RAM."

"But maybe he's right."

"You know that, and I know that. I don't think RAM can even imagine it, though."

"RW?" Jovanna sat up and looked at the digital personality, who seemed to have changed overnight. She had an air of knowledgeable cynicism that Jovanna had never noticed in her before. "You sound different."

"Well, I've learned a lot in a short time. After I went through the family album, I came back and watched you do your research. There were a few things you didn't pursue, but I thought they were interesting, so I checked them out."

"What . . . things?" Jovanna wasn't pleased by RW's implied criticism of her research methods, but she was fascinated all the same.

"Well, Serenity Residence, for one. People go there talking crazy and they come back fully functioning members of society. Well, maybe they're not quite the way they used to be. There were a playwright who never wrote another word after he got out, several professors who retired, and an artist who gave up public exhibitions of his murals to do portraits of corporate bigwigs. But at least they're no more trouble to anyone. Dr. Gruber's stay is scheduled to end next week. He should be a lot quieter when he gets out."

Jovanna felt a chill go down her spine. "What else?"

"I wondered if I could learn anything else about NEO."

"RW! You didn't try to look at any of RAM Main's secret files, did you?"

"No. You told me not to. But I figured since NEO's based on Earth, I'd link into Earth Worldnet. NEO has a primitive little subsystem operating there. I found out a few things about them."

Jovanna felt as if she'd given birth to a monster, but she was fascinated in spite of herself. "Such as?"

"Their main Earth base is in Chicagorg. They're a new group, put together from some other smaller groups. They're strongest in North America, but they have support on the other continents, too."

"What are their aims?" Jovanna asked.

"They say they want to get RAM off Earth."

Jovanna was up now, pacing her small room. She didn't understand a lot about politics, but one thing stood out in her mind. NEO's only terrorist attack she'd heard of had involved damage to property only. The Terrine headquarters had been empty when they bombed it. Even though RAM called NEO terrorists, she felt more frightened of RAM than she did of their small group. Looking back on it, she realized that Vince could have killed her easily in the time he'd had with her, but instead he had hesitated.

She groaned. She didn't know what to think anymore. Vince was a terrorist. Certainly she should have called Security immediately. Yet RAM had called Rachel a terrorist, too, and Jovanna loved Rachel more than she'd loved anyone but her late father.

Her father had been taken away to work at an experimental power station. He hadn't wanted to go and leave his wife alone with five children, but people of their class had no real power over their lives. There had been an accident at the station, and many of the employees, including her father, had been killed.

Jovanna sat down, shaking. She'd never even talked about her father with Rachel. It had been easier to keep her feelings about him hidden, even from herself. Unlike Rachel or Dr. Gruber, she didn't want people to think she was crazy. So she worked hard and stayed quiet, hoping that she'd get recognition because of her exceptional abilities. But RAM worked the way it always had and always would. They would never admit that a woman of her caste could be anything but a mindless drone. If she wanted true appreciation, she must look to people who were willing to fight the system. It was too late to help Rachel, but not too late to help Vince. She took a deep breath, then rose and went to the wardrobe panel to choose the clothes that she would wear on her first day as a NEO agent.

$$\bigcirc \quad \bigcirc \quad \bigcirc \quad \bigcirc \quad \bigcirc$$

Jovanna looked at her wristchrono. It was only 1215, and she had already finished all the work Karenin had left for her. She rarely worked so quickly, but she never before had the motivation that she had today. She took a container of soup from the food dispenser, picked up a plastic spoon, and went back to her desk.

Her first task was to discover where to look for information about the new project. All of the genetics programming was secure, kept for use only by those scientists working directly on the projects. It was easier to delve into the accounting system. While that wouldn't tell her anything about the projects themselves, it would tell her which projects were surrounded with the tightest security and which weren't considered classified. When she knew which project was under the tightest security, she could probe quickly without leaving trails everywhere.

She accessed the fiscal data system and located a file called "General Budget." When she opened the file, she saw that it was the budget report that was furnished to every shareholder in the company. Since everyone employed at Wydlin Corporation received some stock, there would be no secrets here, but she might see something that suggested further exploration.

In addition to the expected operating expenses, there were several projects listed by name, along with their project heads.

She looked at the listings of projects and assigned personnel. Was everyone accounted for? She didn't know, but there might be a way to find out. She printed out the budget report, closed the file, and accessed the personnel listing for Genesis Station.

There were several ways to sort the personnel listing—alphabetically by name, as well as by department, job classification, seniority, salary ranges, and number of shares owned. Jovanna glanced from the screen to the budget printout in her hand and back again. She requested a sorting by job classification and looked under research scientists.

As she expected, the project heads were all research scientists. There was a Dr. Trum, a cybergeneticist who wasn't listed under any project. She requested an expanded listing on Dr. Trum and printed it out. Then she had the computer sort research scientists by several parameters, to see how Dr. Trum compared to the others. He was the highest paid, had the most seniority, and owned the most shares in the corporation. Jovanna smiled. It looked as if she'd found her man.

It might be safer to go ask Dr. Trum what he was up to than to try to discover it through the computer. She had never attempted to get into a scientist's research file before. It could be pretty risky. Scientists were usually sophisticated enough about computer security to provide some unexpected twists in the security surrounding their personal files.

All in all, it probably was safer to go ask Dr. Trum what project he was involved with. Not that Jovanna felt up to it. She had no illusions about her bravery, or lack of it. She considered seeking Dr. Trum out only because she was afraid to approach his files.

Knowing she was procrastinating, but unwilling to take on the danger she knew she would encounter with the next step, Jovanna punched up the office directory for station personnel. She scrolled down the list, looking for his office location. She blinked at what she saw. Dr. Trum was off-station. She looked to see the last date he had been on the station. It was almost two months ago.

Jovanna's reason told her the project *had* to be on Genesis Station. Noah Wydlin wouldn't go to all the trouble to build a station this far from everything just so he could send an important project somewhere else.

Jovanna guessed that Dr. Trum might have been involved in the secret project at one point, but was no longer a part of it. Who had worked with him? She requested the directory from two months earlier and found Trum's location at that time. Then she checked to see who worked near him and found several names. When she matched the names against the departmental charts, she found only one person who had no listed supervisor—someone named J. Wellington Flint.

Well, J. Wellington Flint had to report to someone. Jovanna would bet that it used to be Dr. Trum. The only question was, whom did Flint report to now?

Jovanna accessed the office directory and found Flint. He still had the same office. "Great. Now, who's your nearest neighbor, Flint?" Her eyes widened when she saw the name: Dr. Remus Wydlin.

CHAPTER EIGHT

Jovanna's initial shock was replaced almost immediately with the realization that Dr. Wydlin was
the natural person to be in charge of the new project. After all, he'd founded the company; who was more
trustworthy? And he was the most famous cybergeneticist in the solar system, so his abilities were undeni-
able.

She recalled that Dr. Wydlin had said something the
other night about making RAM pay. If his project had
anything to do with vengeance, she could well see why
it was so secret.

She wasn't sure why NEO was interested in it. Perhaps, not knowing Dr. Wydlin's feelings, they were concerned that Dr. Wydlin might share his work with
RAM. She could tell Vince that NEO didn't have to worry about that, but she doubted he'd believe her. First of
all, she really had no idea what she was telling NEO not
to worry about. She ought to find out.

Luckily, she wasn't as worried about talking to Dr.
Wydlin as she was about approaching the unknown Dr.
Trum. She couldn't simply ask Remus point-blank what
he was working on, but she had another idea. She put a
call through to Dr. Wydlin's office and left a message for

him to call her when it was convenient.

Dr. Wydlin returned her call almost immediately. "Hello, Jovanna. What can I do for you?"

He sounded brisk, not unfriendly, but not much like the man who was so upset three nights ago that she had to help him to his suite. After a moment, she said, "Dr. Wydlin, I've been thinking about what you said the other night about Rachel and what happened to her. You said you were going to—to do something." She couldn't really repeat what he'd said the other night, not on the comnet. She hesitated. Dr. Wydlin's silence wasn't at all encouraging. "I was wondering if there's anything I could do to help."

"Jovanna, you don't know what you're asking." Dr. Wydlin's voice seemed warmer, though, and she felt encouraged. "You have your whole life and career ahead of you. Working for me might . . . jeopardize that."

Jovanna shook her head. "It's not much of a career, Dr. Wydlin, believe me. And it's not likely to be. You're the only person I can think of who might give me anything meaningful to do. That is, if you think there's anything I could help you with." Jovanna knew the physical abilities of some gennies were aided through the use of computer-driven enhancements. Dr. Wydlin was an acknowledged expert in the use of computer implants in basically biological gennies. If he was planning to increase the sophistication of his computer implants, Jovanna was indeed well qualified to help him; she hoped he would see it that way.

"Well," sighed Dr. Wydlin, "as it happens, I could use some help, and a friendly face would be welcome around here. I'll call down to Personnel and see about having you transferred to my project."

"Thank you, Dr. Wydlin," Jovanna said, hardly daring to believe how easy it was.

"Thank *you*, Jovanna," he said, and terminated the connection. Jovanna felt a sudden lump in her throat at his casual yet sincere courtesy. She wasn't used to it, not from people of his caste. It was easy to see how Rachel had become such an uncommon young woman.

Jovanna wished she had asked to help Dr. Wydlin without the prod from NEO. Perhaps she should have told
him why she wanted to work with him. Well, there was
still time.

○ ○ ○ ○ ○

"Are you ready for the grand tour, Ms. Trask?" Dr.
Wydlin's lab assistant, J. Wellington Flint, stood at the
doorway of Jovanna's new office, looking at her from under thick, half-closed eyelids. If he was trying to look
bored, Jovanna thought, he wasn't succeeding. She had
the definite impression that Flint's watery pale blue
eyes missed nothing.

"Yes, I'm ready," she said. Flint indicated with a
sweep of his arm that she join him in the hall.

"This way, Ms. Trask." He led her down a narrow corridor and stopped at a door, which opened as he approached it. "This is my office. If you ever have any
questions or need to talk, the door is always open—
figuratively, that is." He stepped away, and the door slid
closed, as if illustrating his point.

"I see." Jovanna managed a smile. She had no intention of confiding in Flint, but she didn't want to offend
him, either. One corner of Flint's thick-lipped mouth
lifted in what Jovanna took for a smile. It didn't quite
reach his eyes. He continued down the corridor.

"This is Remus Wydlin's office." He waved at a closed
door as they passed, then stopped at the end of the hall.
"And this is the lab section." He pressed his palm onto a
shoulder-high panel beside a double-width door and it
slid open. Jovanna followed him through it.

The first thing she noticed was a large console just to
her right. The lab seemed similar to the corridor they
had come from, except that it was wider and lined with
numerous closed doors. There was a large viewing
screen above the keyboard, in addition to the standard
size screen. Jovanna pointed to it. "What's the extra
screen for?"

Flint tapped several keys on the console. The vision of

a vertically floating, thin, humanlike male came into view. "Barney Number One," Flint said. "This is the view inside his vat. I can also display his vital signs and monitor his implants, together or separately. The screen splits, too." He pushed more keys, and the view of another vat shared the screen alongside the first. As he continued to press keys, the screen went first into four, and then into eight different views, though only the upper-left view had a Barney in it.

"Will there be eight Barneys altogether, then?" Jovanna asked.

"No," Flint said. "Remus is starting with forty. That's all we really have room for without spilling over into the rest of the station. Of course, that's only if the project works this time."

"What do you mean?" Jovanna asked.

"We started this over a year ago, when Dr. Wydlin was still with the company full time. He left before the first group was ready, and another scientist took over the project. He couldn't make it work. The first three batches had to be discarded."

Jovanna shivered. It made her uncomfortable to hear gennies referred to as if they were so many poorly cooked casseroles.

"But now the founding genius himself is back," Flint said, "so we should have our first fully functioning Barney in less than a month, provided your work is all Remus says it will be."

Jovanna bit the inside of her cheek as she tried to think of a suitable reply. She could think of nothing that wouldn't sound either conceited or overly humble, so she changed the subject. "What's in these cubicles?" she asked, pointing to the close-packed banks of doors that extended beyond the computer terminal on both walls.

"The critters," Flint said, with the cynical smirk Jovanna was beginning to find tiresome.

"Do you mean the Barneys?" she asked.

"Yes." He walked over to the first door on the left and pressed some keys on the wall pad. The door slid open

and he stepped inside, beckoning her to follow. A clear
eight-foot-tall vat stood in the center of the room. It contained a translucent, straw-colored fluid. A bony, humanlike naked male floated vertically inside the vat,
nearly filling it. Wires extended from the gennie's cra-
nium, chest, and wrists and led up to a dark box on top
of the vat.

"How tall is he?" Jovanna asked.

"Seven feet. He'll weigh approximately three hundred pounds when he fills out. An incredible fighting
machine," Flint said. "Once he's trained, that is. He'll
be as helpless as a baby when he first gets out."

Jovanna didn't know about that. She planned to teach
the Barneys language via their cranial implants.
They'd have a head start over human infants, which
was a good thing. They'd already be full grown, with little time to adjust to life outside a vat when compared
with the time a human child had to learn and develop.
Jovanna looked at the gennie embryo's peaceful, sleeping face and was struck by how vulnerable he looked.
"He's so thin. And his bones look . . . strange."

"The skeleton is made of a titanium alloy. Don't worry. He'll be extraordinarily resilient once he's finished
growing. Seen enough?" Flint had moved to stand in
the doorway.

After they left, Flint resecured the door. "Remus said
he wants to see you right at 1300. Why don't we go have
lunch now?"

Jovanna hadn't been invited anywhere by a coworker
in all the time she'd worked for Wydlin Corporation.
She wished her first invitation hadn't come from someone so repellent, but it didn't seem polite to refuse.
"Can we both be away from our work at the same
time?" she asked.

"Can we . . . ?" Flint looked at her as if she were mentally defective, then snickered briefly. "Remus isn't concerned at all about things like that. And it isn't as if I
could do your work or you could do any of mine."

Jovanna could see his point. Still, the idea of choosing
when to have lunch was a novel one. It was a small free-

dom, but more than she was accustomed to. "All right, let's go," she said.

Flint took Jovanna out of the secure double doors that separated the Barney section from the rest of the labs and led her to a small break room with utilitarian chairs and tables and a food dispenser unit. "Just like home, eh, Jovanna?"

Jovanna smiled noncommittally and took out her employee identification card to access the food dispenser. She had just removed a plastic dish of deep fried stuyken bits when a pair of hands caressed her shoulders and someone breathed in her ear. "Darling, where have you been? I've been looking all over for you."

Jovanna dropped her dish. Her lunch scattered all over the floor. A small maintenance bot rolled swiftly over from its place in the corner and began sucking up the mess. Jovanna turned around to see Vince standing behind her, smiling mischievously. Flint stood looking at them, clearly intrigued.

"What—what are you doing here?" Jovanna stammered.

"I know we said we'd wait until tonight, but I missed you, Jo," Vince said meaningfully.

He glanced at Flint. "We need to talk. I'm sure your friend will excuse us." Then he grabbed her elbow and pulled her from the room and down the hall.

"What do you think you're doing?" Jovanna whispered angrily when they were out of hearing distance.

"Getting you alone," Vince said, backing her against the wall.

"Do you know how this looks?" she said, looking around to see if anyone was watching. The hall was empty for the moment.

"It looks exactly the way I want it to look," Vince said, suddenly stern. He placed his hands on the wall on either side of Jovanna's arms, hemming her in. "I got tired of waiting for you to contact me, so I came looking for you. I couldn't get clearance to see you in your new office, though. Were you hiding, Jovanna?"

"You idiot!" Jovanna rarely did any name-calling, but

she was perfectly willing to make an exception in Vince's case. "I got assigned to the project! Security's tight!"

"Shh!" Vince said, glancing around. There was still no one in sight. "Yes? What do you have?"

"It's called the Barney Project," Jovanna whispered. "The Barneys are super-strong, cybernetically enhanced warriors, cloned from a single genotype."

"What are their plans for them? To sell them to RAM?"

"No. Dr. Wydlin hates RAM because of what they did to Rachel. If it's up to him, they'll be used against RAM somehow," Jovanna said.

"That's a big 'if,' " Vince said, suddenly close, his breath warm in her ear. Jovanna nearly protested until she heard approaching footsteps and voices. She endured his warm proximity, though it made her feel strange.

"I guess so," she forced herself to return to the subject. "But maybe we can help him. Unless you had something else in mind?"

"It's not up to me to decide. We'll get our orders," Vince murmured as a pair of men in lab coats went by. When they turned the corner, he straightened. "Well, keep me posted, okay?"

"All right," Jovanna said, feeling as if a winter wind had just blown through the corridor. Suddenly she realized how much his being in the lab section had compromised her—in more ways than one. "But don't do this again!"

"This?" He looked at her, his brown eyes innocent.

"Don't come to the lab section. It doesn't look good."

"I'll try not to." He smiled mockingly. "Don't be such a stranger, though, Jovanna. I hate having to wait too long before hearing from you."

"Don't worry about it," Jovanna said sharply. Vince chuckled and walked down the hall.

CHAPTER NINE

J ovanna tapped lightly at Dr. Wydlin's office door.
It slid open, revealing an office not much bigger
than the new one she had been assigned. Somehow Dr. Wydlin had managed to clutter it more than
any office she had ever seen. He beckoned to her from
behind his desk. "Come right in, Jovanna."

She entered and looked for a place to sit. Dr. Wydlin
came out to remove a pile of papers from a chair beside
his desk. "Sit here," he said. "Take a look at the screen."

He pointed toward a wall screen as big as the one
Flint had shown her. On it was a drawing of what
looked like the cross section of a human brain, except
that just below the cerebellum, there was a small,
round metal casing with wires extending into the interior of the brain. "See that?" Dr. Wydlin pointed to the
drawing. "It's an implant I designed especially for the
Barneys. Are you familiar with cranial implants?"

"Somewhat," Jovanna said. "Aren't they used to
stimulate neuromuscular activity in developing gennies, so when they're decanted, their muscles will be
fully developed?"

"That's the standard use," Dr. Wydlin said. "These
implants are more sophisticated, however. When the

Barneys are decanted, I expect them to have learned
language and cultural associations. Enough so that I
can begin a really meaningful education for them."

"What do you mean?" Jovanna asked.

"These gennies are going to be capable of anything a
human can do," Dr. Wydlin said. "However, they'll
learn at a greatly accelerated rate. The fact that they're
so well prepared at the time they're decanted will make
it easier for them to learn."

Jovanna saw the advantage. "So the implants will
stimulate the sense and memory areas of the brain?"

"That's correct," Dr. Wydlin said. "You'll be able to
give them the associations for all the knowledge a typi-
cal Martian child would learn in the first twelve years
of life. It will be as if they had lived twelve years in the
four months they spend in the vats."

"I've imparted language and sociocultural information to computer personalities before," said Jovanna,
thinking of RW, "but I don't have the faintest idea how
to program for sensory input."

"Flint and I have that part of it under control," Dr.
Wydlin said. "If your language program includes any
references to sensation, I have a program that will sort
for that and impart the correct sensation to the Barneys. What you need to do, however, is make sure all the
sensory referents are as specific as possible."

"I see . . ." Jovanna said. It sounded as if she'd be putting in a great deal of overtime. Not that she minded.
The more time she spent around the lab, the more she'd
learn about the project. "Will I have responsibilities
once they're decanted?"

"That will be the fun part," Dr. Wydlin said. "I have a
list of careers that I want the Barneys to learn. They
should be able to begin soon after decanting."

"What kind of careers?" From what Flint had said,
Jovanna had thought they'd all be combat gennies.

"I have a terraformer, an inventor, an artist—even a
philosopher. And there are a few criminal subclasses as
well," Dr. Wydlin looked as if he was both amused and
slightly embarrassed. "They include a computer hacker

and a garden variety space pirate."

"With enhanced strength . . ." Jovanna said thoughtfully. She didn't think any of the Barneys would be "garden variety."

"Anyway, I'd like you to provide all the career skills learning in the same way any Martian would learn it, using computer personalities as teachers where necessary. All the Barneys will have combat skills, of course. For now, we can use standard holographic simulations to help them learn those skills. There will be time later for them to practice live combat if we deem it necessary. But you'll be busy enough as it is, worrying about their cultural assimilation and career skills."

"I'd better get started." Jovanna tripled her estimate of how much overtime it would take to prepare the programs. She wondered how Dr. Wydlin had ever planned to educate the Barneys before she volunteered.

"I'm glad you're so eager," Dr. Wydlin said. "By all means, go right ahead. I'll need the language program as soon as possible for Barney Number One."

Jovanna stood, then hesitated. There was one thing Dr. Wydlin hadn't explained to her. He had never come right out and said that he meant for the Barneys to fight against RAM, but she was sure that was what he intended. It was common knowledge that when RAM manufactured a gennie, they included pro-RAM programming in the design. It would make sense for him to include programming that would make the Barneys despise RAM, yet he hadn't said anything about it.

"About their . . . political leanings," she said delicately. "Shall I program them any particular way?"

"No!" Dr. Wydlin's answer was swift. "If you use any preexisting programs and you find any offensive material in them, I give you permission to delete it. I want them to get a completely honest picture of the world." He looked her in the eye. "Do you know what I mean?"

"I think so." In other words, Jovanna thought, try to cut out any RAM propaganda that might be embedded in existing educational packages. And teach the Barneys about some of the nastier methods RAM used to enforce its will upon its subjects.

"But don't use any of the sensory inputs to give them an uncontrollable aversion to RAM," he said. "I want to play fair, to give them a chance to choose on the basis of facts, not compulsions. Leave the compulsions to RAM."

"All right." Jovanna had known that Remus Wydlin was uncommon, but she hadn't guessed until now just how much integrity he had. She would play by his rules, but she would certainly use every tool he had given her. Which meant that she had to get to work on the cultural programming right away; it would need a lot of pruning. "I'll get right to work, sir."

"Thank you. Good luck, Jovanna." Dr. Remus returned to his desk, and Jovanna went to her office.

○   ○   ○   ○   ○

Jovanna keyed her office door to remain closed and alert her if someone sought entry. Flint and Dr. Wydlin had supposedly left for the night, but she didn't want to take any chances.

Settling herself at her console, she called up RW.

"Hello, Jovanna. It's been a while," RW said, appearing before her.

"Yes. I've been busy," Jovanna said.

"I know. Nice office," RW said.

Jovanna came to the point. "RW, I need your help."

"Yes?"

"I'm in charge of educating the Barneys. They're the new clones Dr. Wydlin is working on. They have computer implants that allow them to begin their education before they're decanted, so later they'll already have the computer schooling many children receive."

RW whistled. "Innovative, ain't he? I thought most gennies were trained more or less like animals."

"Well, certainly most combat and laborer gennies are. But Dr. Wydlin thinks that would limit this group. He says they'll be capable of human levels of achievement."

"Where do I come in?" RW asked.

"I'd like you to be their computer interface. You'll be their teacher. I know it's not much of a job—"

"Not really," Rachel said, grinning. "You could just program a small-memory teacher personality for that, couldn't you?"

"I could, but there are reasons I'd like you to do it."

"First, you could keep an eye on me," RW pointed out.

"You know me too well," Jovanna said dryly. "But I'm also uncomfortable with this project. There may be others—" she was thinking of Flint—"who want to stick their fingers in the pie. You could let me know if anyone tampers with the Barneys' cybernetics."

"Dr. Wydlin's computer security is pretty tight," RW said.

"How do you know?" Jovanna asked.

RW looked at her mischievously. Jovanna threw her hands up in the air. "All right, I'm sorry I asked. Did you get in?"

RW looked annoyed. "No. I've been working on it ever since I figured out you were transferred to this project, but so far no luck."

"Well, cut it out," Jovanna said. "You'll be able to get in tomorrow morning. That's when I told Dr. Wydlin I could have you ready."

"You told him it was me?"

"Well—no," Jovanna admitted. "He's still grieving over you—or Rachel, rather. That brings me to the other thing I was going to ask. Could you make yourself look different?"

Computer personalities were able to alter their appearance at will. So far, RW had chosen to appear as she had first been programmed to appear, like Rachel Wydlin. Jovanna felt uncomfortable asking RW to deceive Dr. Wydlin, but she didn't want to cause him unnecessary pain. RW could be invaluable in helping her keep tabs on the Barneys.

Dr. Wydlin's feelings weren't the only reason Jovanna wanted RW to change her appearance, though. As long as RW continued to range at will through the computer matrix, answering summons from anyone who cared to contact her, there was a risk RAM would discover her. That risk, while it wouldn't vanish completely, would certainly lessen if RW no longer looked like Rachel.

"I remind you too much of Rachel, don't I?" RW said. "Does it make you sad?"

"A little," Jovanna said. "But changing the way you look won't change my feelings about Rachel. It might keep you safer from RAM, though."

"You know what?" RW said. "I don't think they're looking for me as a digital personality. They've sent bulletins all through the Asteroid Belt, and I guess the inner planets, too, but they're looking for Rachel Wydlin, dead or alive. I don't think it ever occurred to them that someone might translate me."

"Well, that's good to know," Jovanna said. "But I'd still feel safer if you'd change your appearance. You can look any way you'd like, you know."

"I know," said RW. "How's this?" Her form wavered momentarily. When it stopped, Jovanna gasped. She felt as if she was looking into a mirror.

"It's . . . all right, I guess," Jovanna said, wondering if RW meant her choice as a compliment. "Uh, why didn't you choose something prettier?"

RW winked. "You're pretty enough for me. Besides, if you programmed me, what form would you come up with?"

Jovanna probably would have taken an existing holo from the file—probably one of the androgynous personalities used for most routine chores on Genesis Station. She had to admit that her own form, unexciting as it was, was more interesting than a file personality.

"You look fine," she told RW. "Now let's train you for your new job."

○ ○ ○ ○ ○

"Mr. Dracolysk? I have the reports." The pleasure gennie's voice was soft, deferential. She made a stimulating personal assistant, Hugo Dracolysk thought. He'd definitely been thinking ahead when he decided to bring Lisa along to Gorgon Station. She was the only real diversion available in his remote training facility.

"Put them on the desk," Dracolysk ordered. He glanced back at his computer screen, reviewing his personal journal until the gennie's movement in his peripheral vision recaptured his attention. He looked at her. "No, don't go, Lisa."

The gennie, who had nearly reached the door, seemed to shrink into herself. She was staring at him wide-eyed, but she turned her face away, hiding it under a curtain of silky brown hair. Dracolysk smiled. This one was going to be most enjoyable. She knew what to expect and was intelligent enough to be frightened, but she hadn't yet become resigned to her fate. They all got so dull after that, and he simply had to discard them and start again. This series had shown more promise than any of the other gennies that he had genetically engineered for pleasure. Of course, even his earliest designs were in great demand for most ordinary purposes. But Dracolysk demanded more spirit in the gennies he designed for his personal use. In the end, they all gave up. But maybe Lisa would last awhile.

He walked over to where she stood and tipped her chin up with a finger and thumb. "Why, Lisa, you're not afraid of me, are you?"

Anger flashed briefly into her brown eyes. Then she seemed to collect herself. She took a breath and said expressionlessly. "No, sir."

"I'm glad to hear it," he said. He walked over to his custom-made red leather divan and seated himself. "Take off your clothes."

Her eyes widened at that, and she looked as if she might say something. He continued to hold her gaze until she finally looked down and began to comply. Dracolysk seated himself on the divan and reached over to open an antique gold box that lay on the teak end table. He watched appreciatively as her dress slid down to reveal a bruised shoulder. That encounter had been highly entertaining. What could he do to make this one as memorable? Watching him, Lisa suddenly flinched. He followed her eyes. She was staring at his hand, which had just extracted a cigarette from the gold box. He smiled. Now he knew what he wanted to do.

"Excuse me, sir." A respectful, genderless voice floated out from speakers that surrounded the large screen on the opposite wall of the room.

"What is it?" Dracolysk said irritably.

"You have a visitor."

"I'm busy. Have him wait."

"Now, Hugo." The abrupt change of the computer's voice made Dracolysk look up, startled. The voice continued, masculine and authoritative, with a faint neo-Swiss accent. "You know perfectly well I don't wait."

Dracolysk motioned to Lisa to pull her dress up as a shimmering form appeared before them. It solidified as much as a digital personality can be said to solidify into the shape of a tall gray-haired man, seemingly in his sixties. "Good afternoon, Mr. Chairman," Dracolysk said. He had always believed it was best to appear unperturbed when the RAM chairman, Simund Holzerhein, decided to call on him. Dracolysk looked over at Lisa, who was poised to leave. "You may go, Lisa," he said, reasserting his control. "We'll resume our . . . discussion later."

Lisa fled as Dracolysk walked over to his office bar and poured himself a glass of Moselle. "What can I do for you, sir?"

"I have an interesting bit of news, Hugo. Do sit down."

Dracolysk saw that Holzerhein now occupied the red leather armchair that stood a few feet from his leather divan. It was the seat Dracolysk usually took when he wished to keep one of his employees on his toes while they had a talk. It annoyed him to see Holzerhein using it, especially since the chairman had no need whatsoever for a chair, but Dracolysk knew better than to say anything. He sat on the divan. "What is it?"

"Your neighbor is up to something."

Dracolysk frowned. He wasn't sure what Holzerhein meant by the term "neighbor."

He had deliberately chosen the Jovian Trojans for his

training station because they were remote and he could have complete control of the environment. There were pirates who sometimes kept bases in the vicinity, but Dracolysk was able to keep them at bay through a careful distribution of bribes. The pirates might have a dozen plots brewing, but he failed to see what they could have to do with him. Still, it would be unproductive to let Holzerhein see his impatience.

Their relationship was a bizarre reversal of the usual business arrangements between humans and digital personalities. Human executives often programmed or hired digital personalities to perform work that was done more efficiently through the computer matrix. As far as Dracolysk knew, Holzerhein was the only digital personality who hired humans to do work that could only be done outside the matrix. The arrangement benefited Dracolysk significantly.

Dracolysk headed a company that trained combat gennies. It gave him a chance to see what the small cybergenetics firms were developing. Holzerhein paid him well for the information and had given him several lucrative contracts as well. Dracolysk had even more reason than most executives to keep Simund Holzerhein happy. "Which neighbor do you mean, sir?" he asked politely.

"I believe you know him—Noah Wydlin." Leaning back, Holzerhein seemed to enjoy the effect his announcement had.

Dracolysk nearly spilled his wine. "Noah Wydlin has a station in the Jovian Trojans?"

"Oh, yes. It's relatively new—only about a year old," Holzerhein said, forming his hands into a steeple and looking at Dracolysk over them. Dracolysk knew that Holzerhein thought less of him for not knowing about Wydlin's station, and Dracolysk was furious with himself for not having discovered it. Then he realized it could have been worse. Holzerhein had undoubtedly made the announcement to gauge Dracolysk's reaction. Dracolysk's surprise had been genuine, which showed that he hadn't kept any knowledge from the RAM chairman. Holzerhein would not tolerate treachery.

"If I may ask, how did you find out about it, sir?" Dracolysk said.

"There was a prison break at one of our more remote
prison stations in the Asteroid Belt several months ago.
The escapee was Rachel Wydlin."

"Noah's crazy sister?"

"Is that what they're calling her?" Holzerhein asked.
"Good. We tried to handle that affair by discrediting her
name as much as possible to keep her from becoming
some kind of champion to the young people. Anyhow,
the escape ship evaded our cruisers and eventually
headed out toward the Jovian Trojans. We destroyed it,
of course, but we began to wonder why it was headed for
such a remote area. I investigated and discovered a
computer link from Wydlin headquarters on Mars to
the station out here. Not only that, but at the time of the
escape attempt, Dr. Remus Wydlin left Mars."

"For—?" Dracolysk asked.

"He didn't take any commercial vessel, and the only
forwarding address we have is 'care of Wydlin Corporation.' He's on their station, of course. They call it 'Genesis.'"

"What do you want me to do, sir?" Dracolysk asked.

"They're up to something over there. Given Dr.
Wydlin's talents and the state of mind he's probably in,
we'd better keep an eye on it."

"Do you want me to do anything about Dr. Wydlin? He
sounds dangerous," Dracolysk said.

"I'm sure he is, or rather, whatever he's working on is.
But first I want to know what the project is. It might
have some value to us. And Wydlin Corporation might
be better taken over than destroyed. I shall make the
decision personally, in any case." Holzerhein stood up.

"Very good, sir. You'll give me the coordinates of Genesis Station?"

"They're already in your computer. Contact me when
you have something to report," Holzerhein said and disappeared.

Dracolysk bolted the last of his wine and went to his

computer. His journal was still up, and he searched it for references to the Wydlins or Wydlin Corporation. It wasn't as if he needed any reminder of one thing about them. Wydlin Corporation still owed Dracolysk Corporation for some training he'd done for them on Mars. They'd had a large account with him at one time, although the old man claimed not to like his methods.

Then the old man retired and Wydlin Corporation started experiencing hard times. Their account quickly went into arrears, but Noah had assured Dracolysk that better times were coming, so he'd been patient.

Dracolysk found a few references to Noah, none of particular interest. He found one mention of Remus Wydlin. Dracolysk had attended a symposium in which Dr. Wydlin had spoken about the future of cybergenetics. Dr. Wydlin believed that the progress of the field to date was nothing compared to what it would become.

Dracolysk had been interested enough to seek Wydlin out later and draw him out in more detail. Dr. Wydlin said something at that time about how shortsighted most developers of combat gennies were. Their creations were undoubtedly strong and damage-resistant, but Wydlin felt they were stupider than they needed to be. He had hinted that he knew how to go about remedying that situation.

At the time, Dracolysk had decided Dr. Wydlin's talk was merely wishful thinking. After all, Wydlin was supposed to be a genius, wasn't he? If he could make smarter combat gennies, why hadn't he already done so? Dracolysk did some dabbling in genetics himself, and he thought he knew what was feasible. What Wydlin was talking about didn't seem possible.

However, Dr. Wydlin knew far more about the melding of biological creatures with computer implants than Dracolysk did. Maybe he had finally come up with something. In any case, it was all Dracolysk had to go on. And he was confident of his ability to convince Noah Wydlin that he knew more than he really did.

CHAPTER TEN

Noah was enjoying the soothing pressure of Marcie's fingers as they kneaded his neck when an annoying buzz intruded on his consciousness. Marcie leaned over to switch on Noah's comnet, then returned to her massage. He sighed, then forced himself to deal with the situation, despite his conviction that his people often had no idea of what a true emergency was. "Yes?" he asked languidly.

It was Commander Andreyev. "Mr. Wydlin, a vessel is approaching—a scout cruiser. Not one of ours, sir."

Noah sat up unhurriedly, signaling Marcie to stop. He'd probably have to deal with this himself. "Identify it and find out what they want." Undoubtedly it was some pirate dissatisifed with the financial arrangement they'd come to. Gretsky, or perhaps Pirelli, might know something about the person they were dealing with and could recommend a course of action.

"Sir, he says he's a friend of yours. Hugo Dracolysk."

Noah would never have called Dracolysk a friend. Indeed, the man was so treacherous that Noah never knew where he stood with him. Noah operated on the principle that Dracolysk usually intended him harm and would move more quickly if Noah ever openly acknowledged the fact.

Noah summoned a smile he was far from feeling and said, "Tell Mr. Dracolysk I'm glad he could come. Have someone show him to my office when he docks."

Commander Andreyev looked surprised but covered it up quickly and signed off. Noah leaned back in his chair and tried to clear his mind and relax. He needed to marshal all his energies for the approaching meeting.

Some time later, Noah heard the door to his outer office slide open. He sat up and faced the door, waiting. Dracolysk entered and walked straight to Noah's desk, smiling broadly. "Noah! Great to see you!"

Noah stood and reached out to clasp Dracolysk's outstretched hand. "Hello, Hugo. Please have a seat." He gestured to some chairs set up a few feet away from his desk and followed Dracolysk over to them. "I have some Venusian coffee if you'd like some."

"Thank you," Dracolysk said. "You know, I had no idea you were a neighbor until recently. I wish you'd told me, Noah. I could have helped you get settled."

Noah smiled to himself. Dracolysk made it sound as if Noah had just moved onto a different floor of the same Martian pyramid rather than into a secret research base. Dracolysk must want something pretty badly to go about things in such a clumsy fashion. Or else—and Noah had to admit this was more likely—Dracolysk was so confident of his ability to get what he wanted that he didn't mind seeming careless. Noah would have to be especially careful. But then, he was always careful when dealing with Hugo Dracolysk.

Noah handed Dracolysk a steaming mug of coffee and sat, smiling. "Your neighborliness is commendable, Hugo. And your curiosity is transparent."

"Curiosity? Not at all," Dracolysk protested. "It's quite obvious what you're doing here."

Noah was momentarily surprised, then realized it was one of Dracolysk's standard ploys—pretending to more knowledge than he actually possessed.

Noah schooled himself to seem merely amused. "And just what do you think we're doing, Hugo?"

"You're working on a new combat gennie, of course. And not just any combat gennie. In addition to the predictable physical improvements, the new gennies will have mental abilities in the human range."

Noah sipped at his coffee to hide his reaction. Dracolysk knew more than Noah thought, but it still could have been a lucky guess. There was no need to let Dracolysk know how accurate his assessment was.

"Your father told me all about it," Dracolysk continued blandly.

Noah choked on his coffee and coughed. The hot liquid burned his mouth.

"Noah, are you all right?" Dracolysk asked.

Noah found a handkerchief in his pocket and dabbed at his mouth, giving him time to formulate a response. "Well, Hugo, I take it back," he said. "You're not curious about what we're doing after all. At the risk of seeming inhospitable, then, just why *are* you here?"

Dracolysk set down his cup and looked at Noah. "At the risk of seeming immodest, I'm the finest trainer of combat gennies in the solar system. So I'm not asking for any favors when I tell you I want to train them."

Noah took another sip of coffee, ignoring his burned mouth. His father already had plans for the education of the Barneys. "You're a fine trainer, Hugo," Noah said. "Why don't you write a proposal, and we'll consider it."

"That sounds like a brush-off," Dracolysk said, feigning injury. "And you've been so tactful, Noah. Well, perhaps it's time to broach a rather painful subject."

Noah assumed he must be talking about the money Wydlin Corporation owed Dracolysk Corporation, even though they had legally settled on a payment plan several months earlier. "Haven't you been receiving your scheduled payments?" he asked sharply.

"Right on time." Dracolysk smiled. Reaching into his breast pocket, he pulled out a gold box and extracted a cigarette. Noah knew Dracolysk smoked; it was one of his costlier and more exotic hobbies. But he'd never known Dracolysk to indulge in front of a social equal without asking permission. Dracolysk was making a clear statement of his advantage. Noah felt prickles of sweat under his arms. What did Dracolysk know?

Dracolysk lit the cigarette, then inhaled deeply. "I'm surprised you've built this station when you claimed to have so many financial difficulties. I'm sure the courts knew nothing about it, did they?"

Of course the courts knew nothing about the station. It had been built and paid for by the time the payment plans were arranged. If Genesis had appeared in their financial statement, its usefulness for classified projects would be at an end. Noah suddenly realized he was holding his cup so tightly he might snap off the handle. He placed it carefully on the table. "Your point, Hugo?"

"Well, now that I've discovered Genesis Station, I feel I ought to bring it to light. We can't have you bilking other unsuspecting people the way you did me. It hardly seems fair, does it?"

Noah's jaw grew tight. "Our financial statement accurately reflects our ability to pay. Go ahead and tell the courts. They'll find no more assets than they did before. Of course, if our present projects are jeopardized, that will affect our ability to work off the debt."

"Ahh . . . I'd hate for that to happen." Dracolysk took a long drag on his cigarette and exhaled. "It's so inconvenient when my good citizenship gets the better of me." He looked around for a place to tap his ashes and settled for his half-full coffee mug. "The thing is, Noah, I suspect there might be something else going on here—something better not investigated. There is the matter of your sister."

"What about her?" Noah's mouth went dry.

"She recently escaped from prison. I'd be disappointed in you if you weren't aware of that, though, Noah. In fact, it's hard to believe you had nothing to do with it. I assume RAM feels the same way, only they haven't found anything to link you with it. Yet. I wonder what they'd find if they searched Genesis Station." Dracolysk leaned back and inhaled again on his cigarette.

Noah forced himself to remain calm. If Dracolysk had wanted to turn him in, he'd be in prison already. Noah strived to appear unconcerned. "You say giving you the Barneys' training contract might inhibit your—what did you call it? Good citizenship?"

"Yes," Dracolysk said.

"Well, I know your work," Noah said. His father would be furious, but there was no getting around it. "I believe that perhaps we can come to some arrangement." He stood and forced himself to shake Dracolysk's hand. It was cool and dry, reminding Noah of a reptile.

"Thank you, Noah." Dracolysk dropped the butt of his cigarette into his coffee mug. "Now, if you could show me the gennies . . . ?"

"Certainly," Noah said. "Would you excuse me, Hugo? I just need to call down and tell them we're coming."

Dracolysk's eyes narrowed. Then he nodded pleasantly. "Of course. I'll step into the outer office."

Noah waited until the door slid closed behind Dracolysk, his eyes riveted to the cigarette floating in Dracolysk's coffee. Then he went into his private washroom and was sick.

○ ○ ○ ○ ○

RW appeared at her usual perch on the edge of the console. "Are you finished?" Jovanna asked.

"Of course. Number Five was easy," RW said, swinging one holographic leg over the other.

Jovanna smiled. "One would hope so." Barney Number Five, who had just finished his general skills training, was due to begin his education as a computer hacker. Finding the programming for that part of his education was, as RW put it, "right up her circuits."

"Uh-oh." RW's eyes went momentarily blank. "Someone wants you." She winked out of sight an instant before Jovanna's commo signal came on.

"Jovanna Trask here," she said. Dr. Wydlin's face came on her screen, a crease between his eyebrows. "Jovanna, could you come to the lab for a moment?"

"Yes, of course, Dr. Wydlin." She rose and found that her knees were shaking.

What could he want with her? They had already met once today, and he'd seemed fine then. Had he discovered that she was providing information about the Barneys to Vince Pirelli? Jovanna prayed that Dr. Wydlin's summons had nothing to do with that.

I'm not cut out for espionage, she thought. Once this project is over, I'll do menial programming tasks for the rest of my life without complaint. She took a shuddering breath and reported to the lab.

A Desert Runner warrior stood on either side of the lab doors when she entered. Jovanna stood uncertainly between them, trying not to be intimidated by the fact that the dark eyes in their short-furred faces were fixed on her. Each wore leather armor covering his torso and arms and carried a pistol and a mono knife, as well as other equipment Jovanna wasn't familiar with. Their legs were unarmored, and the musk of their mottled reddish brown fur, or perhaps just their threatening proximity, made her cough nervously.

When they made no threatening moves toward her, she decided to try to ignore them and discover why she had been summoned. Dr. Wydlin was looking at the large screen above the console. Noah Wydlin stood on one side of his father. On the other side was a tall, dark-haired man in standard RAM business attire. Jovanna didn't remember having seen him around Genesis before. Four images glowed on the screen, each showing a Barney in a different stage of development.

Numbers One through Seven had already been decanted and were visited daily by RW or one of several low-memory backup copies she'd made of herself. Jovanna figured the ones on the screen must be Barneys Eight, Nine, Ten, and Eleven. The most fully developed embryo, Number Eight, looked like a large sleeping human male. Number Eleven, the least developed of the Barneys in progress, reminded Jovanna of a cadaver, its titanium alloy skeleton clearly visible under baggy skin. The hands seemed unusually large; they were already completely functional. Even now they were inhumanly strong, composed largely of titanium alloy and wires.

"Hello, Jovanna." Dr. Wydlin spoke courteously, as usual, but his brow was furrowed. He indicated the dark-haired man. "This is Mr. Dracolysk. He'll be training the Barneys once they're decanted. Mr. Dracolysk, this is Ms. Trask."

Dracolysk turned slowly. He was easily the most handsome man she had ever seen, no mean feat considering the access most members of the Martian executive caste had to genetic engineering and cosmetic surgery. Dracolysk appeared to have taken full advantage of these. His green eyes flickered over her briefly. Then he turned to Noah Wydlin. "Have you told her what she needs to do?"

"I thought you could explain it best," Wydlin said.

Just then Flint entered with Potemkin, the first Barney they had decanted. At seven feet in height and nearly three hundred pounds, he was impressive to look at. Unlike the Desert Runners, he looked completely human, except for his size. His features were naturally asymmetric, like those of a human who had never had RAM-style cosmetic surgery. But they were not unattractive. Perhaps they were blunter than those of most Martians, the nose thicker, the eyes more prominent. Potemkin had brown hair and brown eyes, but the Barneys had a number of different colorations, as well as slight differences in their facial features.

Jovanna had never been this close to a Barney before, and she was surprised at how intimidating she found him. The simple, sleeveless black coverall that was issued to all the Barneys revealed the improbably large muscles of his arms and hinted at latent strength.

She knew, of course, that the Barneys were no teddy bears, but she had been working with their educational programming for so long that she had started to think of them as children. That illusion dropped away at the sight of Potemkin. He looked the room over carefully when he first entered, as if assessing the situation. Whatever conclusions he drew, he kept them to himself, maintaining a neutral expression. Potemkin's physical presence made the husky Desert Runners—Jovanna thought they must be Dracolysk's bodyguards—look thin and underdeveloped.

Potemkin had been decanted for seven months and was just beginning his training as an entrepreneur. He had already learned the rudiments of piloting and combat from holocomputer simulations. When he finished his education, he would be prepared to run every facet of a freight-handling operation, from product distribution to flying and maintaining freighters. How these skills would help Dr. Wydlin make RAM pay for what they had done to Rachel Jovanna didn't know, but she imagined Dr. Wydlin had something in mind.

"Which one is this?" Dracolysk asked peremptorily. As Noah Wydlin began to explain, Dracolysk shook his head. "No, no. I'm sure your attempts at training have met with some success, but I don't want to see the oldest one. You've had the most time with him. Which one has been decanted most recently?"

"That would be Number Seven," Noah Wydlin said.

"Bring him in," Dracolysk said, as if the Wydlins were his servants. Dr. Wydlin's expression froze forbiddingly, and Noah seemed to look a warning at his father. Dr. Wydlin pressed his lips together and turned away.

"Are you sure you need to see Number Seven?" Noah asked Dracolysk. "He was only decanted earlier today, and we generally let them rest for a day or two before—"

"Are you serious?" Dracolysk chuckled. "You'll never get anything like their true potential from them if you baby them like that. It seems I got here just in time."

"Now, see here, Mr. Dracolysk—" Dr. Wydlin began, but Noah put a restraining hand on his father's arm.

"Please, Father. Mr. Dracolysk has a good deal of experience training combat gennies. I'm sure we can work out the details of the handling of the Barneys to everyone's satisfaction." Noah turned to Flint. "Mr. Flint, please return Potemkin to his studies and bring Black Barney in."

"Black Barney?" Dracolysk asked, one finely cast eyebrow arching higher than the other. Flint touched

Potemkin lightly on the elbow, and the huge gennie turned to follow him from the room.

"My father has given names to the different Barneys according to—" Noah saw the look Dr. Wydlin flashed at him and broke off. Then he affected the cynical tone Jovanna had heard her more privileged classmates use when trying to impress each other with how boring they found their wealth and power. "A diverting pastime, don't you think? Not particularly clever, I suppose, but there's not much else to do on a space station."

Black Barney was to be trained as a space pirate, but Jovanna felt sure that Dr. Wydlin didn't want Dracolysk to know that. In fact, Jovana was willing to bet that Dr. Wydlin didn't want Dracolysk in the lab at all. She wondered what had made Dr. Wydlin agree to this unprecedented visit by an outsider.

Flint reappeared, this time leading the seventh Barney. In his sleeveless black coverall, Black Barney was practically identical to his clone brother. His hair was slightly darker than Potemkin's, and his eyes were a steely gray. He moved more slowly. Despite the neuromuscular stimulation he'd received while still in the vat, he was still getting used to actual movement.

Black Barney's expression was also more open than Potemkin's. His eyes searched the room, apparently looking for someone. When he saw Dr. Wydlin, a small, satisfied smile appeared on his face. He obviously already knew his creator, but Jovanna wasn't surprised by that. In the first place, Dr. Wydlin was one of the language referents she had put into the predecanting programming. Also, Dr. Wydlin made it a point to be present at each Barney's decanting and to spend some time with him or her immediately afterward. When proud Martian parents did that at the time of their children's birth, it was called "bonding." At least in Black Barney's case, a bond seemed to have formed between the scientist and his creation.

"Not bad." Dracolysk's tone, as he looked Black Barney up and down, was unbearably patronizing. A muscle in Dr. Wydlin's cheek worked, and Barney, frowning, followed his gaze to Dracolysk.

"He appears intelligent, for a gennie. But I expected that. Let's just check his muscle tone." Dracolysk stepped closer to Black Barney and touched his arm.

Puzzled, Black Barney looked toward his creator for his reaction. Dr. Wydlin looked angry, and Barney, seeing it, turned on Dracolysk with a snarl.

"No!" Dr. Wydlin said, but Barney was already wrenching Dracolysk's arm back viciously. The Desert Runners stationed by the door rushed over. One of them pulled out a rocket pistol, while the other uncoiled a long, flexible tool from his utility belt. Jovanna had never seen a real neurowhip before, but she thought she recognized what it was. The multiple filaments on the end were designed to send an electrical charge into the victim's neurons, inflicting intense pain.

The Desert Runner flicked the neurowhip against Black Barney's bare arm, and Barney gasped in pain, turning to face the threat. He did not, however, release his hold on the white-faced Dracolysk, who swung around in Barney's grasp. The Desert Runner with the whip pulled back to avoid harming Dracolysk, and the other moved to get a shot at Black Barney.

"Dracolysk! Tell your guard not to fire!" Dr. Wydlin said. "Black Barney, let him go."

Black Barney looked at Dr. Wydlin with a puzzled expression, then slowly released Dracolysk. Dracolysk stumbled, then grabbed at the edge of a lab counter to steady himself. Gasping, he put one hand up toward his Desert Runners. "Don't fire."

The Desert Runners didn't move back, but neither did they attack.

"Dr. Wydlin, I believe we would all be happier if this Barney was returned to his cell," Dracolysk managed to say. Dr. Wydlin gestured to Flint, who took one nervous step toward Black Barney, then froze at the gennie's forbidding expression.

"It's all right, Barney," Dr. Wydlin said in soothing tones. "Go along with Mr. Flint and get some rest." The frown on Black Barney's forehead smoothed out, and he followed Flint as tamely as a puppy.

Dracolysk was the first to speak. "Well, that was a bit of excitement! Now that I'm involved, we don't have to worry about that kind of thing happening again."

"Why do you think that?" Jovanna said. She realized it sounded cold and challenging, but she couldn't stop herself. She knew the Barneys were intended to be combat gennies, but in all the time since the first one had been decanted, this was the first incidence of violence she'd heard of. It seemed to her the Barneys would be more dangerous under Dracolysk's tutelage rather than less, if this first experience was anything to judge by.

"Because I know how to deal with insubordination." Dracolysk looked straight into her eyes. Apparently satisfied, he pulled a small computer disk out of his breast pocket. "This is an introduction to my training methods, Ms. Trask. It must be incorporated into their programming. It should be no problem with the Barneys who are still in their vats. However, we have seven Barneys already decanted and in the process of being trained. They also need the programming."

"I'm not familiar with the hardware connections," Jovanna said, reluctant to help Dracolysk in any way.

"That can be arranged, can't it, Dr. Wydlin?" Dracolysk said.

Dr. Wydlin looked as if he wanted to say something, then nodded and turned away abruptly. Jovanna wondered at his acquiescence. The Barneys were his, weren't they? Why put up with Dracolysk's involvement if he found it objectionable?

"Here you are, Ms. Trask," Dracolysk said, holding the disk out to Jovanna. She took it reluctantly. "Mr. Wydlin has arranged a suite for me at the station. If you have any questions, I'm on the comnet."

"Yes, sir," said Jovanna.

"Thank you, Jovanna. That will do," Dr. Wydlin said tonelessly. Jovanna noted Dracolysk's triumphant expression and realized if she was going to get any explanations from Dr. Wydlin, it would have to wait until later.

She returned to her office and immediately inserted Dracolysk's disk into a small slot in her console. Before she took it anywhere near the Barneys, she intended to discover what it contained.

O O O O O

Vince entered Noah Wydlin's outer office and grinned at Marcie. She'd been programmed to be completely faithful to Wydlin, but her aquamarine eyes sparkled at him as she returned his smile. "Hello, Vince. Mr. Wydlin is waiting for you. Go right on in."

"Only if you're sure I can't stay here with you," Vince said, lifting her hand to his lips.

She snatched her hand away, but her smile, if anything, grew wider. "Stop that! I have work to do," she chided him.

Vince looked at her with exaggerated sadness as he walked backward to Wydlin's inner office door, enjoying the flush that spread prettily over her cheeks. When he heard the door begin to slide open, he nimbly turned around and walked into the office.

Noah Wydlin, seated at his desk, gestured to Vince to take the seat facing him. He waited for the door to close before speaking. "I have got an assignment for you."

Vince took the seat indicated, glad that Wydlin had finally found something for him to do. It was days, sometimes weeks, between the times Jovanna found to share information with him. He couldn't complain about that, of course. She'd tell him when she had need of him, and she was risking her cover every time she contacted him. He just hoped that whatever Wydlin wanted, it wouldn't keep him away from Genesis so long that he missed an attempt to contact him. Vince had been worried that he might be assigned to shuttle duty between Genesis and Mars, an assignment that would keep him away from Genesis for two weeks or more at a time. "Yes, sir. What is it?" he asked.

"I have a contract with a nearby company to do some training for me," Wydlin said. "I need someone who's not afraid of the Trojan asteroid field to make regular runs between Genesis and the other station. It's very important to my contractor that the location of his station remain classified, just as it is to me that as few people as possible know about Genesis Station."

"You know I can keep a secret," Vince said, trying not to look as relieved as he felt. It sounded as if it couldn't have been more convenient for staying close to Genesis—and Jovanna.

"Fine," Wydlin said. "You'll make these trips approximately once a week. The first one will be in a few days. And, Pirelli—" he paused, turning a light pencil over and over in his hands—"I'd like you to report to me every time you return. I'm very interested in your impressions of Gorgon Station and of my contractor."

Vince smiled. "I think I understand, sir."

"Good." Wydlin's face didn't change. Vince had the impression of someone who would explode at the slightest pressure. "I'll be in touch."

"Yes, sir." Vince stood. Wydlin nodded and turned toward his computer screen without really seeming to see it. Vince took that as a dismissal and left the office.

O O O O O

Jovanna chewed her lower lip, wondering what to do with the disk Dracolysk had given her the day before.

She called softly, "RW?"

RW rippled into view. "Yes?"

"Do you remember when I told you someone might try to tamper with the Barneys?"

"Vaguely." RW sat up. "Why? Did I miss something?"

"No—at least I don't think so," Jovanna said. "But someone's about to."

"What do you mean?"

Briefly Jovanna described the meeting with Dracolysk and the Wydlins. "I don't like this software. It contains a lot of pro-RAM programming. I'm sure Dr. Wydlin doesn't approve."

"Then why is he allowing it?" RW asked.

"I imagine it's Martian politics. No way to tell without knowing more of the facts. But assuming Dr. Wydlin doesn't want the Barneys programmed to be loyal to RAM, can we do anything about it?"

"Let me take a look at it," RW said. She winked at Jovanna. "I've been studying up."

Jovanna didn't doubt that. RW had evolved immeasurably from the barely functioning personality Jovanna had translated months earlier. RW had a lot of what Jovanna's father used to call "initiative." And she had the advantage of being able to move at the speed of light. RW knew more about the ins and outs of the computer matrix now than Jovanna could ever hope to. Jovanna felt sometimes that she'd created a monster. At least RW was a friendly monster.

RW popped back into view. "You weren't kidding. The disk was filled with codes designed to imprint the Barneys with how utterly godlike the Martian executive class is and how Simund Holzerhein is the godliest of them all."

Jovanna shivered. "Yuck!"

RW laughed. "I'm glad to see I've been a good influence on you, Jovanna. You're starting to sound just like me. The question is, what's next?"

Jovanna chewed on her lower lip. "Dracolysk is bound to check my work. If I destroy the programming or don't use it, he'll know immediately."

"How about a virus?" RW asked.

Jovanna sat straighter. "Keep talking."

"Well, if you can cook up a computer virus—specific to Dracolysk's program, please, since I don't want to catch it, thanks—I'll plant it for you. Just give it a delayed start time so it won't go into effect until after he's had time to examine your work."

"Good idea!" Jovanna said. "I'll start on it tomorrow."

"Why wait?" RW asked.

"I have a meeting with Vince tonight. Then in the morning I'll check with Dr. Wydlin to make sure he wants our help," Jovanna said.

CHAPTER ELEVEN

Jovanna sat alone at the table in Willy's Bar and Grill, letting the conversations of other patrons drift around her and feeling stupid. She didn't know the first thing about barhopping. Not that there were many bars to hop to on Genesis Station. In fact, Willy's, a long, dark room that smelled of fried foods, was the only one. One of the scientists operated it after work as a hobby. Otherwise, it was unlikely a bar would exist on the remote station.

Jovanna's drink sat untouched. When was Vince going to get here? She wished that she could have thought of a less public place to meet. He had asked, "My place or yours?" She'd rejected those two possibilities out of hand. At least at Willy's they could seem to bump into each other.

The door near the bar slid open, and Vince stood outlined in the bright light of the hallway. He walked to the bar and spoke to Willy, then stood looking around the lounge. As he accepted a mug of beer, his eyes settled on Jovanna. "Well, well!" He walked up to her table and pulled out the other chair. "Is this seat taken?"

"No," Jovanna said, wishing she could sound as light and casual as Vince did. "Uh—go ahead, sit down."

Vince sat, then leaned across the table and spoke softly. "Are you proud of me?"

"What for?" Jovanna blinked, wondering what she'd missed this time. Vince always made her feel as if she'd tuned in right in the middle of a tri-dee drama.

"I stayed away and let you call me." Vince leaned forward a few more inches and crooked his finger, beckoning her. Jovanna leaned closer to him, and he took her hands. She was about to pull them away when she remembered their last meeting. Vince was undoubtedly trying to make this meeting look like another romantic rendezvous. It seemed to be his usual style.

"So what's new?" he asked, rubbing one thumb in lazy circles on the back of her left hand.

"Well, uh—" She made herself concentrate on the reason she'd called him. "There's someone else working with the Barneys now—a man named Dracolysk."

"What's he doing?"

"Training, they said. But it's strange, Vince. I'm sure the Wydlins don't want him here. Dracolysk gave me some software for the Barneys' educational program."

Jovanna saw something purple move closer, then stop beside their table. She looked away from Vince and saw a striking brunette in a clingy amethyst dress. The woman ignored her. "Hello, Vince. I thought we were getting together tonight."

Vince looked up at her and smiled. "I thought so, too, Angela. In about an hour, right?"

"Who's your friend?" Angela asked, finally deigning to look at Jovanna.

"Jovanna?" Vince met Jovanna's eyes, then grinned at the brunette. "She's my long-lost sister. We have a lot to catch up on. I'll see you in an hour, okay, Angela?"

Angela didn't look amused. "Maybe. If I'm not there, don't wait all night for me."

"I won't," Vince said cheerfully. Angela's jaw dropped, then she flounced away.

Jovanna felt even stupider than she had while waiting for Vince. "I'm sorry. I hope she wasn't—"

"Just another long-lost sister." Vince patted Jovanna's hand and smiled. "I shouldn't have met you here. I lose more sisters that way."

"I can see how you might." Jovanna found herself smiling in spite of herself. She didn't know whether Vince was disturbed by meeting Angela here, but it was hard not to admire his unfailing aplomb.

"Anyway—" Vince leaned in close to her—"you were telling me about a guy named Dracolysk."

Jovanna filled him in on her discoveries about the software Dracolysk had supplied and the virus she'd given RW to combat it.

"You've been a pretty busy girl," Vince said, an approving light in his eyes. "Have you made a report?"

"A report? You mean to NEO? Uh, I don't know how to," Jovanna confessed. When Vince's eyes narrowed, she said, "I thought you would."

His smile faded and he released her hands. "I see." He put a hand around the handle of his mug but didn't lift it to drink right away. Instead he looked at her for a long moment, then said, "Jovanna, remember what you called me when we first met?"

"You mean 'Vince'?" Jovanna asked, trying to match his earlier lightness.

Vince smiled, but Jovanna could tell he was still disturbed. He sipped at his beer. "Not really. Jovanna, you were expecting me, right? I mean, when I called you 'Dekalb,' you did call me 'Farm Boy,' didn't you?"

"Farm Boy?" Jovanna thought back to their first meeting. There had been something about farming, but what? Then she remembered. "I said if you knew what Dekalb meant, you must be a farmer. I only knew about it from a term paper I wrote once."

Vince set his mug down, frowning. Then he shook his head. "Well, I'd better be going. Call me if you need to." He stood up abruptly and left the table, stopping in the doorway and glancing over his shoulder at her.

Jovanna had the feeling that something had changed, but she didn't know what.

He'd barely blinked when his girlfriend had found him with Jovanna. What could be bothering him so now? Jovanna reached for her glass and took a sip, then choked on the unaccustomed taste of the liquor.

○   ○   ○   ○   ○

Vince pressed the palm lock that allowed him access to his quarters. The door slid open at his touch, but he stood staring abstractedly at the utilitarian room. So Jovanna wasn't Dekalb after all. He'd resigned himself to that in the short time it had taken him to walk to his room. He was extraordinarily lucky that she hadn't turned him in, but it didn't change two basic facts: First, he'd involved a civilian—Jovanna—in a dangerous situation. Second, he hadn't found his NEO contact.

So who was Dekalb? Vince glanced at his computer terminal, then got an idea and approached the unit. Dekalb wouldn't have left him a message on the bulletin board, would he? Could it be that easy? Vince turned on the terminal and accessed the bulletin board. He scanned a number of items, most of which seemed to be notices of various events taking place on the station.

Finally he got to a section that contained more personal notices. One read, "VINCE, DON'T BOTHER STOPPING BY TONIGHT OR EVER. SPEND THE TIME WITH YOUR 'SISTER.' A." Vince felt a slight regret at this evidence of Angela's ire, but it was tempered by the fact that he'd forgotten all about their date anyway. He checked his wristchrono. It was just as well that she was canceling it. He was too distracted by his immediate concerns to worry about her right now.

There was nothing else addressed specifically to him. One notice seemed worth pursuing, however. It read, "F.B., USE #3410 TO CONTACT D."

Vince felt excited. "If F.B. means Farm Boy, then D would mean Dekalb." He quickly pressed keys 3, 4, 1, and 0. A single line appeared on his screen: "CALL ME BY NAME." The person on the other end must be trying to weed out people who were simply curious.

"ARE YOU DEKALB?" Vince typed.

"WHO WANTS TO KNOW?" came the reply.

Vince wasn't excited about committing his code name to the bulletin board, but if this wasn't Dekalb, using it would be the quickest way to find that out. He took a deep breath, then entered, "CALL ME FARM BOY."

After a moment, another line appeared. "GLAD TO HEAR FROM YOU, FARM BOY. WE CAN'T MEET THIS WAY OFTEN. ANY PROBLEMS?"

Vince typed. "NEED TO MAKE REPORT."

Under his line appeared the sentence, "NEXT TRIP AWAY FROM GENESIS, USE FREQUENCY J. ANYTHING ELSE?"

Vince had learned a code for several communications frequencies in NEO training. Frequency J referred to one of several secure channels used for sending information all the way back to headquarters on Earth. "NOTHING ELSE FOR NOW. THANKS, DEKALB."

"NO PROBLEM, FARM BOY."

Vince switched off the computer. Finally he was back on track. He'd have some explaining to do about Jovanna, but maybe Beowulf would forgive him in view of the information she'd provided. He'd find out when he made his first trip to the mysterious Gorgon Station.

○ ○ ○ ○ ○

It couldn't wait any longer, Jovanna decided. She had let the disk sit on her desk for two days, waiting for Dr. Wydlin to talk to her about Dracolysk. Unfortunately, Dracolysk would soon be asking why she hadn't started incorporating his programming into the Barneys' cybernetics. She couldn't put it off forever.

She hadn't sought out Dr. Wydlin. She thought it was up to him to tell her if he wanted to stop Dracolysk, but it suddenly occurred to her that he might not realize what was on the disk Dracolysk had given her. In that case, she'd better inform him immediately.

She went to Dr. Wydlin's office and waited for his answer. She was about to knock again when the door slid open. Dr. Wydlin was seated next to his desk. His eyes looked sunken and his clothing rumpled. His fringe of gray hair looked as if he hadn't combed it for days. "Dr. Wydlin, are you all right?" she asked.

"I'm fine, Jovanna. What do you want?"

Jovanna didn't believe it, but there was no point in challenging him. Her news, if he wasn't already aware of it, would only make him feel worse anyway. "It's the disk," she said. "The one Mr. Dracolysk gave me."

Dr. Wydlin looked up at her suddenly, and she could see a flash of anger. Then his expression became normal again. "It's compatible with our system, isn't it?"

"Well . . . yes," Jovanna said. "It's in simple RAM standard programming language. But I just wanted to make sure you knew what was on it before I followed Mr. Dracolysk's orders."

"My son says Dracolysk knows his business," Dr. Wydlin said. "His methods are not open to question."

"But . . ." Jovanna trailed off uncertainly. It was obvious that Dr. Wydlin didn't want to talk about their problem, but if she went ahead with Dracolysk's programming according to his orders, the Barneys would become loyal to RAM. She couldn't believe Dr. Wydlin was willing to see all his work wasted. "Dr. Wydlin," she began, "you specifically asked me not to use sensory imprinting, but Dracolysk—"

"It's standard," Dr. Wydlin said. "RAM always uses sensory imprinting to make it painful for gennies to be disloyal. They don't want a lot of uncontrollable creatures running around the solar system."

Jovanna ran her fingers through her mop of brown hair. How could she reach him? It was as if he knew exactly what Dracolsyk was trying to do but didn't care. "But he's making the Barneys exactly the opposite—"

"Shh!" He went on, speaking quickly, nervously. "We have to forget all that, Jovanna. Mr. Dracolysk is a good businessman, and Noah says we need to take advantage of his expertise if we want to stay in business. If you want to do well in your career—" he paused, looking into her eyes—"you must give him your full cooperation."

Jovanna didn't really understand all of what Dr. Wydlin was getting at, but one thing seemed clear. They had to at least appear to go along with Dracolysk. And it was going to be very difficult to talk openly anymore about what they had planned for the Barneys. Dracolysk was probably a RAM spy, and the Wydlins knew it, but they were powerless to keep him away from the Barneys. She sighed and wondered how she could make the suggestion she had come here to make. Then a way occurred to her. "I'll do my best, Dr. Wydlin. The Barneys should come out just as Mr. Dracolsyk would like as long as nothing unusual happens."

"Unusual?" Dr. Wydlin frowned.

"Well, there are always computer viruses," Jovanna said, watching for his reaction.

He looked at her piercingly, but she thought he looked hopeful. "I'm sure Mr. Dracolysk's security is very good," he said. A warning, Jovanna thought.

"I'm not saying it isn't," she said. "I'm just saying you can never be absolutely sure about computer security."

"True. Well, if Dracolysk's programming runs into any problems, you can always repair it," he said. Jovanna frowned. Now she wasn't sure whether he wanted her to tamper with Dracolysk's programming or not. This was getting too complicated. She shook her head impatiently. She had to assume she knew Dr. Wydlin, knew what he really wanted.

"I'll repair any problems Dracolysk *finds*," she said, hoping that Dr. Wydlin understood that she didn't mean for Dracolysk to detect anything wrong. By the time the virus had done its work, Dracolysk would already have convinced himself the Barneys were loyal to RAM.

Dr. Wydlin smiled at her. She hoped that meant he realized she would be very careful to leave no traces of any tampering. "Fine." He nodded, as if dismissing her. "I know you'll do your best, Jovanna."

As the door closed, she thought, You bet I'll do my best, Dr. Wydlin. I just hope you and I mean the same thing.

O O O O O

The large double doors of Genesis Station's cavernous spaceport slid open. Two six-foot-tall feathered, bipedal creatures guided a closed, wheeled capsule through the doors. It was large enough to hold the seated Barney that Vince knew it contained. He wondered if the use of the capsule was to guard the secrecy of the Barney project from the others on Genesis, to keep the Barneys from attacking their Falcone escorts, or both.

Jovanna had told Vince about the attack on Dracolysk, and it appeared that Dracolysk wasn't taking any chances. The Falcones—hawklike gennie guards sent to escort the Barneys—were bred for unflagging vigilance. They also bristled with weapons. In addition to the standard laser pistols, they all carried stunners.

"Time to board, Pirelli." Falcone D-2's voice came monotonously through a computerized translating unit that covered his beak. He was the only Falcone outfitted with a translator. The others spoke to each other using a harsh squawking language that resembled no human tongue Vince had ever heard.

Falcone D-2 had remained in the spaceport with Vince while the other Falcones went to get the first Barney and prepare him for transport back to the cruiser Vince would be flying to Gorgon Station. Vince smiled to himself. It seemed that Dracolysk thought Wydlin's pilot was ignorant of whom he was carrying and intended to keep him that way.

To test his theory, Vince said, "I'd be glad to help you with the loading, D-2."

"No!" The Falcone pointed toward the docking bay hatch. "You board now."

Vince shrugged. He was right. Dracolysk didn't want him to see the Barneys, just transport them. He climbed into the cruiser he'd been assigned for the trip and waited until the Falcones signaled him to take off.

As long as he didn't try to approach the Barney, Vince thought the Falcones would probably ignore him. He'd be able to contact NEO headquarters undisturbed.

Vince received the signal that his passengers were ready and requested clearance from spaceport personnel. After several minutes, he was maneuvering through the rough asteroid field above Genesis Station.

He had cleared the worst of the rocks and they were halfway to their destination when Vince tuned to Frequency J. An image of the NEO insignia, a blue and green globe signifying an Earth restored to the condition it had before centuries of pollution and war had virtually destroyed it, appeared on his screen. Vince identified himself as Farm Boy, then busied himself with other tasks while waiting for his communication to travel to Earth at the speed of light.

Nearly two hours later, he was rewarded by the sight of a dark-haired man with gray temples. "Beowulf!" Vince felt incredible relief at seeing the man, a few years older than he, who had introduced him to NEO.

"It's been a long time, Vince," Beowulf said. "We'd almost given up on you. I was trying to figure out how to tell Tia Dolores."

Dolores Garcia y Lopez was the eccentric Chicacorg resident, now in her sixties, who had rescued Vince from the streets shortly after he arrived in Chicagorg nine years earlier. Neither RAM nor the Solar Alliance, the RAM puppet organization that nominally ruled Earth, saw fit to educate children like Vince.

Some of Tia Dolores's once vast family fortune had survived the upheavals of the last several centuries. She still had a few resources and connections, and she housed and taught as many children as she could. Beowulf had been one of her first foster children. Vince came along seven or eight years later.

Beowulf was no longer living with Tia Dolores when Vince was with her, but he came back to visit, and he told Dolores's brood about the New Earth Organization. Vince had wanted to join immediately. He'd been helping Tia Dolores teach the younger children, but as much as he admired her efforts, he needed to do something more active. Though the children in Tia Dolores's care grew to be capable of more than most Earth children, there was little for them to do unless they chose to work for RAM or the Solar Alliance. Neither of those alternatives appealed to Vince. He'd convinced Beowulf of his sincerity and was soon accepted into NEO.

"Give Tia Dolores my love," Vince said, then told Beowulf of the last seven and a half months. He braced himself for the reproach he felt sure was coming, but when Beowulf transmitted his reply, he only said, "You did fine, Vince. It's the best that could be expected.

"About the civilian, this Jovanna Trask. I need you to do one thing when you get back to Genesis Station. Have Dekalb check her out. If he okays her, she'll be fine. We'll have a little induction ceremony for her when this is all over. Just try not to alienate her, okay, Farm Boy?"

"What do you mean?" Vince said to himself, though he suspected he knew what Beowulf was about to say.

"You have a way of making every woman you meet believe she's the love of your life. When they find out they aren't, they tend to make life difficult for you."

Beowulf looked as if he was trying to be stern, but Vince didn't buy it. Beowulf continually ribbed Vince about his women. However, Jovanna had made no secret of the fact that she wasn't interested in him. That was fine with Vince. He preferred more attractive women. Jovanna might look all right if she fixed herself up, but apparently appearance wasn't a priority for her. That was fine, too. He didn't want their relationship to get any more complicated than it already was.

"Don't worry about my bothering Jovanna. She's not my type." Vince knew Beowulf couldn't hear him, but he made the statement anyway.

Beowulf continued. "From what you've told me, it sounds as if RAM's interested in the Barneys. That's not unexpected. The main thing you need to worry about is making sure they don't gain control of them. Wydlin Corporation is probably in danger of a takeover, so stay alert for messages from Dekalb. He's in a position to head off takeover attempts, but he may need your help.

"I look forward to your next report, Hermano," Beowulf said, signing off.

CHAPTER TWELVE

On a morning seven months after Dracolysk first began working with the Barneys, Noah pressed his right hand against the palm lock outside his father's lab while he willed his left hand to stop shaking. He wasn't successful. The computer printout of RAM's buyout offer rattled percussively in his hand, irritating Noah's already frayed nerves.

The door opened and Noah hurried through it, making straight for his father's office. It was locked, and he waited impatiently in front of the security vidcam for his father to recognize him and open the door.

After several moments, it became clear to Noah that his father was ignoring him. It was often difficult to get Remus's attention when he was working. Noah slammed his hand against the door several times. Finally the door slid open.

Remus looked up from his desk with a scowl. "I hope this is important."

Noah strode to his father's desk and flung the printout down on it. "You be the judge."

Remus reached for the paper and looked it over. His scowl changed to a look of puzzlement. "An offer to buy the corporation? Where did this come from?"

"RAM Central. It was forwarded from our headquarters on Mars."

"We don't want to sell," Remus said.

"No kidding," Noah retorted. "But I don't see that we have a choice."

"Why not?"

Noah sighed. For all his father's reputed intelligence, even simple business matters had to be explained to him slowly and patiently. "The offer isn't very good, but it does have some provisions we can live with. For example, you and I would stay on in our current positions. It's the kind of offer RAM makes when they know they can force your hand."

"How do you know that?"

"I just know, all right?" Noah had spent five years with RAM right after his graduation from college, before applying to join Wydlin Corporation. He'd seen other companies swallowed up by RAM and had seen how it was done. "Father, you've played chess, right? RAM is essentially saying, 'check.' "

"They still can't force us to sell."

"True," Noah said, exasperated. "They could just have our creditors press for payment and force us out of business."

"Nobody would gain anything from that," Remus said.

"RAM wouldn't gain quite as much," Noah corrected. "But they can still seize our assets."

Remus looked straight at Noah. "Son, at the risk of seeming conceited, I'd like to point out that I'm probably our biggest asset. Otherwise they would have made this offer before I came back to work here. Refuse it."

"They want the Barneys," Noah said. "I'm sure that has to be it. And they'll get them, no matter what we do. We might as well get something out of it ourselves."

"They won't get the Barneys if I have to destroy every last one of them myself," Remus said, but his voice quavered on the last few words. He finally seemed to be grasping the seriousness of the situation. "But if you're that concerned, stall them."

"How am I supposed to do that?"

"I don't know." Remus said. "You're the one who learned how to do that kind of thing. You might tell them that I won't work for them."

"Oh, that would be great. I'd be signing your death warrant." Noah had spoken without thinking and was startled by the stab of fear his own words caused him. "And what about me? If they've figured out I hired someone to rescue Rachel—"

"They'd have arrested you already," Remus said, but he looked more disturbed than before. "Listen, why don't you tell them you want your lawyers and accountants to look at the offer? That should buy us some time. Maybe something will happen in the meantime."

"I'll try," Noah said. In fact, he'd already told RAM that he had to contact his legal and fiscal departments. He'd hoped that Remus might have an idea that could save the company. Now it seemed that Noah would have to find a way to do it himself. He wished he felt more equal to the challenge.

○ ○ ○ ○ ○

Vince flipped on his compdex and accessed the station bulletin board. Since discovering Dekalb seven months earlier, he'd checked the bulletin board every night. Tonight a message read, "F.B., CALL D."

Vince keyed Dekalb's access code and typed, "FARM BOY HERE."

After a few moments, a second amber line appeared on the screen under his: "J.T.O.K." Vince stared at it, puzzled, until he realized that it must refer to his request for Dekalb to find out if it was safe to trust Jovanna Trask. Vince was relieved that Dekalb had okayed her. He'd been relaying her information to Beowulf for almost seven months.

Another line of type appeared. "NEED HELP. WYDLIN CORP. TAKEOVER DANGER. CAN JT TRANSFER FUNDS TO WYDLIN CREDITORS?"

Vince muttered. Well, Jovanna could probably help

with the transfer. But where were they supposed to get the money? He typed, "WHAT FUNDS?"

"RAM MISCELLANEOUS ALLOTMENTS. I'LL SUPPLY ACCOUNT CODE."

Vince whistled. Whoever Dekalb was, he had some interesting connections. He entered, "CAN DO."

Almost immediately, a line of numbers appeared, followed by the names of about half a dozen corporations and amounts owed to them. Vince turned on his printer and made a hard copy of the information. As it printed out, he put a call through to Jovanna.

$$O \quad O \quad O \quad O \quad O$$

Dr. Wydlin looked nearly as tired tonight as he had when he had first arrived at Genesis Station, Jovanna thought. They were working late, but it was no later than many other nights. As Dr. Wydlin reviewed her report on the programming for Barney Number Fourteen, his mind seemed far away.

Jovanna could stand it no longer. "Dr. Wydlin, what's wrong?"

He refocused his attention on her with an obvious effort. "What? Oh, I'm sorry, Jovanna. Where were we?"

"Never mind," Jovanna said. "Something is wrong. Maybe you need a rest, or maybe—" She hesitated. Sometimes she thought she had gained more of Dr. Wydlin's trust than anyone had since Rachel died, but he was still a very private man. Sometimes she thought about telling him why she'd asked to work with him. He might approve. But Jovanna shrank from telling him that she hadn't been honest with him from the outset. Besides, when she had talked to him about Dracolysk's pro-RAM programming, he'd seemed quite upset. Though she ended up planting the virus to destroy Dracolysk's programming, she'd never told him what she'd done. She simply wasn't sure what she could say to him.

The light on her comnet blinked on, saving her from having to decide what to say next. She smiled apologetically. "Excuse me."

"Please, go right ahead," he said.

She flipped her comnet switch. "Jovanna Trask."

The caller replied in audio only, but she had no trouble recognizing Vince's voice. "Are you free to talk?"

"Not now," Jovanna said. "I'll call you later."

"As soon as possible," Vince said and switched off.

Dr. Wydlin seemed to rouse himself. "Jovanna, there was no need to do that. I'm not doing you any good here anyway. I'll do better tomorrow, I promise."

"Please don't apologize, sir," Jovanna said. Vince could wait. "I just— Is there anything I can do for you? You seem—"

"No, Jovanna," Dr. Wydlin said. "Wydlin Corporation's in a tight spot right now, but there's nothing you can do."

Jovanna looked questioningly at him. He stood and patted her shoulder. "We'll get through it somehow. Now you go see your young man. Tell him I'm sorry I kept you so long."

Jovanna nearly protested that Dr. Wydlin had the wrong idea about Vince, but she stopped herself. Vince had gone to some trouble to make it look as if they had a romantic relationship. It was a reasonably good excuse for why they saw each other from time to time. She'd just have to add it to the other lies and half-truths she had let Dr. Wydlin believe. "Thank you, Dr. Wydlin," she said.

O O O O O

It took Jovanna's eyes a few moments to adjust to the gloom of Willy's Bar and Grill, but finally she saw Vince sitting in a corner booth. As she started to approach him, someone stepped into her path.

"Hello, Jovanna." J. Wellington Flint had obviously had several drinks. He gazed at her unsteadily. "I didn't know you came in here. Care to join me?"

"Sorry, Flint. I'm meeting someone." She tried to go around him, but he moved to block her path again.

"Just for a li'l while, all right? I'm all alone."

Jovanna felt a tiny flash of pity, but it was barely discernible through the distaste she always felt when Flint was around. Reeking of liquor, he was even less appealing than usual. "Maybe some other time."

"Prob'ly won't be another time. We'll all be out of our jobs soon. You know that?"

Jovanna stared at him, wondering what he meant. She felt a firm hand at her elbow and turned to see Vince standing there.

"Let's go, Jovanna," he said, looking at Flint as if he were a Claritas rot beetle. "Excuse us."

Jovanna waited until they were in the hall before saying, "What was he talking about, Vince? Do you know? Have they found out about my working for NEO?" If they had, she was in for worse than losing her job. "I can see why I'd be in trouble, but why Flint?"

"You're the guiltiest person I've ever met," Vince said in a low, amused voice. "It has nothing to do with you personally. I'll tell you about it when we're alone. Do you still object to meeting in one of our rooms?"

In the past, they'd always met in public places. But Jovanna realized that something important was in the wind. "Which one's closer?" she asked.

"Why, Ms. Trask," Vince said, putting an arm around her waist. "I find your eagerness flattering. My room is closer, I think. This way, ma'am."

Jovanna was conscious of Vince's arm around her all the way to his room. She had the definite impression that he was inwardly laughing at her discomfort. When they arrived at his door, Vince activated the palm lock and waved her inside. She turned to face him, ready to scold him at the first sign of mockery, but his face was all business.

"I need your help," he said without preamble.

Vince was the most mercurial person Jovanna had ever met, but at least his businesslike tone was one she could handle. "What kind of help?"

"We need to do a few financial transactions, and they can't be traced back to Genesis Station."

"RW can probably handle it," Jovanna said. "She

could travel through the matrix and initiate the transactions somewhere else."

"Great idea!" Vince pulled a crumpled sheet of paper
from his belt pouch. "I have a code that should let us tap
into RAM's miscellaneous allotments and transfer
funds to some corporations that plan to give the
Wydlins more trouble than they can handle right now.
Maybe she can do it from right inside RAM Main."

"Are you insane?" Jovanna said. "RAM Main? If they
find out—"

"Didn't I just say we can't let them find out?" Vince
asked. "And didn't you say RW could handle it?"

"Well—" Jovanna stared at her feet, wishing Vince
didn't look so contemptuous. Then she got angry. What
right did he have, ordering her to do all these dangerous
things and then getting upset if she didn't jump to obey?
A small voice in her head said that Vince hadn't really
ordered her but had simply asked for her help, but she
ignored it. "I'm not doing anything until you tell me
what's going on!"

His eyes darkened, turning almost black. Then he
took a deep breath, as if controlling himself was an effort. "Wydlin Corporation is in immediate danger of being taken over by RAM if creditors aren't paid off. I
assume you didn't foil Dracolysk's programming to see
the Barneys end up in RAM's hands."

"Oh," Jovanna said, wishing her voice didn't sound so
small. "All right. I'll call RW."

She sat down at Vince's compdex, turned it on, and
keyed in RW's access number.

A moment later, RW appeared. As usual, she looked
like Jovanna's twin, down to the same gray jumpsuit
and low black boots. "Hello, Jovanna. Hi, Vince! Nice to
see you."

"RW? You look different," Vince said.

"Nice touch, huh? Jovanna thought I shouldn't look
too much like Rachel or someone might electrocute me."

"RW chose her own form," Jovanna explained somewhat self-consciously. Before Vince could reply, Jovanna explained to RW what they wanted of her.

"It shouldn't be too hard," RW said. "Vince's idea is a good one. I'll do it from right inside RAM Main. That way, it'll look more like an everyday transaction."

"RW!" Jovanna exclaimed.

"What?" RW asked.

Jovanna still didn't like the idea of RW getting so close to the people who had imprisoned her when she was Rachel Wydlin. However, it did seem like the best way of making the transactions. She threw her hands up in the air. "Never mind. Just be careful, will you?"

RW looked at Vince. "She's the biggest wimp in the world, isn't she? How did you end up with her?"

"Just lucky, I guess," Vince said.

"Someone here has to stop and think," Jovanna said, stung by their comments.

"You think too much, Jovanna. That's your problem." Vince winked at RW, who smiled back.

Jovanna folded her arms across her chest and sat back. "All right, I'm through thinking. When you two finish laughing at me, perhaps we can get started." Vince and RW exchanged glances. As one, their expressions grew almost comically sober.

"I'm sorry, Jovanna," RW said. "Could you give me the code and account numbers, please?"

Jovanna nearly told her to ask Vince for them, but she thought they'd just tease her more. She read the account numbers and the code to RW, who nodded.

"It seems easy enough. If I'm not back in ten minutes, send the digital police." Then her form winked out.

Jovanna wished RW hadn't made that last remark, but she had no intention of letting Vince see her uneasiness. "I suppose now we just wait."

"I guess so. You want a drink?" Vince walked behind his food station nook and opened his refrigeration cube.

"Nothing too strong," Jovanna said and braced herself for the ridicule she was sure was coming.

To her surprise, Vince agreed. "Yeah, I'd rather not either until RW gets back safely. How about some juice?"

"You live well," Jovanna said. Fruit juice was relatively easy to get on Mars, but it was so expensive that few outside the executive class could afford it. Jovanna couldn't imagine how Vince had managed to find any on Genesis Station.

"I have friends who know people, and my job pays pretty well," Vince said, inserting a spout into a vacuum carton to break the seal. He poured a yellow-orange liquid into two clear glasses and handed one to her. "You know, on Earth, four or five centuries ago, most people had juice nearly every day for breakfast."

"Really?" Jovanna sipped. The liquid, an intriguing mixture of sweetness and tartness, had tiny flakes in it. She took one off her tongue and studied it on the end of her finger. It caught the light, looking faintly translucent. "What's this?"

Vince smiled, but he didn't seem to be making fun of her. "Fruit pulp. When they squeeze the oranges, part of the fruit gets into the juice."

"So I'm getting a little fruit with it?" Jovanna said. She took another sip and savored the feel of pulp on her tongue. "Mmmm."

Vince's smile grew broader. "Oh, if Cousin Rosie could see you now. She always made her mother strain the pulp from her juice before she'd drink it."

"Who's Cousin Rosie?"

"She's an ancient relative of mine. She lived back in the twentieth century. My dad taught me to read by using her diary."

"Didn't you have a program for that?" Jovanna asked, suddenly realizing that she knew very little of how children were raised on Earth.

"Croppers don't have computers." Vince's smile turned ironic.

"Croppers?" Jovanna asked.

"Agricultural workers. My mother and father worked the land that used to belong to our family. They hoped one day to earn enough to buy it back. Never got very much out of it, except various cancers." Vince put down his glass as if the juice had suddenly gone sour.

"I didn't know there was any arable land left on

Earth," Jovanna said.

"Well, that's debatable. The family hoped for a long time that the land would recover someday. Some Earth-based RAM subsidiaries sold us fertilizers and pesticides that were supposed to make farming possible, but the chemicals could only do so much. Dad finally realized that he was never going to earn enough from the land to get it back for the family. He realized it too late for himself, but not too late for me."

Jovanna watched Vince, wondering for a tense moment if he was going to cry. A muscle in his cheek worked, and then he let out a long sigh. She wanted to hear the rest of his story. "So you got out?"

Vince nodded. "Yeah. I'd like to see the Pirelli land again someday, but not the way it was when I left. The only way for that to happen is if we take our planet back. NEO isn't very powerful now, I know, but we'll make RAM sit up and take notice someday. Anyway, that's why I joined." He looked up at her suddenly and grinned. "That's what you wanted to know, right?"

His smile no longer mocked her, and she returned it. "I guess so."

"How about you?" Vince asked. "Nice girl, raised on Mars, educated by computer . . . Was it only in fear for your life, or did you have some other reason to help us out?"

"Fear for my life?"

"Don't spare my feelings, Jovanna. I know I blew it." Vince picked up his glass again and took a long drink. "I thought you were my contact. You were lucky that you knew enough ancient Earth trivia to keep me from killing you. I was lucky you didn't call station security as soon as I let you go. Why didn't you, by the way?"

"Well—" She wasn't sure where to start. "I—I've just been tired of never really belonging. I'm kind of an odd person, I know. Scared of things, and not very—" She swallowed a lump in her throat, then attempted the kind of ironic smile she'd seen him flash before. "Not very good-looking. I could never make friends easily. Except Rachel. And then, after I saw what RAM did to her, you came along, and you hated RAM. I thought this was my chance to do something for her, so I decided to help if I could."

Vince was looking at Jovanna intensely, and she laughed, as if her confession was of no consequence. "So now you know my story, too. We're even."

He reached over and put his hand over hers. "Well, you belong now, Jo. I'm glad you're with us."

Jovanna blinked rapidly, but she couldn't stop the tears from spilling onto her cheeks. She stole an apologetic glance at Vince. "Sorry. Rachel used to call me Jo."

Vince grabbed a tissue box from the console and handed it to her. "I didn't know."

"That's okay. I kind of like it, really. I just hadn't heard it for a while."

She dug out a tissue and dabbed at her eyes. She wished she could think of what to say next. She blew her nose to cover her loss of control.

"Hi, guys." RW appeared suddenly, her eyes as bright as if she'd just returned from a vacation.

"How did it go?" Jovanna asked.

"It was sinfully easy," RW said. "You're a good programmer, Jovanna. I couldn't believe how easy it was to get through their security, thanks to what you taught me."

"You mostly taught yourself," Jovanna said, though RW's praise warmed her. Since exchanging stories with Vince, she felt right about what she was doing. In fact, she felt happier than she had since she'd been at the university with Rachel. It was good to have a friend again.

"Well done, ladies," pronounced Vince. "Now we just have to wait and see if Wydlin Corporation can hold its own. Too bad they don't know who they have to thank."

"That's all right," said Jovanna. "If the Barneys destroy RAM someday, that will be thanks enough, don't you think?"

Vince smiled at her approvingly and nodded.

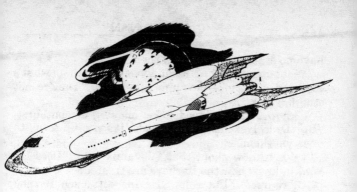

CHAPTER THIRTEEN

Jovanna watched on the screen in Flint's office as three of Dracolysk's Falcones escorted the seventh Barney—Black Barney—back into his cubicle. He had just returned from his second training session at Dracolysk's station. Black Barney waited impassively for the Falcones to leave his cubicle, then removed the upper portion of his loose training suit. A lattice of red welts crisscrossed his back and shoulders. Jovanna frowned. "Why are those marks on his back?"

"All the Barneys have them," Flint said.

"No, they don't," Jovanna said testily. She had seen other Barneys just after they were decanted. Their skins seemed as new as babies. But why shouldn't they? They were babies, in a way.

"I meant they all have those welts when they get back from their training sessions," Flint explained. "Number Seven's are kind of raw now, but the Barneys heal incredibly quickly. In a day or two, he'll only have slight scarring left."

Jovanna shook her head, trying to understand. "Are you telling me Dracolysk beats them?"

"No, not Dracolysk personally." Flint smoothed back a strand of his slick, dark hair. "His trainers do. They have no other way to control them."

"What about reason? What about telling them what's expected of them?" Jovanna said hotly. "They're not stupid, you know."

"I know." Flint seemed to be enjoying her outburst. "But Dracolysk has his methods. It's not up to us to question them."

"I don't know about that," Jovanna said. "Does Dr. Wydlin know how the Barneys are treated?"

"Of course," Flint said. "He inspects each Barney shortly after it returns from a session."

"What does he say about it?" Jovanna couldn't believe Dr. Wydlin approved of Dracolysk's abuse.

"He called Dracolysk after the first one came back looking like that. I don't know what was said. I didn't see Remus Wydlin until the next day, and he never referred to it again." Flint rarely admitted not knowing something. He went on quickly. "I think Dracolysk must have something on him. Ever since his first visit, Remus has been acting strangely. Don't you think so?"

Jovanna knew she wasn't always good at judging such things. All too often she let her own wishes color her perceptions. Now she realized that the depression she'd attributed to Dr. Wydlin's financial troubles hadn't gone away after she'd had RW transfer the funds to keep Wydlin Corporation out of RAM's hands, yet there was every reason to believe the operation had gone without a hitch.

RW had sneaked into the computers of several of Wydlin's creditors to make sure Wydlin Corporation was off the hook. They had saved Wydlin Corporation, at least for the time being.

When she thought about it, Jovanna realized that Dr. Wydlin had never really been the same since Dracolysk's first visit. "Maybe you're right," she said slowly.

She thought her tampering with Dracolysk's disk had cheered Dr. Wydlin at the time, but of course she'd never come right out and told him what she'd done, just as she hadn't told him about the transfer of funds. He seemed not to want to know. She could imagine how he would react to the news that she was working for NEO. She decided she was right to keep it from him, at least for now.

"I'm right more often than you think," Flint said.

Jovanna shook her head, puzzled. What was he talking about? "I'm sorry, I was thinking about something else. Right about what?"

"About people. But you're hard to figure out."

The last thing Jovanna wanted was to have Flint trying to figure her out. Dr. Wydlin seemed to trust him, but Jovanna couldn't imagine ever feeling comfortable with him.

"Maybe there's nothing to figure out," she said. "I'm a pretty ordinary person."

"I doubt that," Flint said. "Remus pulled some strings to have you put on his project, though to put it bluntly, you never distinguished yourself in your previous position. You've been seen several times with that new pilot, Vince Pirelli, who is said to have very discriminating tastes in women. No, I find you intriguing."

Jovanna's flesh crawled. "You watch too much tridee," she told Flint. "I knew Dr. Wydlin before I came to Genesis Station, and he just happened to know that I could handle the Barneys' educational programming and save him some work."

"Uh-huh." Flint's inflection implied he knew there was more to her relationship with Dr. Wydlin than she admitted. It was true, but not in the way that Flint seemed to think. Jovanna realized she was getting angry, but she knew telling Flint off would solve nothing. If anything, he'd think a heated denial proved her guilt. Jovanna had never felt so confused. In the past, her plainness had kept people from speculating about her personal life. Flint apparently not only speculated but also had come to some highly titillating, if false, conclusions.

She was trying to think of an excuse to leave when the message light on the lab comnet began to blink. She leaned over and turned it on, even though it was Flint's office.

"Flint, is Jovanna Trask there? I called her office, but there was no answer." It was Vince's voice on the speaker.

"Yes, I'm here," said Jovanna, relieved at the interruption. "What did you want?"

"We're on for lunch today, aren't we?" Vince made it sound as if they'd planned to meet. In reality, his question was a request for a meeting. They usually met no more than once a week, before Vince contacted NEO headquarters. It seemed safer not to stir up too much comment by being seen together more often. Besides, Jovanna didn't want to interfere with Vince's love life any more than she had to.

"Sure. See you in—" Jovanna checked her chronometer—"say, ten minutes?"

She terminated the connection. "Sorry, Flint." She hoped she sounded more apologetic than she felt. "I forgot I said I'd meet Vince. I've got to go."

When she was almost all the way to the door, she thought she heard Flint murmur, "Yes, there's more to you than meets the eye."

Jovanna hesitated a moment, then realized she didn't want him to know she'd heard him and made her escape. When she got to the break room, Vince was already there waiting for her. It was early for lunch. Since they had the room to themselves, Vince dispensed with his usual hand-holding, though he still stood close enough to speak in a low voice. "What's new?"

"Number Seven just got back from his second training session." Jovanna's food emerged from the dispenser and she carried it to the table. When Vince joined her with his tray, she continued. "Flint let me watch on his monitor. Vince, Dracolysk is torturing the Barneys."

Vince frowned. "How do you know?"

"The welts on his back gave me the first clue," Jovanna explained. "Flint said they all come back like that. Haven't you noticed it?"

"No. I told you, they're very careful to keep me at a

distance when they're loading and unloading the Barneys."

"Well, apparently Dracolysk is using a neurowhip on them," Jovanna said. "Dr. Wydlin may have protested once, but it didn't do any good."

"I wonder what Dracolysk has on Remus Wydlin," Vince said. "Noah wanted me to— Quick, hold my hand!"

"What?" Jovanna stared stupidly at him.

"We're about to have company," Vince said, grabbing her hand. A split second later, Flint strolled into the lunch room. "Hello, Jovanna, Pirelli. I trust I'm not interrupting anything."

"What would you say if I told you you were?" Vince asked.

"Sorry." Flint shrugged and walked to the food dispenser.

Vince lifted an eyebrow at Jovanna as they waited for Flint to make his selection. Flint pulled a tray out of the slot and found a seat at a nearby table. When Jovanna and Vince remained silent, he looked at them and smirked. "Please, don't let me disturb you."

Vince looked at Jovanna. "I'm not hungry anymore. How about you?"

Flint had had the same effect on Jovanna's appetite, though she wouldn't have been as pointed about it. "Me either."

"Come on, I'll walk you back to work," Vince said. As they passed Flint, Vince called, "Enjoy your lunch."

Jovanna repressed a laugh. When they got a few feet down the corridor, she looked at Vince reprovingly.

"What's that look for?" Vince said. "I was polite." He lowered his voice. "To tell you the truth, that guy gives me the creeps."

"Me, too," said Jovanna. "Unfortunately, I have to work with him."

"I always feel as if he's up to something," Vince said.

"Well, if he is, I'll eventually find out about it," Jovanna said with more assurance than she felt.

"Don't get too cocky," Vince said. "He may figure you

out before you get the goods on him."

"Unfortunately, if he finds out the truth about me, he'll know about you, too."

Jovanna hated to sound another note of caution because she was afraid Vince might make fun of her again, but she had to point out the dangers as she saw them.

"That's true," Vince said, surprising her. "Do you have any ideas?"

"What about RW?" said Jovanna, surprised she hadn't thought of it before. "She could carry messages for us. That way we won't be seen together, and you can get your love life back on track."

"Where do I get this reputation?" Vince rolled his eyes toward the ceiling and shook his head, then looked back down at her with a grin. "Good idea. RW won't mind?"

"Are you kidding? She lives for that kind of stuff. Whenever I ask her to engage in any kind of subterfuge, she eats it up."

"She did seem to enjoy moving those funds around, didn't she?" Vince chuckled. "And Noah Wydlin's been positively cheery lately, so it must have worked."

"I think so. RW checked the companies we owed money to in Accounts Receivable, and they've all given Wydlin Corporation a clean slate."

"Good. Well—" Vince patted Jovanna's shoulder almost awkwardly—"take care of yourself. If you need me for anything, call me. Otherwise I'll try to stay out of your way, at least till this operation is over."

"All right," Jovanna said. She felt forlorn. She had come to consider Vince a friend, and now she would be alone again until the operation was over, however long that might be. Of course, she still had RW. She made herself smile at Vince. "You take care of yourself, too."

○ ○ ○ ○ ○

The blue and green NEO globe glowed through the interference on the cruiser's screen, still as difficult to make out as it had been the first time Vince made contact with Beowulf.

"Hello, Farm Boy." Beowulf's image appeared on Vince's screen. "I have some news that I think you'll be glad to hear. Dekalb confirms that RAM is backing off on the takeover for now, since they have no idea where Wydlin got the funds for the bailout. But now they're looking for some other way of absorbing Wydlin Corporation."

"That's good news?" Vince murmured to himself.

"I think the best we can hope for is to keep Wydlin Corporation safe long enough to keep the Barneys out of RAM's hands speaking of which, do you have anything new on Dracolysk?"

Vince told Beowulf about the torture Dracolysk had authorized in the name of training, but he didn't think it would surprise his mentor. Torture was standard practice in the training of Terrines, the gennies most similar to the Barneys. Terrines were even made to inflict injuries on themselves, just to prove that they could take it.

The entire culture of the Terrines was based on who was tougher than whom. Other than the Martians, the only thing Terrines respected was an individual who could physically overpower them. Much of Dracolysk's experience had been with Terrines, so he would be likely to use the same methods with the Barneys.

The Barneys had much less contact with each other than Terrines did, however. Dr. Wydlin had insisted that they keep the Barneys on Genesis as much as possible. Of course, with each Barney born a month later than the one before it, they were all at different stages of development.

"We're up to Number Nineteen, an inventor, now," Vince reported. "He was decanted only a couple of days ago, though. He won't be ready for Dracolysk's training for nearly a month. On this trip, I'll be taking Number Eighteen. I've started making the trips more often ever since Dracolysk added secondary training for the Barneys who have already had the basics. My last trip was

to bring Black Barney home after his refresher training."

Suddenly he realized that Beowulf might not understand his reference to Black Barney. "That's a little
Wydlin humor," he explained. "I'm talking about Barney Number Seven, the space pirate. Dr. Wydlin named
him Black Barney in honor of his calling.

"So do you have any instructions, Hermano?" he
asked Beowulf and waited for his response.

"A space pirate? Very interesting," Beowulf's reply
came while Vince was calculating how much longer he
could let the ship fly on computer before he'd have to
start piloting manually. "He could be a lot of help to us
someday."

Vince was skeptical. How did Beowulf plan to enlist
Black Barney's cooperation? It seemed to him that after
Dracolysk's training, all Black Barney would respect
would be superior strength. He wouldn't even be condi-
tioned to obey those of the Martian genotype. Jovanna
had had RW plant a virus to destroy that part of Dracolysk's programming.

Beowulf was still speaking. "I think we'll have to rely
on the fact that the Barneys are more intelligent than
Terrines. Maybe he'll listen to reason."

"We can always hope," Vince muttered.

"We have a new gadget that just might . . ." Beowulf's
voice trailed off. "Perhaps I shouldn't say anything until we talk it over at headquarters. But keep alert. Dekalb may have a package for you one of these days.
Beowulf out."

The transmission ended, and Vince turned back to his
ship's controls.

CHAPTER FOURTEEN

Two weeks passed before Vince found out what Beowulf's mysterious gadget was. He'd just returned from a Barney run. As usual, Dracolysk hadn't allowed Vince off the ship at Gorgon Station. Vince had been stuck on the control deck for nearly thirteen hours. He'd stumbled off the ship and stretched his stiff muscles as soon as he had returned to Genesis, but the only thing that would really make him comfortable would be a shower and fresh clothes.

He placed his palm on the lock beside his door and entered his quarters. Might as well check the mail, he thought. The problem with a job that called for a lot of travel was that people got nervous when they didn't hear from him in a day or so, so they sent him hard copies of whatever computer mail he didn't immediately respond to.

Vince applied his thumb to a pad much like the one outside the door. A small door beneath the pad slid off to one side, revealing several envelopes and, surprisingly, a small package. Vince picked up the package and hefted it. The return address was Wydlin Corporation headquarters on Mars. He tore it open and found a black velvet jeweler's box.

Inside the box was a silvery bracelet with a number of tiny loops, all containing pale blue synthetic stones. A small paper stuck out from the side of the opened box, sandwiched between the velvet backing and the box. Vince pulled the paper out and unfolded it. It read, "For J.T.'s pirate." Underneath the written message was a hand-drawn yellow ear of corn with green wings on it. All it lacked was a red "Dekalb" emblazoned across the corn to be a credible duplicate of the antique corn sign Vince kept with his gear back at NEO headquarters. Vince went to his terminal and punched in the access code for RW.

She appeared moments later. "Hi, Vince. What's up?"

"You have more personality than every other computer personality I know put together," he said.

"Flattery will get you everywhere, though I suspect that's not why you called me here today," RW said.

"Unfortunately not. Can you get a message to Jo?"

"Aye, aye, sir." RW saluted lazily. "What do you want me to tell her?"

"Just tell her I need to see her in person and secretly. Find out when she'll be alone."

"You've got it." RW disappeared.

Vince wandered over to the cooling cube in his food station nook and pulled out a vacuum carton of orange juice. He had only drunk half a glass when RW reappeared. "Did you miss me?"

"Every second was excruciating," Vince took another swallow of juice. "What did she say?"

"She said to try her at about 2100 hours."

"Twenty-one hundred it is. Thanks, RW."

"No problem." RW's holographic winked out.

It was just 1900 hours now. He had time to freshen up and eat as he planned his visit to Jovanna. Vince stretched and yawned, then headed for the shower.

○ ○ ○ ○ ○

When her door chime sounded, Jovanna glanced briefly at her video monitor to make sure it was Vince before opening the door. He slipped inside quickly, flashing a self-deprecating grin. "Doesn't the superspy routine ever make you feel stupid?"

"Not especially, but you're welcome to if it makes you more comfortable," Jovanna said.

"Ouch!" Vince said. "Enough banter for me. I'll start bleeding if there's much more."

"All right," Jovanna said. The "banter," as Vince referred to it, was just the means she used to feel more in control of herself when she was around him. Focusing on their common goals worked nearly as well. "What's this all about?"

Vince brought a black velvet box out from behind his back. "I brought you something."

Jovanna accepted the box, looking at him suspiciously. "Will it explode?"

"It hasn't so far," Vince said. "I found it in my mail chute today. Go ahead, open it."

Jovanna snapped the box open and looked inside. She saw a silvery bracelet, with a small note lying on top of it.

"It's from Dekalb. Beowulf told me to expect a package from him. This must be it."

"If he's sending you jewelry, you'd better find out if his intentions are honorable," Jovanna quipped.

Vince smiled crookedly. "I think he meant for you to have it."

She read the note. " 'J.T.'s pirate'? Does that mean Black Barney?"

"Probably. Beowulf seems interested in him."

Jovanna removed the bracelet from the box. She held it near the light, examining it. One of the glittering blue stones was flat, thin, and rectangular, rather than oval and faceted like the others. "Hmmm."

"What is it?" Vince asked.

"One stone looks different." Jovanna set the bracelet down under the light, then went to her dresser and opened the top drawer. She pulled out a pair of tiny pliers and returned. She used the pliers to bend the prongs back from the stone, which then slid loose from the facing. As Jovanna suspected, it wasn't a stone at all. She lifted it with her pliers and held it up to the light to inspect it. She chewed on her lower lip, considering. She hadn't done anything with computer hardware since early in her university program. It was at times like this that she was glad she saved everything. She went to a low drawer and dug out her diagnostic kit.

"What is it?" Vince asked.

"A computer chip," Jovanna said. She wiped dust off the case and unzipped it.

"What are you supposed to do with it?"

"That depends on what it's for. It probably has a very simple, specialized function." She pulled the testing board out of the kit and unwound the thin cable that would allow her to attach it to her compdex. Then she searched the side of her compdex for the entry port and put the cable end into it. She laid the chip in a slot in the board, then turned the board on.

Jovanna looked at Vince somewhat apologetically. "I could figure it out myself, but it'll be quicker to have RW check it out." She addressed the compdex. "RW, are you there? I need some help, please."

RW appeared before the compdex. "You rang?"

"Yeah. I have a chip I need identified." Jovanna pointed to her testing board. "I've got it hooked up now. If you could tell us what it's for, it would save me some time."

RW rolled her eyes upward. "You mean my time isn't valuable, too?"

"Knock it off, RW," said Vince. "You love it."

"You know all my weaknesses," RW said. "Okay, give me a minute." She disappeared.

"You said it's for Black Barney?" Jovanna asked Vince.

"I think so. Beowulf said something about NEO's being interested in him. Maybe it's a cooperation chip."

Jovanna looked at him, not sure how serious he was. "You know you couldn't get a Barney to cooperate with one little chip, don't you?"

"Jovanna, pul-eeze," Vince said, doing a creditable

imitation of RW. "I may not be a computer wizard, but I'm marginally literate."

"The question is, if it's for Black Barney, how do we get it into him? I've never done anything with a Barney's hardware after it's been implanted." She had a notion of where she would put the chip if Black Barney's cerebral implant were lying in front of her on a table, but the implant was in his skull now.

RW reappeared. "Hi, guys."

"Did you find out what it is?" Jovanna asked.

"I wouldn't be talking to you now if I hadn't." RW blew on her holographic fingernails, then appeared to polish them on her shoulder.

"Smug, isn't she?" Vince said.

"Hey, when you're good—" RW began.

Jovanna cut her off. "You're brilliant, RW. Now, what does the chip do?"

"It broadcasts a signal." RW's face took on the rapt look it had when she was intrigued by some new subject. "The computer is translating it as an intermittent binary pattern. It's not interested in the signal because it doesn't know what to do with it. Only someone who was looking for it would notice."

Vince said, "You lost me."

"If I didn't know what it was, I'd probably think some computer hack was trying to do some programming and making lots of errors. I'd shut it out of my consciousness after a while. But if I followed the signal, it would lead me right to wherever the chip is. I think you'd call it a homing device."

Realization dawned on Jovanna. "So if it were implanted in a Barney, we'd be able to find him wherever he was."

RW nodded. "As long as he was within, say, twenty miles of the computer matrix, we'd be able to find him."

"Which means within twenty miles of any terminal with access to the matrix," Jovanna explained to Vince.

"Right," RW went on. "At least as long as his implant is functioning. The signal will transmit indefinitely. The neurochemical impulses in Barney's brain will supply power to the implant as long as he's alive."

Vince whistled. "NEO's really taking the long view, then."

Jovanna looked at him, puzzled. "What do you mean?"

"I mean we don't need the chip now," Vince said. "We know where Black Barney is. How long will it take for the rest of them to be decanted?"

Jovanna did some mental figuring. There were to be forty Barneys in all. Nineteen had already been decanted. "Twenty-one months, Martian Standard."

"Remus Wydlin might not keep all the Barneys around quite that long, but he'll probably keep them for a while," Vince guessed. "If he's planning to use them as weapons against RAM, it's better to keep them under wraps for as long as possible. Once RAM sees them in action, they'll try to destroy them or take them over. My guess is that Dr. Wydlin will keep Black Barney and his clone brothers and sisters on Genesis Station for as long as he can, then unleash them all at once."

"Why does NEO want to keep track of Black Barney?" Jovanna asked.

"Who knows?" Vince shrugged. "The question is, can you implant this chip?"

"Not by myself," Jovanna admitted. "But I know who can help."

"Who?"

"Have you ever considered joining the medical profession, RW?" Jovanna asked.

RW smiled broadly. "I've already learned quite a bit from assembling the program for Salk."

"Salk?" Vince asked blankly.

"Barney Number Twenty-four. We haven't started his training yet," Jovanna explained.

"Wait a minute," Vince said. "Do you really think you should be fooling around inside Black Barney's skull?"

"The only other possibilities would be either Flint or Dr. Wydlin. Should I ask one of them?" Jovanna asked.

Vince shook his head. "I see your point. But do you really think it's safe?"

Jovanna didn't see any other option, and she didn't see what good it would do any of them for Vince to worry about the procedure. She needed him to lighten up and show his usual easy confidence. "Look, I'm the worrier in this group. Don't start doing things you're not qualified for."

Vince looked startled, but only for an instant. Then he shook his finger at her. "Don't smart-mouth me, young lady. I'm still your superior in this organization."

"You've been around longer," Jovanna corrected him. "It remains to be seen who's superior to whom."

Vince looked at RW in mock despair. "You see what I have to put up with?"

RW nodded mournfully, but her eyes were twinkling. "Yes, Vince. It looks like you've created a monster."

○ ○ ○ ○ ○

Remus sat with Noah in the lounge of the *Coriolus*, Noah's private space yacht.

Two decks above them, Noah's personal pilot, Gretsky, flew the *Coriolus* in an area of the Jovian Trojans that was far removed from Genesis Station. Noah had told Remus that he trusted Gretsky not to tell anyone where they'd been. Apparently the pilot had performed sensitive missions for Noah before.

Remus gestured toward a large screen built into the bulkhead. It displayed a magnified view of a spherical asteroid approximately one hundred miles below them.

"I'm pleased to say you were right, Noah. This asteroid is even better suited for our purposes than Genesis. Why didn't you choose it to begin with?"

"I thought it was too small," Noah said. "Also too far from the space lanes. However, if I'm right and RAM isn't finished with us, it'll suffice as a safe haven for you and the Barneys. I may need to hide out here for a while, too. I hope you don't mind."

Remus smiled. "Of course not," he said softly. He and Noah had gotten along surprisingly well since RAM's takeover attempt. It was almost as if all the mistakes of

their past had never happened. Perhaps his reconcilia-
tion with Noah was all that was needed to bring order
into their lives. "What will you do after I bring the Barneys here?"

"I'm not sure," said Noah. "I'll have to see what happens. I know RAM won't welcome me back with open
arms. There's always Mercury; they understand the en-
trepreneurial spirit there. Who knows? Maybe your
Barneys will defeat them, and you'll need me to help
run what's left of RAM."

"Perhaps. I certainly couldn't do it. I have no idea how
to run a giant corporation. Which reminds me, when do
you think RAM will make its move?"

"Well, of course I'm not certain, but I think they'll put
it off until all the Barneys are finished. I think they're
especially intrigued by the Barneys."

"So we should have time to build Paradise." Remus
hadn't known till that moment exactly what they'd call
their new station.

"If our luck holds out," Noah said.

Remus nodded and poured another cup of Venusian
coffee. Paradise would be quite different from Genesis.
Genesis had been created for the sole purpose of manufacturing an army of combat gennies. At Paradise, a
few of the Barneys might still need to be trained, but
they would all have been decanted.

As soon as the interior of the asteroid was cored, Remus planned to bring the second Barney, the terraformer Yorder, to the asteroid to create a world that would
live up to its name. Paradise would be a refuge for the
Barneys—a place of safety and peace for the inevitable
times when it was necessary to hide from RAM. He just
hoped it would be finished in time.

Remus raised his mug. "To Paradise," he said.

○ ○ ○ ○ ○

"You're one lucky girl, Jovanna," RW announced
when she entered Jovanna's room.

Jovanna had been about to remove for Black Barney's

implant chip from her bottom dresser drawer. She slammed the drawer. "Have a heart, RW. Couldn't you let a person know you're coming?"

"Sorry." RW didn't look sorry. "But you know what?"

"What?"

"Remus left Genesis Station early this morning. He'll be gone for a while. His destination is listed as company headquarters on Mars."

"It'll take a week to get to Mars and back again," Jovanna said. "The timing couldn't be better." She and RW had been looking for a time when Dr. Wydlin was away from the lab to implant Black Barney's signal chip. They hadn't expected him to leave the station altogether; that was an unexpected bonus. Now all they had to do was get Flint out of the lab for the day.

"Where's the chip?" RW asked.

"I have it." Jovanna opened the bottom drawer again and pulled out the small package that contained the chip. "Are you ready to send the message?"

"As soon as you give it to me."

"All right." Jovanna said. "Signal Flint that he has a private message in his computer mailbox. As soon as he gives you his identification number, print, 'Remain in your quarters today to await special instructions. Discuss this with no one.' Sign it, 'R.W.' "

"Oh, great. You're going to pin this on me," RW said.

Jovanna fixed her digital assistant with a stern look. "You know, of course, that those are also Remus Wydlin's initials."

"I knew that." RW grinned. "I just thought this might be a good time to lighten up a little."

"For you, maybe. You won't make any mistakes."

"Neither will you," said RW comfortingly.

Jovanna hoped the whole idea wasn't a mistake. The message said Flint should keep quiet about the message, but would he be able to resist? She believed Flint was jealous of her closeness with Dr. Wydlin. She hoped that by phrasing the message as she had and surrounding it with secrecy, Flint would take it as a sign that Dr. Wydlin trusted him more than her and would follow the instructions to the letter to prove himself worthy of that trust. It might be a long shot, but it was the best she could come up with.

Jovanna thought of something. "You know you should erase the message as soon as Flint reads it, don't you?"

"Of course." RW peered at her keenly. "You really are nervous, aren't you?"

"A little." She tapped the package containing the chip. "Well, you have your job and I have mine."

"Right." Instead of disappearing, RW stood looking at Jovanna. Jovanna smiled, she hoped confidently, and left.

O O O O O

The autosurgery module stood humming faintly in its usual place in the lab. RW had programmed it so that all Jovanna had to do was wait for Black Barney's skull to be opened, then put the chip in place. Black Barney turned away from the module and frowned down at Jovanna. His voice emerged in a low, menacing rumble. "This is the first I've heard about this."

"And it will probably be the last," Jovanna said, trying to look unconcerned, as if this were a routine procedure. "It's a simple procedure. I just need to replace a chip in your cranial implant."

"Why you?" he asked. "You've never done anything with my hardware before."

"In this instance, I'm the most qualified person." In a way, it was the truth. She was the only person in the lab NEO would trust the job to. If Black Barney took her statement to mean that Dr. Wydlin had given her the task, she wouldn't mind.

"More qualified than Remus Wydlin?" Barney rumbled. His fathomless gray eyes, boring into hers, didn't help her confidence. Somehow she hadn't expected Black Barney to offer any resistance. Jovanna had thought her physical resemblance to his teacher, RW, would assure Black Barney's cooperation.

"Dr. Wydlin isn't on Genesis now." Jovanna hoped her

tone sounded unconcerned, businesslike.

"Pretty strange timing, if I need adjustments," Barney said. Jovanna looked at him searchingly. Something in his tone made her realize that she knew very little about Dr. Wydlin's relationship with any of his Barneys. She had been considering asking Black Barney why he thought Dr. Wydlin would be concerned about one of his many creations, but for all she knew, Dr. Wydlin might be particularly close to Black Barney.

"Actually, it was the only possible timing. Dr. Wydlin can't be involved with this. Do you understand?" As she met his opaque gaze, she hoped some of the real urgency she felt was communicating itself. If Barney took it to mean that she was helping Dr. Wydlin with an intrigue against RAM, so much the better.

"Not really," said Barney. "Explain."

Jovanna had hoped to have as little discussion as possible. She certainly hadn't wanted to lie to Black Barney, but she could see that the big gennie wasn't going to make it easy for her.

"I know what Dr. Wydlin wants for the Barneys," she said. At least, she had known what he was after when he first started to work on them. Since then, RAM interference had made Dr. Wydlin a stranger to her. Still, she thought her employer would favor any plan to use the Barneys against RAM. It was too bad she could no longer talk to him honestly, but she was doing the best she could. Dr. Wydlin would want NEO, the only organization devoted to undermining RAM, to have a way to reach the Barneys; she had to believe that. "And I am trying to help him. Do you understand that?"

"So far," Barney said.

"Good," Jovanna said. "Another thing. Dr. Wydlin has had enough trouble with Mars over the Barneys. He doesn't need any more. So as far as anyone knows, he knows nothing about this procedure." Dr. Wydlin really didn't know anything about it, but Jovanna didn't see any need to tell that to a three-hundred pound gennie.

Black Barney looked back at the autosurgery module, then nodded. "All right," he said.

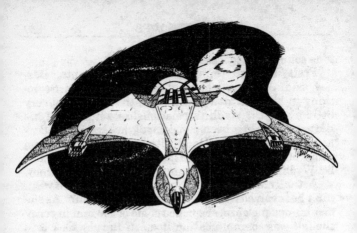

CHAPTER FIFTEEN

I had a feeling things were going too well," Vince muttered to himself. Seventeen Barneys had been decanted since Beowulf had asked him to give the signal chip to Jovanna to implant into Black Barney. He felt a bit uneasy about the fact that he'd been transporting Barneys more quickly than usual to Gorgon Station. Usually no more than two or at the most three Barneys stayed on Gorgon at a time, but with the three he'd just delivered, there were ten there now.

He wanted to make sure Beowulf was aware of what was going on, but now he couldn't make contact. Vince whacked his commo board. He knew, of course, there was nothing wrong with his receiver. The problem was with NEO headquarters. If they were transmitting at all, it wasn't on Frequency J.

He felt a deep foreboding, then forced it to the back of his thoughts. They must be having trouble with the equipment back at headquarters. All of NEO's equipment was salvaged, held together with chewing gum and a prayer. They might be trying to respond on another frequency. If he tried some other frequencies, he'd find them. He set his receiver to scan a narrow band and listened closely.

On the first scan, he heard nothing. He set the scanning sequence to repeat. If he didn't find anything this time, he'd try a wider band. The second time through, he just barely heard something. He narrowed the band and waited for the signal to become clearer.

Just to be safe, he set up to record what he was receiving. It might not ever get very clear, and he wanted to get as much of it as possible. He'd try making sense of it later. After less than two minutes, the signal ended. In case the signal wasn't the hoped-for NEO transmission, Vince continued to scan.

He detected no unusual signals for the rest of his trip to Gorgon Station. Between attempts to raise NEO headquarters, he listened to the disk. He could make no sense of it. He guessed it was a scrambled transmission and tried a number of the techniques Beowulf had taught him for making the message clearer, but to no avail.

○ ○ ○ ○ ○

As soon as he reached his room, Vince opened his belt pouch and pulled out the audio disk containing the strange transmission he'd recorded on the way to Gorgon Station. He looked at the disk, as if by staring at it he could make more sense of it than he had so far. It remained flat, black, and unrevealing. He inserted the disk into his player and plugged the disk player's output cable into a port on his computer terminal. He played the disk again, but he could make no more sense of it than he had during the trip to Gorgon Station.

Ignoring the disk for the moment, he punched up the station network. He checked the bulletin board, scanning the notices, but there was nothing from Dekalb. Well, this time Dekalb would hear from him. He punched in his contact's access code and waited. There was no response. There was no reason for Dekalb to be waiting by his computer on the chance that Vince would make contact. He'd just have to wait until Dekalb was available.

Vince posted a notice on the bulletin board for Dekalb and left the terminal on, set to beep him if there was a message. Then he slipped off his boots and lay down to rest while he waited.

○ ○ ○ ○ ○

A persistent beep woke Vince. His room was dark except for the glow from his compdex screen and the red numbers on the chronometer beside his bed, which read 0133. He shook his head to clear it and tried to figure out where the beeping was coming from.

A flashing line on his compdex screen drew his attention. It must be Dekalb. He stumbled over to the terminal and read, "DEKALB HERE."

"FARM BOY HERE," he typed quickly. "CAN'T RAISE HQ TO REPORT."

Vince waited several tense seconds until Dekalb's reply appeared. "HQ UNDER ATTACK. COMMUNICATIONS OUT."

"Damn!" Vince rose and began to pace nervously. He had tried not to think about NEO's vulnerability to attack ever since he'd been unable to raise Beowulf yesterday. Now he was being forced to think about it, even though there was nothing he could do about it. Then he remembered the disk he'd made. Maybe Beowulf had tried to send him orders. "HAVE ONE MESSAGE. SCRAMBLED," he typed.

After another tense pause, the reply came. "TRANSMIT."

He waited for the computer to encode and transmit the information from his disk, holding his breath until he saw "GOT IT" appear on his screen. After a moment, more words appeared. "STAND BY. I'LL HAVE TRANSCRIPTION ASAP."

This time Vince didn't sleep while he waited. Instead he brought a chair from his kitchen nook to prop his feet on and sat in front of the compdex, waiting. Wearily he glanced at his bedside chronometer. He was just beginning to nod off when another beep from his terminal startled him to alertness.

"DEKALB HERE. SORRY FOR DELAY. MESSAGE WAS SCRAMBLED AND CODED. ALSO NOT NEO TRANSMISSION."

Vince frowned, puzzled. "What was it?"

As if Dekalb could hear him, the message unfolded on the screen. "FROM COL. TISHARENKO, SAC, TO HUGO DRACOLYSK. SENDING RAM ARMADA TO GENESIS AFTER YOU REMOVE BARNEYS. IN-FORM ME WHEN FINISHED."

Vince stared at the ominous, glowing words. Simon Tisharenko had made his reputation as one of the great-est military minds on Mars. And SAC, the Space As-sault Corps, was an elite fighting unit. RAM was obviously through with subtle maneuverings. Vince hadn't expected RAM to make an overt move so soon, but faced with direct evidence of their intent, he had to admit the plan made sense. There were still four Bar-neys who had to be decanted, but even if they were lost in the takeover, RAM would have the remaining thirty-six.

What a time for Beowulf to be incommunicado. Vince had hoped that he'd receive more guidance on this first assignment, especially now, as events took a crucial turn. Maybe Dekalb could help. Vince typed, "WHAT NOW?"

After a moment, the reply came: "SAVE THE BAR-NEYS."

"Thanks a lot," Vince muttered. "I think I could have come up with that on my own." He typed, "SUGGES-TIONS?"

"WILL SEND ORDERS ALLOWING YOU ACCESS TO SHIP FOR ESCAPE."

Vince waited, but Dekalb apparently had nothing to add. "That's all?" Vince muttered aloud. Admittedly, it was better than nothing. "THANKS," he entered.

"YOU'RE WELCOME," came Dekalb's answer. Then the connection was terminated.

Vince figured it was time to involve Jovanna. She was the one who had access to the Barneys, and she might have a few ideas about how to keep them out of RAM's control. It had been months since he'd actually spoken with her. Work on the Barneys had settled into a kind of routine, and there was very little they needed to tell each other about. What contact they did have was through RW. It was a way they'd found to keep their contacts a secret from suspicious characters like Flint.

Vince keyed in RW's access code and waited. A few seconds later, she appeared in front of his terminal, wearing a knee-length white robe and fluffy blue slippers. Her hair was tousled, and she rubbed at her eyes. "What is it?" she asked sleepily.

"Cute," Vince said. As an electronic entity, RW had no need for sleep, but she liked to make a point sometimes.

"It's the middle of the night." RW looked affronted, as if she'd really been sleeping.

Vince had planned to have RW explain the situation to Jovanna, but he suddenly realized he'd rather tell Jovanna himself. She could be annoyingly cautious at times, but at least she knew when to take things seriously, unlike her digital alter ego. "Can you wake Jovanna?" he asked. "I need to talk to her."

"Couldn't you have called her yourself?" asked RW, yawning.

"RW, quit playing around," Vince said. "You know I can't take the chance that someone's monitoring the comnet. Just wake her up and tell her I'm on my way, will you?"

"Oh, all right," said RW. She yawned once more for effect and disappeared.

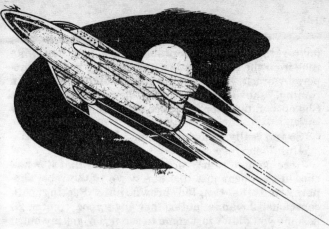

CHAPTER SIXTEEN

Jovanna woke to the annoying clamor of hard cyber-jazz. She blinked, trying to clear her eyes. RW stood at the foot of her bed, looking quite satisfied with herself. "That's done it."

"Done what?" Jovanna asked. "Made me wish it was possible to kill a digital personality? It sure has."

A particularly grating blast of synth-sax blared from the console's speakers, and Jovanna winced. "Turn that thing off! If the jerk next door hears—"

The music stopped suddenly. "Sorry," RW said. "I tried your usual musical choices, but you slept right through them."

"Was there any particular reason you felt you had to wake me?" Jovanna flopped back against her pillows.

"Don't fall asleep again," RW said. "Vince is on his way over here. He asked me to wake you."

"What for?" Jovanna felt herself growing tense.

"He wouldn't tell me." RW wore a childish pout. "He just said he needed to talk to you."

Jovanna looked at her bedside chronometer. Oh-four-eleven. Sighing, she sat up and swung her legs over the side of the bed. Her console chimed, and an image of Vince filled the screen. "Great," she muttered. So much for making herself presentable. She pulled her white robe from the foot of her bed and slid into her blue slippers. A quick, light rapping came from the door. "I'm coming," she sighed, shrugging herself into her robe. She opened the door for Vince, then finished tying her sash.

"So you really do look like that," Vince commented.

"Huh?" she responded.

Vince pointed to RW. Jovanna realized that RW had chosen to appear just like her, down to the robe, slippers, and the tangled brown hair. Feeling self-conscious, Jovanna pulled her own robe tighter. "I assume you didn't just come to see if RW got my outfit right."

"No." Vince looked grim. "We've got problems. RAM is about to move in on the Wydlin Corporation."

"How do you know?" Jovanna's sleepiness vanished.

"This." Vince held up an audio disk. He began to walk up and down her small room, reminding her of a caged animal. "I happened to be in the right place at the right time and eavesdropped on a communication from Simon Tisharenko of the Space Assault Corps to our friend Dracolysk, telling him a RAM invasion of Genesis Station is imminent."

"Why tell Dracolysk?"

"Oh, that's the best part. Dracolysk is supposed to get the Barneys off Genesis before the carnage begins. I guess RAM doesn't want anything to happen to the thirty-odd reasons for this takeover." Vince sat at Jovanna's kitchen nook but immediately got back to his feet and resumed his pacing.

Jovanna felt a cold chill sweep through her. Vince had made the trip to Gorgon Station more often lately, often with three or four Barneys at a time. "He already has a bunch of them, doesn't he?"

"Damn right," Vince snapped. "Ten, last time I counted."

There was no way they would get those ten Barneys back from Dracolysk now, but at least they could keep the rest of them on Genesis. It might buy them some time. Jovanna moved over to her communit, planning to put a call through to Dr. Wydlin.

Vince grabbed her hand pulled her away from the communit. "What are you doing?"

"Warning Dr. Wydlin. Don't you think he should know about this?" Jovanna asked. Vince glared at her, his brown eyes crackling with some unspoken emotion. Jovanna grew tired of waiting for his objection, if he planned to make one. "Honestly, Vince, do you really think we can leave the Wydlins in the dark?"

"We can't let them in on this without NEO approval," Vince said.

"Then get it," Jovanna said. "We can't handle this situation without enlisting the Wydlins' help. Beowulf's got to see that."

"I can't!" Vince slammed his hand against the wall, startling Jovanna into stillness. He seemed to have surprised even himself. He looked at her apologetically. "RAM has launched an all-out attack on NEO. Headquarters is in no position to respond, and Dekalb says other installations have been taken out as well."

That explained Vince's nerves, at least. But it made telling the Wydlins even more imperative, as far as Jovanna was concerned. "Then we have to tell Dr. Wydlin."

"Are you crazy?" Vince demanded. "Just how do you plan to tell him you came by this information? Or does he already know you work for NEO?"

"Of course not." Jovanna resented his implication that she had failed to keep her affiliation secret. "But I can't see the point of keeping it from him now."

Vince sat on her bed and dropped his head into his hands. "You may be right," he sighed. Then he looked up at her. "But let me try something else first. Noah Wydlin asked me to keep an eye on Dracolysk. Until now, I've come up empty. I'll tell Noah about the RAM message instead of you telling Dr. Wydlin."

Jovanna nodded. They might be able to keep NEO out of it while still warning the Wydlins. "All right."

Vince went to her communit and entered a number.

"Noah Wydlin's personal code," he explained. She pulled up a stool next to him. They waited until it became evident that no one was going to answer. Vince frowned. "That should have gotten him." He shrugged, then punched up the directory.

Noah Wydlin's residence and office numbers were both listed. Though he was the CEO of Wydlin Corporation, there was little point in trying to keep his access numbers a secret from the others on Genesis. None of his employees was willing to risk his ire by troubling him at his suite unless absolutely necessary, and his personal assistant would screen any calls that came to his office.

"What time is it?" Vince asked.

"Four fifty," Jovanna said.

"I'd better try the residence, then," Vince said. He punched up the number, and again they waited for a response. There was none. Vince terminated the connection and tried the office code. "I can't imagine him being at his office, but . . ." Vince trailed off. "Maybe he already knows about the takeover and he's trying to avert it." There was no response. Vince punched up the directory again. "I'll try his assistant." After a short wait, a strikingly beautiful blonde appeared on screen. Her hair was disheveled, and her eye makeup streaked, but she was fully dressed.

"Vince, it's you." She sounded relieved.

"Marcie, what's wrong?" Vince asked.

"Noah . . . Mr. Wydlin . . . he's gone," Marcie said. "About half a dozen Desert Runners came with an invitation from Mr. Dracolysk for Mr. Wydlin to come to visit Gorgon Station. Mr. Wydlin looked—" she gulped back tears—"he looked really scared, Vince, but he went with them."

"When was this?" Vince asked.

"Yesterday, about 1500."

"Damn!" Vince turned to Jovanna. "I was still on my way back from Gorgon then. Not that I could have done much about it." He turned back to the screen.

"Marcie, did he say or do anything unusual that indicated he knew what it was about? Or anything that might give someone a clue how to help him?"

Marcie's face puckered. "I—I don't know."

"Think, damn it!" Vince shouted. When his anger had no result, he softened his tone. "Come on, Marcie, settle down. He went with them, right? Did he say anything to you as he left? Did he call anyone?"

"The Desert Runners wouldn't let him call anyone," Marcie said. Then a light seemed to dawn. "But he did ask me to tell Mr. Gretsky he'd have to cancel their appointment."

"Gretsky is Wydlin's personal pilot," Vince said to Jovanna under his breath, then to Marcie, "Did you cancel it?"

"They didn't have an appointment listed," Marcie said. "I checked all through the log. But I called Mr. Gretsky and told him what Noah said."

"And . . . ?" Vince prompted.

"Mr. Gretsky looked puzzled at first, as if he couldn't remember any appointment. Then he seemed to remember and thanked me," Marcie said.

"Good," Vince said, as if what Marcie said made sense to him. "Anything else?"

"No. Vince, will he be all right?" Marcie asked.

"I hope so, Marcie." Vince terminated the connection.

"What's going on, Vince?" Jovanna asked. "Do you know?"

"Not yet," Vince replied. "But I'm going to call Gretsky and find out . . . I hope."

He scrolled through the directory and tried Gretsky's residence. There was no answer.

"He wouldn't be at work now, would he?" Jovanna asked. Vince wasn't listening; he was punching in a new access code. "Who are you calling now?" she asked.

"The spaceport," Vince said. After a moment, a face appeared on the screen.

"Pirelli? How did I get so lucky?" a man in black Wydlin-issue coveralls asked.

"It's nice to talk to you, too, Hearn," Vince said, "but right now I'm looking for Gretsky. Is he there?"

Hearn made a show of looking around, then called to someone in the background, "Is Gretsky around?" He turned back to the screen. "Don't see him."

"Listen, Hearn, could you do me a favor?" Vince said. "Check the log and see if he's taken a ship out."

"I don't have enough to do?"

"Come on. I'll buy you a drink next time at Willy's," Vince said. "Just check back through about fifteen hundred yesterday."

Hearn grumbled, then turned away to work at a nearby terminal. About a minute later, he moved back to his communit. "Are you psychic or something?"

"He's gone?" Vince asked.

"Yep. Took out the *Nike* at 1630."

"What's his destination?"

"Mars," Hearn said.

Vince looked puzzled for a moment. "Was he alone?"

"Negative." Here Hearn looked off to the side, apparently listening to someone who wasn't on the screen. "Felcher says he was accompanied by Dr. Wydlin and another lab coat. This other guy was wheeling one of those capsules."

"Capsules? You mean the kind I'm always transporting?" Vince asked.

"That's what it sounded like. When do I get my drink?" Hearn said.

"We can talk about it when I come in to work. Thanks, Hearn," Vince said, signing off. He turned to Jovanna. "I'm sorry, Jo. It looks like we're on our own whether we like it or not."

Jovanna mulled over Hearn's information. The capsule probably contained a Barney, while she supposed that the "lab coat" was Flint. She'd noticed yesterday that he'd left the lab early, but she hadn't given it much thought till now. "Why would they go to Mars?"

"Obviously the Wydlins have some plan we're not privy to," Vince said slowly. "Though if they had a plan for the Barneys, it escapes me. It looks like they just left them behind on Genesis to fend for themselves."

"Maybe Dr. Wydlin has some surprise planned for

RAM when he arrives on Mars." Though Jovanna couldn't imagine what it would be, it was more comforting to think her employer was prepared. But Vince was right. It was hard to imagine what he planned for the Barneys. If he had a plan, he'd left no one behind to put it in motion.

"Jovanna?" Vince's tone was serious. "We can't take that for granted. I think we have to plan for the worst."

"What, in your opinion, is the worst?"

Vince pushed away from the terminal, stood, and began to pace. "What if he has no plan? Or what if his plan is to save his own skin, no matter what the cost to the Barneys?"

"He wouldn't do that!" Jovanna looked at Vince fiercely. "Those Barneys are like his children. He wouldn't just leave them to whatever fate RAM decided for them."

"Jo, he's an old man," Vince said. "How much energy do you think he has left to fight RAM? Especially now, with Noah in RAM's hands. Dr. Wydlin doesn't seem to be particularly qualified for corporate infighting."

Jovanna hated to admit it, but a lot of what Vince was saying made sense. She had noticed how much fire Dr. Wydlin seemed to lose when Dracolysk started training the Barneys, and how depressed RAM's earlier takeover attempt had made him. Then shortly after RW had saved Wydlin Corporation, he and his son had taken a trip together. They'd come back, it seemed, with a much warmer relationship than when they'd left, and Dr. Wydlin had seemed like his old self since then.

But now another, more serious takeover attempt was planned, and Noah had been abducted. The recent events very well could have discouraged Dr. Wydlin.

"All right," she said. "What do you think is going on?"

"Honestly?" Vince's brown eyes were intense.

"Sure," she said.

Vince looked down, as if groping for words, then met her eyes. "I think he's going to try to cut a deal with RAM."

Jovanna started to protest, but Vince put up his hand. "No, listen. He has one child left—Noah. He's probably not prepared to lose him over the Barneys. No matter how much he cares for his gennies, they aren't really his children. And getting revenge for one lost child can't outweigh wanting to keep the other safe. If I were him, I'd try to arrange for the safety of my son and me, and then do the best I could for the Barneys. I wouldn't blame Dr. Wydlin for doing that. Would you?"

Jovanna swallowed a lump in her throat. "I guess not. So what should we do?"

"I think," Vince said carefully, "that we need to take matters out of Dr. Wydlin's hands."

"How?" Jovanna frowned, not liking the sound of that.

"There's a port in the Asteroid Belt called Barbarosa," Vince said. "It's an open port, not subject to RAM jurisdiction. If we move the Barneys there, they'll have a choice about what to do with their lives."

Jovanna thought about that. Given the training the Barneys had received, it was likely they'd go on to fulfill Dr. Wydlin's original purpose for them—the destruction of RAM. "Maybe you're right," she said.

"I hope so. It's the best I can think of on short notice," Vince said. "There used to be a NEO contact somewhere on Barbarosa. Maybe we can get in touch with him once we're there. NEO could really use some extra bodies right now."

"That's kind of a long shot, isn't it?" RW piped up. "Generally the Barneys aren't team players. Depending on their specialty, they can be pretty independent. Black Barney could be a problem, for example."

"The pirate? Why?" Vince asked.

"It's all in the pirate code, bucko." RW grinned, and the suggestion of a black patch appeared over one eye, then disappeared so quickly Jovanna wasn't sure she'd really seen it. "A pirate only owes obedience to those who can defeat him in battle. The captain earns the right to lead through superior strength."

"Well, Black Barney may not want to join NEO. But

there are others." Vince shrugged. "It's worth a try."

"What do we have to do?" Jovanna asked.

"If Dekalb comes through, I should be getting access to a ship soon," Vince said. "We have to get the Barneys to join us in an escape plan. Or rather, you and RW do. If you can. In fact, it wouldn't hurt to prepare them to aid in their own escape if necessary. Can you do that?"

"Sure," Jovanna said. "RW is still their instructor. You could warn them about this takeover in the course of your regular tasks, couldn't you, RW?"

"Except for those who are on Gorgon Station," Vince said.

"Actually, I can contact them, too." RW grinned. "It'll be slightly less routine, of course."

"Then prepare them, too," Vince said.

"All right, so we warn the Barneys. What else?" RW asked.

"You'll have to learn the correct codes to open their cubicles and to get into the equipment lockers."

"That should be easy," said RW.

"How long do we have to arrange this?" Jovanna asked.

"Not very long." Vince looked at her seriously. "A week at the most. It'll take that long for Dr. Wydlin to get to Mars. Unfortunately if Noah Wydlin signs the Barneys over to RAM before then, we won't even have that long."

RW said, "I can monitor the situation at Gorgon Station and let you know if Dracolysk does anything unusual—like sending ships to Genesis to round up the Barneys, for example."

"Good," Vince said.

"How can we possibly get them ready in less than a week?" Jovanna asked. "We'll need to come up with an escape plan, contact the Barneys, explain the threat—"

"Equip them, give them a signal to watch for," Vince finished. "You're right. We'll be busy. Shall we get started?"

RW's image shifted slightly, and when she came back into focus, she was dressed in a green pantsuit, a duplicate of one that Jovanna owned. "I'm ready."

Jovanna sighed. If they were going to plan this escape, they'd better get started. "I'm ready, too, except I can't get dressed as easily as RW can."

Vince took the hint. "All right. I have a chore to take care of. I'll call you as soon as I'm done and we'll work out the escape plan."

"I'll talk to you then," Jovanna said.

○ ○ ○ ○ ○

Black Barney paced his cell, reliving the combat bout he'd just finished. His opponent had been Barney Number Five. "Call me Quinto," his fellow Barney had said, as if they really had time to call each other anything.

Well, at least the combats with the other Barneys were something like an even match, though Black Barney had defeated Quinto just as he had the others. All the Barneys had the same potential as Black Barney, but it wasn't vital to them to come out on top. It was everything to Black Barney.

The one person he really wanted to fight was Hugo Dracolysk. Dracolysk seemed to think the Barneys lived to please him. Not this Barney. Dracolysk, for all his talk about owning Dracolysk Corporation, was still just a RAM tool. And he planned to make all the Barneys into RAM tools, whatever their own wishes.

And despite Remus Wydlin's wishes, as well. Black Barney wasn't sure why that should matter to him, but it did. Remus was an old man; Barney could easily kill him with one hand if he chose to. But on the two or three occasions Black Barney had actually met with Remus, he had seemed genuinely fond of Barney. When Remus had spoken disapprovingly of RAM, Black Barney had found himself hating the corporation as well.

"Black Barney!"

Barney slowly looked up at the tri-dee screen that hung in a corner of his cell. He always took his time replying to any summons from his trainers, knowing it angered them. This time he was surprised at the image he saw on the screen. It was the digital personality the Barneys knew as "Teacher." She had been the interface for all his computer-based education on Genesis, but he'd never seen her at Gorgon Station before.

"What do you want?" Barney asked.

"Can you escape?" she asked.

She sure knew how to start a conversation. He wouldn't mind getting off this rock, but he wasn't going anywhere until he knew why and where. "Explain."

"RAM is launching a hostile takeover of Wydlin Corporation," his instructor said. "Their first step was to collect as many Barneys as possible at Gorgon Station."

Barney nodded. That would explain in part why there were more Barneys on Gorgon now than he'd ever seen before, even though it interfered with their training schedule and gave him more unoccupied time than he usually had during these trips to Gorgon Station. "Where do we escape to?"

"The Asteroid Belt. You should be able to hide from RAM there until we can figure out the next step."

Barney already knew what his next step would be if he made it to the Asteroid Belt. After all, he was a pirate, and the Asteroid Belt was where many pirates outfitted and staffed their ships. He was ready to do what he had been trained for. "What's the plan?"

RW spoke rapidly. "We're waiting for clearance to take a ship out. When we have it, I'll travel through computer space to Gorgon Station and open the cell doors and equipment room. Then I'll alert you and the other Barneys. You'll be on your own to get to the spaceport. The group from Genesis should arrive within about five hours to pick you up. Do you think you can get there by then?"

"What's going to stop me?" Barney shrugged. Five hours should be more than enough time for ten Barneys to get to the space port unless Gorgon Station had better defenses than he'd yet seen. "All right," he said slowly. He didn't intend to spend the rest of his days serving RAM, which was what Dracolysk seemed to expect. "I'll be ready."

O   O   O   O   O

Jovanna inspected her ragged thumbnail and made herself put her hand in her lap. If she kept chewing her nails,
her fingers would be bloody stumps before RW got back
from Gorgon Station. It had been almost a week since they
had first formed their plan to get the Barneys off Genesis.
If Vince was correct, they had very little time left.

She wondered about Dr. Wydlin. She hoped RAM
wouldn't punish him for what she and Vince were about
to do. She wasn't happy about planning the Barneys' escape without Dr. Wydlin's approval, but there wasn't
much alternative. Maybe if RAM tried to get revenge,
she could get the Barneys to help rescue their creator.

"He'll be all right," she murmured under her breath.
"We'll all be all right."

"Sure we will, Jovanna." RW flashed into view. "But
we'd better get started on this escape thing, because
Dracolysk has just received a coded message from RAM
Headquarters."

"What?" exclaimed Jovanna.

"It looks like party time, as Number Five called it,"
RW said.

"Have you alerted the Barneys?"

"I've told them to be ready, but I haven't opened their
cubicles yet. I haven't said anything to Sattar Tabbibi."
They had decided ahead of time not to involve Sattar
Tabbibi, the thirty-first Barney. RW had discovered
that he had apparently been recruited by Dracolysk as
a personal assistant of some sort. In any case, Dracolysk
spent far more time with Tabbibi than he did with any
other Barney.

"Good. At least the Barneys are ready," Jovanna said.
"But what will we do for a ship? Vince still hasn't gotten one as far as I know."

"I'll tell Vince it's time," RW said. "Maybe he can
think of something else."

"Let me know what he says," Jovanna requested.

RW winked out, and Jovanna brought her ragged
thumbnail to her mouth and bit it vigorously.

O O O O O

Vince lay on his bed staring at the glow panel in his ceiling, wondering if Dekalb was ever going to get back to him. He'd heard nothing since Dekalb had promised to get him a ship. He'd called in sick to the spaceport the past two days to be sure he wouldn't miss any attempt Dekalb made to contact him. He rose from the bed and began to pace. It looked like they were going to have to come up with another plan. With the Barneys' help, maybe they could steal a ship.

"Vince!" RW came into view in front of his terminal. "We've got big trouble. Dracolysk just got a message from RAM. They're launching the takeover attempt."

"That's it!" Vince went over to the compdex. If Dekalb didn't have a ship for him, he'd have to get one himself—at gunpoint if necessary.

He punched in Dekalb's access code. RW looked over his shoulder. "Do you want me to go look for him?"

Just then a line of letters appeared on the screen. "HELLO, FARM BOY. TURN ON PRINTER."

About time. Vince turned his printer on. After a moment, a standard Wydlin mission order began to print out. Vince turned to RW. "Go tell Jo to give the signal to the Barneys, then meet me at the spaceport."

"You got it," RW said, then winked out.

Vince turned his attention back to the printer. Dekalb was giving him orders to take out a medium cruiser, the *Hecate*. Now all he had to do was get the orders and Jovanna down to the spaceport before news of the RAM attack closed it down. Suddenly it occurred to him that he didn't know if Dekalb had any way to get off the station. "NEED A RIDE? PLENTY OF ROOM."

"NO, THANKS, I'M FINE," came the reply.

"OKAY. GOOD LUCK," Vince typed.

"SAME TO YOU," Dekalb transmitted.

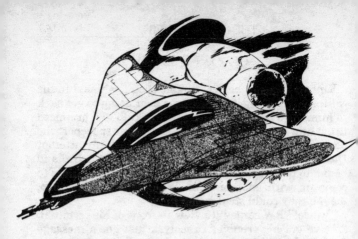

CHAPTER SEVENTEEN

You knew better than this, Jovanna scolded herself as she soaked the throbbing tip of her thumb in a cup of cold water.

"Jovanna, have you been biting your nails again?" RW was right behind her.

Jovanna chose not to answer. "What did Vince say?"

"He just received the orders. He said we should let the Barneys out, then you should get yourself over to the spaceport."

Adrenalin coursed through Jovanna. "All right. I'll open the cubicles here. Are you ready to free the Barneys over at Gorgon Station?"

"Yes."

"Good. Once you get them out, report back here."

"You got it." RW winked out.

Jovanna turned to her terminal and keyed in the code to open the Barneys' equipment cabinets. Then she started a sequence that would transmit a set of escape instructions to the Barneys on Genesis. It would take about twenty seconds for it to play through. Jovanna counted slowly up to twenty, then keyed in the code to open the Barneys' cubicles.

They would be busy outfitting themselves for several

minutes. Wydlin corporation had provided each Barney with a smart suit, a pair of wrist knives, and a rocket pistol. All the equipment was kept in a bank of lockers at the far end of the lab.

Jovanna looked around her office one last time. There was nothing here she needed anymore, and she felt an overwhelming urgency to get out. Once the Barneys were free, Genesis Station would be up for grabs. If she didn't get to the spaceport before the personnel there panicked, Vince might be forced to leave without her.

$$\bigcirc \quad \bigcirc \quad \bigcirc \quad \bigcirc \quad \bigcirc$$

The sergeant who assigned spacecraft had been dubious about the papers Vince had presented to him and had sent him to Commander Andreyev's office for approval. Commander Andreyev spent a full two minutes studying Vince's papers before putting them down on his desk and scrawling his initials across the bottom. "Everything seems to be in order, Pirelli." He seemed annoyed that he'd had no advance warning of Vince's request. "You can take the *Hecate*. Felcher's crew isn't very busy right now. Have them do the launch preparation."

"Yes, sir," Vince said. He was waiting for Andreyev's dismissal when the commander's comnet chimed.

"What is it?"

"Commander Andreyev, RAM cruiser *Hellas* has just requested permission to land on Genesis."

"What the hell is a corporate cruiser doing out here?" Andreyev demanded.

"They say it's a security matter, sir."

"Stall 'em and get me Mr. Wydlin at Gorgon Station." Andreyev cracked his knuckles, his fingers making tiny exploding noises.

Vince wondered whether Andreyev really expected to get in touch with Noah Wydlin. The official word on Genesis over the past week was that Noah was a voluntary guest of Hugo Dracolysk's, but Vince would have thought Andreyev had seen enough RAM politics to know how likely that was. "Permission to leave, sir?" he asked.

Andreyev waved him off distractedly. Vince went to the locker area to retrieve the smart suit he'd brought along for Jovanna. He stowed it, and his helmet, inside the *Hecate*. Then he went to find Felcher to get him started preparing the *Hecate* for launch.

After speaking to Felcher, Vince went to the glass-walled control room in the center of the spaceport dome, hoping to glean any clues he could from the activities there.

Hearn, at the communications console, flashed Vince a feeble smile. "Andreyev's gonna have my hide," he said.

"Why? What's the matter?" Vince asked innocently.

"We've got a RAM ship coming in, and I can't raise the CEO. I called Gorgon Station, but they say they can't reach him."

Vince shook his head. Of course they couldn't—or wouldn't. Getting Noah Wydlin off the station was obviously part of RAM's takeover plan.

"Well, putting off telling him won't make it any easier." Hearn punched a code into his board. Standing off to one side, Vince heard the click that indicated Hearn had completed the circuit.

"Yes?" Andreyev's unmistakable sharp voice came over the speaker.

"Commander, Gorgon Station says they're unable to reach Mr. Wydlin. I told them how important it was, but they said they couldn't help."

"I see. . . ." Andreyev's voice came out quiet and thoughtful. When he spoke again, his voice was more controlled than Vince had ever heard it. "Well, I don't see how we can refuse the *Hellas*. It's always best to co-operate in matters of security. Put me through to them, Hearn."

Vince heard Andreyev ask the captain of the *Hellas* how he could help, then Vince returned to check on the *Hecate*. It wasn't ready yet. He paced in front of the maintenance bay, as if by doing so he could make Felcher and his crew work faster.

"You're driving me crazy, Pirelli," Felcher complained. He waved a wrench at the ship's hatch. "Go inside and get ready for a systems check."

"In a minute," Vince said. He'd just noticed increased activity in the glass-walled control room, which was usual just before a landing. How close was the RAM ship?

"Where's your crew?" Felcher said, turning away from his diagnostic terminal.

"They'll be here any minute," Vince said. He hoped they would, anyway. If the Barneys didn't arrive before the RAM ship landed, they might never get off Genesis Station. The Barneys were now primed to rebel against RAM; Vince doubted they'd submit to anything. If the *Hellas* landed before they could get off the station, there'd be one hell of a mess.

Vince heard the roar of an approaching spacecraft. After it subsided, he could hear the ship's seals being fitted to the docking hatches.

Felcher lifted an eyebrow. "Sounds like we got company. Wonder who it could be?"

Commander Andreyev emerged from his office and strode to the docking bay where the ship was arriving. All activity on the maintenance and docking levels stopped.

"Must be a big wheel of some sort," Felcher commented. The hatch to the docking bay opened, and a long line of troopers in red RAM uniforms marched from the ship and formed into a double row. Andreyev's face grew white as he stalked to the end of the aisle they'd formed and waited. Nearly a minute later, a RAM captain emerged from the hatch. Andreyev stood stiffly at the end of the double row of troopers as the captain approached.

The captain walked to the end of the line where Andreyev stood. "Commander Andreyev? I'm Captain Dorn, of RAM's Space Assault Corps. In accordance with the Mars Judicial Code, item twelve, subheading four-A, dealing with collaboration with an enemy of the state, the assets of Wydlin Corporation are being seized.

We are here to account for the assets of this station and to take Dr. Remus Wydlin into custody."

Andreyev frowned, apparently taken by surprise. Vince was a bit surprised himself. He had thought the takeover attempt wouldn't begin until RAM had Dr. Wydlin in custody, or at least accounted for. Andreyev spoke carefully. "Dr. Wydlin is not on the station. He should be on Mars by now."

Dorn stared at Andreyev coldly. "We already have his son, Noah Wydlin. There is no danger to the personnel on this station as long as everyone cooperates. I want to know the location of Dr. Wydlin and of the genetic mutants he calls 'the Barneys.' "

Andreyev, still frowning, said, "I'll put a call through to Dr. Wydlin at his lab and living suite immediately, though I'm sure he's not on Genesis. I'm afraid I'm not familiar with the genetic mutants you mentioned."

Vince had the impression that Dorn was highly aware of his audience. There was a quick movement by Dorn, accompanied by the dull thud of his fist meeting Andreyev's midsection. Taken off guard, Andreyev let out a surprised "Oof" as he doubled over.

Dorn signaled to two of the troopers, and they each took one of Andreyev's arms and pulled him upright. As Andreyev gasped for breath, Dorn looked at him, his expression outwardly pleasant. "I didn't catch what you said, Commander. Once again, where are the Barneys and Dr. Wydlin?"

Still gasping for breath, Andreyev shook his head. Vince realized Andreyev had already told Dorn everything he knew, but Dorn apparently believed he was being defiant. As the troopers held him up. Dorn punched him in the stomach again, then delivered a blow to his jaw. Andreyev sagged.

"We need a quieter place to talk." Dorn's deadly calm expression was even more frightening than if he'd revealed some emotion. His eyes roved over the group of workers near the maintenance bay and settled on one of Felcher's assistants.

"You! Show us to the commander's office!"

The assistant looked terrified, but he hastened to obey the RAM captain, leading the way for Captain Dorn and the two troopers who supported Andreyev. The remaining troopers took up positions in the control room and throughout the maintenance and docking levels of the space port's interior.

One trooper stationed himself not ten feet from the maintenance bay that housed the *Hecate*. Felcher's face took on a mulish look. He turned back to the *Hecate*, signaling to his other assistant to return to the task that the *Hellas*'s arrival had interrupted. Vince felt an overpowering admiration for Felcher at that moment. "How can I help?" he asked.

Felcher's face became exaggeratedly pleasant, as if he'd be damned if he'd let these RAM troopers see any dissension among the inhabitants of Genesis Station.

"Well, Pirelli, we were talking about running a systems check. Why don't you take the controls?"

Vince performed the systems check, responding to Felcher's requests with extreme care, even though he ached to know what was going on outside the *Hecate*. Finally he heard a low whistle from Felcher over the comnet. "Something's up."

"Why? What's happening?" Vince asked.

"More RAM troopers coming off the *Hellas*," Felcher reported. "And my assistant just got back from Andreyev's office. Seems some of the gennies have escaped from the lab section. That captain must be sending the troops after 'em."

Vince couldn't stand it any longer. He climbed down from the cruiser's control deck and left the ship to see what was happening. A line of troopers was passing through the main door that led from the spaceport to the rest of Genesis Station. The spaceport doors closed behind the last of the RAM troopers.

A scream from the direction of Andreyev's office punctuated the tense silence that hung over the spaceport. The station personnel stood stock still, trying to avoid Dorn's notice. Vince didn't blame them.

Some minutes later, the spaceport doors slid open, and

Vince, like everyone else in the room, felt his gaze drawn like a magnet to the person who stood there. Jovanna seemed impossibly small next to the nearly seven-foot-tall troopers who guarded the doorway. It looked as if she was asking to be admitted. Vince couldn't see their expressions, but the stiffness of their posture gave him little reason to think Jovanna would get her way. Just as he'd decided to try to convince the soldiers that Jovanna was his girlfriend who had come to visit him at work, one of the troopers stepped aside and motioned Jovanna to sit in a chair a few feet away from the door.

Jovanna looked around the spaceport. When she saw Vince, she smiled slightly. Unfortunately, if she meant to be reassuring, the effect was negated by the fact that she sat ramrod straight, her hands tightly clasped together.

Felcher said, "Well, Pirelli, I'm satisfied with the systems check if you are."

Vince nodded, despite the fact that he could barely remember having performed the check. Felcher stepped back in front of his terminal and examined the readout. "Refueling's finished, too. We can move her up to the launch bay now."

"Fine," Vince said. Felcher keyed a sequence into the computer. Through the hatch, Vince heard the elevator begin to move the ship from the maintenance bay up to the launch bay.

The sequence was nearly complete when the door from Commander Andreyev's office slid open abruptly. Dorn stormed out, white with fury, followed by the two troopers. "Where's Bay Eight?" he barked.

The question was directed to a nearby maintenance worker, who was too terrified to do anything but stare openmouthed at him. Vince stepped forward and called to the captain. "Over here."

Dorn swiveled to look at him. Vince returned the look levelly. Dorn approached him. "Is someone preparing for takeoff here?"

"I was," Vince said. He inclined his head toward

Dorn. "With your permission, sir."

Dorn's lips spread in a slow smile. "I'm too busy to consider your request immediately, Mr.—?"

"Pirelli," Vince supplied.

"Mr. Pirelli. As I was saying, I can't allow you to leave immediately, Mr. Pirelli. And I find your timing very interesting." Dorn held out his hand. "Show me your orders."

Vince considered reaching instead for his rocket pistol, but there were twenty RAM troopers nearby for whom he'd make an easy target. He picked up his printed orders from where they lay on Felcher's console. "Here they are, sir."

In no apparent hurry, Dorn took the orders and looked them over. After nearly a minute, he looked up. "Noah Wydlin's authorization code. Good enough—or it might have been, say, an hour ago. But the purpose of your trip seems rather vague, Mr. Pirelli. Where were you going?"

Vince felt a muscle in his cheek begin to twitch, and he willed it to be still.

"That was intended to be classified, sir."

Dorn's eyes took on the look of steel. "Ah, classified. I can understand your not wanting to say it in such a public place, then. But you'll tell me, Mr. Pirelli. Let's step into the commander's office for a minute, shall we? He doesn't seem to be using it right now. Apparently he's feeling a bit under the weather." Dorn gestured to the troopers behind him, and they took up positions on either side of Vince.

Vince looked around the spaceport, trying to assess his chances of escaping. The other RAM troopers had moved closer, ready to back up the two flanking Vince if it became necessary.

"Well, Captain." Vince smiled crookedly at Dorn. "I guess I'm all yours."

CHAPTER EIGHTEEN

Dracolysk's office at Gorgon Station was the most luxurious office Noah Wydlin had ever seen off Mars. The real red leather divan, flanked by ebony tables, must have cost Dracolysk a fortune. Noah nearly laughed aloud, thinking about the price of furniture at a time like this. Still, it was easier than thinking about what must be happening back at Genesis Station and whether his father was safe.

No, he wouldn't worry about that. Remus had to be safe. They had worked the plans out in painstaking detail. Gretsky would have known at the first mention of a "canceled appointment" that it was time to take Remus Wydlin to Paradise, listing their official destination as Mars. Remus could then arrange with Gretsky to ferry as many of the Barneys as possible to Paradise.

"Cognac, Noah?" Dracolysk asked from behind the bar. He had opened a cut crystal decanter and was reaching for a matching snifter.

Noah did not reply.

"No? You remind me of Tabbibi," Dracolysk said, waving a cut-crystal stopper in the direction of the brown-haired Barney who stood alertly near the entrance to the office. Sattar Tabbibi was the thirty-first Barney and had apparently replaced Dracolysk's Desert Runners as his personal bodyguard.

Dracolysk put the stopper back on the decanter. He walked around the end of the bar, then settled himself in the wing-backed chair that faced the red divan Noah was sitting on. "Tabbibi never indulges, at least, not when he's working. I rather like that trait in a gennie. I don't understand why you feel that way, however."

Noah met Dracolysk's gaze but did not answer. He'd speak when there was something worth talking about. Dracolysk shrugged, pulled out a cigarette from the gold box on the low table between them, and lit it.

"You must be thinking, 'Why doesn't he come to the point?' The truth is, this is getting rather boring. We've been over that territory, and I don't believe we're any closer to a resolution than when you first arrived." Dracolysk inhaled deeply on his cigarette, then exhaled, speaking through a fog of blue smoke. "Or am I wrong? Will you sign the order turning the other Barneys over to me? It would certainly ease the tension around here."

"Go to hell," Noah said.

Dracolysk chuckled. "Even if I do, it won't help, Noah. I only wanted your signature so I could save a bit of face with Simund Holzerhein. If I can show him the order, at least he'll know I tried. Other than that, my request has little significance. RAM has already launched the first attack against Genesis Station."

Noah couldn't help himself. He leaned forward, prepared to strike out at his tormentor. Quickly Tabbibi moved toward him, and he sat back. "When?"

Dracolysk consulted his wristchrono. "About ten minutes ago, I'd say. The first ship arrived to collect the Barneys and take your father into custody. More ships will be arriving within the next hour or so, just in case the first runs into any opposition. But it won't, will it? I believe we've timed this quite well."

When Noah made no reply, Dracolysk continued. "I doubt you were expecting RAM to move this soon. Otherwise you never would have accepted my invitation to visit, would you?"

Noah knew better than to say he had a pretty good idea what Dracolysk was up to when he summoned Noah to discuss "terms of the sale of Wydlin Corporation," especially since it was delivered by six Desert Runner warriors. Noah only hoped that his meek surrender had bought his father enough time to escape from Genesis Station before the RAM troops arrived. If his father had managed to escape with even one Barney, someday Noah would be rescued no matter where RAM imprisoned him.

The comnet's chime saved Noah from having to endure any more of his captor's boasting. "Excuse me," Dracolysk said, approaching his desk.

"Mr. Dracolysk, there's been a disturbance in the training barracks." His secretary sounded frantic.

Dracolysk's languor disappeared instantly. "What kind of disturbance?" he asked quickly.

"The Barneys have escaped, sir. They killed at least four guards and injured more than that."

Dracolysk ground out his cigarette viciously. "Where are they now?"

"A guard who managed to escape said they were at the equipment cage. He overheard them saying something about getting to the spaceport."

"I see . . ." Dracolysk said. "Close the spaceport tunnel immediately. Order a complete security shutdown. And tell Colonel Tarish to capture them, Lisa. Alive."

"Yes, sir."

Dracolysk turned to Noah. "Well, Noah, it seems you weren't without contingency plans after all. How did you manage it?"

Noah had no idea how the Barneys had freed themselves, nor why they had chosen this critical time to do it. He had no intention of admitting that to Dracolysk, however. "It doesn't matter, does it? If I were you, I'd concentrate on what you're going to do about it."

O   O   O   O   O

Black Barney fastened the equipment belt around his waist, hooking two loaded rocket pistols onto the belt. Next to him, Number Eight, Stalin Khan, tucked some extra "smart" ammo clips into a belt pouch. He noticed Black Barney looking at him and smiled beatifically. "I believe in being prepared, don't you?"

Before Black Barney could respond, a female Barney stepped between them. "How do I look?"

It was Number Thirteen, Lilith. She turned, displaying a lithe, muscular, six-foot-eight-inch frame encased in a shimmering gray smart suit. Barney looked her up and down. "Very well equipped."

"Flatterer," she said, giving him a smoldering glance.

Khan chose that moment to interrupt. "Look, you two, I like a bit of fun as much as the next gennie, but we have to get moving. At least one of those guards got away. He's had time to raise an alarm by now."

"You're right, unfortunately," Lilith sighed. She turned to Barney, unable to resist one more flirtatious gesture. "Well, Captain, would you care to lead?"

Because of his training as a pirate, Black Barney had been accepted as the de facto leader, which suited him fine. He nodded to Lilith, then called out so that the others in the equipment area could hear him. "Let's go!"

Smart-suited Barneys looked up from lockers and chests. "Come on!" Black Barney said. "We have a ship to catch."

Quinto spoke up. "You have a way with words, Pilgrim. *Vamanos!*"

Barney led the others from the equipment cage to the corridor that led to the tunnel that cored through the asteroid to the Gorgon Station spaceport. Potemkin and Rembrandt kept an eye out from the last rank, to avoid any nasty surprises coming on them from behind.

As they approached the door that opened onto the tunnel security checkpoint, Lilith nudged Black Barney. "Do you think they're expecting us?"

"Can't hurt to be prepared," Black Barney grunted, springing his wrist knives. Then he turned to face the others. "Lilith and I will penetrate as far into the area as we can. When the rest of you get through the door, stay together." He nodded to Lilith and broke into a run. Starting half a step behind, Lilith caught up with him a moment later. The automatic door barely had time to open before they barreled through it.

Black Barney sensed the others running up to join him, and then he was in the midst of the Falcones. Dracolysk's gennie guards, with their sharp talons and beaks, were fierce fighters, but they didn't worry Black Barney. They couldn't move as quickly as the Barneys could, for one thing. But then, very few living beings could match the Barneys for speed.

Black Barney plunged one of his knives into the throat of the Falcone who blocked his way. Beside him, Lilith pushed her knife into the vitals of a bird-man and wrenched it upward. The two Falcones collapsed at virtually the same instant. Barney lifted his dead opponent and threw the corpse against the throng, knocking two of the Falcones to the floor.

Lilith simply let her dead Falcone drop and sprang for her next opponent. Barney went for the nearest Falcone to his right. Stalin Khan pushed through the gap between Lilith and Barney and threw himself at a pair of Falcones who had seemed intent on driving a wedge between Black Barney and Lilith.

"Thanks, Clone Brother," Barney said, evading a Falcone's claws to thrust his wrist knife into the soft spot under his opponent's rib cage.

"No problem," said Khan, swiftly disemboweling his foe. Behind Khan's back, Black Barney saw the flash of a taloned hand about to slash down on Khan's back. He shouted, but before Khan could turn to deal with his attacker, the Falcone crumpled to the ground. Barney saw the flash of Lilith's feral smile before a movement at his side caused him to whirl to face a new opponent. Quinto appeared beside him, slashing at one of the Falcones.

As Black Barney advanced into the area, the rest of the Barneys followed, forming a solid phalanx against the Falcones who blocked the tunnel to the spaceport.

Several bloody moments later, when Black Barney

looked around for a new opponent, he saw no one left to
fight. His eyes took in the heaps of dead Falcones scattered throughout the area.

"We make a pretty decent army," Quinto observed.

"That's what we were created for." Stalin Khan, several yards away, sheathed his wrist knives.

"Yeah, well, let's get our pretty decent army out of
here," Black Barney said, moving to the tunnel hatch.
The hatch, which had stood open all the previous times
he was in this area, was now closed. It was operated by a
console that stood on a shelf beside the opening. Barney
stepped up to it. The screen was blank, so he keyed in a
request for on-line help. A moment later, a well-
modulated voice said, "This area is on security alert.
This terminal will not operate until the alert is lifted."

"What's the problem?" Quinto asked.

"The terminal won't work," Barney said.

"I'm all for breaking the sucker down," Quinto said.

"Good idea," growled Barney, who had been considering the same action himself.

He looked at the hatch, trying to figure out what it
would take. He tried to turn the small wheel in the center, but it didn't budge.

"Allow me." Ochoa Varilla joined Black Barney at the
door. Ochoa had been trained as an engineer and was
well acquainted with the workings of space stations as
well as the ships that traveled between them. He examined the door. "I've seen these before. Short of an explo-
sive charge, we won't get it open. At least not today."

"So what's next?" another Barney asked. Black Barney frowned, trying to think of an answer.

Just then a small humming sound came over the terminal's speaker. A breathy female voice said, "We need
a report, Tunnel Station."

"Report this, Honey," said Quinto. "We just took out
your—"

Barney came over and clamped a hand down on Quinto's shoulder warningly. Then he spoke into the speaker.
"Who is this?"

A tense silence followed his question. After a moment,

another voice—a man's this time—came over the speaker. "Tunnel Station, report."

Barney recognized the voice. "Well, well. If it isn't Hugo Dracolysk! How the hell are you? What happened? You run out of stooges to do your work for you?"

There was another pause before Dracolysk said, "Which Barney is this?"

"Call me Black Barney," he said, to the guffaws of his companions.

"What's your number, mutant?" Dracolysk snapped.

"Mutant is such an ugly word," Barney said. "Especially the way you say it, Dracolysk. It's a good thing we're leaving, or I'd have to teach you some manners."

Dracolysk laughed harshly. "You're not going anywhere. The only tunnel to the spaceport is sealed."

There was a short silence, and then Dracolysk spoke again, his voice now smooth and calm. "You're all very valuable property, as I'm sure you know. I think we'd all be happier if you'd just return to the barracks. I don't know what Noah Wydlin told you, but his problems with RAM have nothing to do with you."

"Ha!" snorted Lilith.

"Is that you, Lilith? I'm especially hurt that you'd want to leave, after all we've meant to each other."

Barney wasn't sure what Dracolysk meant, but he couldn't miss the cruel tone of his voice nor the bright red spots that burned in Lilith's cheeks. When Dracolysk went on, his tone was once again businesslike. "I'm giving you all five minutes to get back into your cells. I think you'll agree that's more than generous."

"Give this guy a medal," muttered S'mahl, a dark-skinned Barney.

"Any Barney who hasn't surrendered within that time will be hunted down and killed," said Dracolysk matter-of-factly. "You're not so valuable that I'll risk any more damage to my property. Do you understand?"

Black Barney looked around at the others. None of them seemed interested in surrender. He was about to tell Dracolysk to stuff it when Stalin Khan spoke up.

"We understand, sir. Thank you for your generosity."

"Are you cr—?" Barney began, but Khan grabbed him by the arm and pulled him away from the console. Khan signaled to Quinto to cut off the communications link.

"Of course I'm not crazy," Khan said crisply. "We have five minutes of free movement if we pretend we're giving up. We'll have no time at all if we defy him openly."

Black Barney had to admit Khan had a point. "All right," he said. "So the question stands—what next? I'm open to suggestions."

"We can't get through that hatch in the next five minutes," Ochoa Varilla said with conviction.

"I say we get to Dracolysk and convince him to open the door for us," Lilith said. "Or kill him—whichever seems easier." Mutters of agreement greeted her words. "I know a way to get to him."

"Where will he be, though?" asked Stalin Khan.

"Probably in his office," said Lilith. "He has a nasty little mobile sculpture on his desk. It works kind of like a sonic stunner, except you're still conscious after he turns it on. It just makes you too dizzy to stand or move. He has it set to work against the Barneys' genotype. I'll bet he thinks that'll keep him safe."

"It sounds pretty convincing to me," Quinto said.

"Someone just has to disable it," said Rembrandt. "I'll volunteer."

"Fine," said Black Barney.

"Wait a minute," Ochoa Varilla said. He opened a small door in the console and pulled out a tool kit. He searched until he found a roll of fibrous material Barney couldn't identify. He snipped two small strips from it, then rolled the strips into two balls. "Put these in your ears," he said to Rembrandt. "I'm not one hundred percent sure it will work, but it should shut out some of the sound waves."

Black Barney signaled to Lilith. "Take the lead with me. You can show us to Dracolysk's office and warn us if anything seems unusual."

"Yes, Captain." Lilith pointed off to the left, toward an unfamiliar corridor.

"This way."

CHAPTER NINETEEN

The Desert Runners will provide your Barneys
with a challenge, don't you think, Noah?" Dracolysk said, reaching for a cracker spread with
beluga caviar. Noah's eyes focused on the large screen
Dracolysk was watching. It revealed that the Barneys
had just reached the atrium level of the administration
tower and were battling to get to the elevator. Dracolsyk had dispatched a squadron of his Desert Runner
warriors to the atrium to hold off the Barneys. "I must
admit, these Barneys of yours are good, though."

Black Barney had just killed two Desert Runners simultaneously, slicing a knife across each one's throat in
one smooth, deadly swipe. Khan and Lilith fought on
either side of Black Barney. Behind the three in the
front, two Barneys had climbed on the shoulders of
their clone brothers and were firing rocket pistols at the
Desert Runners who hovered just beyond the melee.

Noah held his breath. One of the Desert Runners
raised his own rocket pistol. He aimed unhurriedly,
then shot at the gennie called Heisenberg. Heisenberg
nearly fell off backward, then sighted the Desert Runner who had shot him. As the Desert Runner squeezed
off a second shot, Heisenberg fired, his smart bullet

smashing into the Desert Runner's face. The Desert Runner collapsed just as Heisenberg sagged, pulling his fellow Barney to the ground.

Black Barney, Khan, and Lilith had battled their way farther into the atrium, allowing more of their companions to close ranks with the Desert Runners.

"They're in their element now," remarked Dracolysk, as unperturbed as if they were watching a match in the Coprates Duel Pits. "My Desert Runners won't fire into close melee, and as remarkable as their own strength is, they can't beat the Barneys hand to hand." He brushed crumbs from his fingers and stood up. "I'd say it's time to retreat gracefully."

"Retreat? To where?" Noah asked. "The spaceport is sealed off, isn't it?"

Dracolysk looked at him as if he were feebleminded. "Of course. We won't leave the station until it's all over, Noah. We'll simply go up to the top level. The Barneys will look for me here first. We may be able to eliminate a few of them if they do. Tabbibi, wait in the outer office, please."

When Tabbibi was gone, Dracolysk pressed a few keys on his computer. An abstract metallic sculpture on his desk began to vibrate, starting a multitude of tiny, snakelike pendants that hung from it to jingle.

He turned to Noah. "I call it 'the Gorgon.' It produces sound waves that affect the central nervous system of any targeted species, disrupting the balance of the affected creature so completely that he can't even walk without falling. It's currently set to work on the Barney series, though I can adjust the frequency to work on other gennie types as well." Dracolysk turned away from Noah and opened a drawer. "They'll find another obstacle or two before they can get to us. In the event that they do arrive up on the pyramid level, we'll still have Mr. Tabbibi on our side."

It occurred to Noah that Dracolysk didn't have Tabbibi now. And with the Gorgon operating, Tabbibi would be at a severe disadvantage if Dracolysk did call for him. There would probably be no better time to reverse the situation. Noah quietly inched around to get in position to attack.

Just then Dracolysk turned, aiming a rocket pistol at Noah. "And in case you were going to try anything, I wouldn't advise it. Unlike the Barneys, your market value is the same dead or alive."

Noah put his hands up. "You always did know your markets, Hugo."

"Thank you," Dracolysk said. "Now, shall we join Mr. Tabbibi?"

O   O   O   O   O

Lilith put her hand on Black Barney's arm and pointed at a door near the end of the corridor. "That's the door to Dracolysk's outer office."

"Where are the guards?" Barney asked. Dracolysk was never seen without a pair of Desert Runners flanking him, and in most areas of Gorgon Station there was a Desert Runner or a Falcone guard posted every twenty yards or so. The area near Dracolysk's office was curiously empty.

"We've killed a lot of them," Rembrandt said, straining to look over Barney's shoulder. "Maybe we already took out the ones who are supposed to be here."

Their opposition had grown thinner since the battle in the atrium. They'd run across a few isolated guards as they'd made their way up to the twenty-ninth floor, but they had presented few problems. Still, Barney thought there should be more guards at the station. And if there were, they wouldn't leave Dracolysk undefended.

Rembrandt was starting to put his earplugs in. "Skip it," Barney said. "We're not going in there."

"But Dracolysk—" Rembrandt began to protest.

"Dracolysk isn't there," Barney said. He turned to Lilith. "What's upstairs?"

She shrugged. "I've never been up there. I think Dracolysk said something about a big laboratory. And maybe some meeting rooms."

"All right. We go up quietly. Keep your eyes and ears

open," Barney said. "If we run into a pack of Desert Runners or RAM troopers guarding a door, that's where we'll find Dracolysk. Let's go."

They took to the stairs. Barney had decided earlier that it was too easy for Dracolysk to control the elevators, possibly trapping or killing them. When they reached the next level, Barney signaled for quiet before he opened the hatch.

The hall was deserted, and the four doors he could see were all closed. He stepped out of the hatch and listened. He didn't hear any voices, but he had no intention of going up to the top floor without making sure this one was empty. The others joined him soundlessly. Black Barney began to walk down the hall. As he approached the first door on the left, it opened with a sudden, heart-stopping whoosh. Barney's rocket pistol was in his hand, but all he faced was a long table with perhaps a dozen chairs. He stepped away, and the door closed again.

The first door on the right opened as easily as the one on the left had, and the room behind it was similarly unoccupied. Barney was beginning to breathe more easily as they approached the next door. When the door slid open, Barney just caught the faint tinkling of chimes before someone hit him unexpectedly from the side and knocked him to the floor. Lilith was on top of him, yelling, "Get away! It's one of Dracolysk's stunners!"

Khan fell to the floor and was looking around helplessly, but the rest of the Barneys managed to get out of range before they were stricken. Rembrandt stuffed his earplugs in grimly, then moved quickly down the corridor and grabbed Khan by the leg, pulling him away from the door. With no one in front of it to activate the door, it slid closed soundlessly.

"Nasty stuff," Black Barney grunted.

Khan tried to rise up. He got to his knees before falling. He tried to stand several more times without success, then closed his eyes. "How . . . long does it . . . last?"

"About eight hours," Lilith said.

"Wonderful," Khan gasped. "I hate to . . . admit it, but I . . . can't walk."

"I'll carry you," said a blond Barney named Grotowski.

Khan's eyes remained closed. "Thanks."

"Well, folks, anybody want to open any more doors?" asked Quinto.

"I will," said Black Barney. He didn't want to ignore the one door that remained on this level. Giving the door that hid the stunner a wide berth, he approached the last door. It hid another empty meeting room. Barney reported this to the others.

"Good," said Rembrandt. "We didn't need any more surprises like the last one."

"Are we ready to go up now?" Lilith asked.

Barney shrugged. "As ready as we'll ever be."

○   ○   ○   ○   ○

"I wonder why they haven't reached my office yet." Dracolysk frowned, looking away from the tri-dee screen that showed a closed-circuit view of his office. He had been watching expectantly, as if he couldn't wait to see the Barneys' reaction to his trap. Several of Dracolysk's top scientists and executives also crowded around the video display.

"Maybe they got caught in traffic," Noah said from his seat some distance away on a low lab stool.

Tabbibi stood watch over Noah closely, scrupulous about keeping him away from Dracolysk. Noah looked around at the interior of the glassteel pyramid. All the remaining nonmilitary personnel of Gorgon Station were there, some talking in excited whispers while others simply looked terrified. The only inhabitants of the room who seemed remotely prepared to deal with the Barneys, provided they made it this far, were Tabbibi and Dracolysk's two remaining Desert Runner warriors. Above the lab, the stars twinkled through the glassteel roof of the pyramid. Noah looked out, wondering where Paradise was from here and hoping his father was there. Noah heard the sounds of rocket pistols being fired beyond the lab's secured double doors.

"They can't be up here already!" Dracolysk screamed, as if he couldn't believe the Barneys' rudeness in failing to walk into his trap. "They must have bypassed the office!" Dracolysk frowned, then entered another sequence into the computer keyboard beneath the screen. Noah stood, using the rungs of his stool to get a better look at the tri-dee screen.

The view of Dracolysk's office disappeared, giving way to a shot of the wide corridor outside the lab's double doors. Statues of every species of gennie that Dracolysk had bred or trained rose from pedestals lining the walls. Red-uniformed RAM troopers crouched behind every available piece of cover, firing furiously at the remaining Barneys. The Barneys continued to advance in uneven spurts, darting from doorway to doorway, returning the fire of the Martian troops as they moved relentlessly closer.

Noah caught occasional glimpses of the action on the screen. He noticed that Black Barney and Lilith had advanced close enough to engage their foes hand to hand. Barney faced two RAM troopers. It took him mere seconds to slit their throats. When a third leaped into the breach left by his fallen companions, Barney wound one arm around his foe's waist, pinioning him. Then he stabbed the trooper's side and sliced at an upward diagonal. The unfortunate trooper grabbed at his midsection, trying to hold his entrails in. His uniform grew dark with blood. Noah stared at the carnage as if hypnotized.

The Barneys advanced inexorably. Noah could count only seven of them now, but those seven were cutting down Dracolysk's RAM reinforcements with incredible efficiency. Noah heard Dracolysk's voice, low and venomous. "You've displayed your power, Noah. Now call them off."

Noah looked away from the screen and focused on Dracolysk, who now stood beside him.

"I repeat, tell them to stop," Though Dracolysk ap-

peared to be in control of his emotions, Noah knew his
foe would never appeal to him unless he was desperate.

However, Noah had no power over the Barneys. His
father was adamant in his belief that the Barneys were
eventually to be their own masters. "Otherwise," Remus had said, "we're no better than RAM. We'd simply
be building preprogrammed slaves for ourselves."

Noah could ask the Barneys to stop the killing, but
given their frenzy, he doubted that he'd be successful.
However, there was no reason for Dracolysk to know
how little influence Noah really had. "Why should I?"
he asked in the calmest tone he could muster. "So you
can turn them—and me—over to RAM? Sorry. I'm not
interested."

A thunderous boom sounded at the lab's double doors.
Noah looked back at the screen. The Barneys had lifted
one of the statues from its pedestal and, holding it hor-
izontally, were using it to batter the lab doors. Dracolysk pulled at Noah's sleeve, suddenly as humble—and
as desperate—as one of the derelicts who thronged the
entrance to the Mars-Pavonis Space Elevator. "What do
you want, Noah? Name it!"

Noah looked at the screen and considered. The Barneys rammed the doors again, and another shuddering
boom filled the lab.

"Noah, be reasonable!" Dracolysk grabbed at Noah's
arm.

Noah pulled away, then met Dracolysk's eyes. "Open
the spaceport tunnel." Dracolysk first looked as if he
would refuse. Another concussion shook the doors, and
Dracolysk pushed the computer operator out of the way
and swiftly pressed keys. He turned to Noah. "It's done.
Now call them off."

"That's a good beginning," said Noah, trying to think
of another demand to divert Dracolysk from discovering
his lack of power over the Barneys. The lab shuddered
again. At the blow, the lab doors parted slightly, their
metal surface warping inward.

A pair of hands appeared at the gap, as if one of the
Barneys was trying to enlarge the opening. The execu-

tives and scientists scattered, hiding behind cabinets
and counters as Dracolysk's Desert Runners pulled out
laser pistols and began firing at the door. The hands
moved out of the gap.

"Call off your Desert Runners!" Noah shouted. Dracolysk looked at him as if he was insane, and Noah explained feverishly, "They'll just make the Barneys
angrier. I can't promise anything if you keep provoking
them."

"You mean you can't make them obey? Then why the
hell am I talking to you?" Dracolysk shouted. The doors
shook from another battering. Dracolysk flinched at the
sound.

"You trained them," Noah said calmly. "Why don't
you make them obey?"

A long, dusty screech filled the room. Noah watched
as the top of one of the doors was forced out of its track.
The Desert Runners positioned themselves to attack
the first Barney through the door. Noah saw movement
out of the corner of his eye and turned to see Dracolysk
lurching back to the computer console.

Noah dove at Dracolysk, but before he could reach his
enemy, Tabbibi whirled in front of him, wrist knives
flashing.

"No!" Dracolysk shouted. Tabbibi stopped his advance on Noah but didn't take his eyes off him. "He's
mine," Dracolysk said, raising his rocket pistol. "You
stop the Barneys."

Tabbibi hesitated, then stepped around Noah, heading for the doors. Dracolysk stepped back but kept his
pistol aimed at Noah. "You're more trouble than you're
worth, Wydlin."

A metallic scrape sounded behind him, and Noah
glanced over his shoulder. A final kick from one of the
Barneys had released the loosened door from its track.

As it fell inward, the Desert Runners began firing into the approaching Barneys. A smoking hole appeared
in Black Barney's shoulder, but he seemed oblivious to
the pain. He charged the Desert Runners, his face a
snarling mask of rage. Tabbibi stood staring, his expres-

sion more confused than fearful. Noah wondered if he
found it difficult to attack another Barney. Well, he
wasn't going to wait for Tabbibi to overcome his reluc-
tance, no matter what its source.

"Barneys!" Noah called. "The spaceport tunnel is
open! Run for it!" He felt a sharp blow to his lower back
at the same moment he heard the explosion of a smart
bullet. He tried to turn and face Dracolysk again but
found that his legs wouldn't obey him. He gripped the
edge of the console and managed to pull himself around.
Another smart bullet exploded in his chest. He fell awkwardly, sprawling over the computer console. He felt
numb all over now, unable to speak or move.

Dracolysk slid along the edge of the room, not looking
at Noah. He thinks I'm dead, thought Noah. As the
sounds of the fighting seemed to grow distant, Noah realized Dracolysk was right, or would be soon. He managed to lift his head and look back at the Barneys. One
of them—he couldn't remember this one's name—
hoisted a Desert Runner into the air and ran full tilt at
one of the glassteel windows. The window frame bowed
outward, and the Barney stepped back and swung the
Desert Runner around in a circle over his head, then
hurled, throwing him at the weakened area.

A buzzing alarm sounded, and a computer voice said,
"Danger! Inner containment compromised on thirty-
first floor. Evacuate and pressure-seal the area."

The message repeated as Noah's vision grew dimmer.
Well, if he wasn't going to survive this, at least Dracolysk wouldn't survive either. If the inner containment
of Dracolysk's tower was destroyed, the pressure loss
would cause an immediate, catastrophic explosion. And
Noah didn't think the Barneys would let Dracolysk out
before that happened. Before Noah's vision faded completely, he wanted to see the look on Dracolysk's face.
Noah turned back to where he'd last seen Dracolysk,
but no one was there. He blinked, trying to clear his vision, but he still couldn't see Dracolysk.

Noah's head drooped, and he couldn't lift it again.
And then everything ceased to matter.

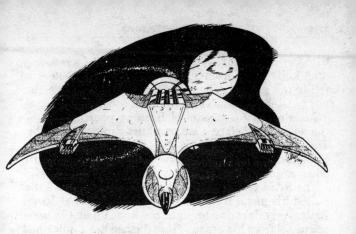

CHAPTER TWENTY

The RAM troopers were about to march Vince away when Jovanna saw the desperation in his eyes. He quickly looked away, as if embarrassed that he'd revealed his fear.

"Wait!" Jovanna called. Vince looked reproachful, and she glared back at him. Did he expect her to just let him be tortured? The captain turned to look at her.

"Don't you have better things to do than question innocent bystanders? The station's in an uproar. Aren't you going to maintain order?" Jovanna demanded.

"You're not helping matters, young lady," the captain said. "In fact—" he gestured to one of the RAM troopers—"bring her along for questioning as well."

The trooper grabbed Jovanna's arm and pulled her back to where Vince and his two guards stood. "Nice going," Vince mouthed to her. She ignored him and tried to think of some way out of this. Perhaps she could distract the RAM captain with just enough information to make him think she was cooperating with him.

There was a hiss of large automatic doors opening. The captain froze momentarily, then began barking orders. Jovanna noticed that the spaceport doors had opened. The troopers there were locked in a struggle

with two of the Barneys. One Barney pulled a red, drip-
ping knife away from a trooper's throat just before he
fell to the ground. The other trooper died when a Barney twisted his head sideways with a sickening crunch.

Jovanna saw a stream of Barneys pouring through
the doors just before a smart bullet exploded near her.
The captain, clutching his chest, sagged to the ground.
She glanced around and saw that Vince was looking
down at the captain, a rocket pistol in his hand.

The RAM trooper who stood between her and Vince
pulled his pistol from his holster and aimed at Vince.
Reflexively Jovanna brought her knee up and knocked
the pistol from his grasp. Vince flashed her a quick look
of gratitude before dealing with the other trooper.

Jovanna dove for the pistol on the floor, then turned
and aimed it at the trooper who'd lost it. Fear was written on his face. It was good that he didn't know she had
no idea how to shoot it. "Get down on the floor," she ordered him and was relieved when he complied. She
turned around to see what was happening.

The Barneys were enmeshed with RAM troops, who
had converged on the main doors. Vince was shooting
into the massed red uniforms. He turned and saw her.
"Get into the ship!" he yelled. "Bay Eight! Get RW to
prepare the launch bay for takeoff!"

Jovanna clanged up the metallic stairs to the launch
bay level. The hatch didn't budge, and Jovanna stared
at it stupidly for several seconds before noticing the
computer keypad next to it. "Oh, great," she remarked
to no one in particular. "How am I supposed to know the
code to open one of these?"

She forced herself to think. The code wouldn't be particularly difficult. It would be used too often for that. On
a hunch, she spoke into the speaker between the keyboard and the screen. "Request help," she said.

"What kind of help do you want?" came a familiar
voice, and RW's image appeared on the small screen.

Jovanna felt dizzy with relief. "First I want to get into
this ship. Then prepare the bay for the launch sequence.
Where did you come from, by the way?"

"After I got back from Gorgon Station, I checked the lab. Since the Barneys were gone, I figured they were here. Did you know RAM has a ship here? Someone just planted a virus in the station computer system."

Jovanna sighed. "What kind of a virus?"

"I was about to check that out," said RW. She looked past Jovanna at the battle raging on the lower level of the spaceport. "I see the Barneys have arrived."

Jovanna looked over her shoulder. The Barneys were slowly pushing back the mass of RAM troops. Vince crouched behind a computer console, reloading. Jovanna turned back to RW. "They're fighting half the RAM troops in the solar system. RW, we've got to get off this station. Find out about this virus, but be careful."

"Will do," RW said just before winking out.

Jovanna gripped the rail overlooking the lower level of the spaceport. She looked down at her right hand, surprised to realize that she still held the rocket pistol she'd taken from the RAM trooper. She glanced down at the place where she'd told him to lie, but he was no longer there. Frantically she tried to locate him. She finally saw him moving in a half-crouch. She wouldn't have blamed him for trying to get back to his ship, but he wasn't moving in that direction. Instead, he was intent on something else. Jovanna followed his line of vision and saw that he was heading straight for Vince.

She screamed a warning to Vince, but he couldn't hear her over the fighting. Raising her trembling hands, she pointed the rocket pistol at the trooper and squeezed the trigger. A sound like a tiny engine ignition roared in the gun's chamber, and a dart of golden fire sped from it. The rocket bullet struck a cabinet several feet ahead of the trooper. Vince turned around and, seeing the new threat, fired at him. The trooper fell, and Vince returned his attention to the melee before him.

The RAM troops crouched behind cover and were trying to pick off the Barneys. Jovanna saw the dark-skinned female that Dr. Wydlin had named S'nee firing a rocket pistol. When it ran out of ammunition, she threw it down and advanced on her enemy, who stood paralyzed with fear. By the time he raised his pistol to fire, S'nee had pulled out one of her wrist knives.

S'nee sliced through his arm, causing the pistol, with the trooper's hand still attached, to clatter to the floor. As he stared in horror, S'nee plunged her knife into his torso, then pulled it upward and out again. Jovanna looked away when S'nee, grinning, licked the bloodied knife as the trooper, wide-eyed, slumped to the floor.

A Klaxon blared suddenly. After a moment, Jovanna determined that it was coming from the RAM ship. Troopers near the ship moved toward it quickly, slipping through the hatch with practiced precision. The first Barney, Potemkin, was facing a RAM trooper when the alarm sounded. As the trooper tried to retreat, Potemkin sprang for him, knocking him to the floor. A wide red slash appeared in the trooper's throat before Jovanna realized Potemkin had drawn his wrist knife.

"Jovanna!" RW called from the screen behind her. The digital personality wore an urgent, worried expression for the first time in Jovanna's memory. "Bad news," RW gasped. "The virus attacked the station's life support system and the attached alarm system. I couldn't stop it, Jovanna. No one without a space suit will be able to survive after about fifteen minutes."

"Good lord!" Jovanna cried, feeling a stab of shock. She quickly surveyed the combat below. Most of the Barneys were still wreaking havoc on RAM troops, preventing them from returning to their ship. Potemkin and Matsuo had blocked the entry to the RAM ship and were denying entry to the now-frantic troopers.

"We don't have time for this!" Jovanna screamed at the Barneys over the *ah-ooga, ah-ooga* of the Klaxon. "Let the troopers go! We've got to get out of here!"

No one heard her. She started for the stairs, then yelled back to RW, "Open that hatch and get ready to start the launch sequence!" Then she clattered down the stairs.

She elbowed her way through the melee and finally caught a glimpse of Vince ahead. "Vince !" she yelled. "Stop! Listen to me!"

A cruelly tight vise clamped around her upper arm, and she felt someone swing her around as if she were a hollow plastic doll. She found herself staring at a red-haired female Barney whose sea-green eyes showed no expression whatsoever. "Paris Joan," Jovanna breathed as she recognized the clone warrior and mystic.

Paris Joan's eyes flickered, and surprise came into them. When she spoke, her voice was calm and well modulated, in complete contrast to the mayhem around them. "Teacher. Why have you come?"

Jovanna waved her arm in the general direction of the *Hecate*. "You've got to stop fighting and get the Barneys into the cruiser in Bay Eight. The life support is failing for the whole station."

"But the RAM troopers—" Paris Joan began.

"Let them go!" Jovanna shouted. "You can fight RAM another day, but not if you don't all come right now!"

"I'll tell the others," said Paris Joan, making a small, formal bow. She closed her eyes and took two slow, deep breaths. Then she strode toward Potemkin and Matsuo. They were engaged with a knot of troopers who were trying to get past them to the ship.

Potemkin glanced at Paris Joan as he twisted the neck of a trooper. When the trooper slumped to the ground, she stepped over him toward Potemkin, her whole attitude one of relaxed concentration. A trooper ran up, apparently planning to attack Joan while her back was turned. Before Jovanna could shout a warning, Paris Joan backhanded the approaching trooper, lifting him off his feet. He landed several yards away.

After a short conversation with Joan, Potemkin nodded and stepped away from the *Hellas*'s hatch. Paris Joan turned to face out into the spaceport and uttered a high, keening wail that cut through even the insistent Klaxon, and the Barneys all turned to look. Potemkin raised his right hand, palm out, then pointed to Jovanna. "Follow me!" she yelled. For those who couldn't hear her, she made a broad beckoning gesture with her arm, then bounded back to the stairs that led up to the launch bay. Before she reached the stairs, Jovanna

heard the sound of running feet behind her. She felt a
hand snatch at her arm and began to run faster.

"Wait, Jo! It's me," yelled Vince. "What's happening?"

"Station life support . . . about to lose it," she puffed,
wishing she were in better shape. Vince nodded,
grabbed her arm, and pulled her up the stairs.

When they got to the top, Jovanna looked down. The
Barneys had abandoned the battle and were following
her. She turned and followed Vince through the hatch,
mentally thanking RW that she had remembered to
open it despite all the distractioins. She scrambled up
the ship's ladder, not stopping until she reached the control deck on the top level of the cruiser. Vince was already strapping himself into a chair. RW stood nearby.

"Vince, are we ready to go?"

"As soon as everyone's on board," snapped Vince.

Matsuo appeared in the ladder opening. "Where do
you want us, Teacher?"

Jovanna nudged Vince. "Several of the Barneys are
qualified on ship's operations. Need any help?"

Vince addressed Matsuo. "We need a communications
officer, a sensor operator, one or two of you in the engine
section, and six more on weapons stations. The rest of
you get to the crew quarters and strap in for takeoff."

Matsuo looked at Vince as if he were someone's pet
dog, then turned back to Jovanna. "Teacher?"

It was gratifying that the Barneys trusted her. She realized it was because she looked like RW, but they
might as well get used to trusting Vince. "Do whatever
Vince says." Matsuo disappeared down the opening.

Jovanna turned to Vince. "What should I do?"

"Strap yourself in," he said briefly, not taking his eyes
from the computer screen. She started to sit near him
but he barked, "Not there!" and waved vaguely toward
a seat near the hatch. She hurried over to it. Potemkin
and S'nee climbed into the control deck, taking positions on either side of Vince.

"RW, can you handle the station's part of the launch
sequence? I just need you to operate the bay doors. To

hell with clearance at this point," Vince said.

"Sure." RW wore an expression of calm concentration. "Are you ready?"

"As ready as I'll ever be," Vince said, settling his hands on the console before him.

"See you on Barbarosa," RW said.

"Right," Vince replied. RW waved briefly at Jovanna, then disappeared.

Jovanna felt her throat tighten. RW had been invaluable so far, and Jovanna wished she could travel on the *Hecate* with them. But like most digital personalities, RW used too much memory to be contained on a ship's computer. She'd reach Barbarosa by traveling through computer space. They'd have to survive without her.

A few seconds later, the ship vibrated with the pressure of the engine roaring to life. Jovanna clung tightly to her seat, as if her straps might fail. Then the thrust of the ship pushed her back into the seat more thoroughly than the straps or her own hands could ever do.

After a few moments, Vince looked away from his instruments and addressed Potemkin, who sat at the communications console. "Monitor communications back at the station. If you can pick anything up about the *Hellas*, I want to know about it."

"*Hellas* is transmitting," Potemkin said. "The signal is scrambled, though. I can't make any sense of it."

"I'll bet it's a RAM coded distress signal. Keep trying," Vince said. He turned to S'nee on his left. "Seen anything on radar?"

"Not yet. The *Hellas* hasn't moved."

"If we get another ten minutes away from Genesis before the *Hellas* launches, they'll never catch us," Vince pointed out.

After what seemed like hours, S'nee reported, "No launch from Genesis station." Jovanna let out a breath she hadn't been aware of holding. Vince grunted an acknowledgment and turned to Potemkin. "Get anything else on that signal from the *Hellas*?"

"Not yet," Potemkin said. "Wait. They've stopped transmitting."

"Why would they stop transmitting?" Vince asked.

Potemkin frowned, operated several instruments, and listened. "Because they're receiving."

"Receiving? From whom? Where?" Vince demanded.

"I can tell you, Captain," said S'nee from her seat at the radar station. She pointed at her screen. "About twelve spacecraft, on course to Genesis Station."

"Can you identify them?" The grim look on Vince's face indicated to Jovanna that he expected the worst.

A few seconds later, S'nee said, "They're RAM, Captain. Two battlers, four light cruisers, six medium cruisers. A regular small armada. RAM's serious about taking over Genesis."

"We already knew that," Vince said shortly. "Well, we'll just have to get past them. I hope your clone brothers have been able to convince the spaceport personnel on Gorgon Station to let us land there. That'll make life a lot easier." His hands flew over the controls. "Potemkin, order battle stations. I'll try to evade them."

"Vince!" Jovanna spoke for the first time since launch. "We can't fight all those ships!"

"You don't think so?" Vince asked in mock surprise. He jerked his head toward the two Barneys. "Let us worry about that, okay? Especially since the alternative is to end up like the people on Genesis."

Stung, Jovanna sat back in silence.

Vince swung the *Hecate* into a tightly banked curve. "That'll take us out of their immediate flight path," Vince said. "Let me know how many break off to follow us, S'nee."

S'nee nodded. After a minute, she said, "It looks like we got all four of the light cruisers and three of the mediums. The battlers are still in formation, though, heading for Genesis."

"Good," Vince said, glancing at the radar display. "On this flight path, we should be able to outrun those medium cruisers. We'll take out the light ones and be home free."

CHAPTER TWENTY ONE

A ll right, here's what we need to do," Vince said over his commlink. "I'm going to concentrate on evading those medium cruisers. I need the Barneys manning the weapons to take out the scout cruisers as fast as they can. With reasonable luck, we'll be out of range of the medium cruisers before they can do us any harm."

"Got it," growled one of the Barneys.

Vince glanced at the tactical display and saw the four small green blips representing scout cruisers split into two pairs and approach the *Hecate*. The first pair was coming in at four o'clock, while the second pair swung wide to come in on his tail. A pair of tiny points broke away from the green blips at four o'clock. "Ready lasers to take out incoming missiles at four o'clock," he said. "Now! Fire all weapons at will!"

At the order, Vince saw several green dots leave the circle that represented the *Hecate*. They sped toward the scout cruisers, who managed to destroy most of the incoming projectiles. The *Hecate* also destroyed one incoming missile at a distance. The other missile continued on toward them, and Vince braced himself just before an explosion shook the *Hecate*.

"Damage report!" he demanded.

"We've been hit in the engine section," Matsuo said over the link. "Nothing too bad. We're working on it."

S'nee, watching the tactical display, hooted triumphantly. "One of our K-cannon missiles hit a scout. She's drifting."

"Not for long," said an unidentified Barney over the commlink. "We'll finish her next time."

"No!" cried Vince. "Concentrate on the others. We don't have to kill them, just keep them from following us." He turned to S'nee. "Any other good news?"

"Looks like the other one at four o'clock took a hit, but she's still following."

Vince looked at the screen. The pursuing medium cruisers had lagged so far behind they were almost off the display, but the remaining scout cruiser at four o'clock was closing in, and the two who'd swung wide were now at six o'clock and matching his speed.

"Whoever's on the K-cannon, if you could take out that bandit at four o'clock, I'd appreciate it," Vince said. "Acceleration gun and starboard laser, back him up. All others, direct your sights at the pair on our tail."

Vince looked at his speed indicator, frustrated at the *Hecate*'s disappointing performance.

His piloting skill gave him no advantage now; *Hecate* was a tub compared to the streamlined scouts that pursued them. All he could do was let the Barneys deal with their enemies. He looked back at the tactical display. Another round of fire was being exchanged.

"Damn!" cursed a Barney over the commlink. "She took out our big missile."

"But I took out her incoming one," said another. "We'll get her next time."

Vince continued to watch the tactical screen as two more incoming missiles exploded some distance from the *Hecate*. "Nice work, aft lasers," Vince said. Then he saw two hits register on one enemy scout and three on the other. He watched to see if they were crippled, but they both kept coming. The remaining scout at four o'clock was closing fast.

Vince watched the display as more projectiles sped away from the *Hecate* and the three scouts who remained returned fire. A moment later, the cruiser that had been following them at four o'clock exploded into green fragments on his screen. Huge chunks of debris blew past the cockpit, and Vince heaved a sigh of relief. "One more down. Good job. Get the last two, and we're home free."

"We're working on it," a Barney's voice came back over the link. "But make that one, Captain."

At that instant, one of the ships on the *Hecate*'s tail turned into a rapidly disintegrating ball of green on the tactical display. "Three down, one to go," Vince said.

"Not for long," said the raspy voice Vince associated with the Barney manning the K-cannon. Another round of missile and laser fire burst from the *Hecate*, aimed at the lone scout on their tail. The scout returned fire, showing no signs of veering off.

"That scout's taken a lot of damage," S'nee said, reading a line of numbers at the top of the display. "You'd think they'd get the hint."

Vince couldn't believe what he was seeing. The scout and the *Hecate* became one large blip on the screen, as if the scout was intent on ramming their ship. "Doesn't make any sense," he muttered. The scout was too small to do much damage to the *Hecate*, and in a collision, the smaller ship would surely be destroyed. Then he realized what the scout must be attempting. It was getting close enough to train all its weapons on one area of the *Hecate*—probably the control section—and cripple her that way. *That* made sense; Vince might try it himself if he were a small ship attacking a larger one.

"Not today, sucker," he said, banking the *Hecate* away from the pursuing scout. An explosion shook the *Hecate*. A quick glance at his control panel told Vince that the ship had suffered no damage to her controls or sensors, but she seemed to have slowed considerably.

"We got the scout, captain," S'nee, on his left, said. Vince looked at the tactical screen and saw the floating green dots of their last enemy ship.

"Damage report," Vince said.

"That last hit gave us some bad problems with our engine," Matsuo said. "Nothing irreparable, but we'll be down for a while."

"How long?" Vince asked.

"Maybe an hour," Matsuo said.

"We need it in half that time," Vince said. The medium cruisers they'd evaded earlier weren't that far behind them.

"I'll do my best, but we're dealing with a radiation leak," Matsuo explained.

"Understood," Vince said. "All right, I'll take her deeper into the asteroid field, and we'll sit tight while you make repairs. Maybe they won't find us if we're not moving."

○ ○ ○ ○ ○

S'nee's tension communicated itself to Vince immediately. The gennie's posture became even straighter than usual.

"What is it?" Vince asked, though he had a good idea. It had been over an hour since they'd cut their engines, but the life support was still operating. Whether their energy use, or simply the heat of their bodies, had been detected, it made little difference.

"Three RAM medium cruisers. *Tikhov*, *Gale*, and *Graff*," she said. "And they're paying a lot of attention to us. I guess we don't look much like just another rock, after all."

A shrill whistle sounded from the commo board. "This is RMS *Tikhov*, Captain Podkayne commanding. Identify yourselves."

Potemkin raised a questioning eyebrow at Vince, who shook his head. "Don't respond. No point in making it too easy. . . . Matsuo," he called down to Engineering. "How are we doing?"

"Not bad, Captain," Matsuo's voice came over the link. "I just need to test out a few more things."

"Well, don't get involved in anything you can't drop

at short notice," Vince said. "We may need to move in a hurry."

"Company?" Matsuo said.

"We have the *Nina*, the *Pinta*, and the *Santa Maria* trying to decimate the Indians," Vince said.

The RAM captain's voice barked from the console. "We've identified you now, *Hecate*, not that there was ever much doubt. That ship is RAM property. If you surrender immediately, no one will get hurt."

Vince snorted, then called down to Matsuo again. "We've got to move now, Matsuo."

"Go ahead," Matsuo said.

Vince powered the thrusters and angled the *Hecate* away from the three RAM ships, navigating through the asteroids with precision. "Are they with us, S'nee?"

"They're still back there," she reported. Vince flew the *Hecate* into an area of the asteroid field where the rocks were closer together and more numerous. Once they got through this more treacherous part of the asteroid field, they'd have an almost clear shot to Gorgon Station. Vince expected that they'd have outrun the *Tikhov* and company long before the trip got easier. He had experience in navigating this section of space on his side, since he'd often made the trip to Gorgon Station.

"Those pilots are better than I thought," Vince muttered.

The RAM captain spoke again. "*Hecate*, we don't want to destroy the Barneys."

"We don't want that either, *Tikhov*," Vince said, continuing to thread his way through the asteroids as fast as he could safely manage. "Unfortunately, it's hard for us to believe you after a RAM squad destroyed all life on Genesis."

"That was an error. The guilty parties will be punished."

"We can believe that," Potemkin said over the open channel.

"Rest assured, we'll conduct a full inquiry into the incident on Genesis," *Tikhov*'s commander said. "We believe the Barneys have been misled by enemies of the state, so I'm sure you won't be held responsible. We'll find new owners for you, and you'll be able to contribute to society."

"Why doesn't that make me feel any better?" Potemkin commented dryly.

The *Hecate* cleared the worst of the asteroid field, and Vince was considering whether to turn back into it when a glance at the tactical screen told him that he'd have difficulty making it past the three RAM ships arrayed against him. They had kept pace, but Vince knew they had no fuel to waste after their long space voyage. If he could stall *Tikhov*'s attack until they could no longer pursue, he might live to tell his grandchildren about this.

The voice of the *Tikhov*'s commander turned steely. "I'm getting tired of this. I'd prefer not to kill you, but my orders are clear. You pose a threat to RAM security. We take you into custody or destroy you. It's up to you."

S'nee grabbed Vince's arm and signaled him to look at the tactical display. Another lone ship had appeared there, heading for the *Hecate* at twelve o'clock.

"Identify," Vince mouthed to S'nee, then addressed the *Tikhov*. "You make a good point, Commander. None of us wants anything unfortunate to happen."

"Then cut speed and come around. We'll escort you back to Genesis."

Vince looked at his companions. The Barneys were clearly against surrendering. Jovanna looked terrified, but when she saw him looking at her, she clamped her lips together and tried to look brave.

A chime sounded on the combat tactical sensor, and Vince turned to examine the readout. The new ship was listed as the *Medusa*, a heavy cruiser bristling with armaments and registered to Hugo Dracolysk. Apparently the RAM cruisers had radioed Dracolysk for help.

The last thing they needed was yet another enemy ship bearing down on them. The situation had looked bad enough before. With another heavily armed ship against them, they didn't have a prayer. The Barneys wouldn't like it, but he had no choice but to surrender.

Surely one day some of them would escape from RAM.

Vince could feed RAM some story about taking Jovanna hostage. If they bought it, she wouldn't have to suffer much. The only one he knew wouldn't escape RAM's wrath was himself, but that couldn't be helped. He spoke carefully, avoiding the eyes of the others on the control deck. "I'm cutting speed, *Tikhov.* I'll come around as soon as you inform your reinforcements about my actions. I don't want them taking any potshots at us."

"What reinforcements?" *Tikhov*'s commander said.

"That big freaking—" Vince stopped suddenly. *Tikhov* must not be in communication with the *Medusa.* He thanked a merciful providence for RAM's internal distrust or whatever it was that had kept the *Medusa* from contacting the RAM cruisers. *Medusa* would be out of *Tikhov*'s sensor range for several more minutes. Vince decided to try a sudden, steep climb. If it worked, it would leave the *Medusa* and the three RAM medium cruisers staring at each other, scrambling to figure out what had happened. Vince winked at S'nee, then addressed *Tikhov*'s commander again. "My mistake. I was certain you'd radioed back to your fleet for help by now."

"Listen, you nasty little pile of terrorist scum," *Tikhov*'s commander said, "you'll never see the day I need reinforcements to deal with the likes of you."

"Now, now, don't get testy. I'm coming around now, sir," Vince said.

Vince started his swing a little wider than necessary, then pulled *Hecate*'s nose up sharply. *Tikhov*'s commander communicated his displeasure immediately, firing a barrage of missiles at the *Hecate.* The *Medusa* continued on her heading, straight toward the space *Hecate* had just occupied and now facing the three medium cruisers head-on. "Releasing chaff," came the welcome message from a Barney on weapons deck. One explosion followed another as the missiles came into contact with the chaff field. After several moments, S'nee announced, "All incoming missiles destroyed."

"Nice job," Vince called down to the weapons deck. He turned back to S'nee. "Do we have any company yet?"

"*Tikhov* and company are turning to pursue," S'nee reported. "*Medusa* is continuing on her present heading."

"What the—? Why?" Vince looked at the screen and turned to Potemkin. "Monitor communications between *Medusa* and *Tikhov*." By this time, *Tikhov* had *Medusa* in sensor range. Whatever came of the exchange between ships, Vince wanted to hear it.

"This is RMS *Tikhov*," its commander was saying. "Our sensors identify you as RMS *Medusa*, registered to Dracolysk Corporation. Confirm, please."

"Confirm this, *Tikhov*!" replied a deep, growling voice. It sounded somehow familiar, reminding Vince of Potemkin's voice, only it was more menacing.

"Vince, the *Medusa* has fired on the *Tikhov*," S'nee blurted.

The communication between the *Tikhov* and the *Medusa* continued as the growling voice said, "This vessel has been renamed the *Free Enterprise*, Black Barney commanding. But you can call me 'sir,' you RAM tub jockey."

His statement was followed by several explosions. "The *Tikhov* has taken two hits," S'nee reported gleefully.

Vince looked at Jovanna. "Could that really be Black Barney?"

"I recognize the voice," Jovanna said. "And if you're asking if Black Barney could steal a ship from Gorgon Station, the answer is yes."

"*Tikhov* is returning fire," S'nee reported. "The other RAM ships are moving to encircle the *Medu*—the *Free Enterprise*."

"Can he fight his way out?" Jovanna said.

"He's outgunned right now. Let's even things up," Vince said. He swung the *Hecate* around and headed back to the battle.

S'nee yelped triumphantly, and Vince glanced at the tactical display to see why. The *Tikhov* no longer existed; green specks like dust motes were dissipating away from the area where it had been the last time Vince had looked. However, the *Free Enterprise* had taken several hits.

"Black Barney, this is the *Hecate*, from Genesis Station. We've come to assist you," Potemkin said over the communit. If there was any reply from the *Free Enterprise*, it was lost in her next round of attacks. Her K-cannons and missile launchers roared just moments before she launched a load of radar-confusing chaff. The resulting static made communication impossible, but Vince guessed his message had gotten through, since the *Free Enterprise*'s next attack concentrated on the two remaining RAM cruisers.

Vince could see that RMS *Gale* had some bad hull damage as he got closer. The *Graff* didn't look particularly bad. He decided to attack the *Gale* first, reasoning that once she was out of the way, he and Barney could finish off the *Graff* at their leisure. "Target the *Gale*," he said into his commlink as he brought the *Hecate* around to bear on her.

Committed to attacking the *Free Enterprise*, the *Gale* didn't have time to change her tactics. She managed to get one missile off, targeted on Barney's ship before receiving a full barrage of hits from both the *Hecate* and the *Free Enterprise*. The *Gale*'s hull, already damaged, burst apart in a spray of orange fire.

"Great minds with but a single thought," Black Barney said over the commlink. Vince heard an explosion through the link, but the *Free Enterprise* still remained on the screen.

"Barney? Are you all right?" Vince asked.

"I'm fine," Barney replied, but his voice sounded strained. "Now, let's take out that last one so we can get out of here."

"I don't think so. You look like you're in bad shape, *Free Enterprise*," the RAM commander mocked. "You're history the next time we hit you."

Vince brought the nose of the *Hecate* around to gain a better approach to the combat area and saw what the

captain meant about the *Free Enterprise*. She had taken
damage to her hull and engine, and one of the K-
cannons the *Free Enterprise* had been using to such dev-
astating effect had been hit, leaving a charred lump in
its place. "Don't underestimate the *Hecate*," Vince said
into his link, hoping to divert the *Graff*'s attention.

As if on cue, the Barneys on the *Hecate*'s weapons
deck let loose a barrage of missiles and laser fire. Unfortunately a pair of missiles already released from the
Graff were speeding toward the *Free Enterprise*.

"Come on, Black Barney, launch your chaff," Vince
urged under his breath. Barney needed to protect the
Free Enterprise, not worry about attacking the *Graff*.
But apparently Black Barney preferred offense to defense, which somehow didn't surprise Vince. A missile
sped from the remaining K-cannon of the *Free Enterprise*, but the *Graff* was hit before it could arrive as the
Hecate's weapons began to take their toll on the *Graff*,
battering her hull and destroying part of her engine.

An explosion blossomed near the forward section of
the *Free Enterprise*, followed seconds later by another,
but the *Free Enterprise* was still there. "Barney, you're
one lucky gennie," Vince said over the link. "Now will
you let me take care of the *Graff* and get yourself out of
range?"

There was no response from the *Free Enterprise*. Before Vince could repeat his question, the K-cannon pro-
jectile from the *Free Enterprise* struck the *Graff*, and
she went up in a roiling sphere of flames.

"All right, Barney, you did it!" Vince exclaimed.
There was still no response from the *Free Enterprise*.
Vince looked at Potemkin, who said, "We're transmitting. They should be reading us." Potemkin examined
the communit's controls and repeated, "*Free Enterprise*,
do you copy? *Free Enterprise*, this is the *Hecate*. Come
in."

A few moments later, a throaty female voice shouted
as if she were some distance from the communit, "I
copy, *Hecate*. Our control deck is in pretty bad shape."

Vince's elation vanished with the news. If the control

deck was that badly damaged, they couldn't hope to repair the *Free Enterprise* before every RAM ship within fifty thousand miles had come to investigate. But even more importantly, Vince wondered why Barney hadn't answered. "Any casualties?" he asked.

"I don't know," the female voice said. "Black Barney looks pretty bad, but I'm having trouble getting close enough to tell for sure. Request assistance."

"We copy," Vince said. "Prepare the crew to abandon ship. Repeat: prepare to abandon ship. We'll send a medic and a team over to assist."

"I copy," the voice said.

Vince looked expectantly at Potemkin. "Can you assemble a team?"

"You damn betcha," Potemkin replied, rising.

Vince concentrated on maneuvering through the debris from the RAM cruisers toward the *Free Enterprise* so the rescue could be performed as efficiently as possible. He heard a familiar voice, sounding small after the full, heavy voices of the Barneys. "Can I help?"

Vince turned and saw Jovanna sitting in her seat by the ladder. He had forgotten, during combat, that she was even there. "Have you ever used a rocket belt?"

She looked at him uncertainly and said, "I don't think so."

He rolled his eyes. "Jovanna, either you have or you haven't."

She looked embarrassed. "Well . . . no, then."

"This isn't the time to learn. Just try to stay out of the way," he said. She looked angry, but Vince didn't have time to baby her now. He turned his attention back to the controls. "Oh, hell, she's drifting! S'nee, get a readout of the *Free Enterprise*'s angle of drift, will you? I'll try to stay with her."

Vince tried to match the *Free Enterprise*'s speed and direction until S'nee produced the readout, then programmed the flight computer to match the crippled ship's path.

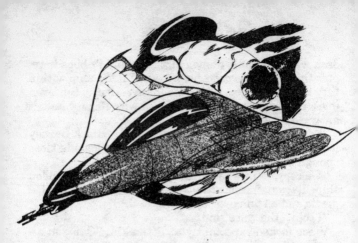

CHAPTER TWENTY TWO

Jovanna woke to a hand on her shoulder. She sat up, blinked her eyes open, and squinted into the darkness of her cabin. "Vince? Is that you?"

"Yeah. We're cleared to land on Barbarosa. Before we do, see if you can raise RW to look for our NEO contact."

"You mean you don't know where we're going? I thought you had a plan," Jovanna said testily. She was still angry with Vince. Ever since they'd boarded the *Hecate*, he'd treated her like an idiot.

Vince spoke with deliberate patience, as if she were three years old. "Beowulf had a plan. I'm just doing the best I can, considering the fact that I have no support."

Jovanna ground her teeth. What was she if she wasn't support? Maybe she couldn't shoot guns or fly spaceships, but Vince would never have made it this far without her, nor would the Barneys have come with them if it hadn't been for her. She had half a mind to leave Vince on his own as soon as they landed, but she had no idea how to get around on Barbarosa. The place was rumored to be full of cutthroats and thieves.

"You can use the computer on the bridge to contact RW." Vince crossed her small cabin and stood in the doorway. The light outlining his body hurt her eyes. She remembered how she thought Vince looked like an angel when they first met. Now she had no such illusions. He looked at her impatiently. "Are you coming?"

She wanted to tell him to contact RW herself, but she decided she'd prove she could be professional even if he didn't appreciate it. "Yes, I'm coming," she grumbled.

O   O   O   O   O

As Vince and the Barneys prepared the *Hecate* for landing, Jovanna established a link to the Barbarosa computer network. Her companions were busy, so she had time to browse through the network to see how it was organized. The Barbarosa net tapped into RAM Main. There was access to Infonet, Mediabloc, and the other major services of the largest computer in the solar system, but it seemed that nearly half the transactions on Barbarosa were protected by some degree of security, a higher proportion than Jovanna had ever seen before.

As she was scrolling notices to see if RW had left a message for her, she saw one for Farm Boy. "Vince!"

"What is it?" Vince said, coming to stand next to her.

"Could that be for you?" Jovanna asked, pointing.

"I certainly hope so," Vince said. He nudged her, apparently wanting her to relinquish her seat to him.

"Did you want me to move?" she asked, annoyed.

He looked puzzled. "Yes . . . if you don't mind."

"Help yourself," she said, springing out of the seat.

Vince looked at her with a puzzled expression, then shook his head and sat at the console. He entered the access number that was displayed in the "Farm Boy" message, then typed, "FARM BOY HERE."

After several moments, a line appeared under Vince's. "WHAT IS YOUR BIRTH DATE?"

"02-23-24" he typed.

"GLAD YOU MADE IT, HERMANO," replied the screen. "IT'S BEEN A ROUGH FEW WEEKS."

Vince reached out, grabbed Jovanna's hand, and held it tightly. She looked at him, puzzled, and he pointed at the screen. "Don't you see that? It's Hermano!"

"Yes, I see it. What's wrong?" she asked.

"Wrong? Nothing's wrong. That's Beowulf!" He jumped up and hugged her. Then he seemed to notice what he was doing and let go of her self-consciously. He cleared his throat, and a foolish grin spread over his face. "We used to call each other 'Hermano' about a hundred years ago."

He returned to the computer. "WHAT'S NEXT, HERMANO?"

"FIND A BAR CALLED ACHERON IN TORTUGA STREET. ASK FOR ME."

"I COPY." Vince typed, then signed off. He stood and turned to Jovanna. "Let's go."

"Go where? We have twenty-six Barneys along, and four of them are badly hurt," Jovanna said. "Do we parade them through the streets?"

"We'll wait here," Potemkin broke in. "None of the injuries are too serious. Even Black Barney is stable."

Vince looked at Jovanna. "See?"

"I don't—" Jovanna began, but S'nee interrupted.

"We'll live," the dark female said. She winked. "You two run along. Have a good time."

"Come on." Vince grabbed Jovanna's hand, ignoring the objection she was starting to form.

O O O O O

Barbarosa lived up to its reputation as far as Jovanna was concerned. The asteroid was a haven for every pirate, smuggler, and outlaw in the solar system. There were also tourists, rockhoppers from all over the Asteroid Belt, and an occasional Martian who enjoyed slumming. The wealthier, and more cautious, visitors stayed and played in the entertainment dome at the opposite end of the hundred-mile-long asteroid from the spaceport dome. Only those less fortunate or those with covert business ever strayed into Barbarosa's unevenly lit interior tunnels.

Tortuga Street, beneath the spaceport dome, thronged with seedy inhabitants who had nothing better to do than lounge outside gambling dens, brothels, pawn-shops, and tenements. Jovanna tried not to walk too close to Vince. First of all, she hated to earn any more of his disdain, and secondly, she had the feeling that the denizens of Tortuga Street could smell fear a mile away and would not hesitate to take advantage of it.

Vince had already given her a rocket pistol and hol-ster to attach to her utility belt. She tried not to think about what might happen if she had to use it. Vince had looked amused when he gave it to her. "You probably won't need this, but we're asking for trouble if you go underground without it. Try to look as if you know what it's for." Jovanna grimaced and held back a reply.

"Here we are," Vince said, pointing to a pair of black doors. On the right door, in simple block lettering, was the word, "Acheron."

Jovanna followed Vince closely as he approached the doors. The doors didn't open at his approach, although they looked like the usual automatic doors.

"What do you want?" a surly, throaty baritone voice said from a speaker beside the doors.

"Friendly, aren't you?" Vince said sarcastically.

"You want friendly, get on the monorail and go to the pleasure dome," came the discouraging reply.

"I thought this was supposed to be a bar. How do you survive if you won't let customers in?" Vince asked.

"We're more on the order of a private club." The voice sounded amused. "To join, you need to be recommended. Now, if you can find a member to recommend you, tour-ist, then we'll open up. Otherwise don't waste my time."

Vince's frown disappeared. "Is Beowulf a member?"

After a pause, the voice said, "Are you by any chance Farm Boy?"

"Farm Boy it is," Vince said. The doors slid open, re-vealing a long, dark room dominated by a bar. Several small round tables stood along the room's length. At the far end, Jovanna could just make out a curving stair-case leading up. A lone female bartender, mostly re-markable for the depths to which her neckline plunged, stood looking at them as she polished a glass.

"Welcome to Acheron," she said. Jovanna tried not to stare. It was the same baritone voice they'd heard over the speaker. Other than her remarkable cleavage and the timbre of her voice, she seemed ordinary enough. She was reasonably attractive, but no knockout.

A door behind the bar slid open. A small, dark-haired girl sauntered out and stared at them curiously.

"Why are you out here?" the woman asked sternly.

"I want a snack." The girl was looking from Jovanna to Vince, a winsome smile curving her lips.

"Get back inside and finish your lesson," the woman said.

"But, Ma—"

"You heard me." The child turned and stomped back through the door. The woman looked at Vince. "You looking for Beowulf? He's upstairs."

"Thanks," Vince said, pulling Jovanna toward the dimly lit stairs. She nearly tripped in the darkness. At the top of the stairway, a door slid open to admit them.

The hall was lined on the left side with doors. The first door opened, and a short, solid man with black hair, prematurely gray at the temples, hobbled toward Vince, supporting himself with a cane. He embraced Vince with one arm. "Good to see you, Hermano." He smiled at Jovanna. "And you must be Jovanna. I'm Beowulf. It's good to finally meet you. Come on in."

They entered a small, well-lit room with an unmade bed, a small chest with a compdex on top, and a table with two chairs. Beowulf apologized as he quickly straightened the bed. "Sit down and tell me what happened. I've heard about the takeover on Infonet, but as you know, we've been pretty busy ourselves."

"What happened to you?" Vince asked.

"The limp is only temporary," Beowulf said. "RAM made a simultaneous raid on most of our Earth-based headquarters just before you learned they were planning to take over Wydlin Corporation. We had to scatter, and what little communication we still have is through the computer matrix. A few of us are on Barbarosa. I was afraid I'd never see you again, Hermano."

Vince smiled crookedly at his mentor. "Surprised?"

"Vince, if it had been anyone but you, I'd have said it couldn't be done."

"I had help." Vince said and gestured toward Jovanna, who was surprised by the praise, however faint. "And if it hadn't been for Dekalb, we'd probably never have made it. Have you heard anything from him?"

Beowulf's smile faded. "Not a word. What happened?"

Vince told the story of the rebellion and escape, and then Beowulf filled Vince in on RAM's attack on NEO's Earth-based headquarters. Jovanna's attention wandered as Vince asked about people she didn't know and installations she'd never heard of. She came back to the conversation with a start when she realized they were talking about Wydlin Corporation again.

"Dekalb told me not to worry about him, but I can't help it. It's hard to believe he's all right," Vince said.

"Do you want me to look for him?" Jovanna said. Beowulf looked at her questioningly, so she explained. "On the computer network, I mean. I may be able to find out which Wydlin personnel survived the RAM raid." While she was checking, maybe she could find out what had happened to Dr. Wydlin as well.

Beowulf shook his head. "I only knew him by his code name, Dekalb." He turned to Vince. "Iroquois was his contact at NEO, just as you were mine. And Iroquois was killed in Chicagorg."

"Do you have a clue to Dekalb's identity?" Jovanna asked.

"I believe he worked in the financial division at Wydlin. Most of the information Iroquois got from him related to financial concerns."

"That's a start," Jovanna said, going to the compdex.

"Wait, Jovanna," Beowulf said. She turned to look at him, and he said, "I already know who survived the Wydlin takeover."

Jovanna didn't like Beowulf's tone. She tried to ask, but somehow she couldn't make the question come out.

"You lived through it and so did Vince." Beowulf put one hand on top of Jovanna's, as if trying to comfort her.

"The broadcasters on Infonet had Vince's name since it was on the flight orders he used to get the escape ship. They didn't know your name, and they could only guess at the number of Barneys."

Jovanna recovered her voice enough to say, "Were we the only ones?"

"Yes," Beowulf said.

"What about on Mars?" Vince asked. "Dr. Wydlin should have been on Mars at the time of the takeover. What happened to him?"

"He never arrived on Mars," Beowulf said. "It's hard to piece the truth together from Infonet stories, but RAM reported they intercepted a ship registered to the Wydlins near Jupiter. There was combat, and the Wydlin ship was destroyed. RAM, of course, is saying the Wydlin ship fired on them first—"

"Sure," said Vince, obviously skeptical.

"It wasn't till later that they figured out that Dr. Wydlin was aboard the ship," Beowulf said. "By that time, they'd already searched both stations for him and tried to exact cooperation from the Wydlin employees in their inimitable RAM style. The whole operation was a public relations coup for RAM."

"How?" Vince frowned.

"The entire Wydlin Corporation, and the threat it posed to the security of the Martian people, was 'sterilized.' That's the official Infonet line, of course. What it means is that when RAM didn't get exactly what they wanted from the employees immediately, they simply killed everyone in the corporation."

"Noah Wydlin?" Vince asked.

"Well, there's a bright spot," Beowulf said. When Jovanna looked at him hopefully, he shook his head. "No, I'm sorry. I didn't mean that Noah lived. I just meant that the little rebellion you had the Barneys stage on Gorgon Station took all of Dracolysk Corporation with it. The station was destroyed along with everyone on it."

"No loss there," Vince said. "Except possibly for Noah Wydlin."

Jovanna said nothing. Maybe Vince thought it was good that a whole station was destroyed, but she didn't see how the destruction of Gorgon Station was less of a tragedy than Genesis. There had been innocent people in both places. Perhaps Vince didn't think any Martians could be considered innocent. She wondered what he thought of her now that their operation was over.

"You did manage to save some of the Barneys, though," Beowulf said into the silence.

"Twenty-six." Vince roused himself. "One of them is Black Barney—the one we planted the signal chip in."

"Good," said Beowulf. "Maybe someday that will come in handy. If NEO ever recovers, that is."

"It's that bad?" Jovanna asked.

Vince stared at her. "Haven't you been listening? Iroquois, the general, and over half the Command Council were killed. Our best Earth bases were destroyed. We're in worse shape than when we first banded together."

Jovanna blushed and made no reply. Beowulf patted her shoulder. "Lay off her, Vince. Let's think about what needs to be done right away and worry about restructuring NEO later."

"You're right," Vince said. "And the first problem is the Barneys."

"The original plan was to try to recruit them," Beowulf explained. "There's not much left to recruit them to, but we can try. They'd make a real difference to NEO right now."

"All right, we'll go work on it," Vince said.

"You get started on that," Beowulf said, "and I'll contact whatever other NEO people I can find. If we're going to try to bring the Barneys into the organization, we'd better have it look as if there *is* an organization."

"Right. Come on, Jo," Vince said.

"Wait a minute." Beowulf held up his hand. "Jovanna was brought into NEO more or less by accident. She could walk away right now and probably talk her way back into Martian society." He looked at Jovanna. "We can sure use you, Jovanna. I just want to make sure it's your choice."

Jovanna hadn't realized she had a choice. She figured
Vince would tell Beowulf she wasn't NEO material. He
seemed to have forgotten the help she'd given him on
Genesis Statioin. She feared he'd always think of her as
a Martian and therefore somehow untrustworthy.

But if Jovanna had needed anything else to convince
her that she wanted to stay with NEO, Beowulf had just
said it. She knew so much already that she could, by reporting to RAM, destroy what little was left of NEO.
Beowulf apparently trusted her not to do it. She smiled
at him. "Count me in."

$$\bigcirc \quad \bigcirc \quad \bigcirc \quad \bigcirc \quad \bigcirc$$

Vince clanged the hatch of the *Hecate* closed behind
them and yelled, "We're back!" There was no reply. He
looked at Jovanna. "What could the Barneys be up to?"

"How do I know?" Her voice was cold, and Vince
looked at her closely. She hadn't been the same since
they'd escaped from Genesis, but he figured he was
over whatever was bothering her when she committed
herself to NEO. Now he wasn't so sure.

She brushed past him and began to climb the ship's
ladder. "Let's find them."

He shook his head at her moodiness and followed her.
Their footsteps echoed through the ship. Finally, on the
medical level, they heard signs of life.

A familiar voice floated out from the infirmary. "And
then just when I thought the sentry program would hit
me with an energy bolt, it zapped right past. It never
even saw me."

"RW?" Jovanna said expectantly, going through the
door. Vince followed close behind and saw RW leaning
on the edge of Black Barney's berth. The Master Pirate
was asleep, probably lulled by RW's incessant chatter.

"Boy, am I glad to see you!" the digital personality
said. "This guy is no fun at all."

"He almost died," Jovanna said. "Where have you
been, anyway? And where are the other Barneys?"

"I hid out in the matrix until you landed," RW said. "I

found out something really interesting, but by the time I got here to tell you, you'd already left. So I told the Barneys instead."

"What exactly did you tell them?" Vince asked.

"That RAM Internal Affairs Division is really interested in the *Hecate*. They're sending someone here to investigate."

Jovanna turned pale, but Vince couldn't worry about her nerves just then. "Where are the Barneys?"

"They left," RW said. "The other three injured ones could walk, so the rest took them along. Lilith said she'd be back for Black Barney as soon as she found someplace safe for him. But that was a couple of hours ago. That IAD team could arrive any time now."

"We have to get out of here," Vince said grimly.

"Where to? Acheron?" Jovanna asked.

"You took the words right out of my mouth," Vince said. "Let's get Black Barney out of here while we still can."

O O O O O

Jovanna rapped lightly at Black Barney's door. There was no answer, which surprised her. Black Barney had been almost completely healed last night when she had last seen him. He'd complained of cabin fever, despite the fact that not too many hours earlier he'd been unable to walk ten yards without help. She had planned to ask him if he wanted to get out for a while, an opportunity she thought he'd leap at.

Vince had said something last night about finding a job on a pirate cruiser for Black Barney. He'd left a couple of hours ago to speak to a pirate captain. If he had any luck and Barney agreed, the super-gennie could be on the ship by tonight. She knocked louder. There was still no answer.

Something was definitely not right. Jovanna punched the access code into the keypad beside Barney's door and watched it slide open. As she feared, the room was empty. She ran down the hall to Beowulf's room and

hammered at his door. After a moment, it slid open and
she went inside.

"Jovanna," Beowulf said. "What's the matter?"

"It's Black Barney," she said. "He's not in his room."

Beowulf grabbed his cane. He was moving better than
he had two days ago when they first came to Barbarosa,
but he still needed more time to heal properly. "Damn!
Did he leave on his own?"

"I—don't know." Jovanna wondered why Beowulf
would expect her to know.

Beowulf got to his feet. "Let's check his room and see
if there are any signs of a struggle. If someone abducted
him, though, it's unlikely we wouldn't have heard
something." He started across the room. "He probably
just decided to leave like the other Barneys did. Maybe
he left us some clues."

Just then the hall door chime sounded, and Beowulf's
vidscreen filled with Vince's image.

"Good!" Beowulf said. "Vince can help us search. Let
him in, will you, Jo?"

Jovanna pressed a few compdex keys and went to wait
at Beowulf's door. Vince entered through the hall door,
followed by Black Barney. "Lady, our problems are
solved!" Vince said, grinning.

"You mean Barney was with you?" Jovanna said,
looking from Vince to Barney and back again.

"I wasn't about to let Pirelli arrange my life until I
saw this ship he was talking about. It'll do," said Black
Barney.

"We were worried about you," Jovanna said, then realized she was probably the only one who had been worried. She sat down, determined not to say anything else
to embarrass herself.

"Sorry," Vince said. "I didn't even know Barney was
following me. He didn't let on until I was in the spaceport dome. He should make an exceptional pirate."

"So what happened?" Beowulf asked.

"The captain of the *Rusty Scupper* is willing to give
Barney a try."

"No big surprise," Beowulf said. "Barney's the best

warrior they're ever likely to see. When do you start, Barney?"

"Today," Barney said.

"But that's not the best part," Vince said. "We convinced the captain that Barney was the answer to his prayers but that we needed a favor before Barney would agree to come on board."

"What—?" Beowulf began.

"We've been wondering what to do about Jovanna, right?" Vince said.

Jovanna stared from Vince to Beowulf, unaware that they'd been making her a topic of discussion. "You've been talking about me? When?" she asked. Beowulf looked embarrassed.

Nonplussed, Vince went on. "Anyway, the captain said he'd take Jovanna to Mars with a story about finding her in a survival pod in the Asteroid Belt. His crew will back him up. So, Jo, you'll be able to go back and work for RAM."

Jovanna's mouth dropped open. So they had her future all mapped out, did they? "What if I don't want to work for RAM?"

Beowulf put his hand on her arm. "It was mostly my idea, Jo. I'm sorry we didn't ask your opinion sooner, but I didn't expect Pirelli to move this quickly."

Jovanna looked at Vince with disgust. "Yeah, he's a regular ball of fire, isn't he?"

"But, Jo," Beowulf said, "if you could get a job with RAM, we'll have a better chance of staying a step ahead of them. I'm not excited about reorganizing NEO just to have RAM squash us again."

"But I'd be all alone. I thought I could be with you for a while." When she realized she was looking straight at Vince, she quickly looked away.

"Jovanna, to get RAM to accept you, we have to move quickly," Beowulf said. "If you're missing for too long, they'll wonder where you've been and what you've been doing."

"We have a pretty good story for you—about how I used you for a hostage—but the longer you're gone, the less likely RAM is to accept it," Vince said.

"You're just trying to get rid of me," Jovanna accused him. "You think I'm worthless because I can't shoot or use a rocket belt like you can. If it hadn't been for me—"

Beowulf interrupted her. "Jo, you're wrong. Vince recommended training to make up for some of your deficiencies, but we both really want you in NEO."

Beowulf made Jovanna feel a little better, but not much. She looked down at her hands. "How am I supposed to get this NEO training while I'm working for RAM?"

"We have another operative on Mars," Beowulf said. "She'll meet you occasionally for training sessions once you feel confident RAM trusts you."

"What will you be doing?" Jovanna asked Vince. She bet he wasn't going to be hidden in some boring job.

"I'm on the task force to find a new headquarters for NEO," Vince answered. "Then I'm supposed to help recruit and train new pilots."

"Listen, Teacher," growled Barney, "while you hang around here arguing, I'm getting calluses on my butt. Either do what they say so I can start work on the *Clogged Drainpipe*—"

"*Rusty Scupper*," Vince corrected.

"—or I'll just walk," Barney continued, staring at Vince expressionlessly.

Vince turned to Jovanna. "Well, Jo?" Jovanna hoped that, despite the impatience Vince had shown with her during the trip to Barbarosa, he'd remember how much help she'd been on Genesis Station and they'd work together again. Vince had been her first real friend since Rachel Wydlin, and she would miss him. But judging by the expression on his face, the feeling wasn't mutual.

She looked at the others. Barney looked back at her with his characteristic unrevealing expression. Beowulf just seemed anxious.

She threw up her hands. "All right," she said. "I'll try."

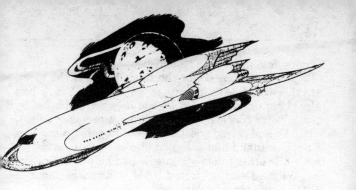

CHAPTER TWENTY THREE

Twenty-one years had passed since the survivors of RAM's takeover of Genesis had gone their separate ways.

Vince stood at attention and checked his blue uniform. His mirror reassured him that, despite his forty-three years, he was still trim, muscular, and clear-eyed. It hadn't been easy to accomplish, considering he hadn't flown an active mission in over two years.

On the way to his appointment with Beowulf, he realized he wasn't the only NEO officer who had brushed up on his spit-and-polish. All of Salvation, NEO's main military installation, had taken a new lease on life since NEO and its allies had bested RAM in confrontations near Earth and later off Vesta in the Asteroid Belt.

Vince had to give the credit to Buck Rogers. When the twentieth-century fighter pilot had been revived after nearly five hundred years in a cryogenic capsule, he'd immediately conceived of one risky scheme after another, each calculated to bring RAM's wrath down on NEO. Contrary to Vince's—and almost everyone else's—expectations, everything Rogers touched turned to gold. Thanks to Buck Rogers, RAM had finally acceded to

Earth's demands for independence.

Rogers had come in for the lion's share of the glory, but there had been plenty to go around. Vince had missed out on all of it. He wished he wasn't affected by such a petty concern, but it rankled him nevertheless. When he had raised questions about Rogers's plans early on, Command had assigned him to remain on Salvation while other pilots—people he had helped train, like Col. Wilma Deering—forced RAM to knuckle under to NEO's long-standing demands.

Vince had been left out of the most important events in NEO's history. Having suffered through it, he had no intention of letting his life continue on its current course. It wasn't all over yet with RAM.

They had shown how well they could be trusted when they agreed to let Earth resume its own government and then kidnapped its new governing body and laid waste to its major cities in one massive, well-coordinated attack.

NEO still needed people who could ferret out RAM's stratagems, and Vince knew he was one of those people. He was going to ask to be reassigned to Intelligence.

Outside Beowulf's office, he paused to take a deep breath, then rapped at the door.

"Come in," Beowulf's familiar voice called as the door slid open. Beowulf looked up as he entered, and Vince realized his old commander wasn't getting any younger either. His hair, once gray only at the temples, was now the color of steel. Despite Beowulf's best efforts to stay in shape, his waist had gotten thicker. "Hello, Vince. Excuse me—Major Pirelli." Beowulf sounded amused as he took in Vince's formal appearance. "What can I do for you?"

"Sir, I've come to request a change in assignment."

Beowulf frowned. "You having problems where you are? Hamilton hasn't said anything."

Colonel Hamilton was Vince's superior officer in the Training Corps and a reasonable man to work for. "No, sir. That's not it," Vince assured Beowulf. "I'd just like to make more of a difference to the organization. There are plenty of competent pilots who can teach flying."

"But there's something you feel you can do better than the ordinary pilot?" Beowulf said. "What is it?"

"I want to be reassigned to Intelligence," Vince said.

Beowulf nodded thoughtfully. "That's a bit more exciting than nurse-maiding young pilots. I thought you seemed frustrated about that when all the excitement around Hauberk and Vesta was going on."

Vince said nothing. He was as good as any of the pilots who had taken part in those battles, yet his own big mouth had kept him out of them. He'd learned caution from that experience.

"Our Intelligence Division has gone through some significant changes, Vince. NEO has now become a highly visible political entity, and there are those who say we shouldn't engage in subterfuge anymore," Beowulf said, shaking his head. "As if all of RAM's actions are completely aboveboard."

"What are you saying? That we have no Intelligence Division anymore?"

"Not at all. It still exists," Beowulf said. "But we've found we have to be more subtle. Which is not one of your strong points, I'm afraid."

"What do you mean? I've shown I can infiltrate. What about my work at Wydlin Corporation?"

"Twenty-one years ago, Vince," Beowulf reminded him. "You're a little out of practice, don't you think?"

"I'll pick it up again," Vince said.

Beowulf looked at Vince through narrowed eyes, as if trying to gauge just how much to say. "What if I told you we have a project in mind that you might be qualified for? It'll require initiative, but you're not short on that. None of NEO's old guard has forgotten how you spirited the Barneys away from RAM."

Beowulf's mention of an event that was so far in the past made Vince feel ancient, but he made himself focus on the subject at hand. "Can you tell me anything else about this project?"

"We need a group of agents to work out of the Asteroid Belt," Beowulf said. "However, the way we envision it

now, it would entail your working with Jovanna Trask
again. Would that be a problem?"

Vince blinked. He knew Jovanna still worked for
NEO, but he'd lost track of her after all these years.
Still, he had nothing against her. If anything, it was the
other way around. She'd made no secret of her annoy-
ance at being sent back to Mars, and he felt that she
held him responsible. He hadn't heard from her since
they had parted company after the Wydlin affair, and he
hadn't wanted to invite her recriminations by trying to
contact her. But if working with Jovanna meant he
could get some excitement back into his life, he was all
for it. "I don't mind if she doesn't," Vince said.

"We'll find out how she feels, then," Beowulf said. "I'll
set up a meeting with Jovanna. If she's willing to work
with you, I'll approve your reassignment."

"I understand," Vince said, wishing he could be sure
Jovanna would agree. Still, he was glad for the chance.
And he would figure out how to talk Jovanna into it; it
was his one chance to recapture the excitement he'd felt
when he first joined NEO. "Thank you, sir."

Beowulf, smiling, shook his head. "You're welcome,
Major Pirelli. Dismissed!"

Vince delivered a crisp salute, turned on his heel, and
left Beowulf's office before flashing a heartfelt smile.

○ ○ ○ ○ ○

Jovanna looked at the chronometer on the office wall.
It read 1837—one hour and thirty-seven minutes past
time to get off work—but Mr. Sorin had asked her to
stay, and she had a reputation for devotion to her super-
visors. That served two purposes, of course. It placed
her above suspicion—everyone knew Ms. Trask was too
mousy and obedient to consider doing anything disloyal
to RAM. She also found it possible to stay as late as necessary any time she wanted. Security thought nothing
of seeing Ms. Trask in her cubicle until midnight.

It was only a problem on rare occasions like tonight,
when she had a NEO contact scheduled in the evening.

Well, her contact might have to wait. A few feet away, the door to Sorin's office slid open, and Jovanna busied herself looking over some property transfers.

"Ah, Ms. Trask, hard at work, I see." Sorin tried to sound genial, but Jovanna sensed the tension in his voice. There were personnel changes going on all around the office, and he had enough experience with RAM politics to be worried by them.

"I have the rest of the parameters we need to consider as we absorb Universal Biomed's assets. Could you look them over tonight and have any questions ready for me first thing tomorrow?" Sorin asked.

"Certainly, Mr. Sorin," Jovanna said, taking the printout he held out to her. "Shouldn't you go home, sir? You look exhausted." And the longer he hung around, the later it would be before she could leave.

"I am a bit tired," Sorin admitted. "Will you be all right here alone?"

"Sir, if you don't mind, I thought I'd take this home with me," Jovanna said. "I have a terminal there if I need one."

"That's fine, Ms. Trask. Good night." Sorin smiled at her nervously and disappeared into his office. Jovanna shook her head, glad once more that RAM did not consider her promotable. The farther one rose within the corporation, the more susceptible one's position seemed to be, although RAM board members might have more security. For Jovanna's purposes, her low-level, invisible job was perfect. She stuffed the papers Sorin had given her in her carryall and left the office.

The Coprates monorail stopped in front of the pyramid where Jo worked, and she headed straight for it after satisfying herself that no one was watching her. Jovanna had learned to maintain a heightened awareness. When she first came back to Mars twenty years ago, RAM had pretended, after an intense questioning session, to accept her story about being taken hostage by Vince Pirelli. But she'd been followed, and her communications were kept under surveillance. RW had surfaced briefly to warn Jovanna, then reappeared three years later to let her know when she was taken off RAM's suspect list. Then, after a training period, Jovanna's life as a NEO informant began.

Jovanna took the northbound monorail to the fourth stop, then checked once again to make sure no one was watching her. She got off the train and headed for the monorail station's women's lounge. The lounge consisted of two rooms. The first was a long locker room, its floor covered with worn, dirty carpet. The back room was a restroom with sinks and stalls.

Jovanna slipped a small key card out of a concealed slit in her carryall and inserted the card in one of the wall lockers. Someone in the restroom had just turned off the water. Jovanna moved away from the locker, pretending to search her carryall for something while the woman finished drying her hands and left.

Jovanna returned to the locker, pulled out a large, gold pelosaur-skin purse, and tucked it into her carryall. Then she went into the restroom, finding an unoccupied middle stall and pulling the door closed behind her. She checked her wristchrono; it was only 1853. She wouldn't be late for her meeting after all. She waited in the stall for two other women to leave before beginning her transformation. By 1857, the lounge was silent.

Jovanna hung her carryall on a hook, pulled out her black purse, and opened it.

A curly blonde wig and stretchy emerald bodysuit sprang out, contained until then by the purse's tight fastenings. With the ease of long practice, she exchanged her sensible, practical gray suit for the emerald bodysuit. After putting on the wig, she reached back into the purse and pulled out the gold pelosaur-skin boots that matched the purse.

After she finished dressing, she checked herself in a mirror before finding a locker for her carryall, which now contained her everyday clothes. No matter how many times she transformed herself, Jovanna couldn't get used to the change. Her eyes, usually nondescript, always looked wide and exceptionally green when she dressed in what she called her "blonde tart get-up."

Sometimes she rather liked it, but tonight she had no time to stop and admire herself. Her contact would be waiting.

The monorail was nearly empty when she got back on it. It was still the dinner hour, a little early for the club crowds on Marineris Boulevard. The boulevard wouldn't start to get really busy for a half hour or so.

Marineris Boulevard, though it attracted a different clientele than that which frequented the Coprates Duel Pit, had one thing in common with that staple of Martian civilization. It was one place where members of the executive and manager castes, including off-worlders, mingled freely. The boulevard lined the north canyon wall of Coprates Chasm, where the chasm-dwelling executives and the rim-dwelling managers both had easy access to its pleasures.

The clubs on Marineris Boulevard featured musicians from the manager class. Many of them, though unwelcome in most of the chasm because of their lower social standing, were admired by off-worlders and members of the manager class. Many younger, avant-garde members of the executive class, who enjoyed feeling as if they were more sophisticated or broad-minded than their fellows, managed to find their way to Marineris Boulevard as well.

It was a good place to bump into someone without attracting much attention, which was why Jovanna liked to meet her NEO contacts here. Not that she met with them that often. Most of her communications with Beowulf took place through RW. Occasionally special circumstances required a meeting in person. She got off the monorail at the Marineris stop and headed across the skywalk to the designated meeting place.

Ric's Cafe was illuminated in small, warm patches by shaded table lamps and wall sconces. The house band was already playing, its featured performer fingering the keyboard in a slow, languorous piece that sounded vaguely nostalgic, though she didn't specifically remember having heard it before.

Though her contact was always a different person, he

usually dressed as a wealthy Mercurian, identified by a
gold sash. She saw someone with a gold sash at the bar,
so she found a seat near him. When she ordered her
drink, she could feel him looking at her, so she turned to
try her password on him. She found herself meeting the
admiring brown eyes of Vince Pirelli. Flustered, she
turned back to the bartender and waited for her drink.

As she reached into her purse to pay, Vince moved
closer and said, "Can I get that for you?"

"I'm supposed to be meeting someone," Jovanna said,
wondering if he recognized her. He hadn't given his part
of the password yet. Possibly he wasn't her contact, but
then why would he come to Mars? It wasn't as if there
was nothing for him to do, with all the changes NEO
was going though.

"Maybe if you hide he won't find you," Vince said,
smiling mischievously.

"Aren't you meeting anyone?" Jovanna said. She
paid the bartender, who'd been growing impatient.

"Besides you? I forget," Vince said.

This had gone on long enough, Jovanna decided. Now
she remembered how complicated her relationship with
Vince had been before. Whether he recognized her or
not, it was time to do her job.

"Nice music, isn't it?" she said. "Nobody plays piano-
harp quite the way Sam does."

Vince blinked as she said her half of the password,
then smiled a slow, lazy smile. "I'll see if he'll play 'As
Time Goes By.' I believe that's your favorite."

It was Vince's half of the code, probably culled from
some ancient Earth source. Most of NEO's passwords
were obscure references to Earth's history or culture.
Jovanna looked at Vince closely, trying to decide whether he'd known who she was before she said her half of
the password. He seemed to recognize her now, but he
also seemed to be taking her appearance, though quite
different from the way she usually dressed, in stride.

"Let's move," he suggested. "Too much traffic here."

Knowing how much easier it would be to avoid eavesdroppers outside, Jovanna led Vince from the cafe, and

as they passed groups of people along the boulevard, she said, "It's been a long time."

"Too long," Vince said, smiling. "The years have been good to you, Jo. Are you any older than you were when I knew you before?"

"Twenty-one years older," she said.

"I know that, but I can't believe it to look at you," he said. "On the other hand, I feel every year of it."

Jovanna studied Vince. Other than a few fine lines around his eyes, he didn't seem much older. Certainly the way he talked to women was pretty much the same, she thought. And he hadn't gotten paunchy as so many RAM executives did when they reached their forties. Of course, there was always cosmetic surgery, which was how most executives coped with advancing age, but she doubted that Vince had resorted to that. Terrans, unless they aspired to Martian careers or social goals, didn't tinker with their appearance the way wealthy Martians did. "You look fine," she told him.

He smiled. "Thanks. Surprised to see me?"

"Yes, actually," she said. "I thought you'd be some big wheel at headquarters by now."

"I've been little more than a glorified nursery school teacher," he said. "But I asked for reassignment. I wanted to work with you again."

Jovanna stopped short. Whatever she'd expected him to say, it hadn't been that. Why was he saying this now, when back on Barbarosa he had seemed to be in such a hurry to get rid of her? She studied the darkening late summer sky for several moments before answering. "I didn't think you thought much of me. You certainly seemed impatient with me the last time we worked together. Remember?" She turned back to look at him.

He looked embarrassed. "Well, I've trained a lot of raw kids since then. You're no worse—in fact, a darn sight better—than most of them."

Jovanna resumed walking. "Thanks . . . I think."

Vince matched her stride. "Would you work with me again, Jo? You seemed upset with me the last time I saw you."

Jovanna glanced at him. He was right; she had been angry with him, and she still wasn't sure about all the reasons. She'd felt like such a dolt next to his calm self-assurance, and she hadn't liked the feeling. She found that she didn't like it any better now.

She'd learned how to take care of herself since she'd last seen Vince—how to handle herself in a fight, how to use a gun, even how to kill if necessary. The one thing she hadn't learned was how to come out and say what she really felt. Well, she wasn't too old to keep learning. She took a deep breath. "I was angry. I didn't think you gave me enough credit for my help."

"You were right. I didn't give you enough credit," Vince said slowly. "I'm sorry, Jo."

She looked at him, startled. Somehow she hadn't felt that getting an apology from him would be so easy, and she was puzzled. Could she have been wrong all this time about why she'd been angry with him?

She thought back to their time together on Genesis, remembering what it was like. The hardest thing, she thought, was that she hadn't been truthful with Dr. Wydlin about her NEO affiliation. Then he'd disappeared—probably died—at the time of the RAM takeover without ever knowing the truth. She'd always felt vaguely guilty about his death. Maybe it was time to exorcise that specter as well.

She walked over to the stone railing that lined one edge of the boulevard and leaned forward against it, barely noticing the twinkling lights of the pyramids that spread out through the chasm below. It was an accustomed reflex by now, checking for irregularities in the wall's smooth surface that might conceal listening devices. Then she looked up at the sky, which had grown just dark enough for stars to begin appearing. "I also blamed you for Dr. Wydlin's death."

"What?" Vince's jaw dropped open. He recovered from his surprise and frowned. "Why?"

She looked at him, realizing she didn't really have an answer. She tried to come up with one. "Because we planned the Barneys' escape without even trying to contact Dr. Wydlin or help him. I never felt right about that."

"You never said anything about it at the time," Vince said. "In any case, I doubt we could have done things any differently."

"I still wish we had tried," Jovanna said.

"You haven't really changed, have you?" Vince's irritation was obvious. "You still stew about things."

She turned on him, stung. "Why did you even bother to come here?" It was obvious it hadn't been for the pleasure of her company.

A speculative look crept into Vince's face, and he turned away from her and looked out into the twinkling lights of the chasm below.

Jovanna realized Vince had come for a specific purpose. "You need me for something, don't you?" she asked.

Vince hesitated, then said, "Headquarters needs a small group of operatives that can move quickly." He leaned close to her. "We're looking to operate out of the Asteroid Belt. It's a promising recruiting area, and we'll be able to blend in there. And it's a prime place to pick up information that isn't otherwise available."

Jovanna felt a stir of excitement. If Vince was asking her to become part of such a group—he hadn't actually said he was—it would be a chance to escape the RAM labyrinth. Maybe she could recapture the feeling of belonging that she had back on Genesis Station, when she and Vince were working so closely together.

She made herself speak as if his answer didn't matter. "Where do I fit in? Or do I?"

"You and RW both do, if you're both willing," Vince said. "We need someone to provide a home base and—" he lowered his voice even further—"someone with connections to a certain pirate."

Jovanna knew who Vince was talking about, but she hadn't had any contact with Black Barney since they left Barbarosa twenty-one years earlier. "I thought he worked for Buck Rogers now."

"Well, yes and no," Vince said. "If Rogers were anywhere to be found, I'm sure he'd still have Barney's loyalty, but he's off with Wilma Deering on some secret project. And Barney hasn't kept in touch with us."

"So now we know what we planted that signal chip for," Jovanna said thoughtfully. That was another thing she hadn't told Dr. Wydlin about, but she didn't think she ought to bring it up with Vince right now—not if she wanted to hear more about this new assignment.

"We don't want to operate in the belt without the sanction of the Rogues' Guild," Vince said. Black Barney reputedly controlled the Rogues' Guild, a loose confederation of pirates, freebooters, and information brokers who congregated mostly in the Asteroid Belt between Mars and Jupiter.

"I'll see if RW can locate him," Jovanna said.

"Not till we're settled in the belt," Vince cautioned. "We don't know how Barney will react, and I for one don't want him calling for us on Mars."

"Of course not," said Jovanna. Black Barney wasn't noted for his subtlety. "Assuming we get his approval and recruit this group, what next?"

"Our work will be what you might call politically sensitive," Vince said. "Things that NEO, now that it's become such a high-profile entity, needs to distance itself from. We don't have our first assignment yet, but Beowulf assures me it won't be long."

Jovanna had been waiting for an assignment like this ever since her work on Genesis Station had ended. Now that she saw Vince again, she realized that she'd never felt completely competent around him. He had called all the shots back on Genesis, and she'd simply gone along for the ride.

She had spent only half an hour in Vince's company, but Jovanna knew nothing had changed between them, even though she felt she'd learned a lot since then. But the tension she felt with him was not a good enough reason to pass this opportunity by. It might take some time for her to prove herself to Vince, but it was the chance she'd been hoping for.

"All right. Count me in," she said.

CHAPTER TWENTY FOUR

An unremarkable door on Tortuga Street slid open to the pressure of Vince's thumb on the pad beside it. It was coded to accept only two people—Vince and Jovanna.

Vince climbed a dark staircase and entered Jovanna's apartment. Jovanna was at her computer terminal. The screen was filled with numbers that were meaningless to Vince. RW was there as well, seated on the edge of the console, looking like Jovanna had twenty years ago—a bit too thick-waisted, with stringy, mousy brown hair, her eyes colorless. Jovanna's looks had improved since then—she'd changed from somewhat flabby to lean and muscular, and she wore her hair in a shorter, more flattering style now.

"Are you ready?" Jovanna asked. Vince nodded. Jovanna turned to RW. "I'm just getting the slightest hint of Black Barney's signal. I don't think he's in the Asteroid Belt. The question is, where do we look?"

RW looked blank, as she always did when evaluating data. "Don't worry, I'll find him."

"All right," Jovanna said, nodding. "Let us know when he's on the way, RW."

"You bet. See you," RW said and winked out.

Jovanna stood abruptly, turning away from her terminal. "Do you think Barney will bite?"

"I'd bet on it," Vince said. "The question is, how hard?"

○ ○ ○ ○ ○

Master Pirate Black Barney leaned forward in his captain's chair on the bridge of the *Free Enterprise*. He kept his eyes focused on the tactical display his second mate, Peg, was monitoring. RMS *Venture* should be coming into sensor range within the next thirty minutes, and Barney meant to relieve her of the load of atomic fuel she was transporting to Luna.

It was risky, attacking them within a day's travel from Mars, but he'd rather do it here than when the *Venture* got closer to Luna. They were crazy on Luna, certain to take offense at any combat action near the generous territorial space they claimed for themselves. Not that Barney was afraid of them, but Buck Rogers had some kind of alliance with the Lunies and might not appreciate Barney's annoying them.

A shrill buzzing sound indicated that security had been breached. Barney's security officer, Xeno, instantly began operations at his terminal, trying to determine the reason for the alarm. Black Barney stalked to Xeno's terminal, staring over his security officer's silvery crew cut at the screen.

Before Xeno could pin down the source of the breach, however, a faint roaring sound and the smell of hot steel reached Black Barney's senses. He moved until he stood where the sound was loudest, near the lift door, and stepped back. "Over here." He signaled to Xeno.

Xeno pulled his rocket pistol from his belt and approached the bulkhead. Black Barney's second mate Peg joined Xeno, also training her rocket pistol at the breach. The thin flame of a plasmatorch burst through the bulkhead, then moved upward, making a neat line.

Barney tried to imagine who might be crawling through the innards of his ship and why he would use a plasmatorch to get onto the control deck. Of course, if someone—say, from Engineering—got stuck between the bulkheads, the plasmatorch might be the only way to free himself. But Barney had a hard time imagining who could have gotten through such a cramped space.

It wasn't likely there was a spy on the *Free Enterprise*. Barney was pretty careful about whom he recruited, and Xeno had never yet allowed someone who wasn't a crew member—or a prisoner—onto the ship. However, Black Barney's crew remained alert to any possibility, which was why Xeno and Peg waited, pistols drawn, for the torch-wielder to emerge.

The plasmatorch turned at a right angle and started cutting a line about a foot and a half above and parallel to the deck, continued for another foot, and then made another angle downward, continuing down to the deck. Moments later, the torch hissed abruptly, and the cut-out area of the bulkhead was pushed down toward the deck by a pair of long-fingered, furry silver hands.

A small, silver-furred face emerged. Golden, lemurlike eyes peered out at them. "There you are, Captain," the creature said when he saw Black Barney. His voice was improbably high-pitched but well modulated. He looked perfectly comfortable, despite the fact that every person on the bridge was staring at him.

"Galen!" Peg exclaimed. "Why aren't you in the med unit?"

Barney remembered picking up the Tinker about a month earlier, after looting an expeditionary cruiser he was on. He hadn't remembered the Tinker's name before Peg said it. Barney did remember that the Tinker had been offered a position in the Engineering section as soon as it became obvious that he wasn't badly hurt. Tinker engineers were the best in the solar system. However, unlike many Tinkers, who were genetically designed for technical skill and manual dexterity, Galen was not an engineer. He was trained as a medic, so the first mate, Skrug, assigned him to the med unit.

"I want to see the captain," Galen replied nonchalantly, and he began to move toward Black Barney before

Xeno cut him off. Barney watched to see how the newest member of his crew would react to Xeno's implied threat, but Galen seemed unfazed. He leaned to one side, peering around Xeno's knees, and said, "With your permission, Captain?"

"Search him, Xeno," Black Barney said. Galen looked more like a child's stuffed bedtime companion than a threat, but Barney hadn't survived over twenty years as the most feared pirate in the solar system by leaving anything to chance.

Xeno searched the Tinker thoroughly, then turned to Black Barney. "He's clean."

Galen harrumphed. "As if I'd be stupid enough to make such an entrance and bring a weapon with me."

That answered Black Barney's unspoken question; obviously the Tinker had come to the bridge by design, not by accident. The question that remained was why. Barney waited silently for Galen to explain.

Galen looked at Black Barney, as if waiting to be questioned. As Barney stared at him, the Tinker cleared his throat. "I have a problem, Captain."

"You have at least two problems then," growled Skrug from his post at the ship's systems monitor. "I assigned you to Engineering this morning, and that's where you're supposed to be." Skrug's red mustache bristled with outrage. Galen clamped his mouth shut, apparently displeased to be interrupted.

"Go on, Tinker," Black Barney said.

"Your first mate introduced the problem rather neatly," Galen said. "I'm not an engineer, I'm a physician."

"You're a pain in the neck," Skrug interrupted. "Doc asked me to reassign you . . . says he can't work with you."

A low growl started in Barney's throat at the interruption. Skrug shut up.

Galen wasn't as sensitive to Black Barney's moods, however. "It's not my fault Doc's barely competent. He's just jealous," the Tinker retorted.

Barney's fist smashed down on a nearby console, bringing instant, complete silence to the bridge. "So what's your point?" Black Barney roared. "You want to get reassigned to the med unit?"

"No, sir," said the Tinker. "I want to get off the *Free Enterprise*. I'm no pirate."

Peg gasped, and Barney could see the shocked expression on her face out of the corner of his eye. The *Free Enterprise* was the most profitable pirate ship in the solar system, and her crew was paid handsomely. It was practically unheard of for someone to ask to leave. Of course, Galen had ended up on the *Free Enterprise* by accident. Still, his request took Barney by surprise.

Black Barney pondered what to do. Galen's unauthorized entry onto the bridge was, to say the least, a breach of discipline. Barney didn't believe the Tinker meant any harm, but he couldn't let it go unpunished. There would be time to sort out what to do with Galen after they finished with the *Venture*. Barney was just about to confine the Tinker to his quarters when the security alarm sounded again.

Before Xeno could return to his computer, the main screen in the front of the bridge filled with an image. Black Barney looked at it for several moments, not trusting his eyes. It was Teacher, the digital personality who had been his educational interface when he was on Genesis Station. It had been twenty years since he'd seen her last, and seeing her now, with no warning, was somewhat of a shock. Two surprises in less than fifteen minutes were two too many for him.

Teacher's eyes settled on Black Barney, and she nodded, satisfied. "I thought I'd find you here. I have some friends who need to talk to you. They'll meet you at Acheron, in Barbarosa." She disappeared instantly, and the main screen once again showed the view from the front of his ship.

The silence on the bridge was deafening. Black Barney clenched his fists and shouted, "Xeno!"

"Yes, Captain?" Xeno said.

"Put the Tinker in the brig, if you can find a cell that you think will hold him. I'll deal with him later."

As Xeno removed Galen, Barney fumed. Who dared to

contact him this way? How had they even known where
he was? His reputation was built on the fact that, while
he had the means to locate almost anyone—or
anything—he wanted to find, no one could find him unless Barney wanted him to.

Black Barney moved deliberately back to his captain's chair. "Lay in a new course!" he bellowed.

"Sir?" Baring-Gould, his astrogation officer, swiveled
away from his console to look questioningly at Barney.

"To Barbarosa!" Barney growled. He saw the members of his bridge crew exchange glances before his first
mate, Skrug, cleared his throat, his bright red mustache bristling.

"Permission to speak, Captain?"

Barney favored Skrug with a chilling gaze but nodded. Skrug was careful and smart; he wouldn't be first
mate on the *Free Enterprise* if he wasn't. Barney generally listened when his bridge officers felt the need to say
something, then did what he wanted. It let them feel as
if they had some say in things, but it also kept them
from bothering him too often.

"This smells like a trap, Captain. Who is it who wants
to talk to you? I don't like any part of it," Skrug said.
The others—Xeno, Baring-Gould, and Peg—were all
nodding in agreement. Barney himself agreed, but it
didn't make any difference.

"Got to go," Barney said. "Bad for business, people
finding me when I don't want to be found."

Skrug's bright blue eyes looked searchingly at Barney's, then he nodded. "I'll get a team together to go in
with you."

"No!" Barney said. "Just you and Peg. Xeno, you keep
track of all shipboard personnel while we're on Barbarosa. No communications offship till we're back on
board. Understood?"

Xeno nodded. It was good to have crew members who
didn't need everything spelled out for them, Barney
thought, though if one of the clever suckers had come up
with a way to betray his captain, he'd wish he hadn't.
And if it was the Tinker, Galen, he'd better enjoy the

view inside the brig, because it would be the last thing he ever saw.

"Course laid in for Barbarosa," Baring-Gould said.

"Let's go," said Barney.

O   O   O   O   O

"He just docked," RW announced, her voice coming through Jovanna's terminal speaker.

"That's it, then," Vince said, rising. "I'll wait for him over at Acheron."

"I'm coming, too," Jo said.

"It's your funeral," Vince said.

Jovanna wished he had put it a different way. She moved to a wall panel near her kitchen and pushed against one corner. It slid up, allowing them to enter a narrow passage that contained pipes and wiring. After Vince joined her in the passageway, she pressed on the back of the panel, waiting as it settled back into place. The space was claustrophobic, but it provided access to the room above Acheron that Lanni rented to them.

Jovanna had never learned the whole story of Lanni's life or why she had been so helpful to them when they first landed on Barbarosa with the Barneys. Beowulf said she had been bred as a pleasure gennie, and someone in NEO had rescued her from slavery to RAM. In spite of her taciturn personality—or perhaps because of it—Jovanna was glad to have her for an ally now.

They arrived at Vince's room above Acheron. Jovanna slipped the concealing panel back into place before asking, "Want to meet him up or down?"

"Downstairs, I think," Vince said. "That way maybe he'll only tear up the bar and not the whole building."

"Good point," said Jovanna.

A couple of men were seated at a small table, speaking in low whispers, when they arrived downstairs. From her usual post behind the bar, Lanni raised her eyebrows when she saw Vince and Jovanna come downstairs. "Expecting company?" she asked softly.

"Soon," Vince said.

Lanni addressed the two men at the table in her rough baritone. "Finish your drinks, and then it'll be time to go, gentlemen."

"We're not through talking," said one of them, a small bony-faced man.

"You can talk somewhere else," Lanni said.

"Listen, Lanni," said the other man, "we've got business here. We're in the middle of some delicate negotiations."

"Well, take 'em somewhere else, Rex," she said. The buzzer signaled that someone was at Acheron's front entrance. Lanni looked down at the screen she kept under the bar to discover the identities of her patrons before admitting them. She looked up at Jovanna and Vince and nodded.

They'd wanted to keep Black Barney's presence at Acheron secret, but there was no way Rex and the bony-faced man could avoid seeing Barney now. Vince shrugged, and Lanni pressed the door control.

The door slid open, and Black Barney filled the doorway, glaring into the dimly lit bar. Lanni chose that moment to disappear into the back room. The bony-faced man took one look at Barney and tried to crawl under a table. Rex stared at the door, his mouth open. "You wanted to see me?" Barney asked, striding up to Rex.

"Uh, no, Black B—I mean, no, sir," Rex said. "That is, I'm honored to meet you, of course, but—"

His protests were cut short when Barney lifted him off the ground by his collar. "Somebody here wanted to see me," Barney said, "and I want to know who right now!"

"I did," Vince spoke up. Jovanna moved next to him. Barney dropped Rex, who scrambled to his feet and ran to the door, only to be blocked by a man and woman who stood there, rocket pistols drawn.

"What do we do with him, Captain?" asked the man, a beefy, balding redhead with a sweeping mustache.

Barney's eyes remained glued to Vince. "Get him out of here."

A second later, Rex was on the street. When Barney's red-haired henchman stepped back inside, Vince point-

ed under the table at the bony-faced man. "He shouldn't
be here either."

Barney pushed the table over on its side with a re-
sounding thud. Cowering and whimpering, the man
seemed unable to move. Barney hooked his foot under
the man's midsection and booted him toward the front
door. As Barney's assistants stepped aside, he crawled
swiftly out the door. The door slid closed behind him,
sealing Acheron's gloomy interior.

Barney turned back to Vince. "I'm wondering why
you called me here today and how the hell you knew
where to find me."

Vince indicated the two by the door. "Do you want
them to hear this?"

The red-haired man took a step forward. "He's trying
to trick you, Captain. We're not leaving you alone with
him."

"You think I can't take care of myself?" Barney asked
the man, seemingly amused. "Relax, Skrug. You're
staying."

Jovanna watched Barney turn back to stare at Vince.
If Vince objected to Barney's companions, he said nothing about it. She just hoped that what they were about
to discuss wouldn't leave this room. But given Barney's
reputation for iron control he exercised over his crew,
she figured that if Barney agreed to help, he would see
that their secret was safe. Barney turned his attention
to Jovanna. She forced herself to return Barney's gaze
levelly. "Do you remember us?" she asked.

Barney's eyes narrowed, but he said nothing. Jovanna
swallowed hard, then continued. "I worked on your educational programming on Genesis Station. Vince saved
you from becoming a RAM pawn and brought you here
to Acheron."

Something flickered in Barney's eyes, but Jovanna
wasn't sure how to interpret it. "You look different," he
said.

"People change in twenty years," Jovanna said.

"True." Barney's expression didn't change. "What do
you want?"

"We just want your approval to operate on Barbarosa," Vince said.

Barney was at Vince's side before Jovanna realized that he had moved. He grabbed Vince's arm and twisted it up behind his back. Vince gasped in sudden pain.

Barney growled, "You don't interrupt someone in the middle of business to ask for that. How did you find me?"

Vince looked as if he was trying to answer, but he couldn't speak because of the punishment Barney was inflicting.

"Let him go," Jovanna said quickly, trying to remain calm. "He can't answer you while you're breaking his arm."

Barney lessened the pressure but did not release his grip. "How did you find me? Do you have a spy on the *Free Enterprise*?"

"No!" Vince gasped. "You have a microchip—it broadcasts a signal."

Barney let him go. "Where?"

"In the computer implant Dr. Wydlin used for your predecanting education," Jovanna said. "It sends a code that only two people can recognize."

Barney turned his unrevealing gaze on her. "Which two?"

"Jo, don't—" Vince began, but Jovanna ignored him. She didn't think it would help matters for her to hold out on Black Barney now.

"RW—she's the digital personality you know as Teacher—and I." Jovanna thought about telling Barney that he had allowed her to implant the chip himself, but she stopped herself. He'd probably figured that out already, and if he hadn't, she didn't want to draw his attention to the fact. There was no telling how he'd react.

Barney looked her over for a long, uncomfortable moment. "Then you and your digital personality are very dangerous to me."

"They're no threat," Vince protested. "They helped you escape from Gorgon Station during the RAM takeover of Wydlin Corporation."

"That was twenty-one years ago," said Barney. "What have they done for me lately?"

Jovanna looked at Vince, who seemed no closer to an answer than she was. One thing about Black Barney, you couldn't expect him to show loyalty for past help. She remembered RW saying that the only loyalty Barney really understood was the code of the pirate, and that a pirate obeyed the person who could defeat him in combat.

"You seem like big trouble to me. And I don't leave trouble sitting around waiting to happen." Barney moved closer, his huge shape dwarfing her, his face just inches from her own. "Why should I let you live?"

For the first time in recent memory, Jovanna was frightened. She tried to answer, but she couldn't think of anything to say. Mercifully Vince came to her rescue. "You forgot something important, Black Barney. We're from NEO."

Black Barney straightened and turned to look at Vince. Apparently he hadn't thought about that before. Buck Rogers was rumored to have defeated Black Barney, so Barney gave Rogers his unquestioning loyalty. Buck Rogers and NEO had the same goals, and Rogers demand an explanation if Barney harmed any of his NEO compatriots. Barney looked back at Jovanna expressionlessly, and she wondered if even their connection with Buck Rogers would be enough to convince Barney to help them.

"We're not asking for much," Vince said. "We want your approval to operate on Barbarosa. Sometimes we may need to know who to talk to, to gain certain information. Most of all, we need to recruit a few people to join us. You should know who we can trust."

Barney's eyes narrowed, still fastened on Jovanna, as if he was trying to decide whether *she* could be trusted. Then he looked away from her abruptly and addressed Vince.

"You don't want anyone else to know you're from NEO?"

"Not until we're sure they're trustworthy," Vince

said. "That's where you come in."

Barney glared at him. "I don't need people knowing about that damned signal chip. And I don't want you using it to find me."

"Only in an emergency," Jovanna promised. Barney stood still, without speaking or looking at her.

Jovanna looked at Vince, hoping he knew some way to reach Barney. Vince shrugged and gave it a try. "Barney, we won't abuse it. I promise."

After several tense moments, Barney replied, "All right." He sat down, his huge frame dwarfing the chair. "What do you need first?"

Vince put his hand carefully up to his shoulder, the one Barney had nearly wrenched out of its socket. "Offhand, I'd say a medic would be good."

Barney threw back his head and laughed. "That's easy! I have an extra one on the *Free Enterprise*. You can have him."

"An extra medic?" Jovanna asked.

"We took him off a ship we captured about a month ago. He's a good medic . . . he says." Barney had a secret amused look, as if he was enjoying some private joke. "He's not much of a pirate, though. What else do you need?"

Vince and Jovanna had discussed the question before and had decided to keep the size of their crew small. Still, they needed someone to help keep their cruiser, the *Geronimo*, in tiptop shape. And they could always use some extra help in a fight. "We need an engineer, and we need someone like you," Vince said.

Barney lifted an eyebrow, and Vince explained. "I'm not trying to recruit you, Barney. I mean we need someone with muscle who's handy with weapons."

Barney stood up. "I'll get 'em. If you want me, call me the regular way. Understand?"

"We understand," Vince said. Jovanna moved next to Vince as they watched Black Barney lead his two companions out into the greenish light of Tortuga Street.

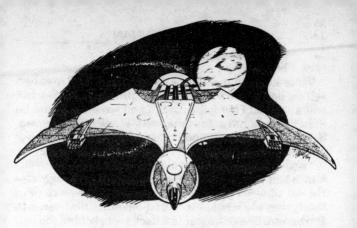

CHAPTER TWENTY FIVE

Jovanna wandered over to the window to look down at Tortuga Street below. It was a little before 1700, and few people were out. People with legitimate business didn't conduct it on Tortuga Street. Those with more clandestine purposes held their meetings behind closed doors, and usually at night. The faintly green artificial light of Tortuga Street was lowered nightly at 2100, then brightened again at 0700. Jovanna wondered idly if there were any other denizens of Tortuga Street looking out onto the street from narrow windows. If there were, she would never see them, just as they couldn't see her. The external side of most of the street's windows projected a mirrored surface, preventing anyone from seeing inside. Tortuga Street kept its secrets.

Though little appeared to be happening, Jovanna knew it was different beneath the surface. She felt a nervous energy, despite her best efforts to remain calm. She considered going back to their cruiser, the *Geronimo*, despite Vince's instructions to get some rest. She didn't feel at all tired. She knew why Vince had sent her back to her apartment. It was the only way he could think of to get their new engineer, Sandra Starseeker, to take a break.

Vince knew that Jovanna could now take care of herself on Barbarosa's mean streets. But he'd told Sandra, who thought of herself as tough and streetwise, that he didn't like to have Jovanna walk alone on Barbarosa. Sandra had agreed to accompany Jovanna back to her apartment near Acheron.

"While you're there, grab some sleep for yourself," Vince had told Sandra. Sandra was Lanni's daughter—the dark-haired girl who couldn't have been more than four years old when Vince and Jovanna first came to Barbarosa. She still slept in a back room behind the bar. She'd been looking for a way off Barbarosa when Vince and Jovanna began recruiting their crew. Lanni had suggested Sandra for their engineer, and she'd turned out to be a good choice, working as hard as Vince asked her to and then some.

"I'm not tired," Sandra had protested.

"You've been working for ten hours straight. Yesterday it was fourteen. If you keep this up, when we finally get our assignment, you'll be in no shape for it," Vince had said. "Go ahead, take a break. I'll expect you both back here at 0900."

Jovanna had played around with her computer for about an hour, but she hadn't found anything interesting or helpful. She thought about returning to the ship now that she'd delivered Sandra safely to Acheron, but she knew she ought to rest as well. Vince was right; RW could be returning any time now with their first assignment from Beowulf.

Vince didn't seem to think they were ready, but the assignment couldn't come too soon for Jovanna. It was all right for Vince and Sandra to fuss endlessly with the *Geronimo*, though Jovanna wasn't sure the ship really needed it. It occurred to her that Vince was going out of his way to get the new group to spend time together in order to get used to each other. She had the definite impression that he was nervous about the upcoming assignment, that it was extremely important to him that they succeed.

Jovanna knew it was important to have the *Geronimo* in top condition, but she felt as if she was just getting in the way. The ship's computer was already in excellent shape, so she didn't feel as if she was really contributing to their efforts. All she was doing now was waiting for someone to hand her busywork.

Their medic, Galen, kept himself busy organizing the *Geronimo*'s sick bay. However, he was adamant about not wanting any help. Jovanna couldn't help smiling at the incongruity of the small medic, whose voice reminded her of a child who had inhaled helium. He spent countless hours cleaning and arranging his instruments and equipment, a frown of concentration on his furry silver brow.

Galen might have been a little more amenable to assistance had not Sandra immediately offended him by talking about how cuddly he was. One look at Galen's face told Jovanna that he did not find such comments amusing. Now he seemed determined to prove to the crew of the *Geronimo* that he could handle his duties like anyone else.

So mostly Jovanna had sat around the cruiser, trying to stay out of the way. Their warrior, a Desert Runner named Rolf, had the same problem, though he'd never said as much to Jovanna. From his demeanor, Jovanna didn't think he ever would. Rolf didn't seem to be the confiding type.

Rolf had come to them rather poorly equipped, and Jovanna had first supposed that he was inexperienced as well. She revised her estimate when Vince gave him some money to outfit himself. He had returned with state-of-the-art battle armor that included specially made gauntlets that would allow him to use his most formidable natural weapons—his claws. He had shopped wisely in other ways. Vince hadn't been stingy with the amount he'd given Rolf, but Jovanna was still amazed by the variety of personal weapons Rolf had returned with—laser and rocket pistols, a mono knife, even a rocket rifle.

Rolf had satisfied himself that the *Geronimo*'s weap-

ons systems were in good working order, picked out his
cabin, and established himself there. He emerged only
for meals and exercise, or if one of the others asked him
to help with some task. He wasn't consciously surly; he
just didn't talk much. Black Barney had certainly tak-
en Vince's request to find someone like himself seriously. Of course, Rolf wasn't as strong as Barney, but
then only the other surviving Barneys—eleven at last
count—could even approach Black Barney's formidable
strength. Rolf was strong enough, though, and he had
an inbred ferocity that rivaled Barney's.

Vince hadn't quite known what to think of Rolf, and
he'd asked Barney why he brought Rolf to them. "I'm
surprised you wouldn't want him for your own crew,"
Vince had said.

"I don't hire Desert Runners," Barney had replied,
refusing to elaborate. Jovanna had puzzled over the
statement for a while until she remembered that Dracolysk had employed Desert Runners as bodyguards back
on Gorgon Station.

A chime from her computer console interrupted
Jovanna's musings, and as she moved away from the
window, RW shimmered into view. "Got your assignment."

"Does Vince know?" Jovanna asked.

"I saw him first. He said for you to collect Sandra and
head back to the ship."

"Tell him we'll be there as soon as we can," Jovanna
said. RW winked out, and Jovanna pressed Lanni's access code.

"Yeah?" Lanni answered.

"Lanni, it's Jovanna. How's Sandra doing?"

"She's finally asleep," Lanni said. Jovanna felt regret
at having to disturb Sandra's rest, but she was too eager
to hear about their assignment to wait, and she figured
Sandra would feel the same way.

"Sorry," said Jovanna. "I need to talk to her."

"I'll get her," Lanni said. "You heading out?"

Jovanna knew it was difficult for Lanni to ask that
question; at first she had tried to remain as ignorant as

possible of Vince and Jovanna's activities, but now she had a daughter involved.

"I don't know yet," Jovanna said.

"Just a minute," Lanni said, her baritone voice sounding even more subdued than usual.

A few moments later, Sandra appeared on Jovanna's monitor. "What's up?" Unlike her mother, she spoke in a normal voice. She was making an effort to seem as if she hadn't just been roused from a sound sleep.

"Vince wants us back on the ship," Jovanna said.

"Do we have a job?" Sandra asked, her pale, strong-boned face growing more alert.

"Yes," said Jovanna.

"I'll meet you downstairs. Five minutes," Sandra said and clicked off.

Jovanna ran a comb through her hair, then went to her window and checked the street again as she always did before leaving the apartment. She saw nothing out of the ordinary.

Sandra hadn't yet emerged from Acheron, and Jovanna was about to go into the bar to wait for her when she felt an uncomfortable prickle, as if someone was watching her. She looked around reflexively, but she saw no one on the street. She was considering whether she ought to return to her apartment and use the comnet to warn Sandra of her suspicions when the door to Acheron slid open. Sandra emerged. "Ready when you are," she said.

"Come on," Jovanna said, grabbing her arm and pulling her toward the end of the street where Barbarosa's lift cars stopped. Sandra looked puzzled but kept pace with Jovanna's rapid stride. Soon the younger woman was huffing and puffing.

"What's the hurry, Jo?" she asked, straining to catch her breath. "I want to impress headquarters, too, but I won't be very impressive if I'm in the med unit with a heart attack."

Jovanna pulled Sandra around the corner and stopped, giving her time to catch her breath. "I think we were being watched," she said to Sandra in a hushed tone.

"Damn!" Sandra said. "Are they following us?"

Jovanna glanced around warily. This close to the lift car station, there were a few more people about, but none of them seemed to be paying any particular attention to Sandra and Jovanna. Jovanna no longer felt what she had felt for that uncomfortable moment outside Acheron. She shrugged. "I don't think so. Maybe I was imagining it. Instinct never was my strong suit. I should leave that kind of stuff to Vince."

"He's something, isn't he?" There was no mistaking the admiration in Sandra's tone. Despite Jovanna's repeated admonitions to herself to think of Vince only in the most businesslike way, she felt annoyed by Sandra's reaction to him.

"He knows what he's doing," Jovanna forced herself to say casually. The lift shaft was just ahead, and a chime signaled the approach of one of the lift cars. Jovanna quickened her steps, and Sandra matched her pace. The lift doors opened and they sprinted the last few steps to the car.

Jovanna found an unoccupied padded tube and wriggled into its harness. Sandra took the one next to her, and the car started its rapid ascent. "Jo?" she said suddenly. "Can I ask you something?"

"I guess so." Jovanna said. Up till now, Sandra had seemed pretty tough and blustery. This tentativeness was something new.

"There isn't anything going on between you and Vince, is there?"

Jovanna blinked in sudden surprise. She'd half expected a question about Vince, but not one about herself. She wasn't sure how to answer. A simple no would have been the easy answer, but somehow that seemed to be too simple.

Until the last month and a half, she hadn't seen Vince at all for twenty-one years, but she'd thought more about him during that time than she would have thought possible. Maybe it was because there were no other men in her life to think about. One or two men had shown an interest in her, but they were generally bland, low-level RAM manager types. There had been no one she was really interested in. Besides, with her double life, it hardly seemed fair to get involved with someone. How could she have a relationship when she couldn't be honest?

She hadn't been honest with Dr. Wydlin about her involvement with NEO, nor with Barney when she'd installed his signal chip. The first deception had haunted her for a long time after she learned that Dr. Wydlin apparently hadn't survived the RAM takeover. The second deception was just now coming back to haunt her. Barney obviously didn't trust her, and it was casting a shadow over his dealings with her.

At least she'd always been pretty honest with Vince. Maybe that was why she felt the way she did about him, which was . . . what? Attraction, certainly, but she resented him at the same time. Even though she'd been with NEO for nearly as long as Vince had, she didn't feel anywhere near his equal, and it rankled. She'd had the training now, and she knew she had made a genuine contribution to the organization over the years. But when Vince came back to ask for her help in starting this team, he'd made it seem as if he was doing her a favor.

Well, as long as Black Barney was so important to their efforts, she wasn't really Vince's equal, especially since Barney barely acknowledged her existence. Maybe when they really got established she'd feel more in control.

"Jo? Are you in there?" Sandra was asking.

"What? Oh . . . sorry," Jovanna said. "Is there anything between Vince and me?" She smiled ruefully, then answered honestly, "We've known each other a long time, Sandra. I'd say we're friends. But I'm not his type."

She watched a smile light up Sandra's hazel eyes, and she felt only a slight twinge as she mentally acknowledged that Sandra was, indeed, Vince's type.

○ ○ ○ ○ ○

As Jovanna and Sandra approached the bay that
housed the *Geronimo*, Jovanna once again had the feeling that they were being watched. Unable to help herself, she turned quickly and saw Black Barney bearing
down on them. "What are you doing here?" she asked
when he came near.

His only response was to look right through her. She
swallowed, then went on. "I'm not sure Vince will want
you on board. We've just received a communication
from headquarters."

"He'll live with it," Barney said.

Sandra nudged Jovanna. "Maybe Vince asked him to
come, Jo."

"No," Barney said.

"Then how did you—?" Sandra began, but Barney cut
her off.

"I heard you were on your way here," Barney said,
looking at Jovanna. That explained why she'd had the
feeling of being watched. Barney certainly had the resources to keep an eye on her if he'd a mind to. His tone
was insulting, but she swallowed it. There was little
else she could do, after all.

"Well, we'll see what Vince says," Jovanna said, entering the docking bay.

Sandra and Barney followed her. She heard voices in
the crew lounge. When she entered, she saw Vince, Galen, and Rolf gathered around the holo display area.
RW was in the middle of the group, looking like the life
of the party.

"Hello, Barney." Vince noticed the big gennie's presence at once. "What can I do for you?"

"I said I'd help you," Barney said, not seeming in the
least pleased about it.

Vince looked at Jovanna, who shrugged. He addressed Barney. "You already have. You arranged this
dock space for us, helped us locate Galen and Rolf—"

"She said you've heard from Beowulf," Barney said,
jerking his thumb to indicate Jovanna. "What's it all

about?"

Vince looked torn, as if he wasn't sure he should answer, then shrugged. "After all the help you've been, I don't think Beowulf would mind your knowing about it."

As long as Barney remained loyal to Buck Rogers, Jovanna reasoned, he'd never jeopardize a NEO operation. Still, she wasn't pleased about Barney's presence. Maybe she was oversensitive, but it seemed as if he was displaying his distrust of her, as if he was here to make sure she didn't foul up. She quickly realized how ridiculous that was. Barney had no particular reason to dislike her.

"Are you ready?" RW asked.

"Go ahead," Vince said.

"Here's your background, then," RW said. "Vince, do you remember an operative named Casimir Pulaski?"

"Sure," Vince said. "He's been with NEO for about ten years."

"Well, I quote: 'Pulaski needs help. Seems urgent. Look for him on Thebe,' " RW said.

"Thebe?" A crease formed between Vince's eyebrows. "RW, don't you have any more than that? I know Thebe is a satellite of Jupiter, but I didn't think it was settled."

"Thebe is one of Jupiter's inner moons," RW said. "Its orbital radius is 138,000 miles, diameter forty-five miles, period of revolution sixteen hours. There have been several attempts at settlements, but none have been successful for more than a few months at a time."

"Then why is Casimir there?" Vince asked.

"He communicated with headquarters about two weeks ago," RW explained. "He told them he thought he was onto something big, but that he needed to make a certain contact before he would have any details. Two days ago, he got on a line to Salvation's computer and transmitted one word only: 'Thebe.' They haven't been able to contact him since. It's not clear to Beowulf whether Pulaski is actually on Thebe, but he obviously wants someone to go there."

Vince looked at Jovanna. "So we go to Thebe and see

if we find out what Pulaski wants us to know."

Jovanna nodded, then remembered how furiously he and Sandra had been working to prepare the *Geronimo*. "Is the ship ready?"

Vince looked around at their newly assembled team, and Jovanna felt her attention drawn to them as well. Galen was wearing a concerned frown. Rolf had risen to his seven-foot height, his hackles rising and his claws extending from their usual retracted position. Due to his gene-encoded ferocity, he might be difficult to control once he was in combat, but they'd known that when they had decided to take him on.

Sandra's eyes were brighter than usual, as if the challenge of the mission was just what she'd been waiting for to bring her to life. Jovanna couldn't miss the way Sandra's obvious eagerness brought a spark to Vince. He smiled at Sandra, then answered Jovanna. "Sure, we're ready."

"All right," said Barney from his place near the lounge door. All eyes turned to him, and he continued. "I have to make a stop at the *Free Enterprise*. I'll be back in ten minutes."

His words were met with shocked silence. Finally Jovanna found her voice. "Are you coming with us, Captain?"

"Yeah," said Barney, looking at her with fathomless gray eyes. "You have a problem with that?"

"I thought you only traveled on the *Free Enterprise*." Galen's golden eyes were huge in his furry face.

"Not this time," Barney said. "I'm having some work done on her. It'll take too long to get her ready to launch. I want to know what's going on on Thebe without the Rogues' Guild's approval."

Jovanna wasn't sure he was telling them his real reasons, but the alternative—that he was watching over them, perhaps because of his loyalty to Buck Rogers—was too unbelievable for her to accept.

CHAPTER TWENTY SIX

The *Geronimo* had begun her second orbit of Thebe, and the tension on the bridge was starting to get to Vince. "Have you spotted anything yet, Sandra?" he asked.

"Still scanning," Sandra said. "Wait! I'm picking up an energy source."

"Any life forms?"

Sandra swiveled to examine her infrared pattern sensor. "Right there."

Vince looked where Sandra was pointing. On a two-dimensional representation of Thebe's surface, a point of light flashed. Beneath it, a readout of its coordinates appeared.

"Are they sending or receiving any communications?" Vince turned to look at Jovanna, who was monitoring the *Geronimo*'s communications system.

"None," Jovanna said. "What do we do now?"

"We go in and have a look," Vince said, though they all knew it wasn't likely to be that simple. There was no telling what they might find.

"Do you want me to hail them?" Jovanna asked.

"No." Vince decided. "No, I'll take the *Geronimo* in and we'll look for signs of settlement and check out the lay of the land before we commit ourselves."

At least, Vince hoped that was how it would work. He also hoped their approach hadn't already been detected. He had to make sure the team understood the delicacy of the situation and that when they landed, Rolf, in particular, wouldn't decide to attack first and ask questions later. Vince knew that Rolf and Sandra were both new to this, but he didn't plan to let their inexperience hinder their mission. "Jo, get me full on-board communications," he said.

Jovanna pressed a sequence of keys. "You've got it."

Vince decided on a no-nonsense approach. It would make very little impression to Jo or Black Barney, but Galen and Sandra might benefit from it on their first mission together. Vince also hoped it would keep a lid on Rolf, at least for a while.

"This is Major Pirelli speaking," he said. He caught Jo's wry look out of the corner of his eye and glanced at Sandra, who, unlike Jovanna, seemed impressed.

"We're going down to the surface. Suit up as quickly as possible. Whoever's down there probably doesn't know we're here yet, and I'd like to keep it that way for as long as possible.

"Remember, this is a rescue mission. You fire on my orders only. I don't want to find out later that someone accidentally killed Pulaski. Now, let's get ready."

Vince fitted his helmet into the neck flange of his smart suit, turned on his air recirculating unit, and checked his seals. Jovanna and Sandra had come to the control deck prepared to leave the ship and had only to don their helmets and check seals. After receiving confirmation that the others were suited up, he took the *Geronimo* out of orbit and brought her into landing position near the coordinates Sandra had pinpointed earlier. Finally he flipped on the reverse thrusters and set the *Geronimo* down like the cherry on a sundae.

Vince unharnessed himself and floated toward the ship's ladder, then looked back to make sure the others were following. Sandra was grinning at what Vince guessed was her first landing on a gravityless world, but when she saw Vince looking at her, her expression became serious. Jovanna, already unharnessed, floated toward the ship's ladder. She grabbed her compdex along the way and slung it over one shoulder.

"All set to check their security," she said, her voice coming into his helmet's built-in commlink.

"Good." He moved aside to let her pass. "Go on down and get started. We'll join you in a minute."

Jovanna raised her eyebrows and looked meaningfully from Vince to Sandra, but Vince wasn't in the mood for teasing. "Knock it off, Jo," he said.

Sandra arrived at the ladder port. "Knock what off?"

"Nothing," Jovanna said. "I'll see you down by the air lock." She pulled herself down the ladder and out of sight.

O O O O O

Jovanna let herself down the ladder as quickly as she could. She had already tapped into Thebe's computer system when Galen appeared, followed quickly by Rolf and Black Barney. Her feet nearly came out of the straps she'd hooked into to keep from floating back up the ladder when she saw Black Barney. She realized now why, despite the fact that Barney was probably RAM's best-known enemy outside of Buck Rogers, his victims couldn't describe his appearance. Instead of the standard helmet, Barney wore a dark, menacing mask that revealed nothing of his face. Convex black goggles concealed his eyes.

With an effort, Jovanna returned to her task. When Vince and Sandra arrived, she had her assessment ready. "We're within twenty meters of the entrance, Major. I can't tell you if there are any guards, but I do have an idea what kind of security we're dealing with. You enter through a hatch that goes through a couple of pressurized rooms to a lift that goes down to the main computer room. Four corridors lead away from the main computer room, corresponding roughly to the four points of the compass, with rooms off each corridor.

Most locks are numerical code devices. The entry hatch
to the complex uses a pressure sensor alarm system."

"What does that mean?" Rolf asked.

"It means that when the pressure changes, as it will
when we open the inner air lock, an alarm will sound
inside the complex," Jovanna said.

"So much for the theory that Thebe is uninhabited,"
said Vince. "They seem to have quite a setup here. Can
you knock out the alarm system?"

"What if Pulaski set it up himself?" Jovanna asked.

"We'll just have to live with that possibility," Vince
replied. "I doubt that Pulaski would have the resources
to do something as elaborate as that all by himself, and
I sure don't think he'd do it without NEO having knowledge of it. It's far more likely he stumbled onto someone
else's operation, and in my mind, that means RAM."

"Good. I can't think of anybody I'd rather tangle
with," Rolf growled. Jovanna remembered he'd once
been owned by a RAM subsidiary.

"On my orders only!" Vince reminded him sharply,
then turned to Jovanna. "How about that alarm?"

"I wish RW were here, but Thebe's computer is too
small to hold her," Jovanna said. "Give me a minute."

The alarm didn't seem much different from other
alarms she had foiled on Mars. On those occasions, however, she usually had had RW's help. Jovanna chewed
her lip, trying to remember the program that would destroy the alarm without alerting the whole system.

When she was satisfied, she punched several keys and
watched her compdex screen. "That did it," she said after several moments.

"Next question," Vince said. "Is there any way to get
more specific information about what's inside there?"

"Like tapping into their security vidcam display if
they have one?" Jovanna asked.

"That'd be a good start," Vince said.

Jovanna called up a list of the size and functions of
Thebe's computer. The system was the smallest mainframe she'd ever seen. It had very few functions, but
there were several programs of interest besides the sta-

tion layout and the alarm system. As she had expected, there was a line to the security vidcams. There was also a log of arrivals and departures, which would be of interest if Pulaski happened to be mentioned in it or if it gave any clue as to who ran the installation.

Unfortunately both these applications were currently being monitored, and she might be detected if she tried to tap into them. She told Vince of her findings.

"Can you take the vidcams off-line? It may give them some warning, but at least they won't know our exact location," said Vince.

"If you say so," Jovanna said.

She began to enter a sequence, but Vince interrupted her. "Wait!" He looked around at the others. "As soon as she finishes this, we're going in. Are you all ready?"

The others nodded their assent. Vince looked at Rolf. "Remember, you attack only on my order."

"I heard you the first two times," Rolf said.

Barney grunted. "If this were my crew, vat scum, you wouldn't be on it for long."

"Then we're both lucky it isn't," Rolf said.

"Ready!" Jovanna said sharply, interrupting the growl that was forming in Barney's throat.

"Come on," Vince said, as he moved to open the ship's air lock. "We don't have any time to waste. Let's go!"

Vince pushed away from the *Geronimo*, using the jets on his rocket belt to maneuver in the direction of the entry hatch. He secured a line and signaled to the others to join him. By the time Jovanna arrived, he and Barney had already opened it.

Vince waved her through, and as the others joined her, she checked her compdex. So far there was no evidence that anyone inside had detected the disabled alarm. As to their reaction to the missing vidcam display, that was anyone's guess.

"Go ahead," she told Vince. He nodded to Rolf, who closed the outer hatch, then turned the wheel to the pressurized inner chamber that was their first stop on the way to the rest of the complex.

The inner chamber was small, and their group was

packed together tightly when they were all inside. There were only four wall handles to keep them from floating to the ceiling. Vince motioned to the others to use them, then hooked his hand into the crook of Sandra's elbow.

Barney refused to use a handhold, but he was tall enough to hold himself down by pushing one cybernetically enhanced hand against the ceiling. "This stinks," he proclaimed, apparently referring to their crowded conditions rather than the smell of the room, since none of them would remove their helmets. In case they became separated, the commlinks in the helmets would keep them in communication with each other.

"What's next, Jo?" Vince asked. Jovanna squirmed, trying to bring her compdex around so she could see the map displayed on its small built-in screen.

"The next room leads to the lift shaft," she said.

"Is it bigger than this one?" Barney asked.

"Somewhat." Jo studied the wall panel, which contained a keypad. "Sandra, can you take the cover plate off and find someplace I can tap into it with this cable?"

Sandra squeezed over to look at the keypad, then applied herself to the task with fierce concentration. After several moments, she held the cover plate in her hand. "Try there," she said, pointing. "It's a port for performing repair diagnostics."

Jovanna's cable plug fit the port Sandra had indicated. Jovanna pressed the command sequence that would make her compdex generate endless strings of random numbers. It was several uncomfortable minutes before it came up with the right combination.

The door hissed open. Pressed against the door, Vince popped through it before he could grab on to anything, followed closely by Black Barney. Rolf followed next.

Jovanna heard the hums of lasers and the blast of a rocket pistol. She let go of her compdex, allowing it to float by its strap as she drew her laser pistol and approached the door.

CHAPTER TWENTY SEVEN

At the other side of the room was a pair of closed lift doors. Two large greenish-gray humanoids with mottled, scaly skins and long muzzles stood in front of them. As Jovanna watched, Black Barney pulled himself by the room's wall handles toward the larger of the two guards. Rolf aimed his rocket pistol at the other. Jovanna saw Vince lying, unmoving, against the ceiling just beyond the doorway.

Jovanna looked behind her. Sandra was pulling out her laser pistol. Galen looked uncertain what to do.

"Stay out of the doorway!" Jovanna shouted. "Vince is hurt. Sandra, cover me while I pull him in here."

Sandra nodded. Jovanna holstered her pistol and let go of the wall handle, letting herself float up to the ceiling. Her compdex drifted toward her face, and she quickly pulled it away. She negotiated the top of the door with some difficulty but managed to get through. Sandra's pistol whirred once as she reached Vince. Jovanna grabbed his booted foot, but he pulled it away.

"What the hell are you doing?" Vince glared at her.

"I thought you were dying. Excuse me," she said. A rocket bullet zinged toward them, and Jovanna thought she felt an impact in her back. She checked herself for injuries and found none. Unfortunately, her compdex was another matter. The bullet had lodged directly in the screen. She turned her attention to the combat.

The guard Barney had attacked was dead and had floated to the ceiling. "That's one good thing about fighting in zero gravity," Barney cracked over the link. "You don't trip over the bodies."

Rolf had zeroed in on the other guard. As Jovanna watched, Rolf fired again. The guard dropped his pistol, which floated up to the ceiling. Barney pushed the guard backward, and his feet came out of the anchoring loops. He floated upward to join his companion on the ceiling. Rolf turned to Vince and dead-panned, "I didn't wait for your order. Sorry."

Vince had just reached one of the wall handles. He returned Rolf's look levelly. "That's all right. I promise you, neither of these guys is Pulaski."

Galen pulled himself into the room and touched Jovanna's arm. "You were hit, weren't you? Where?"

Jovanna shook her head. "Not me, but my compdex is shot. Literally." She held the instrument in front of her, displaying its ruined screen.

"What does that mean?" Vince asked her anxiously.

"I won't be able to tell what's in Thebe's computer until I get to one of their terminals," she said.

"So it looks like we have to find one," Vince said. "The main computer is down one level, isn't it?"

Galen interrupted, insisting that he look everyone over, starting with Vince. Galen was apparently satisfied that Jovanna was uninjured, so she went over to inspect the dead guards. Their gray smart uniforms were unlike any Jovanna had seen; there were no markings denoting rank nor were there any insignia that might tell whether they were attached to RAM or any other corporation. They seemed similar to Terrines, but their faces were more elongated and had a more reptilian aspect than any Terrines she'd seen before. She shuddered at the length and sharpness of their teeth.

Vince joined Jovanna. "Any clues?"

"I can't see any sign of their affiliation, if that's what

you mean. No corporate or planetary insignia. They're well equipped, though." She pointed at the belt packs, bristling with pistols and other paraphernalia.

Vince fingered a guard's uniform. "It looks military, but no military I'm familiar with," he said.

"How come there're no rank markings?"

"They may be able to detect each other's rank through scent or some other exotic sense," Vince said, loosening the collars of the gennies and looking around their necks. "No identification tags, either. Apparently the less information they carry, the less outsiders like us can learn about them. I doubt that's accidental."

"So who are these guys?" Jovanna asked. "RAM?"

Vince shook his head. "I have no idea. This installation—and these gennies—are an incredibly well-kept secret. If they're RAM, I'd be willing to bet that very few know of their existence."

"I never heard of them, and I've been in and out of RAM security files a time or two," Jovanna said.

By the time Jovanna and Vince finished looking at the gennies, Galen had finished his inspection as well. Only Black Barney had taken a hit. A charred depression dimpled his chest plate where one of the guards' lasers had pierced it. The armor had resealed itself.

"You should take your armor off so I can treat that," Galen told him.

"Get lost," Barney responded.

"Doesn't it hurt?" Sandra asked.

He regarded her for a moment, then said, "I've had worse. Can we get going?"

"Right. Let's get to the computer level," Vince said.

They entered the lift and grabbed handholds. The car sped downward. As it began to brake, Jovanna noticed that she wasn't the only one who'd drawn a gun. Only Galen's remained on his belt, but his long fingers gripped his medikit tensely.

The doors whooshed open. Jovanna held her breath as Barney and Rolf pushed out. She waited for a burst of fire and was relieved when none came. Ahead of her, Vince exited the lift. Jovanna moved after him and felt

Sandra and Galen close behind her.

They had entered a large, circular, low-ceilinged room. One door stood at the northernmost point of the circle, and there were two others at points ninety degrees to the left and right of it. The room was empty except for a small unattended mainframe computer that filled the center of the room. Jovanna started to approach it, but Barney put out a hand to stop her.

"Where do the doors lead?" he asked.

"I don't know," Jovanna said. "If I can use the computer to call up the map or the vidcam display, I could tell you."

"Can you remember anything about the floor plan?" Vince asked.

Jovanna closed her eyes, trying to conjure a mental image of the map she'd called up earlier on her compdex. Her eyes snapped open. "Four spokes! There's a door behind us, near the lift shaft."

"Wait." Barney looked at Vince. "Let me check back there for any surprises. You!" Barney pointed at Rolf. His voice was pitched so low that Jovanna felt as if she were reading his lips rather than hearing him over the commlink. "I'm going around on this side. You watch for anyone trying to come around on your side. The rest of you, stay put unless I call you."

Jovanna didn't like to think about what would make Black Barney call for help. The master pirate eased himself around the corner. Several seconds later, Jovanna heard Barney's low growl, followed by several sounds of laser pistol fire. Rolf tensed noticeably but managed to stifle any impulse to join the unseen fray.

Vince's forehead creased, but before he could tell Rolf to go help Barney, two doors burst open and Jovanna saw several more of the gatorlike gennies firing at them. Rolf returned fire at the gators in the west door, closest to him. Sandra slid her foot into a floor strap and began firing at the gators in the east door, who were exchanging fire with Vince. Jovanna decided to help Rolf. His bulk made it hard for Jovanna to get a clear shot around him. Finally she muttered, "The hell with it," released her grip on the handle beside the lift door, and allowed herself to float up to the ceiling so she could maneuver to shoot past Rolf's head.

Lying prone on the ceiling was disorienting. She missed with her first shot but hit one of them on the second. The injured gator fell backward into the dark doorway. Rolf had killed at least two of the creatures, because she could see them floating up to the ceiling. But at least two others were still firing from the cover of the west doorway.

A sound behind her drew Jovanna's attention, and she looked back in time to see a gator pulling himself along the handles on the outer wall of the lift shaft, intent on Rolf. The gator's yellow eyes met hers, and he switched his aim to her. She fired, and the beam from her laser seared into his smart uniform. His shot went wild and he snarled, grabbing at his chest. A wicked black hole appeared in the ceiling perhaps an inch from her head. She scrabbled back along the ceiling, trying to get partial cover from the lift shaft.

Before she got there, the gator's next shot struck her in the side. She gasped at the heat, but her suit reacted to the assault almost immediately, dispersing the shot's intensity. Nevertheless, her hand trembled, and she wondered if she'd be able to aim accurately.

She pursed her lips together and steadied the laser pistol. The gator braced to fire again. Suddenly a black gloved arm snaked around the gator's chest and tore him, handle and all, from his hold on the wall. Another gloved hand, holding a reddened knife, flashed toward the gator's throat. As the gator and his attacker bumped up against the ceiling, the knife traced a red line across the gator's throat. After a moment, the creature ceased to struggle. Black Barney pushed himself down from the ceiling and moved gracefully toward the rest of the party.

Barney ignored Jovanna. She glanced back at the door she and Rolf had been firing toward. It gaped darkly, gray-clothed bodies floating in front of it. Rolf had moved into the round computer room, his attention fo-

cused on the east door, where Vince and Sandra had
been concentrating their fire. Apparently they hadn't
been as successful with their opponents as Rolf and Barney had. There was no sign that any of the gators at
that door had taken any major damage.

Rolf fired his rocket pistol, felling one of the gators.
The remaining gators returned the fire, and three thin
red beams struck Rolf almost simultaneously.

The big Desert Runner grabbed at his chest. Galen
pushed past Sandra and headed toward Rolf. The distance between the foot brackets, installed for creatures
with far longer strides than Galen's, caused him some
problems, but he struggled on. Barney snarled and
floated up to the ceiling, then pushed his feet against
the lift shaft, launching himself toward the east door.
The gators hesitated at the sight of Barney's bulk hur-
tling straight toward them. Before they could react,
Barney had kicked downward, his boot crushing the
first gator's head into the wall. One of the others aimed
his laser pistol at Barney, but at the same moment, a
beam from Vince's gun opened a smoking hole in his
chest. Barney pulled down hand over hand along a ver-
tical line of handles, then used one hand to twist and
snap the injured gator's neck.

Jovanna brought up her pistol to aim at the guard
who remained in the doorway, but before she fired, a
beam sliced out from Sandra's gun and hit him. As he
clutched at his chest, Jovanna fired, also hitting him.
His body suddenly went limp, then floated upward.

The room was silent. Jovanna looked around. No
more gators appeared. Galen busily tended to Rolf, who
was pale but still conscious. Sandra leaned back against
the lift doors. "Whew! I'm glad that's over!"

Vince pointed at the rectangular bank of screens and
keyboards in the center of the room. "You want to take a
look at this, Jo?" he asked.

Jovanna moved over to the computer and studied it.
On the east, south, and west sides were three terminals.
On the north side of the rectangle was a commo board.
Jovanna moved clockwise around the rectangle. The

east computer screen showed a map display, the south displayed a log, and the west had a split-screen display showing two small rooms with occupied bunks.

Vince joined her. "Got anything?"

She pointed to the vidcam display. The room displayed on the left side of the screen contained a Martian male in standard RAM business attire as he mumbled in his sleep, restrained in his bunk by straps. If this was a RAM installation, the executive obviously got on the wrong side of somebody. The right side of the screen showed a cell that contained a blond man lying strapped to a wall bunk.

Vince grabbed Jovanna's arm and pointed to the right side of the screen. "Can you magnify that view?"

"Sure." Jovanna set the vidcam to enhance the figure in the bunk. The features on the blond man's face became clearer. He was obviously Terran, and his smart suit seemed rather the worse for wear.

Vince's grip on Jovanna's arm tightened. "That's Pulaski! Where is he?"

Jovanna read the bottom of the screen, then moved to the south terminal to look at the map display. She pointed at the door to the east of the lift shaft, where several gator corpses still floated. "Second room on the right, down that hall. Hang on a minute. I'll see if I can figure out the sequence to unlock it from here."

As she worked, Vince spoke to Barney and Sandra, and the three moved to the east hall. The door had swung closed, but at their approach, it slid open again. "We're going in, Jo," Vince called. "When you get the cell open, sing out!"

"You'll be the first to know," Jovanna assured him. Then she looked back at her screen and noticed that the cell door was now listed as open, although she hadn't done anything with it. "What—?" she murmured to herself, then called out, "Vince!"

Barney growled loudly, "What the—?"

Jovanna looked at the vidcam display just as a gator entered the cell and rushed toward the startled figure. The gator lunged at Casimir, who tried to fend him off, but his straps restricted him. The gator sank his teeth into the NEO agent's arm, snapping through what circuits remained of the smart suit. Casimir gasped in pain and grabbed the injured arm, then began growing noticeably paler. Next the back of Barney's dark helmet appeared, blocking most of the screen, but Jovanna didn't wait to see what would happen next.

"Galen!" she yelled, unstrapping herself from the computer station. He looked up, and she pointed toward the door their companions had just gone through. "They need help down there!"

Galen looked at the door, then glanced back uncertainly at Rolf, whom he hadn't quite finished treating.

"Go ahead," Rolf said. "I'll be all right."

Galen grabbed his medikit and stretched his foot toward the next strap on the floor, but this was no time to watch him struggle. Jovanna pulled his nearly weightless body out of the strap and tucked him under her arm as if he were a sack of flour. Then she kicked away from the floor and maneuvered toward the corridor down which their companions had disappeared.

"Let go!" Galen struggled under her arm. Just then Jovanna bumped to a stop against the wall near the corridor, and Galen freed himself from her loosened grip. He looked at her angrily. "Was that necessary?"

Jovanna pointed at the corridor that lay before them. "Sorry, Galen," she said, "but there was one gator still alive, and he attacked Pulaski."

At her explanation, Galen pushed himself around the corner and down the corridor.

"You coming, Galen?" Vince's tense voice came over the commlink.

When she finally arrived at the cell, Galen had anchored himself to a bed strap and was examining Pulaski. The gator, apparently dead, floated at the top of the cell. Barney, Sandra, and Vince watched Galen work. Jovanna approached Vince. "What happened?"

"The gator was stationed outside the cell door when we came into the corridor," Vince said. "When he saw us, he charged into the cell. Barney got down here first, saw the gator attacking Casimir, and pulled him off."

"Did he have to kill him?" Jovanna was getting tired of all the questions they had found so far without any answers. If they couldn't bring Pulaski around, maybe they could have gotten some answers from the gator.

"Barney didn't do it," Sandra said. "The gator bit himself in the wrist. He was unconscious just seconds after Pulaski."

Galen looked at Vince. "Pulaski's dead. I'm sorry."

"What about this guy?" Jovanna said, pointing upward at the floating gator.

Galen looked thoughtful. "Pull him down to the bunk. I can't treat him up there."

Barney turned to face Jovanna, and she had the sense that he was regarding her carefully, but under his mask, his expression was impossible to see. However, he tugged the unconscious gator over to the Tinker physician and held him in place.

Galen examined the gator and shook his head. "He's dead, too. It looks like they both succumbed to some sort of venom with paralytic properties. Fascinating."

Galen opened the gator's mouth carefully and, with a long instrument, probed around inside. "There's an organ behind the gum ridge that secretes a fluid. I'll take a sample. I can check later to see if I'm right."

"Obviously the gator had orders to make sure Pulaski didn't live to tell us anything," Vince said. "It looks like he killed himself rather than submit to questioning."

"Great," said Jovanna. "So we still know nothing." The numb expression on Vince's face reflected his own disappointment. "I'm sorry, Vince. Casimir was a friend of yours, wasn't he?"

"I knew him," Vince said, "though only slightly. Still, I hate the fact that we just missed rescuing him. And you're right, we still know essentially nothing of what he wanted to tell us. Hell of a start for our first mission."

Jovanna knew how much this mission meant to Vince, and it was important to her as well. She was about to suggest returning to the computer to see if they could learn anything there when Barney spoke up.

"Don't you want to know what Pulaski said before he blacked out?" Barney asked.

"He said something?" Vince asked excitedly.

"Yes," Barney said, turning his masked gaze on Jovannna. "In spite of someone's best efforts."

Jovanna stared at him, shocked. So he really did suspect her of something. This was getting ridiculous.

"Well?" Vince said to Barney. "What did Casimir say?"

Barney turned back to Vince. "Not much. He said, 'The Red Warrior's coming back.' Then he muttered something like, 'Operation Far Star.' "

"So now we have some leads. Sort of." Vince looked at Barney. "You have connections. Did Pulaski's last words mean anything to you?"

"No," Barney answered simply. He held up one finger "Wait a minute."

After several moments of tense silence, Barney said, "Communication from the *Free Enterprise*. There's an unidentified cruiser approaching Thebe, maybe an hour away. Skrug thinks it broke away from a small RAM fleet that's orbiting Jupiter."

"I thought the *Free Enterprise* was back on Barbarosa," said Jovanna.

"That's what I wanted you to think," Black Barney said.

"Hey!" Rolf's deep voice over the commlink broke into their conversation.

"What is it?" Vince asked.

"You better get back in here quick," Rolf said. "The commo board just started beeping. Someone is hailing the complex."

"We're on our way." Vince started for the cell door. As Jovanna tried to follow him, she felt a viselike grip on her arm. "Not yet, Teacher." Black Barney clearly had no plans to release her. Astonished, she looked about helplessly as the others, unnoticing, left the room, leaving her alone with Black Barney.

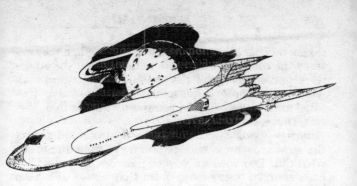

CHAPTER TWENTY EIGHT

What are you doing?" Jovanna said.

Black Barney reached over and snapped the seals on her spacesuit helmet, then removed it from her shoulders. Jovanna gasped involuntarily, then realized that breathable air would not be a problem. The complex in Thebe provided an atmosphere that approximated Mars. Barney must have realized that, and she should have also, since neither Pulaski nor any of the gators had needed to use masks or helmets to breathe.

Black Barney's voice came through a speaker on the front of his helmet. It sounded metallic, distorted by static, even harsher than his voice ordinarily was. "Relax, Trask. I'm not going to kill you. Yet. But I don't want you communicating with whoever is trying to reach this station. I took your helmet off to get you off the commlink, nothing else."

It was all incomprehensible to Jovanna. "Why? What do you suspect me of?"

"Shut up," came his unhelpful response. "Come with me. We're going to find out who's trying to communicate with Thebe."

He followed the same route Vince and the others had

taken, pulling Jovanna along with him. When they entered the computer room, she could see that the others were gathered around the communications terminal, watching it tensely. After a moment, she heard an irritated male voice over the terminal. "This is Red Warrior, Thebe. Report immediately!"

Barney approached the others, stopping out of view of the screen. Jovanna tried to pull away from him to see what the "Red Warrior" looked like. Barney pulled her back sharply. "Stay away from that screen and keep your mouth shut."

"What—?" Jovanna started, only to feel Barney's strong hand close over her mouth. Helpless, she waited for one of the others to notice her plight, but they were all staring at the communit screen, oblivious to what Barney was doing to her.

"Thebe, we received your distress signal. I want a full report, or I will assume that the installation has been contaminated and needs to be sterilized. Do you read?"

Barney's hand tightened over Jovanna's mouth, and he moved closer to the group in front of the terminal. "You're not transmitting?" he asked Vince.

"No way. He's wearing a RAM uniform. I think we've found out who's responsible for this complex, if there was ever any doubt," Vince said. His voice inside the helmet sounded muted to Jovanna, since she wasn't receiving it over the commlink anymore, but Jovanna could still understand him.

"Good," Barney said. He removed his hand from Jovanna's mouth and flipped a switch on the underside of his helmet. "*Free Enterprise*, have you been monitoring all communications to Thebe?"

Barney was silent, apparently listening to the response. "All right," he said after several moments. "Destroy 'em. Report to me when you're finished."

Vince had apparently just noticed the way Barney was holding Jovanna. "Jo, what's going on here? Why did you take your helmet off?"

"Ask Barney," she said.

"Barney?" Vince looked at the big gennie.

Barney was looking at the inside of Jovanna's helmet, inspecting her commlink with special care. "It's all right." He handed it back to her. "Here. It doesn't look like you have any extra linkups in there."

"What are you talking about?" Galen asked. Jovanna put her helmet back on and resealed it.

"I wanted to make sure she couldn't talk to anyone besides us," Barney said.

Jovanna had had enough. "If you suspect me of something, why don't you just come out and say it?"

"I will when I'm ready," said Barney. He turned back to Vince. "For now, we'd better blow this pop stand. You've found everything you're going to find here."

"We haven't gone through the computer," Jovanna pointed out. "And what about the other prisoner?"

Vince looked puzzled for a moment, as if he couldn't place who she was talking about. "You mean the RAM executive in the other cell? What about him?"

"He looks to me like the only person who might be able to tell us anything about Thebe," Jovanna said.

Vince nodded. "You have a point." He moved over to the vidcam display screen. The Martian prisoner continued to mumble, but he still didn't seem to be conscious. "Galen, how soon do you think you can bring him around?"

The Tinker physician pulled himself over and looked at the screen. "Hard to say. Depends on the cause of his unconsciousness. It could take some time."

"Which we may not have if the Red Warrior gets past the *Free Enterprise*," Vince said.

"Wait," Barney said. He flicked the switch on the underside of his helmet. After a moment, he said, "The Red Warrior didn't get past the *Free Enterprise*. His ship is gone. No survivors."

"There are still RAM ships around Jupiter," Galen pointed out. "You might want to transport the prisoner up to the *Geronimo* and have me treat him there."

"Good idea," Vince said. He looked over at Rolf. "Rolf, how are you feeling?"

"Fine," the Desert Runner replied, but Galen shook

his head fiercely.

"Don't even think about having Rolf move him. He has injuries of his own to worry about." Galen pointed to Black Barney. "How about the pirate?"

Barney turned his silent regard on Galen, who returned the look with calm equanimity. Jovanna wasn't surprised that Vince hadn't thought of asking Barney to carry the prisoner first. Despite his incredible strength, Barney didn't strike most people as a beast of burden. However, he was the reasonable one to ask for help now.

"Barney, would you—?" Vince began, but he was cut off by Barney's unequivocal response.

"No."

"Look, I'm sorry, Barney. I wouldn't ask you except—"

"Never mind, Vince," Sandra said. "You and I can move him."

"No," Barney said again.

"*Now* what's the problem?" Galen asked in an exasperated tone.

"He's from RAM," Barney said. No one said anything for several moments, as if they were waiting for Barney to go on.

Finally Vince said, "We can see that. But as Jovanna pointed out, he's our best chance of finding out what's going on here."

"I doubt that." Barney's voice was cold. "He's probably a plant. Just like your Jovanna Trask."

"What?" Jovanna said. Barney turned to look at her.

"You heard me." Barney jerked a thumb toward the vidcam display. "I say you and your friend should stay on Thebe and wait for your RAM comrades to rescue you."

"Where do you get these ideas?" Vince asked hotly. "Jovanna is a NEO agent."

"So she says. But I say she's worked for RAM ever since the Wydlin takeover," Barney said. "How do you know she's not selling NEO secrets to them?"

Jovanna looked at the others to see if they were believing Barney.

Galen's eyes looked even larger than usual, and Sandra looked confused. Rolf had snarled at the mention of RAM, and she saw a closed look coming over his face. Even Vince looked nonplussed for a moment. Then he shook his head. "I've known her since before the Wydlin takeover. She's one of us. I'd stake my life on it. Buck Rogers will—"

"Buck Rogers will thank me for disposing of the garbage," Barney said. "I promised him I'd keep an eye on things while he was gone, and that's what I'm doing."

"It's not up to you," Vince said.

"Oh?" The big gennie sounded amused. "Who's going to stop me? Even if you could get her past me, you'd have the *Free Enterprise* to deal with. I say she stays here."

Jovanna realized that nothing Vince could say would make any difference. Probably nothing she could say would make a difference either, but she had to try. "Is it too much to ask why you think I'm a RAM spy?" she asked.

"I don't like you," Barney said. It surprised Jovanna how much that unadorned statement hurt, but she pushed her feelings aside and listened to the rest of Barney's argument. "But that's not the main reason. You have control of all the information this group receives. None of the others knows as much about computers as you do. You can tell them whatever you want, and they have to believe you."

Jovanna was puzzled. "What do you think I've lied about? Everything I've told you about this complex is true. You've seen that."

"It's not what's true. It's what you left out," Barney said. "Like the one gator conveniently left alive to kill Pulaski before he could tell us what was going on here."

"I didn't know anything about him!" Jovanna protested. Barney said nothing, and she looked at the others. She wondered if Barney's accusations were starting to convince them, but it could have been that they were just as dumbfounded as she was.

Apparently Barney could make these accusations, but

there was nothing she could do about it. Of course, if
they questioned the RAM executive, he might tell them
something that would vindicate her, but Barney might
say they'd worked the story out ahead of time. And if
she found something in the computer, he could say she
made it up or planted it. There was literally no way she
could prove herself innocent. Only information from
some independent source would be even remotely be-
lievable to Black Barney. And there was no time for
that with a RAM fleet as close as it was.

Jovanna nearly laughed out loud. She thought she'd
come a long way since joining NEO. True, she was no
great hero, but she had learned a thing or two about
courage—at least physical courage.

Saying what she really felt was still extremely difficult for her, she had to admit. When she and Vince had
argued about Dr. Wydlin, she had backed down rather
than try to come to any resolution.

Then when they'd met up with Barney again, she had
avoided telling him that the signal chip he hated so
much was the chip she had implanted in him. She'd
avoided telling him because she was afraid he'd be so
angry he'd refuse to deal with the team if she was on it.
She was really still a coward after all.

And now she found that what she'd thought was pru-
dence wasn't helping the team. She knew Black Barney
as well as Vince did, yet Barney refused to trust her.
And if he had his way, she would be turned over to RAM
because she hadn't been honest with him to begin with.

What bothered Jovanna most was that their mission
was doomed to fail if they didn't get more information
from the other prisoner. It was bad enough that she'd
made Barney angry with her. She'd pay for that if they
left her behind on Thebe. But, far worse, the whole team
might botch this mission simply because he didn't trust
her. That was something Jovanna couldn't allow. Since
Barney believed the Martian executive was a plant,
he'd never let him off Thebe, and he probably wouldn't
let her anywhere near the computer.

How could she get Black Barney to trust her enough

to agree to rescue the RAM executive so Vince and the others could question him? If she could just get Barney to agree to that, she'd accept staying behind on Thebe. Maybe she'd even find some useful information here to send back to NEO before the RAM fleet arrived.

She doubted that RAM would be merciful once they found her, but she decided not to think about that now. Right now, she had to convince Black Barney to let Vince take the executive off Thebe.

Vince's voice brought her back to the present circumstances. "I can't let you do this," he was saying to Barney. "Jovanna is a member of our team. In fact, if it weren't for her, we wouldn't be here." He gestured to Rolf, Sandra, and Galen. "We'll stop you no matter what it takes." The others looked troubled. Already the team was in danger of coming apart.

"No, Vince," Jovanna said. "That isn't the way. I don't think there's any way for me to get off Thebe."

"Don't be ridiculous, Jo. I can't let Barney—"

"You can't stop him, Vince. You're serious about this, aren't you?" Jovanna said, turning to Black Barney.

"Yes," Barney said through his opaque black mask.

"It's my own fault," Jovanna said. It was probably too late to make any difference, but it couldn't hurt anything to be honest with Barney now. "It's the signal chip, isn't it, Barney?"

"What about it?" Barney's voice was ominous.

This is probably a mistake, Jovanna thought, then almost laughed aloud. What was she afraid of? She was already doomed to spend the rest of her short life on a deserted moon of Jupiter. How could things get any worse? "I misled you about the chip twenty years ago, and then when you came to Barbarosa, I didn't come clean, even though I suspected you'd figured out the truth. I don't blame you for not trusting me."

"So . . ." Barney continued to stare at her. "Remus Wydlin knew nothing about it?"

"No," Jovanna admitted. At the time, she'd rationalized the action by telling herself that Dr. Wydlin would have approved if he hadn't been so tangled up in RAM politics. She knew now that Barney wouldn't have much patience with any rationalizations.

"And now you can find me any time you want," Barney said.

"Not for long," Jovanna reminded him. "Once you leave Thebe and RAM takes me into custody—" She stopped, confused. Barney believed she was in league with RAM. He would expect Jovanna to lead RAM straight to him once the fleet rescued her.

"Wait a minute," Vince said. "Jovanna implanted that chip on Beowulf's orders. If you're out for revenge, take it out on NEO, not on her."

"Shut up," Black Barney said. He turned to Jovanna. "Well, Trask, I never expected you to give me the courtesy of an apology, but it couldn't hurt if you did."

"An apology?" Jovanna didn't know what she was expecting Black Barney to say, but that hadn't been it. The idea of Barney wanting her to apologize was one she'd never have thought of. She shrugged. "I've already blown it about a hundred and ten ways. What would you like me to apologize for?"

"How about for treating me like a tool, for starters? You could have told me what the chip was for when you first put it in."

"I didn't think you'd—"

"Agree?" said Barney. "Probably not. But then you and NEO and even Remus Wydlin were so busy thinking about how you were going to use me and the other Barneys that you never stopped to think that we might want to make our own decisions. Which is interesting, since from what I can make out, one of the things Remus Wydlin hated about RAM was the way they used gennies as slaves."

"You're right, Barney. I should have told you what the chip was for," Jovanna admitted. "I should have been honest with Dr. Wydlin and with you."

"It wasn't your secret, Jo," Vince protested.

"It shouldn't have been a secret at all. Not from the Wydlins," Jovanna said. "Sorry, Vince. I was just so glad to be included back in those days that I did what-

ever you said to do. Even things I believed were wrong.
At the risk of beating a dead horse, we should have been
more honest with Dr. Wydlin. We were on the same side.
I let you keep me from saying what I really felt, Vince.
Hell, my opinion is as good as yours."

"Did I ever say it wasn't?" Vince looked faintly puzzled at her outburst.

"No," Jovanna admitted. "No, you didn't. I did that to
myself." She suddenly felt she liked herself more than
she had in years. She turned back to Barney. "To be honest, Barney, it never occurred to me that you could make
a reasoned decision. I'm sorry. I know that sounds terrible, and I'm not proud of it now. But I knew you before
you were even decanted. Maybe since all my background was in computers, it was hard for me to think of
you as a real person with any desires other than those I
helped program into you."

"Remus Wydlin called it education, not programming," Barney reminded her.

"That's right," Jovanna admitted. "And I guess I
didn't really know what he meant until now. Well"—
she looked at Barney wryly—"at least I know what to
apologize for. I'm sorry I didn't respect you as a person."

She waited for his response. When he answered, he
gave no indication of whether or not he accepted her
apology. "All right, Trask, I'll give you the benefit of the
doubt for now. I imagine if I don't, Pirelli will do something stupid so I have to kill him, which would be uncomfortable for everyone concerned. I'll check out a few
things with Beowulf. If he backs up your story, I'll still
help your team." He turned to Vince. "Otherwise, Pirelli, I'm unavailable until NEO deals with her."

Jovanna felt as if he'd slapped her in the face, but at
least he wasn't leaving her to RAM. She knew Beowulf
would back her up. But there was one thing she wanted
to be sure of before they left Thebe. "What about the
prisoner? Are we taking him?"

Barney shook his head. "You have some nerve, you
know that, Trask? I'm still not sure I can trust you. Why
would I allow you to bring that Martian slug along?"

"Because he might hold the key to what's been happening here," Jovanna said patiently. "If you still really think I'm in league with RAM, why don't you keep us separate? You can take me back on the *Free Enterprise*. Put me under something like house arrest, if you like. I'm sure the others on the *Geronimo* can control one unconscious Martian businessman."

"I can live with that idea," Black Barney said slowly. "Except that you go on the *Geronimo*. Sleeping Beauty comes with me on the *Free Enterprise*. I'll deliver him to Beowulf. It'll give me a chance to get a few things straightened out with NEO."

"Whatever you say," Jovanna said. Then she remembered about Thebe's computer.

"Barney, just one more thing."

"Now what?" Barney asked.

"There might be something useful on this computer. I suppose you don't want me investigating it—"

"You suppose right," Barney said. "But I see your point. I'll have my people look it over. If there's anything there, I'll see that Beowulf gets it."

"But—" Jovanna began.

Barney looked at her. "I'm beginning to think you don't trust me."

Jovanna swallowed. If she ever expected Barney to forgive her, she'd better show some trust in him. "All right. I'm sure they'll know what to do."

Barney looked at Vince. "Satisfied, Pirelli?"

Vince nodded. "Do you want us to shuttle you up to the *Free Enterprise*?"

"No. I'll wait for them here. You take the *Geronimo* and go back to the Asteroid Belt. When we finish here, I'll take the prisoner to Beowulf for questioning."

Jovanna didn't quite know what to say, but she wanted Black Barney to know she was grateful for the chance he was giving her. "Thanks, Barney."

He looked at her, or at least his black goggles were aimed in her direction. "Don't thank me until you hear from Beowulf, Trask."

CHAPTER TWENTY NINE

Vince's comnet chimed. Jovanna, hoping RW
was finally reporting back from Beowulf,
nearly tripped Vince as they both hurried to
answer it. "Ladies first," she said.

Vince grimaced, rubbing his shin. "Especially when
they wear metal-tipped boots."

Jovanna made a face at him. Even as she took the seat
in front of the screen, she could feel Vince move in close
behind her so that he could see the screen. She flipped
the switch to answer. "Yes?"

"Hi, Jo, Vince." Sandra appeared on the screen, with
the familiar murkiness of Acheron in the background.
So it wasn't RW. Jovanna smiled, trying to hide her disappointment. If Sandra was disturbed to see Jovanna in
Vince's room, she didn't show it. "Have you had Infonet
on today?"

"No," Jovanna said. "Why?"

"I saw a still shot of our prisoner. We were about to
access the story, but I thought you'd want to know about
it," Sandra said.

"We? Who's there with you?" Jovanna asked.

"Just Rolf," Sandra said.

"Do me a favor. We may as well all watch it together."

Jovanna glanced at Vince to see if he agreed with her spontaneous decision, and he nodded. "Call Galen and meet us up here. We should be hearing from Beowulf at any time, so we'll all be together for it."

"You bet," Sandra said and terminated the connection.

"They'll be right up," Jovanna said.

Vince nodded, but he looked glum.

"What's the matter?" Jovanna asked.

"I just wish we'd heard something—anything—about the mission. It doesn't look good, seeing a news story about the prisoner before we're told anything." A knock came at Vince's door. Sandra and Rolf appeared on the security camera, and Vince opened the door. "Where's Galen?" he asked.

"He's on his way," Sandra said. Galen had a room a few doors down on Tortuga Street.

Rolf walked over and stood in front of Vince's terminal, which they hadn't yet tuned to Infonet. It was as close as he'd probably get to telling them he was anxious to see the news item they'd gathered to watch. Jovanna had had her doubts whether Rolf would make much effort to fit into their team when they'd first recruited him, but despite his very different personality, she believed he was well on his way now. She smiled at Vince. "Rolf will never last until Galen gets here. For that matter, neither will I. Why don't you go ahead and access the story?"

Sandra had already pulled a chair from beside Vince's small table and scooted it over in front of the terminal. The others joined her. The image of a beautiful brunette getting into a jet limousine came up, and a newscaster's voice began speaking.

"We have an update on the abduction of Baron Anton Turek. The Baroness Anastasia Turek, nee Valmar, left her Coprates villa today for an undisclosed location. Sources close to the family report that she received word about her husband and left to negotiate his release."

The woman on screen entered the jet limo, someone

closed the door, and it zoomed away. Then a still image of the man they'd rescued from Thebe appeared.

"The Baroness reported her husband missing two weeks ago. Baron Turek is a vice president in RAM's prestigious Economic Affairs Division. Friends of the family speculated that a ransom might be sought, but no demands were immediately forthcoming."

The image on the screen changed to one of a large space yacht. In front of it were two lines of men in RAM uniform, forming an aisle leading to a door. The announcer continued. "Several minutes ago, this Space Assault Corps squad arrived to escort Baroness Turek on her journey. General Simon Tisharenko, the supreme commander of the Space Assault Corps and a cousin of Baroness Turek, arranged the escort."

A knock at the door distracted Jovanna. A quick check of the security camera revealed Galen, and she opened the door.

"What's going on?" Galen asked. Jovanna started to fill him in on the news story when a phrase from the terminal caught her attention.

". . . yet another act of villainy from the notorious space pirate, Black Barney," a middle-aged man in the red uniform of a RAM general was saying. "This time we will crush him once and for all." The image then blacked out, signaling the end of the story.

"What was that all about? I missed the last part," Jovanna said.

"That was Tisharenko," Vince said, chuckling. "Barney is demanding a ransom from Turek's family. So now RAM thinks—at least it's the official story—that Barney's responsible for Turek's disappearance."

A shimmering near her terminal caught Jovanna's attention, and she turned to see RW taking shape.

"Sorry it took so long," RW said. "Beowulf asked me to check out a few things before he sent me back."

"What did he say?" asked Rolf. RW looked at him, surprised. Jovanna figured Rolf was probably the first person RW met who took her sudden appearances for granted.

"Beowulf?" RW said. "He said congratulations."

Vince and Jovanna exchanged glances, and Jovanna said, "Does he consider the mission a success?"

"Close enough," RW said. "Beowulf said he was sorry about Casimir Pulaski, but he doesn't blame you for not having arrived in time. From what they've pieced together, it's lucky you got there in time to rescue Turek."

"So it was all right to have brought him back?" Jovanna asked. She had wondered about Beowulf's reaction when they sent a RAM executive to Salvation, even though she was sure Black Barney had taken every precaution to keep its location secret.

"He must have been able to explain about Thebe," Sandra prompted.

"Not really, but Beowulf found out he was Pulaski's contact," RW said.

There were murmurs of surprise and approval through the room before RW went on. "You see, Turek found a reference to Far Star in a RAM database. Data piracy isn't his thing, so he asked Pulaski to help him. Then he was grabbed and brought to Thebe. They nabbed Pulaski two days later, probably just after he sent that message about Thebe to Beowulf. Actually, Beowulf was able to piece a few things together, both from what Turek told him and from what Barney got out of Thebe's computer."

"And?" Vince asked.

"Well, RAM's use of Thebe is quite recent and very covert. It's not even known to most people in RAM's Internal Affairs Division. The Red Warrior apparently had complete control of Thebe, though what his purpose was, we still don't know. He was a special operative who had IAD's cooperation, but he didn't report to them. He reported directly to the Holzerhein family."

"So we know that whatever Turek and Pulaski got into, it was highly classified," Vince said impatiently. "But we knew that already. What's next? For us, I mean."

Jovanna thought that Vince wouldn't really believe he'd proved himself to Beowulf until he received hard

THE GENESIS WEB 279

evidence, probably in the form of a new assignment. But Jovanna needed her own form of vindication. She wasn't ready to think about their next task until the loose ends from this one were tied up.

"Why did Beowulf send Turek back to Mars?" Rolf asked. Apparently he wanted the loose ends tied up.

"That's the good part." RW settled onto her usual perch on the edge of the console. "Now that Red Warrior is dead, Turek can go back to Mars safely. There's no evidence to indicate that anyone other than Red Warrior has any interest in him."

"Not the Holzerheins?" Vince asked.

"Beowulf asked me to check that out," RW said. "I discovered that Red Warrior had had no communication with the Holzerheins for some time before he took Pulaski into custody. Both Pulaski and Turek were abducted, rather than arrested openly. Which means that Red Warrior was the only one who knew about Anton Turek's NEO connections."

Jovanna could understand why Beowulf would want to keep a NEO operative so highly placed in RAM, but if she were Turek, she'd be reluctant to rejoin RAM. "It still seems dangerous for Turek to go back."

"He's not worried," RW said. "He told Beowulf that as soon as he rejoins his family, he'll be so well protected that even if RAM finds out anything, they'll have to deal with him through the court system."

That made sense to Jovanna. According to the Infonet story, Turek was linked with the Tisharenkos and the Valmars, two of the most powerful families on Mars, outside of the Holzerheins. No, RAM couldn't simply dispose of Turek even if they did find out about him.

Vince seemed satisfied as well. "He does seem to have good connections. And if RAM does prosecute him—say, for data piracy—this Operation Far Star is bound to leak out."

"Exactly," RW said. "Turek doesn't think RAM wants that to happen, and neither does Beowulf. However, Beowulf does want NEO to know what it's all about. And so that'll be your next assignment."

"Wait a minute. So Beowulf thinks Turek is safe. That's great." Rolf's voice dripped cynicism. "But what makes NEO think they can really trust this guy? One little contact with Pulaski?"

"I knew I was forgetting something," RW said. "Of course, the way you guys interrupt me—"

"What did you forget?" Jovanna cut RW off before she could really get started.

"We already know Turek," RW said, then looked at them as if she was enjoying this.

Vince looked at her skeptically. "What are you talking about?"

"You should know him, Rocketjock," RW continued. "You knew him as Dekalb about twenty-one years ago."

"Dekalb!" Vince looked at Jovanna, then back to RW. "I thought he was dead."

"No, he survived. Dekalb—or Turek—was in transit to Mars at the time of the RAM takeover. That was why he had so much trouble getting the ship for you and why he wasn't killed during the takeover. He barely escaped criminal prosecution, due mostly to his family connections, but RAM kept an eye on him for a long time after that," RW explained.

It sounded reasonable to Jovanna. She remembered having to maintain a very low profile for several years after she returned to Mars.

RW went on. "He only recently started meeting with Casimir Pulaski and sharing information with him."

"Wait." Jovanna had to know how Barney's discussion with Beowulf had gone. "Did Black Barney—?"

"He and Beowulf had a private talk. I wasn't invited." RW looked momentarily miffed. "But Barney said to tell you he'd continue to help the team."

"Great! So what's next?" Vince asked, all business.

"Slow down, Major," said Sandra teasingly. "Don't we get a little time to celebrate after our victory?"

"Victory!" Vince practically exploded. "Listen, rookie, you've got a lot to learn. We barely managed to stumble through that mission. Don't get a big head."

Sandra flushed deeply, and Jovanna took immediate

pity on her. She was just young and enthusiastic. Jovanna would have thought, with the feelings Sandra had for Vince, that he would cut her a little slack.

"Come on, Vince," Jovanna murmured.

Vince was still wound up. It was obvious Beowulf's approval hadn't yet sunk in. "If it hadn't been for Black Barney—"

"Yeah, yeah, we'd have been toasted several times over," Jovanna said. Sandra smiled. Galen chuckled. Even Rolf's expression seemed less severe than usual.

Vince started to glare at her, then grinned sheepishly. "I was being a jerk, wasn't I?"

Jovanna smiled back. "Not a complete one. But we might as well enjoy Beowulf's first message."

"What was that?" Vince frowned, trying to remember.

"Congratulations," Jovanna reminded him. Now that she knew there was no question about her NEO loyalty, she felt that she had earned his praise.

"He did, didn't he? Well"—Vince smiled—"I guess we can get back to training later."

"You'll have to," RW chimed in. "Beowulf said he'd be sending you orders for your next mission soon."

"All right. You can get back to whipping this team into shape tomorrow, Major." Jovanna nodded toward Sandra, Rolf, and Galen. "But let's give these rookies a little credit first."

Vince looked at their three new team members, then looked back at Jovanna. "Do you think they'll do?"

"Why shouldn't they?" Jovanna said. "They're nowhere near as pathetic as I was, and I learned."

Vince smiled. "You're right. You *were* pretty pathetic, Jo."

"And—?" Jo prompted.

"And you learned," Vince admitted. "All right, let's celebrate. First round is on me." He went to his cooling cube and pulled out a vacuum pack of orange juice. "Terran 2458," he said, waving it aloft. "A very good year."

Invaders of Charon Series

A New Dimension in Outer Space Adventure!

Book Two: **Nomads of the Sky**

William H. Keith, Jr.

The mysterious, dreaded Space Nomads take Vincent Perelli prisoner, forcing him to fight a ritual battle for survival before he can seek the Device, a missing RAM artifact that may save the life of Buck Rogers.

Available November 1992